THE PROUD VILLEINS

THE PROUD VILLEINS

Bridges Over Time
Book I

Valerie Anand

St. Martin's Press
NEW YORK

Library of Congress Cataloging-in-Publication Data

Anand, Valerie.
    The proud villeins / Valerie Anand.
      p. cm.
    ISBN 0-312-08282-7
    1. Great Britain—History—Norman period, 1066–1154—Fiction.
I. Title.
PR6051.N34P76   1992
823'.914—dc20   92-1583
                                   CIP

First published in Great Britain by Headline Book Publishing PLC.

First U.S. Edition: September 1992

10 9 8 7 6 5 4 3 2 1

This book is for Susan and David
by way of thanks
for so many happy evenings round the fire with glasses of
wine setting the world to rights

Acknowledgements

My thanks go to Phoebe Phillips Editions for permission to use the quotations from Anne Savage's translation of *The Anglo-Saxon Chronicle*.

My thanks also go to the Oxford University Press for permission to use the quotation from Marjorie Chibnall's translation of *The Ecclesiastical History of Orderic Vitalis*, 1969–81.

Contents

PART VI   DANGEROUS DREAMS AD 1215

THE PROUD VILLEINS

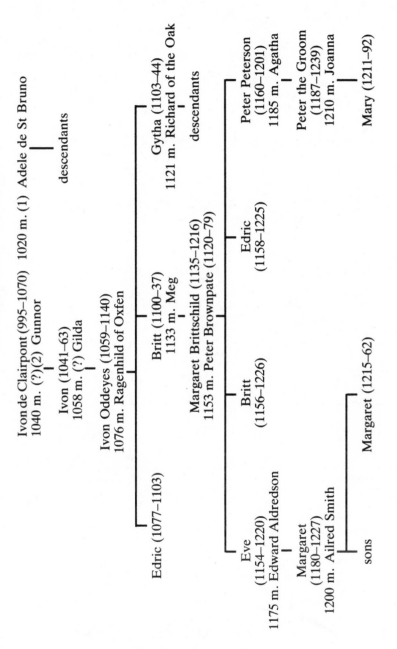

PART I

Sir Ivon de Clairpont,
AD 1040

1036 Alfred, the blameless atheling, King Ethelred's son, came here and meant to go to his mother, who was in Winchester . . . but [Earl] Godwin hindered him, set him in captivity, and drove away his friends . . . some they sold for money, some killed wretchedly . . . nor was a more bloody deed done in this land after the Danes came.

The Anglo-Saxon Chronicle

Chapter One

The Captive

The man who had once been called Sir Ivon de Clairpont knew of three things that might confuse a scent trail: sheep, water and loose sliding stones like those of the scree up which he had just frantically scrambled.

And none of them was going to work.

He had realised that the moment he heard the hounds in the distance and recognised the bass voice of Eric Olafsen's brindled monster Odin dominating the rest. Plainly, neither the sheep-pen through which he had run before he fled from the farmstead at noon, nor the stream down which he had waded as he made his way south-east out of Eric's Dale into the next valley, had confused Odin. Odin (oh God, please send down a thunderbolt and blast that four-footed demon into hell) hunted with his muzzle raised, scenting the air through which his quarry had passed rather than the ground his feet had trodden. Nothing short of witchcraft, thought Ivon de Clairpont bitterly, would defeat Odin.

Simple desperation had sent him bolting up the scree but now, as he lay flat on his stomach behind two massive grey boulders, listening to the thunder of his heart against the rough ground, he knew that he was trapped.

By peering between the boulders, he could see the ground below the scree. Advancing through the valley into his line of vision, near enough already to be recognisable, were big blond Eric, his younger brother Niall, his twelve-year-old son Bjorn and two strapping cousins. Eric's farmstead was a peculiar, sprawling place by the standards of a Norman used to a tidy hierarchy of lords, tenants and peasants. Eric presumably owed allegiance of some sort to the Earl of Northumbria, but the Dale was his own, and the assorted kinsmen with whom he shared it apparently recognised his ownership without feeling any sense of inferiority. They lived in long-houses built close to Eric's bigger, original one, so that the farmstead appeared to be growing into a species of village, but they tended to gravitate to Eric's house for meals, a habit encouraged by the women, who could cook companionably and in bulk. Eric's relatives argued cheerfully with him across the dinner table day after day, tossing opposing opinions on whether to plant oats or barley, or when to start the midsummer shearing, disrespectfully back and forth as though they were his equals.

Eric's father had been a Danish Viking who had come to England with

3

King Cnut and settled. Ivon supposed that this was the way people lived in Denmark. He considered it extraordinary, and undignified.

But there were no arguments going on at the foot of the scree, he noticed grimly. The importance of recapturing a runaway thrall was something on which Eric and his kinsmen would be in perfect agreement. Each man carried a knife, a bow and a laden quiver and each had a hound straining on a leash. Odin of the supernatural olfactory powers tugged at that held by Eric. The two of them were in the lead and Odin was veering towards the place where Ivon had climbed the scree.

The afternoon was warm. Stone outcrops glittered; in the heather and the shaggy grass which grew to his left, where the scree ended, bees hummed and grasshoppers creaked. He was sweating heavily after his climb. The scree was steep and at the age of forty-five he was not as vigorous as he had been. Moisture dripped into his eyes and he wiped them impatiently. He'd prefer to see the foe coming. Of course it was only sweat that was blinding him. A Norman knight didn't weep, not even in the utmost reaches of despair, not when facing death or pain or slavery, not even when the third attempt to escape from bondage had failed, exposing him to God alone knew what retribution this time. He'd had to keep his pallet for three days and sleep on his stomach for more than a week, last time.

Absurdly, as he lay there, he found himself once more thinking of Adele.

He thought of her often these days, which was strange, for he had never as far as he knew even liked, let alone loved, the wife his father had found for him. The word most descriptive of Adele was *sharp* and the adjective applied equally to her voice, her nose, her snapping black eyes and the points of her elbows. He'd been pleased when she gave him children, naturally, but not unduly grieved when the third confinement killed her.

Only, since his enslavement, he had not had a woman. There were plenty of thrall-women in Eric's household and no one would have minded, least of all the women themselves. One – that brazen little sandyhaired vixen Gunnor – had been giving him the eye since the day he arrived, even while her own man was still alive. After the man's death last year, she had become a positive nuisance and all the more so because at times he had been tempted.

But if no one else in Eric's Dale cared a straw that, once, Ivon had been a knight, he himself would never forget it. His son and daughter by Adele were safe in Normandy, being reared in the households of knights in a manner suitable to their father's rank and no child of his should ever grow up to anything less, least of all to thralldom. And so, the last woman he had slept with, five years ago now, was Adele and in this bleak, inhuman world of servitude among strangers, she had come to represent normality for him, the rights and duties of manhood, the shapes and scents of home. At this moment, he would have pawned his soul to be back in her embrace. He had never done her justice, he thought wryly. Her voice might have

4

reminded him of broken glass but she had been a good wife none the less, her body well-shaped, her skin smooth and her willingness unfailing. He put his damp face against the boulder in front of him and his arms crept round it as if to cuddle it. His need for comfort was as great as that.

Below, Odin bayed. Ivon shuddered. But even the fear of what Eric might do to him when he caught him was now not as potent as the misery of understanding, at last, that not only was Adele gone for ever, but that this third attempt at flight had failed, and he would never now see Normandy, or the wide vale of Clairpont, again.

Four years ago (only it felt more like four centuries), Sir Ivon de Clairpont had been a respected senior knight in the service of the great Abbey of St Simeon, from which his family held their land. The abbey in turn held lands from the Count of Boulogne in return for providing him with twelve knights for his household. Which was how Ivon had come to be seconded to the Count, and then further seconded to a protégé of his when the said protégé set out on an official visit to England.

English politics had never interested Ivon, and he knew only the barest details of the story behind the visit. But he did know that there had once been an English king called Ethelred who had been deposed by a Danish invader called Cnut. By 1036 both Ethelred and Cnut were dead but one of Cnut's sons was ruling England while Ethelred's two sons were in exile in Normandy. The Count's protégé was the younger of the two, a man called Alfred Atheling. *Atheling*, Ivon was told, was an English word meaning king's heir, and the younger brother bore the title equally with the elder. In England, the elder son did not automatically inherit.

The Atheling's mother still lived in England (having after Ethelred's death adroitly married his supplanter Cnut). She had asked her sons to visit her but they feared treachery and so only Alfred was going. 'Well protected,' the Count had said. 'He's to take a force of six hundred. I'm lending them to him.'

It had been an ill-chosen number, Ivon thought in retrospect. Not enough for real protection against the forces that the English king had at his command, but enough to look as though Alfred had a bid for power in mind. That he still called himself *Atheling* would have reinforced that. He should have called himself Alfred Ethelredson and taken six men, or kept the title Atheling and taken six thousand. The attempt to compromise was a disaster.

Ivon did not know how the betrayal had been managed: whether Alfred's mother had been in it or not, whether the great Earl Godwin who had met the party at Dover on her behalf were involved, or taken by surprise as he seemed to be.

He did know that they had been escorted inland to a little walled town (the English referred to it as a burgh) called Gildenford. Their hosts had pointed out the kingcups in the river meadows, dusting the grass with gold, and said that the burgh's name meant Gilded Ford. They dined in a small hall there, which belonged to the English earl. But there wasn't enough room for them all to sleep in it and: 'You're to lodge here and there in the burgh,' the Atheling explained.

No one liked it. In this land ruled by Alfred's rival, Alfred's men were strongly inclined to keep together. They did not in the least want to be parcelled out in tens and twelves here and there in a strange place.

But there was no help for it. Ivon and nine others found themselves sleeping by the fire in a house belonging to a blacksmith. Ivon, uneasy, took a long time to fall asleep and when he did, it was for the last time as a free man. He woke in the dead hours to find the room full of men with the bearded faces and the distinctive leathern- and chain-mail of English housecarles. Three stood holding flambeaux to provide light while two, with drawn swords, guarded the smith and his family and the others dragged Ivon and his companions to their feet. He stood there helpless with a dagger at his jugular while his hands were bound.

He had occasionally heard men, when speaking of some terrible thing they had seen or experienced, say: 'I can't remember it clearly now.' Ivon only wished his own memory were so obliging.

The Massacre of Gildenford was famous now, or infamous. In making his escape, Ivon had not dared to use it, but there was a well-marked track through Eric's Dale; people came through the Dale and sought a night's lodging there quite often. Merchants came, pedlars, minstrels, people travelling to weddings or fairs. From their conversation Ivon, who after a while acquired far more Norse-English than he was prepared to admit in Eric's presence, learned what he had not known before, the fate of Alfred Atheling himself, who had been taken away from Gildenford, transported to a place called Ely, given a mock trial and blinded, and had since died. He learned that the story of Gildenford, of the Atheling's fate and the treatment meted out to his followers had gone swiftly round the whole country and from the shocked undertones in people's voices, he understood that their horror echoed his own.

Against his will, his memory preserved a series of ugly sights and sounds. The forced march through the darkness, stumbling because their captors' flambeaux shed confusion rather than light. If anyone fell, he was yanked roughly up again and cursed. The caves where they were kept for the rest of the night; the rocky walls; the faces of friend and foe, coming and going in the torchlight. The stomach-griping sense of approaching evil.

The English earl, Earl Godwin, his gold arm-rings and huge garnet cloak-brooch glittering, coming into the caves before dawn and appearing to remonstrate with the leader of their captors. The leader's thick finger as he drew it expressively across his throat. Ivon remembered staring at the ground for fear someone should see the horror in his eyes and shutting his teeth to hold back a wave of sickness. If you were a knight you were prepared to die by violence, but fighting, with a sword in your hand, not like this, like a helpless sheep. And then the sheer enormity of the numbers involved, hitting him like a lump of rock. *What, all of us?* he thought. *Six hundred?*

6

And then the discovery, next day when they were herded out on to the hillside above the town, that it wasn't to be quite as bad as that. Not quite. There were all of sixteen or seventeen survivors.

He didn't want to remember. He wished the scene wouldn't come back to him so often in the dreams which made him cry out and disturb the other thralls sleeping to either side of him in the straw in Eric's longhouse.

He had seen bloodshed before. He had seen battles. He had once made a pilgrimage to Rome and fought off robbers on the way, killing three. But this . . .

The Atheling himself wasn't there but as far as Ivon could see, all his companions were. They died by lottery. The leader of the English soldiers and his men lined them up in rows, shoving them so that they sat down heavily, and went along the rows spearing every tenth man. Then they started again, killing every tenth survivor. And so on . . .

From the moment in the caves when he understood that he was probably about to die, Ivon had made up his mind to say nothing, to show no fear, to command his face, his voice and his bladder. He held on to that resolution though some of those around him did not. There were many who like himself took refuge in contemptuous silence, but others called down curses and some broke down and pleaded wildly. All, at the last, fought, twisting in their bonds, trying to kick, spitting up at the faces of their slayers. When his own final moment came, he decided, he would issue one comprehensive curse and kick his murderer in the groin if he possibly could.

But the count of ten passed him by again and again and when the survivors numbered less than twenty – just a handful of them left amid the carnage on that stinking, squalid hillside, amid the pitiful heaps of blood-stained clothing that had been their comrades – then, suddenly, the slaughter stopped. Their tormentors conferred, with sly sidelong glances towards the prisoners, and bursts of laughter.

What had followed, the branding iron and the crude jeers as the knight became a slave, had been for Ivon worse by far than death.

Eric Olafsen was not among the butchers, which was fortunate for Eric. If he had been, Ivon would have found a way to kill him long ago. Eric, as far as Ivon had been able to make out since, had simply been making a rare visit to London to haggle for some specimens of a thick-woolled breed of sheep which presumably wasn't yet obtainable in the north. Ivon and his fellow-captives were taken to London, their feet secured under their mounts' bellies, and their captors evidently let it be known that they had human merchandise for sale. Strangers came to the hall where they were being kept in fetters, to stare and bargain. Ivon could remember sitting dejectedly on the floor, looking at the chains which had now replaced the ropes round his wrists and wondering if it were possible to will oneself into dying, and being suddenly prodded to his feet by one of his jailers with a spear-butt, to meet the eyes of a blond-bearded man in a rust-coloured tunic, who was pointing at him.

He was made to walk about and his sleeves were pushed up to show the sword-muscles in his arms. The blond man tried to speak to him and Ivon, staring at him inimically, did not answer. The man turned to a group of others, of similar appearance, who were apparently with him, and there seemed to be a mild argument. He gathered in the course of it that the blond individual's name was Eric. Some sort of consensus was reached and all of them then took to arguing with Ivon's jailers. Then they went away.

One of Ivon's fellow-prisoners knew some English. 'They've bought you,' he said. 'They got you cheap.' He suddenly grinned, the first grin any of them had achieved since Gildenford. 'Do you know why?'

'How would I? I can't understand their gibberish. They sound like animals,' said Ivon fastidiously. 'All growls and gutturals. All right. What did they say about me?'

'That you're of – er – mature years . . .'

'Middle-aged. I'm over forty. Go on.'

'And you've been a knight. So you may not have that many years left in you and you're likely to be insubordinate. That blond fellow said he was doing our captors a favour, taking you off their hands, and one of his friends there – or maybe they're brothers; they look alike – doesn't want him to buy you at all. But the big blond one said the farm was isolated so you'd find it hard to escape, and you've got good muscles, so he'd take you at a third the normal price. He got you for half-price in the end, after a bit of haggling. At least you've robbed these . . . these . . .'

'Churls,' said Ivon, 'swaggering in their masters' clothes.'

'Yes. You've done them out of a fair amount of profit.'

'That's the only good news I've heard in weeks,' said Ivon. 'And it's probably,' he added, 'the last good news I'll ever hear in my life.'

The blond man and his companions came for him the next day. They made a journey by boat, down the River Thames and northward up the east coast and then by way of another river to the city which his captors (he would not think of them as owners) in their uncouth dialect called Jorvik but which he now knew was the ancient city which other people called York.

He had, of course, attempted to escape on the way. He considered Eric's assessment of him to be an impertinence but it was remarkably accurate. They were casual, on board ship, about keeping him fettered and he tried to appear sullen and resigned. On the second day of the journey up the coast, they put in at a small port for provisions. Finding, as the ship set out again, that he was within swimming distance of land and with his hands free, Ivon promptly dived overboard.

The rowers changed course smoothly and he was pulled out of the water within minutes. He was beaten up in an efficient, dispassionate manner and then Eric came and looked at him and with the back of his hand flicked the brand on Ivon's forehead. The gesture said, plainly: 'How far do you think you'll get with that thrall's mark on you?'

But he wasn't left loose again until the last stage of the journey, which was by pony, along the banks of an unnavigable stream. He was made to help drive Eric's new sheep and he was allowed to have his hands free from then on. Thralls, after all, had to work.

There were still times when he couldn't believe it. How could anyone seriously suppose that he, Sir Ivon de Clairpont, was going to spend the rest of his life here in these bleak foreign moorlands, grooming oxen for a man who was no more than a well-off churl who stabled the oxen in question at one end of his own hall, planting oats for him, feeding sheep, mending harness and – in winter – shovelling away the snow from the paths that linked the longhouses together?

The other thralls regarded him with a mixture of alarm and amusement, as though he were a slightly dangerous madman. They had all been born into bond status and couldn't see much wrong with it. They were fed and housed, weren't they? And they weren't the ones who had to worry about it, or face the ridicule of their kinsfolk when Eric's new sheep turned out to be quite unsuited to life on the chilly upland pastures round Eric's Dale, and died, every one of them, in the very first blizzard.

In the struggle to retain his self-respect, Ivon made a fetish of not understanding, and never speaking, what he considered to be their barbarous northern language. But in spite of this, a rough-and-ready communication did develop, and his fellow-thralls managed eventually to convey most of their views to him and there were those good-natured ones who tried to coax him into acceptance.

But that was a concept which revolted him. Thereafter, although he could not help but work, eat and sleep in close proximity to them, he could and did keep his mind aloof. In his very first week at Eric's Dale, when he was sitting miserably on a bench in the trodden-earth yard, cleaning dirty ox harness because if he didn't he wouldn't be fed, he had looked up and seen a hunting eagle and yearned to have wings too, on which to surmount the imprisoning hills that bounded the Dale. He began at that moment to plan his next escape.

He would have to find his way to York and then, somehow, on to a ship bound downriver and across to Normandy. The main difficulty would be reaching York. On the journey to Eric's Dale, they had left the ship, on which Eric had simply bought passages since he apparently didn't own it, and gone on by barge to a small fortified burgh where Eric's ponies were waiting in the care of a friend or kinsman – Ivon didn't know which – who lived there. Then had come two and a half days of riding, north and then west, along the banks of that tumbling stream. But there were streams everywhere in this land and one looked very much like another, and the bleak moors stretched in all directions. He had seen what they were like in bad weather; how the clouds sank down and covered them. To escape safely, he needed much more detailed information than he had.

He waited, gleaning what he could from such conversation as he could understand in the household and from Eric's passing guests, taking pains meanwhile to behave quietly, in order to make Eric and his tribe of kinsman watch him a little less attentively. It all took time. It was nearly two years before he felt he could risk the attempt.

He buoyed himself up meanwhile by imagining how his return home would be. He would go straight to his home at Clairpont, which he had inherited from his father. He pictured it in his mind: the fortified farmhouse like a miniature castle, standing in its broad vale with the low, wooded hills – so different from the steep moorlands of Eric's Dale – all round it, and the river winding through. The road to his gate led across the river by way of a stone bridge with three arches. It was a famous landmark, visible from a long way off whichever direction one came from and it had given the estate its name. He presumed that the place was being cared for somehow until his son was old enough to take charge. He would ride over the bridge and announce himself. He would sit that day beside his own hearth and sleep that night in his own bed. He would send word to the Abbot of St Simeon's and to the Count of Boulogne, saying that he had returned to take up once again whatever duties they required of him. He could, if he wished, marry again.

He consoled himself at night, curled up in the straw, by making these pictures in his mind.

When he finally fled he believed he had made careful preparations. But he was caught in mist before he was two hours on his way and by the time Odin came up with him, he was thoroughly lost and so bitterly cold that he was almost relieved to be recaptured. He had hated himself afterwards for that moment of relief. That was a sign of servitude. Only a man with the mind of a slave thought his master's roof better than death in the open.

Therefore, he began to plan his third attempt at once, even while he was still recovering from Eric's chastisement. And this time, he thought, it would have worked but for Odin. He had taken care to watch the weather and, furthermore, he hadn't had to steal anything in order to pay his way.

Last time, he had filched some silver coin from an untidy guest, a risky proceeding for which he could have been killed if anyone had discovered the theft. He'd thrust the coins under an outcrop before he was recaptured. This time he'd been very lucky. As he lay pressed against the earth, the gold arm-ring hidden under his brown tunic sleeve pressed into the muscle of his right arm. Another of Eric's guests had given it to him, publicly, last Yuletide, because Ivon had noticed that the man's pony was lame, and had tended it. He had meant to sell the arm-ring in York. He could have bandaged his head to hide the brand, and pretended he'd been in a fight.

Fastened to his belt were two other objects which were also digging into him. One was a little knife. Even thralls were issued with these, to cut their food or the thongs of haybales. It was small but sharp. The other object was his talisman: an old bone dagger-hilt. When as a young man going to Rome, he had fought and killed that gang of robbers, he had broken one of their daggers in the fight and kept its hilt as a memento, attracted by the curious, eastern-looking pattern carved into it. The dagger had seen a lot of no doubt lawless service and in one place the pattern had worn smooth.

There Ivon, who was handy at such things, had engraved his family device, an arrangement of curved lines arching over wavy lines, to make a stylised river bridge and thus represent the name Clairpont.

The hilt was worthless, or his captors would have seized it from him at Gildenford. But to Ivon, it had infinite value. He fingered it now, remembering.

Below, Eric had pulled Odin to a halt. Bjorn stood beside his father. The others were spreading out along the foot of the scree, knowing what to do without discussion, thinking in unison as only the closest comrades, or blood relations, could. Eric himself was scanning the hillside where a few pebbles, disturbed by Ivon's frantic all-fours ascent, still rolled and trickled. He tilted back his head and funnelled his hands round his mouth. 'Holloa! Ivon, are you up there? Can you hear me?'

Behind his boulder, Ivon rose slowly to his feet. He too made a funnel of his hands. 'So you do know what my name is!'

'So you do understand my language!' retorted Eric. 'I've thought so for a long time! Come down, you fool! Or we'll send Odin and the pack up to fetch you!'

'No!'

For, after all, he did not have to surrender. He had made his decision the moment his fingers touched the old bone dagger-hilt, a reminder of the days when he was a man and a Christian. Those days were long over. No thrall could call himself a man, and the inhabitants of Eric's Dale were only nominally Christian. The only priest Ivon had ever seen in the Dale was a traveller passing through and marriages, he had been scandalised to observe, were conducted by the old handfasting ceremony without a representative of the church in sight. He saw how, unwittingly, he had let the Dale change him, for the decision he had just made, he would once have rejected instantly as contrary to Christian law even though it would give him back his manhood. Now the manhood seemed the more precious and his chosen course the only one possible in honour. His belt knife would do the job, he thought, fingering the point. It was keen enough. Yes! He had done with slavery. He stood up as a free man to bandy words with Eric, his reluctantly acquired Norse-English thick and ungrammatical but good enough for this.

'I will not come down! I am not your property!'

'Yes, you are! I got you half-price, you bloody-minded Norman, but I still gave eight good ounces of silver for you!'

Eric sounded fairly good-humoured. He had probably rather enjoyed the chase and, though insistent on his rights, he was a naturally easy-tempered man. As far as rank went, he was such a man as once had marched at Ivon's back. He was also such a man as Ivon, once, would have liked very much.

'More fool you!' Ivon now bellowed. 'I was a freeborn man who'd done no wrong! I was following my liege lord's orders! Is that a reason to make me a slave? Listen! I'm going on my way now!' He wrenched out his belt knife and pointed up the slope with it. 'If you send up the dogs I'll kill them if I can! If I can't, I'll come rolling down with this . . .' he did not know the word for heart but jabbed the knife vigorously towards his own chest '. . . here!'

Eric would never let him go, of course. He'd lose too much face. These were Ivon de Clairpont's last moments on earth but at least he had been the one who chose to make them so. He was in command of his destiny again and he felt mad and lighthearted, as if he were drunk. He turned his back on Eric and his staring companions and set off without more ado up the slithering scree.

Odin, seeing his quarry retreat, sprang forward, dragging on his leash and baying. But Eric did not loose him.

He spoke instead to his son and Bjorn, his movements flowing one from another as smoothly as though they were oiled, unslung his bow, took a shaft from his quiver, drew and shot, and Ivon rolled down the hillside towards them, not with a knife in his heart but with an iron-tipped arrow accurately transfixing one ankle.

'What am I to do with him?' said Eric wearily to his kinsmen and his wife Maria. He had summoned her from the private quarters where she and the other women were weaving, to join the conference in the hall where those who had been with him on the manhunt were taking off their boots and shaking their heads over the impossibility of ever finding a way to deal with a man like Ivon.

Big, brownhaired Maria was a woman of sense. The farmstead had prospered since the day Eric had brought her home from her father's farm twenty miles to the north. She had encouraged Eric's cousin Halfdan to go to Jorvik to learn the blacksmith's craft; had urged that they should trade in York to bring in money and new goods and animals. Her skill at the loom and her ability to train other women were such that they had cloth for sale now as well as to the calfskins and raw wool and Halfdan's ironwork. She'd reared and educated and personally arranged good marriages for four daughters as well as presenting Eric with Bjorn. Her counsel was valued in the Dale.

'I've no stomach for beating him again,' said Eric frankly. 'I'd be within my rights but Bjorn's arrow has done enough. Even if he lives, he'll go lame all his days. For another thing – I bought and paid for him but he's above me and always will be. In war, he'd best me and we both know it. What do you say, Maria?'

Maria bore the name of the Mother of God and came from a far more Christian family than her husband. She never made a to-do about it, and her daughters had all been married by the old handfasting rite, but she kept a crucifix on the wall of the private chamber. And once in a while, when asked her opinion on a problem, her attitudes would surface.

'Why not give him his freedom?' she said. 'He should not have been made a slave. He was a knight and a Christian. I have often wished you had never bought him.'

12

'So have I,' said Eric in heartfelt tones. 'But set him free I cannot. It would give the other thralls ideas. He has not earned the right to freedom by showing loyalty. On the contrary, he's made repeated attempts to escape! No, Maria.'

'Your husband is right.' Halfdan the Smith did not approve of Maria's presence in this conference. His own wife knew her place; he made sure of that. 'Your kindheartedness does you credit as a woman,' he said to Maria, 'but it would cause more trouble than it solved, to let this thrall go free.'

'By modern law,' said Maria mildly, 'a man of Ivon's rank should have been ransomed by his family or his lord, not sold.'

'That's an English custom,' said Halfdan shortly. 'Here in the north we keep to the Danelaw, as our forefathers did. Your husband has paid good silver for this man Ivon's person and Ivon himself came here in the following of a man who was marching on to someone else's soil with six hundred troops. He is a captured prisoner of war and it has always been the custom to sell such men.'

'That's true. Yes.' Eric's brother Niall spoke in agreement and the boy Bjorn nodded vigorously.

'That was the past,' said Maria. 'And our forefathers were not Christian men.' For once she had said it out loud, putting the Christian position against the ancient Viking laws, and the spark in her eyes showed that she knew it. 'We are more enlightened now,' she said firmly.

'Soft!' said Halfdan.

'The lord he followed here,' said Maria, 'was blinded and died of his injuries. Some might say that his sufferings were enough to ransom many men, not just one.'

'Your husband still paid out that silver.'

'Enough, Halfdan,' said Eric calmly. Silence fell at once while they waited to hear what he had to say. Eric Olafsen wielded slightly more authority than Ivon, who equated authority in the home with his father's harsh, peremptory shouts, had understood. 'Maria's point is good,' Eric said. 'What was done to Ivon's lord is indeed an argument for setting him free. But my thralls would never understand it. And even if I took the risk of causing jealousy and unrest among them, what of Ivon himself? I said, he will be lame for life. And his family I suppose think he is dead. His lands if he has any will be in other hands. Would he be welcome or would he be just a limping ghost? To my mind, he could be better off here.'

'Can't we just sell the man?' Orm, the second of the cousins who had helped to pursue Ivon, spoke impatiently.

'Would anyone be fool enough to buy him?' Halfdan let out a bark of laughter.

'Very few, now,' said Eric soberly. 'Past his youth, incurably sullen, and lame . . . no. No. What I want is a way to make him settle for being here, other than thrashing him senseless. In any case,' he added, 'he's ready to destroy himself if I do, and possibly even if I don't. Then what will I have for my eight ounces of silver? So – what do we do?'

13

Maria, inclining her head in acceptance of the decision that Ivon could not be set free, said thoughtfully: 'He brings to mind . . . a ship that needs an anchor. Gunnor likes him.'

'He won't let Gunnor become his anchor,' said Eric gloomily. 'I offered her to him once. He made out he couldn't understand me, so I fetched her and joined their hands and looked at him with eyebrows *so* . . .' he put his features into a classic expression of enquiry '. . . but he wrenched his hand away and said one word. *Child!* he said. Then he pointed to his brand and shook his head as if he wanted to shake it right off. I think he meant he wouldn't breed thralls.'

'He wasn't laid flat with a smashed ankle, then,' said Maria serenely. 'He is now. He's helpless and in pain. And Gunnor has some skill at healing. We all use the remedies she brews, at times. Let Gunnor see what she can do.'

Chapter Two

The Thrall-Woman

If he could have died, he would. Men did die, often, of injuries such as this. Loss of blood, gangrene, shock, could all kill. But although no longer a young man, he was healthy and death didn't come for the asking. The shattered ankle was agonising but the flow of blood, roughly staunched by Eric with Ivon's own tunic, allowed itself to stay staunched and the wound refused to suppurate. The iron tip of the arrow which had brought him down was fire-new from Halfdan's smithy and carried no infection. Even the shock-fever went down after three days. Ivon de Clairpont lay on his pallet, failing to die, and cursing.

The pallet, to his helpless fury, was in the hut where lived the young thrall-woman Gunnor, who had been making eyes at him since the day he arrived in Eric's Dale.

A few of the Dale bondfolk had huts of their own, although most ate their main meals in the hall each day. Gunnor's deceased husband had built theirs. It was a low, squat, one-roomed affair with a thatched roof and next to no light inside. But like the longhouses it had stout double walls with brushwood and rubble sandwiched in between them, and was plastered inside with daub. There was a stone-lined fire-pit where Gunnor cooked minor meals and brewed medicines and there were shelves for her pots and jars and bowls. A small barrel of her own home-brewed ale always stood in one corner. The bed she provided consisted of an unbleached cloth on top of a pile of heather, and an old fur rug for a covering. Fur rugs which had become shabby were automatically passed down from Eric and his family to their thralls. This one had worn bald in places but it still offered adequate warmth when the northern summer night was chilly. He was away from the noise and hurly-burly of the longhouse. Physically, he was being well looked after.

Only, Gunnor was always there.

It had been Maria in the first place who had washed the wound, setting the broken bone and binding it in such a way that the arrow hole could still be uncovered for further cleansing. But now it was Gunnor who applied salves and poultices and changed the dressings and she did so with a degree of skill which astounded him. One expected the lady of a household, a woman like Maria, to be knowledgeable about such things but he had taken it for granted that a bondwoman like Gunnor would be

15

ignorant. That she was nothing of the kind was annoying, a disturbance to the natural order of things.

Despite his wish to die, there were times at first when he was forced to feel grateful to Gunnor for the relief she brought him, for to begin with the pain was so bad that it was almost tangible, like a leaden boot encasing his foot and lower leg.

He resented this, too. He did not want to be grateful to a thrall.

Over some matters, the resentment far outstripped the gratitude. He could not leave his pallet unaided when he wanted to relieve himself and three times a day, Gunnor, laughing merrily at his outraged demands that she should fetch a man, insisted on helping him.

Gunnor laughed often, which was a further cause of irritation. Ivon was not and never had been a man much given to laughter, except at a certain kind of tough, soldiers' humour. The laughter of sheer light-heartedness seemed to him a sign of trivial-mindedness. He did not respond and this only amused Gunnor more. She would trace the line of his high cheekbones and the creases between his nostrils and the corners of his mouth with a mocking finger and call him 'Old Woodenface'. He pretended not to understand.

It was after the pain and fever had subsided that he noticed how much time she was spending with him. 'Always there,' he had said to himself during those first few days, but now he saw that this was literally true. She never seemed to be called to her usual work of cooking or weaving, but was apparently free to stay in her hut with him all day. She was cleaner and tidier than usual, too. Her little pointed face was not grubby as it used to be, and her pale red braids looked as though they had been washed. She wore her usual coarse, dun-coloured clothes, a long, tight-sleeved underdress with a shorter, looser garment on top, but even these had apparently been brushed, and she generally wore a necklace of some sort.

It finally occurred to him that she must have permission for all this, and possibly even orders.

Had she, indeed! He lay back on his pallet with his eyes closed and thought that over. Eric had tried to wish Gunnor on him before, apparently believing that he might by that means be reconciled to captivity. Well, Eric could forget it! Even when he was still a freeman, at home in Normandy, Ivon had never amused himself with serf-women as some men did. Bondwomen were little more than animals and a man with self-respect didn't go with an animal. Least of all when he had no chance of raising his offspring from the dirt. The private oath of celibacy which he had sworn when first he came to the Dale, would hold him.

Since he didn't appear to be dying, therefore, he had better recover as quickly as possible and escape from his nurse. That morning, he sat up and made it clear that he was tired of the soft oatmeal porridge he had been eating, and wanted solid food.

Gunnor immediately took to bringing him delicacies.

16

One of the worst things about slavery had been the gastronomic deprivation. He was ashamed of this. A man who had lost his liberty and his home and seen his comrades massacred should be beyond whining about such mundane matters as his palate. But although as a soldier he had been used when necessary to eating whatever provender came his way, no matter how poor, when he was at home in Clairpont, or dining among the other household knights at St Simeon's or at the Count of Boulogne's table, he had eaten excellent dishes, and a variety of them. As a thrall in Eric Olafsen's household, he ate the fare of the lowly day after day, week after week, year after year. And he minded.

The food at the Dale was sufficient in quantity; Eric did not starve his belongings, whether four-legged or two-legged. But the thralls' food was both coarse and repetitive: salted meat and fish more often than fresh even in summer; dark bread, flat, flavourless griddle cakes, oatmeal porridge, boiled beans, thin ale or well-water to drink.

When fresh meat was available, at celebrations or when the spare animals were slaughtered in November, the best cuts went to the family and the thralls had what was left. The most toothsome item which ever came his way nowadays was a kind of spicy sausage which, although made from the nastiest meat left-overs, was flavoured with herbs and garlic and, compared to the rest of his diet, was almost exciting. But this too had palled by now. When Gunnor appeared with a chunk of more or less refined bread on which reposed two slices of roast sucking pig with crackling, his mouth watered uncontrollably in expectation of pleasure.

'Where did you get that?' he asked in his awkward English.

'The mistress give it to me. They're having a feast. Master Niall's wife had a son this morning. The first two babies she had just died at once but all's well this time and Eric said we must drink *waes hael* to him and her.' She had left the hut door open to let in the daylight and now squatted beside him to watch him eat. 'You've been used to good food like the master eats,' she said. 'I can see it. I'll try what I can do.'

'Don't trouble,' said Ivon, forcing the ungracious words out and trying to ignore a tantalising vision of the Count of Boulogne's Christmas table, complete with roast haunch of venison, ducks cooked with apples and raisins, porpoise, hare, salmon steaks swimming in delicate sauces, and cinnamon cakes.

Gunnor took no notice of him. Next day, she brought a chicken into the hut and cooked it herself, in a pot, adding herbs to the juices. The day after that she brought some of the honeycakes which Maria and the other freewomen made and usually reserved for themselves and, as was now her habit, sat on the floor by his bed to watch his enjoyment.

Ivon ate the offerings, felt constrained to smile at Gunnor, and because the door was once more open, clearly saw the happiness which at once lit up her triangular little face. It was a fox-shaped face, he thought. It went with her fox-red hair. It was wide across brow and cheekbones and narrowed sharply to a pointed nose and chin. These, unexpectedly,

17

reminded him of Adele. So did the bright, penetrating glint of Gunnor's eyes, although hers were greenish-grey, not dark as his wife's had been, and they were set in a freckled, wind-reddened countenance which was nothing at all like Adele's smooth olive complexion.

He at once felt newly ashamed, for encouraging her, for permitting himself, even for a moment, to compare a bondwoman to his well-bred wife. He wondered suddenly whether Gunnor, who had almost certainly been told to seduce him if she could, would be made to suffer for it if she failed.

He preferred not to know. Cautiously, he said: 'I'll be fit to sleep in the hall again soon. 'I'm a trouble to you. I shall tell them how well you've cared for me and I hope they'll reward you for it.'

'You're no trouble. Dunno about rewards. They won't bother.' At least she didn't seem frightened when she spoke of her owners. 'But it's dull in here, ain't it?' His knowledge of her tongue was now good enough to tell him how rough her speech was. No, she was *nothing* like Adele. 'You're away from the hall and missing all the tales and songs,' Gunnor said. 'You missed all the uproar at the feast for Niall's son. It was funny.'

'Uproar? Funny?'

'Yes. They had a contest,' said Gunnor, 'at making up songs about this story and that. Master Eric went round the others, pointing at each one and saying what he was to make a song about. First one had to make up something about Beowulf killing the monster – you've heard about Beowulf?' Ivon nodded; a desire to know what the songs and stories were about, with which the Dale folk enlivened the dark winter evenings, had gone a long way towards making him pick up the language. 'Well, when he got to his cousin Halfdan, he told *him* to make verses about Hallgerd.'

She seemed to expect some kind of response but Ivon remained blank. Gunnor sighed and, in a kindly voice, proceeded to enlighten her ignorant foreign charge. 'Hallgerd is one of the women in the Sagas. She and her husband were once besieged in their house and her husband was holding off his enemies by shooting at them with his bow. Then his bowstring broke so he asked Hallgerd for some of her long hair to make a new one. But because he'd once struck her, she refused, and he was killed.'

'She *refused*?' The note of admiration in Gunnor's voice scandalised him into comment. 'She let him die because . . . ?'

'Yes.' Gunnor nodded, amused by his indignation. 'But the point is, Master Eric told Halfdan to sing about Hallgerd because Halfdan's always hitting his own wife and they all say it's not right, that he's got no reason to. Well!' Gunnor settled herself more comfortably, her greenish eyes fixed on his face. 'The mistress, she'd got out her elderberry wine, that she and the women make themselves, and Halfdan's wife had had some of it, or I reckon she wouldn't have dared – but she upped and started clapping her hands! And then Halfdan goes all crimson in the face and jumps up and drags her out of the longhouse. Niall and Eric

18

tried to stop him but he just shook them off, and we haven't seen Halfdan's wife since though the thralls as live in their longhouse say there was a big fight in there, because he started knocking her about but she fought back for once and kicked him and threw things.'

'What happened about the competition at the feast?' asked Ivon, bemused.

'Oh, it went on without 'em. Master Eric said he couldn't interfere. But no one thinks that's the end of it,' said Gunnor, clearly looking forward to future instalments of the drama. She stood up. 'That wound wants dressing. I'll see to it.'

She duly saw to it, and came and went as usual throughout the rest of the day, chattering about this and that. But lying awake that night, with the door shut and the curious, slightly fetid odour which Ivon privately called 'the thrall stink' in his nostrils, he knew that he had failed in a resolution. He hadn't taken it consciously, only instinctively, but it still mattered and he had let himself down. He had allowed himself to be interested, just for a few minutes, in the people and affairs of the Dale.

Next day, after Gunnor had gone out as she always did at first light to fetch water from the well, he heard shouting in the distance. When Gunnor reappeared, in haste, slopping the bucket, she was laughing. 'Told you it wouldn't be the end of it, didn't I?' she said.

'Told me what wouldn't be the end of what?'

'The business with Halfdan and his wife.'

'Shouldn't you say *Master* Halfdan?' The thralls of the Dale did not always use the titles *Master* and *Mistress* when discussing their betters and it still startled him. Had the serfs at Clairpont called him Ivon behind his back?

'No, why? They can't hear and Halfdan's a proper bastard, any road,' said Gunnor disrespectfully. She grinned. 'She's divorcing him and going home to her people, over westwards somewhere. She says she's going to get a better husband. He's trying to pretend he's divorcing her because all she's given him is that grizzling little girl that she's welcome to take away, but the truth is she's set on taking the bairn anyway and you should have heard them slanging each other and each of them bawling that the other one was lying to save their pride! She'd got the little one clinging to her and wailing, and Halfdan was trying to get at her and Niall holding him back . . . what a joke!' Gunnor knelt by the fire-pit, checked that the fire, damped down by clods overnight, was still smouldering, and began to rouse it up again with twigs from the basket she kept handy. 'They're in the master's hall now. The master came and fetched them inside. He said if there was going to be a divorce, it all had to be done according to custom with an attempt to put things right and if that don't work, a proper announcement about the marriage ending, in front of witnesses. But I don't reckon he'll try very hard to make her stay. He's never liked the way Halfdan treats her and nor has the mistress. Halfdan'd be rude to the mistress if he dared. He thinks women are dirt.' She glanced up sideways. 'Were you married, ever?'

'Yes.'

'Is that why you kept running off? To get back to her before someone else grabbed your place?'

'No. She died,' said Ivon stiffly. 'Before I left Normandy.'

'That's sad.' Gunnor sounded genuinely sympathetic. 'Children?'

'One boy, one girl. There would have been another boy but he came too soon and they both died.'

'What was your wife like?' Gunnor blew on her fire and the blaze crackled into cheerful life. She reached for cooking pot and oatmeal jar and began making porridge. Everyone in the Dale breakfasted on that boring porridge; at this time of day it was inescapable. Gunnor gave him another sidelong look. 'Was she beautiful?'

'She was pleasing.'

'Pleasing!' This restrained enthusiasm awoke her ready laughter. 'Was she good at it?' inquired Gunnor outrageously.

He felt his face go as stiff as his voice as he answered: 'That's a rude question.'

'On, come on! What were you like as a husband? Were you a bully like that Halfdan?'

It was extraordinary how helpless a man felt when he couldn't walk. There was an instinct to placate the person who looked after you, however humble their status might be. He wanted to put on a haughty face and refuse to reply but instead found himself compelled to an answer of some sort. 'There was no question of bullying. She did her part and I did mine. We understood and respected each other.'

'Doesn't sound much fun.'

'Marriage isn't meant to be fun. But,' said Ivon sternly, 'it's meant to be for life. In Normandy, people marry before the priest and they can't part and remarry at will.'

'Halfdan's wife is lucky she's not Norman,' said Gunnor candidly. 'You don't like him either,' she added.

Ivon was silent, because she was right and having his mind read felt like an intrusion. He decided after all to be in a huff. Gunnor glanced at him and busied herself with the porridge. When she brought it to him, she said in a gentler voice but with even more perception: 'You must get tired, talking our language all the time, don't you? Tell me some words in your language. What are the words for one, two, three?' She held up the appropriate number of fingers for each, to make sure he understood.

This at least was harmless. 'Un, deux, trois.'

She repeated them, while he scooped porridge into his mouth with a wooden spoon. Her pronunciation was dreadful but when he shook his head and made a face, she only laughed. As she took the empty bowl from him, one of her fox-coloured braids almost fell into it. She caught it back with her spare hand and flipped it at him. 'How do you call this?'

'Hair? You mean hair . . . ?' He knew he sounded distracted, but she had now dumped the bowl on the ground, reached out and picked up a lock of his own hair, which like his beard had grown because he had no tools fit for barbering himself, and laid it across her palm beside her own braid. 'Mine is red. Yours is black, *very* black.' Her face was uncomfortably close to his. He could smell the animal femaleness of her. Her gaze sharpened. 'Your eyes,' she said. 'They ain't the same colour. Fascinated me, they did, from the minute you got here. Never seen eyes like yours before.'

Ivon shifted uneasily on his bed. The peculiarity was noticeable only at close quarters. Gunnor must have been observing him closely for a very long time. Well, so she had. He knew that. It made him very uncomfortable indeed.

His father's eyes had been the same. The left eye was an indeterminate blue with a brown inner ring round the pupil, while the right eye was all light brown. Ivon had never gone in much for looking into mirrors and in the days when he was a shorthaired, clean-shaven Norman, had usually been barbered by someone else. But occasionally he'd felt impelled to borrow a proper silver mirror and examine his own face and then, of course, he had seen the oddity for himself.

In relation to his father, he never gave it a thought, but in himself, he thought it a blemish. But Adele had never minded and nor, apparently, did Gunnor, who now put her head on one side and observed: 'Pretty.' He tried to pull his hair away from her and succeeded only in jolting his ankle, hard enough to make him shut his eyes and grit his teeth. Sweat broke out on his forehead and Gunnor at once concernedly stroked it. The effect of this was horrific and took him by surprise. He kept his eyes shut and prayed she wouldn't notice. But the morning was already warm and he had let the rug slip aside. Gunnor sat back on her heels and laughed and as his eyes flew open, she reached out to lay a maddening hand on the little pyramid his manhood made beneath the loose hose which he had insisted on wearing (if Gunnor had had her way, he wouldn't have had any clothes at all; He'd got them back by pleading).

'How is this called?' she enquired.

Ivon swayed forward and struck her. She fell sideways, her hand going to her face. He was sorry at once, because he had behaved just like Halfdan, whom he considered to be an ill-tempered churl, and because however outrageous Gunnor had been, she had cared for him and eased his pain. He waited for her to tell him that he was just another Halfdan but instead: 'I s'pose you think I ought to call you Master! You'd like me if I wasn't a thrall!' Gunnor flung at him, and scrambled to her feet and fled.

When he rolled down that scree with Bjorn's arrow in his ankle, he had crashed from a mental high place too. In an exalted frame of mind, he had sworn to take his own life, but down in the slough of agony and fever and being cared for like a helpless child, he had let go of his resolve.

It was time to remember it again.

Consider, after all, the choice before him. On the one hand, a lifetime of dishonour and despair as a slave, not only for himself but for the unborn progeny who were now a serious risk. Immobilised here in Gunnor's hut, he was as thoroughly trapped as he had been on the scree. Gunnor had run away but she'd surely come back to her own hut and she was a menace to his integrity. His body was aflame for her, and her little fox-face, her sharp greenish eyes, danced before his inner eye in elfin enticement.

She would win. He and his seed after him would live out their lives as thralls unless he turned to the alternative.

Unless, as he had tried to do before, he fled for refuge to that ultimate, pure and impregnable stronghold: death.

Only now, he had no knife. Eric had taken it away and he ate all his food now with his fingers, or a spoon.

He could of course refuse to eat at all. But he doubted his own strength of mind when Gunnor offered him titbits. Besides, she would probably fetch Maria. He had once seen a thrall in this house take to refusing meals out of anger at what he thought was some injustice or other. Maria had summoned two other thralls and made them hold him while she herself held his nose with one hand until his mouth opened. She then ruthlessly spooned porridge into it. It might be as well not to try conclusions with Maria.

What he needed was to get his knife back. When he was healed, he would presumably be given it back anyway but that might well be too late.

She took her time over returning but when she did, he was horrified to see that she was embarking on a new tactic of seduction. She smiled and set about tending his wound as though their quarrel had never happened. And she had fresh clothes. They looked as though they had been made over from some of the freewomen's gowns. Instead of her dull thrall's garments, Gunnor now wore a colourful sleeveless affair in soft green wool with yellow flowers embroidered round the neck opening, over a long dress in a pleasing shade of russet. She leaned over him to see if he was awake and he realised that she had not only had a wash in the interim, but a luxurious one. She smelled of lavender.

'I want a piece of wood,' said Ivon loudly. 'Any kind of wood, but about this big.' He used his fingers to frame the size he meant. 'And a little knife. I want to . . .' His crude English was good enough for the everyday but he didn't know any words for *carve* or *whittle*. He made gestures to explain his meaning. '. . . make something,' he said.

After a few puzzled moments, during which he went through it all again, Gunnor nodded and slipped away. But when she returned, Eric was with her.

He and Maria had come occasionally to see how their damaged property fared, but had never lingered. This time, however, Eric stood by the bed, stooping his head a little under the low thatch, and tugged at his blond beard for some time, without speaking. At length, he said:

22

'Gunnor tells me you want a knife to make something with wood.'

'I want something to do. Time goes slowly. I can't stand without help yet. I want to make a . . . a present for Gunnor. She has been kind.'

'If I let you have the wood and a knife to carve it with, will you swear not to harm yourself? Will you swear to use the knife only on the wood?'

'When I was a knight,' said Ivon bitterly, 'my word could be trusted. Now that I am a slave, my word is nothing. No, I won't swear.'

Sharp in the mind as ever, Eric thought, staring at him. He's a handsome man, with those strong bones. Even the odd eyes are . . . pleasant. He is no monk. He should want to do other things with Gunnor than make toys for her. Perhaps if he is amused, occupied, his defences will falter. He would breed strong children.

'I'm not sure I can trust you,' he said. 'But I'll risk it.' He turned to Gunnor. 'Fetch him what he wants.'

He had meant to act as soon as he got hold of a blade, but Gunnor had earned her little keepsake, all the more so because he had been so rude. She must have thought him graceless. And besides, she had heard him tell Eric what the wood was for and her face when she put the knife and the piece of pinewood into his hands was bright and expectant. For all her experience, she was in years not much more than a child. She should have her gift. He could wait that long.

'What shall it be?' he asked her. 'A dog?' He had seen her sometimes stroke the dogs which wandered round the longhouse. Even Odin would wag his tail and push his brindled head under her hand. Gunnor nodded, enthusiastically.

He had acquired the knack of carving small figures, and decorative patterns, when he was a boy. He had made toys for his children. It wasn't the sort of skill a knight considered important, but it had given him pleasure and he liked to do it well. He therefore set about his task slowly and with great attention to detail. It would be the last time he ever practised this or any skill, and the process of ending one's life, he felt, should involve some kind of ceremony; if not a moment of dramatic declaration when besieged halfway up a scree, then some ritual act performed to perfection. This, then, should be his ritual.

He worked on the carved dog, on and off, for three days. This was partly because, although Gunnor had moved his bed nearer the door for the sake of the light, he could not work much when it was cloudy. But it was also – as he gradually recognised – because he was not only finicking over detail but also putting off the final moment. He swore silently at himself and speeded up. None of that nonsense, Sir Ivon! You will die, my friend, and like it!

Gunnor had sat with him less frequently while he made the carving, perhaps sensing that he wished to work without distraction. She was not there when at last he finished it. He examined it with care. It was good; he knew that. He had persuaded Gunnor to sharpen the knife that morning on the excuse that he needed a keen blade to complete the ears, and it really had made a difference to the ears, which were alertly pricked and subtly hollowed. The carved dog looked repellently like Odin; probably Odin had been in his mind and had come out through his fingers. But since Gunnor actually liked the creature, he thought she wouldn't mind.

She would come soon with his dinner. She had not repeated her cruder attempt to seduce him but what he thought of as her secondary campaign was continuing. She still wore unusually colourful clothes and washed in scented water and brought him treats to eat, and her eyes, her smile, her voice, the very movements of her body, continually said to him: Try me, I'm good. He dreamed about her sometimes at night and had been driven, several times, to do what he hated doing, and had been told by his father's chaplain was very wrong, and relieve his own longings. It was high time to give Gunnor her present and depart.

He lay for a while, looking up at the thatch, and then turned his head towards the door. He could see a segment of sky with cloud drifting across it, and a distant shoulder of hill, green under a pelt of bracken. He wished he could see a church tower somewhere, or that the little pile of belongings by his bed – clothing, shoes, his belt with the bone dagger-hilt still attached to it – included some religious emblems.

Well, he must pray without them. 'Forgive me, Oh Lord, for what I am about to do. I can see no other way. I am sorry.' Some impish voice within him added: 'Why did You have to make animals like Odin?'

He heard Gunnor's footsteps and there she was, smiling, red braids hanging forward over the breasts that her dress wasn't loose enough to hide, and a girdle of dyed yellow cord wrapped round sturdy hips. Gunnor's chin might be narrow but her pelvis was made for child-bearing. Ivon had gathered from her that before she was sixteen, she had had two babies by her deceased husband, although neither had lived, because, like their father, they were prone to chest illnesses. It must have been hard on her; Ivon could understand why she wanted another, stronger man. But why did the little minx have to choose him?

He held out the carved dog. 'Here it is. To say thank you.' He pointed towards his bound ankle. 'It is mending. I shall soon be trying to stand on it again.'

Gunnor took the toy from him slowly, searching his eyes. For once, there was nothing provocative in her own; she seemed to be trying to read his mind. He took her hand and folded her fingers round the gift. 'Yours,' he said. 'Thank you.'

A small, work-hardened palm closed over the back of his hand. Her sadly questioning expression hurt him. He felt sorry for her, as though he were going to betray her. Well, in a fashion, so he was, and he had better get on with it. 'I'm thirsty,' he said. 'Gunnor, the mistress lets you bring me nice things to eat. Would she let you bring me just a little elderberry wine? Enough so that we could both sip it? Then we can drink to the gift.' He had an inspiration. 'We could drink *waes hael* to my ankle. I first heard that phrase in the south,' he added inconsequentially.

'Comes from there, I suppose, Master Eric started using it after he'd been down there. It means *be well*. I'd like to drink to you getting better but the mistress is that careful with her wine. Even for you . . .'

'Just ask her,' he said. 'If you just ask her, I'll . . . I'll give you a kiss.'

To his distress, her face lit up as if the sun had shone on it. She set the little carving on the shelf and darted out of the hut. He watched her go with real sorrow. But he must not weaken now. As soon as she had gone, he sat up straight, pulling up his tunic and feeling in nervous haste for his heart. He would need to thrust hard and accurately, to make a quick end. There might well be a hideous mess; a punctured heart could spout like a fountain. Gunnor would be the one who found him and he regretted that but . . .

It was easy enough to discover his heart. It was hammering violently as if to protest at its imminent destruction. He positioned the knife-point. Don't stop to wonder what lies beyond. Don't think: This is the last time I shall see this hut, that thatch, the sky out there. *Do it.* He gripped the hilt with both hands and braced his muscles. He spoke in a whisper. 'Father, into thy hands . . .'

There was a shriek, a thudding of feet. The light from the door was briefly obscured and then something warm and herb-scented descended on top of him and small but very strong fingers seized his hands and the knife and dragged the blade back from his heart. He shouted and fought, trying to throw her off, ignoring the warning jab from his ankle as he lurched from side to side. 'Let go, let me alone, let me *alone*, I say . . . I don't want to hurt you . . . give that knife here . . . !'

'I won't, you shan't . . . !'

'I will! Leave go, get away from me . . . give that *here* . . . !'

But Gunnor had had the advantage of surprise and she knew the trick of bending back a little finger to loosen a grip. She sprang away to the far side of the hut with the knife, his only escape route, firmly gripped in her fist. 'I been afraid . . . you'd do summat like this!' She was gasping for breath and sobbing at the same time. She leaned against the wall. 'I've been scared ever since you asked for a knife and wouldn't give your word to the master. And today, when you tried to send me to Maria, there was that in your face . . . I didn't go away. I crept back to the door and peered through the crack. And I *saw* . . . you was going to do yourself in!'

'Why didn't you let me? Sooner or later I'll do it, Gunnor. So why not now?'

Gunnor was crying openly. She wiped her palm across her eyes and nose. 'Because I say not, that's why!' She took a long breath and looked at the knife in her hand. She wiped her face once more and stepped forward, halting just out of his reach. Her eyes met his and now they were steady and hard. 'I've cared for you; you're grateful. You said it yourself. You made me a gift.'

'Yes, but . . .'

25

'But you owe me more than a little wooden dog thing. You owe it to me not to let me do this!'

'Stop that!' He was off the bed somehow, hopping, lurching, propping himself on the wall with one hand, risking the toe of the injured foot against the earth floor, grabbing at her. She had the knife aimed at her own side. 'You fool, you little fool!' His balance was too uncertain; he could not get himself away from the support of the wall. 'Very well!' he said angrily. 'Do it, then. If you're mad enough to kill yourself for me, it's not my fault. I can't stop you.' An unpleasant thought came to him. 'Gunnor. I know quite well that you had orders to . . . to look after me and perhaps more than that . . . will they blame you if I die? Are you afraid of what they'll do to you?'

Gunnor stared at him. She was still gripping the knife although she had let the point droop towards the floor. 'The mistress told me to make you happy if I could. She said she'd help. The master was there and he laughed and said I'd need luck and he wished it for me. They never said they'd do anything to me. I ain't frightened of them! It's you! I can't live without you; I *won't* live without you! Ever since the day you first come to the Dale, I've . . . you . . . .' She stumbled over her words. 'I only want you,' she said at last. 'Not any other men. Just you.'

'But, Gunnor!' Ivon was sweating with embarrassment. 'You're a fine girl. There must be many men ready to marry you. Even a freeman might . . .'

For an astonishing moment, he thought she was going to stab him herself. '*Even* a freeman,' said Gunnor savagely. 'Yes. That's how you think of us, don't you? I'm just a thrall, summat so low I ain't human; can't feel! *Even* a freeman! You think we're just animals. That's the truth, in't it?' She advanced and he found himself recoiling from her anger, stumbling backwards and sitting down heavily on his bed. Gunnor stood over him. 'Just animals. Stupid like animals. I've pounded the right herbs to poultice your wound and I can read your mind half the time – such as now – but I'm just a stupid *animal*, am I?'

'No, no, no, but . . .' He floundered in a mire of words, hampered by more than a language which was not his own. He wanted to explain that no, of course she wasn't a fool, but she *was* a thrall and a knight was . . . well, it was the difference between a scruffy pony and a destrier bred through generations for purposes of war. A pony might be admirable, goodhearted, intelligent, but you didn't mate it to a destrier, not if you wanted the foal to be a fine war-horse. He couldn't explain anything of the sort. She would never understand.

Gunnor did not give him time to speak in any case. She was raging on. 'You say no but you mean yes. You think that bondfolk are no more than cattle. You think that when I say I can't and won't go on living unless you're here, I'm just on heat like a cow! Well, let me tell you that I know all about that, about just being randy, and this in't the same. Even if you never speak to me or let me touch you, ever again, it won't change anything, I still won't live unless you're near me. And I'll tell you something else. You don't just think I'm nothing, you think you're nothing as well, because you're a thrall now too. That's why you want to kill yourself. Well, you shan't. Why should you? The rest of us put up with being thralls; so can you.'

'Now it's you that doesn't understand,' he said. 'I've been a freeman, a warrior, a landholder. Now I've come to this, and yes, by God, I do despise this! And I have contempt for people who accept it. If you were the same as us, you'd all run away or kill yourselves.'

'Why?' said Gunnor. 'Sun's warm, stories are good to listen to, snuggling together's sweet. Just living's worth something.' She tossed the knife across the room and sat down beside him. 'Must've been terrible, losing your freedom. You think I don't know that? You ain't talked to me much about what you did before you were captured, but I know enough. The master and mistress told me a bit. I'd give you your freedom if I could. But all I can do is . . . is look after your wound and bring you the things the mistress lets me have from her table and talk to you and . . . and . . . but I might do more,' said Gunnor, looking not at him but away across the hut, 'if you'd let me.'

Ivon had drawn up the knee of his good leg and was resting his forehead exhaustedly on it. The enormous tension, the long, slow, tight-winding process which had brought him to the point of placing the blade against his heart, had given way. If Gunnor were to hand him the knife now and walk away, he could not use it. His mind and body ached once again with the need which had made him, on the scree, take a boulder in his arms: the childish need for comfort, for somewhere to lay his head and rest.

Gunnor had turned to him again and once more read his mind. She put an arm gently round his shoulders and sat like that, quietly holding him. For a while, they sat still.

She was strong and firm and rounded. He had never talked to her, either of Gildenford or of his life in Normandy, because he had thought she wouldn't understand.

And probably she could indeed understand only some of it. But if he did tell her, she would try, he thought, to share. She would understand what he felt even if she could not imagine the life he had lost.

He laid his head between her friendly breasts and began to talk, and presently he did what he had sworn he would never do, and gave his seed to Gunnor the thrall and his line to the future, in a country not his own.

He was anguished afterwards and lay for a while with his arm thrown across his eyes. 'Yes, it was good,' he said in answer to her anxious enquiry. 'But what have I done? My sons will be serfs.'

He had already experienced Gunnor's ability to look into his mind. In later life, her gift of seeing further than others was to grow more marked still.

27

She was silent for a moment, so that he took his arm away from his eyes to look at her. She was gazing into the distance, as though seeing something he could not.

'For a long time, perhaps. For as far as the eye can see,' said Gunnor. 'But perhaps, not for ever.'

PART II

Ivon Oddeyes: Northumbria,
AD 1065–74

Never had William shown so great a cruelty . . . In his rage he caused crops, herds and flocks, food and utensils of every kind to be destroyed. In this way, all the sources of life north of the Humber were wiped out . . . more than a hundred thousand individuals of all ages and of both sexes perished.

Orderic Vitalis

Chapter Three

The Ravens Fly East

'Your grandfather was a good bit different when your father was alive.'
Ivon Oddeyes' grandmother Gunnor said this often.

Sometimes she varied it. 'Your grandfather was different when old Eric
was alive. The old master got to treating him like a friend in the end but
this Bjorn, he's jovial enough among his own but to him a thrall's a thrall
and *he* won't mellow.' But mostly, Gunnor put old Ivon's increasing testi-
ness and tendency to dwell in the past, down to the loss of the man who had
been his son, and had fathered Oddeyes. 'It goes against nature for a man
to see his son die before himself. He never set much store by his daughters
and maybe rightly, for they weren't lucky.' His father, Oddeyes gathered,
had had several sisters but none of them had thrived. Disease or childbirth
had carried off all but one of them before the epidemic came that within
one month wiped out half the population of the Dale in a welter of raging
fever and bloodstained diarrhoea. Numbered among its many victims were
Gunnor's last surviving daughter, both Oddeyes' parents, all but one of
Bjorn Ericsen's children, and Eric and Maria themselves. Halfdan the
Smith was one of the fortunate few who recovered from it but the young
cousin he had been training as his assistant had died. Halfdan had not
married again after the divorce which was now part of the Dale's folklore,
so now he ran the forge by himself, and unaided made the horseshoes and
arrow-tips and ploughshares and utensils which the Dale so badly needed,
to use and to sell.

Ivon Oddeyes could barely remember his parents. Instead, he had
Gunnor and his grandfather Old Ivon and a couple of aunts, his mother's
sisters, the wives respectively of Orm the Shepherd and Snorri the
Cowman, who made him casually welcome in their huts among their own
children. They were usually busy, however, caught up in the eternal
round of work which made up the lives of the thrall-women: grinding flour
for bread each day, baking, sweeping, feeding animals and helping Master
Bjorn's wife Estrith and the other freewomen to weave and stitch to keep
the household clad. He therefore lived mostly with his grandparents,
which suited him.

He revered his grandmother, responding instinctively to her forceful
personality and unconcerned by her somewhat peculiar appearance.
Gunnor at forty-six was the second oldest woman in the Dale and looked it.

31

She had lost half her teeth and acquired a nutcracker profile, while the fox-red hair had long since faded to a dust colour, streaked with white. She was also far from clean. Gunnor had once taken trouble to wash in order to woo Ivon de Clairpont, but it didn't come naturally and now she had reverted to nature. At close quarters, she smelt.

But she had a formidable reputation for herbal remedies and wound-healing and also for foretelling the future. Even Bjorn respected her and sometimes sought her advice. This impressed Oddeyes considerably. If his grandmother could make Master Bjorn (who usually behaved as though the bondfolk didn't exist) address her so politely, then she must be wonderful.

The only person among the Dale bondfolk who was Gunnor's equal was his grandfather, whom she defended when he started on his tales of a past which no one else in the Dale could share.

'He goes on and *on*,' Oddeyes sometimes heard his aunt Dreda Ormswife grumble to the other women as they dragged buckets from the well or pounded dough side by side. But Gunnor was proudly loyal to him. 'When folk grow older, they think back to their youth. He can't help it and it eases him to talk about the past.'

'It's bad for the boy,' Dreda said once, in Oddeyes' hearing. 'He was the same with the lad's father, always stuffing him up with tales of belonging to a great family and dreams of getting back to it one day. It used to unsettle Red and it'll unsettle Oddeyes too if the old man ain't careful.'

'He wants it to,' said Gunnor. 'It's partly my doing,' she admitted with a snort. They were shaping bread and she slapped it about with a hard, irritated hand. 'I foretold that his seed would get back one day to where he come from. But I ain't sorry I said it. It felt true and it still does and it gave him hope. He'd have died years back if he hadn't had that.'

'He's still not doing right by the lad,' said Ymme disapprovingly. Spare, stooped Ymme was genuinely the oldest of them all. She was three years older than Gunnor, and the personal thrall of Bjorn's wife Estrith, who had inherited her from her mother-in-law Maria. On grounds of both age and position, Ymme considered that she ought to be senior to Gunnor, whose lustre as the wise-woman of the Dale she envied. 'Remember the business over the child's name?' she said grimly.

'Well, the master put a stop to that,' said Gunnor. Her gap-toothed smile was sour. 'Like I expected he would. It was the same with Red.'

Oddeyes had not been called that at his birth. Nor had his father been originally labelled Red. Both of them, at old Ivon's insistence, had been called Ivon after him and furthermore had been baptised by Christian rites. In Red's case, Old Ivon had performed the rites himself but by the time his grandson Oddeyes was born, a priest had taken to visiting the Dale, riding over now and then from Trygg's Thorpe, the hamlet which had grown up in the valley to the north, and the third Ivon had had benefit of clergy. At each baptism, Old Ivon had said the same thing. 'The child is a de Clairpont, the descendant of Norman knights. He must carry the family name. We won't be slaves for ever.'

Eric Olafsen had been present at both ceremonies and had neither interfered nor commented. But even Eric, naturally good-natured and growing increasingly tolerant with time, never encouraged his thralls to think of themselves as anything other than that. Old Ivon's son had his father's odd-coloured eyes but his mother's fox-red hair was more immediately startling. Eric nicknamed him Red and somehow saw to it that he was always known as that.

Old Ivon's grandson, by the end of his first year, was developing the same hair, but in him the odd de Clairpont eyes seemed more noticeable. Eric took to addressing him and referring to him as Oddeyes and found frequent occasions for doing both.

It was a natural, understated process. Half the people in the Dale were called by nicknames. Dreda herself had been originally named Gundreda but had had it shortened to distinguish her from an older Gundreda. But understated or not, it had worked once more. Before another six months had run, everyone but his grandfather had given up calling him Ivon.

'Might be best,' said Ymme, 'if his granddad would call him what the rest of us do. Or there'll be trouble one day, I can see it coming.' She nodded several times, wisely, with pursed lips. Dwelling, in portentous tones, on the dark side of life was one of Ymme's methods of drawing attention away from Gunnor. Bjorn had once called her a malevolent crone and he resolutely refused to drink any of the possets she sometimes brewed by way of challenging Gunnor. 'She drops ill wishes in with the herbs,' said Bjorn.

'Well, he's fixed in his ways now and he won't change,' said Gunnor, referring to Old Ivon. She put another loaf to bake on the flat stones at the edge of the longhouse fire-trench, reached for another batch of dough and casually overrode Ymme's latest bid for sibyl status by adding in meaningful tones: 'What will be will be.'

Ymme and Aunt Dreda were tiresome, Oddeyes thought, and slipped out of the hall. He wanted to find his grandfather.

Oddeyes revered Old Ivon, in fact, as much as he did his grandmother, but in a different way. He was not afraid of Gunnor but Old Ivon sometimes scared him. Indeed, his grandfather was good at scaring people. The old brand on his forehead was puckered and ugly, and he had a trick of looking at people such as Aunt Dreda down his high-bridged nose, with no smile on his hard brown face, which reduced them to a pulp of anxious agreement and scuttling servitude, as though he were one of the masters instead of another thrall.

When he talked to Oddeyes, which he often did, it could be alarming because it was frequently incomprehensible, and if Oddeyes didn't understand, Old Ivon would show impatience, or even cuff him.

Yet the old man fascinated him. As he grew bigger, Oddeyes was acquiring duties which kept him occupied for much of the day. He had to scatter grain for the poultry that clucked and scratched round the longhouses, and in summer he was sent to the fields to throw stones at the birds which tried to steal the crops. But he sought Old Ivon out whenever he could. His grandfather did not stay in his hut during the day, but, being lame, he was never hard to find. He was always either by the fire-trench in the main longhouse or else, in good weather, on a bench in the trodden-earth courtyard in front of the main longhouse, working with his hands, mending things or making small items of furniture. If Oddeyes came to squat beside him, Old Ivon would not interrupt his work, but he would begin, in that puzzling, demanding, exhilarating fashion, to speak.

'Never forget who you are.' He said that over and over and Oddeyes knew that he meant his grandson must never forget he was a de Clairpont. Oddeyes was rather confused as to what a de Clairpont was but he understood that it meant being different from the other thralls. His confusion was the worse because no one else seemed to think that he or his grandfather were anything but thralls, whose purpose in life was to serve the people who lived in the longhouses, especially the master of the biggest one. In return the master fed and housed them and if enemies should come, would defend them. Everyone else in the Dale took this arrangement for granted. It was only his grandfather who ever questioned it. But when he did, he opened a door in Oddeyes' mind, through which shone the sunlight of another country. Confusing or not, Oddeyes loved it.

'I was a freeman when I was young, boy,' Old Ivon would say. 'More than that. I was a knight, a noble warrior, in Normandy.' Oddeyes often wondered where Normandy was and what a knight might be, but questions made Old Ivon impatient. 'You're bred from a proud line. Just bear that in mind.' Old Ivon would then fix him with the unmatched eyes which they both shared and sigh. 'You don't even speak your own language. If I try to teach you a word or two, you can't pronounce it right. You talk like a Norseman. Bah!'

Old Ivon himself spoke northern English with a thick nasal accent. Some of the Dale people laughed at it, which did nothing to improve the old man's irascible temper.

On the day that Oddeyes came to sit with him while Gunnor was in the longhouse thumping dough and keeping Ymme in order, Old Ivon added something new. 'We Normans come from Norse stock but we went south and mixed with the Latins; we're different. We use the French tongue and we're proper Christians. And *our* family was prosperous. I held land in Normandy, lad, a whole valley . . .'

'Like this?' said Oddeyes. He had never been out of Eric's Dale and for him the word valley meant this one, with the fields and cattle meadows splashed across its floor and a swift, boulder-strewn river running through; steep-sided hills on either hand where sheep grazed, and trees growing only in a few places where the slope was softer.

'No, not like this. Wider, shallower, and the hills all round were lower. They weren't covered with grass and bracken and heather like these, they were thick with forests full of game. We had a river running through the valley, but it was slower than this one and it wound in great loops. There was a bridge you could see miles away, even from where the road first topped the hills.' Old Ivon's voice had grown distant and so had his eyes; he was gazing at something within his own mind, and describing it. 'Clear Bridge, that's what Clairpont means. Not that I stayed there after I was seven. I was sent off to another big household to learn my trade. I was page to great people, my boy. I served at table and held water for splendid lords to wash their hands. Mighty men, they were, with great prowess in war. But they'd never bring their swords into the hall. They'd come to dine wearing fine wool and silk. Swords and armour were for the practice field, or for war itself, though I spent time enough, too, learning to care for the mail and the weapons and how to use them.'

Bjorn and the other freemen had weapons and mail. These hung on the wall just inside the door of each longhouse. There were two-handed swords with intricately chased hilts and there were axes of various sizes, some so huge that only a full-grown man could lift them. There were scarred old circular shields, made of leather stretched over wood, with an iron boss in the middle. Old Ivon sneered at these, saying that a shield should be elongated to protect its owner's legs. Occasionally, these things were taken down and the Dale freemen would have a practice bout or two and instruct their male offspring in martial arts. But when this happened, the thralls had to watch from a distance. There were boys of Oddeyes' age among the masters' children and these had toy swords to play with. They were not allowed to share these games with the bondmen's children and Oddeyes couldn't imagine being permitted to touch a real weapon.

Nor could he imagine what his grandfather meant by 'splendid lords'. He had heard, vaguely, of a being called an earl but he did not connect this with the idea of a lord since what Dreda had actually said was: 'If you don't behave, Earl Tostig will come in the night and eat you.' Oddeyes assumed that an earl was something like the trolls which featured sometimes in the stories round the fire in winter.

He supposed that 'lords' might be something like the Dale's master, Bjorn and his kinsmen. But they, although they were powerful and had to be treated with caution and could stop working if they felt like it, and though they wore bright-coloured wool on occasion and owned garnet and amethyst cloak-brooches, nevertheless had daily tasks and working clothes very like those of their thralls. At ploughing and planting and harvesting, master and bondman worked side by side as a matter of course. The lords his grandfather talked about would surely never have done that. They remained, for him, mysterious.

When Old Ivon got on to his life as a grown man, however, he talked about things still harder to imagine. Ponies the boy had seen but his grandfather had apparently once ridden about on enormous animals called war-horses. 'Much taller than any pony, sleek-coated, splendid and fiery . . . we trained them to rear on command and trample a foe.'

Mounted on this fabulous steed, Old Ivon had gone to war. And he had been knighted. While Gunnor, in the longhouse, was deciding with grim satisfaction that she had gained the upper hand in her feud with Ymme, Ivon was trying to explain to Oddeyes what knighthood meant. '. . . it was a solemn event. I had to pray in a chapel beforehand and then take a bath and there was a ceremony in my suzerain's hall . . .' (What on earth was a suzerain? Oddeyes wondered.) '. . . then, my boy, I was one of a brother-hood of trained warriors of good breeding. That is what being a knight means. Of course, it isn't always so formal. Men are knighted on the battle-field sometimes as a reward for valour and sometimes a lord will knight a loyal servant on the spur of the moment and that's still a knighthood. But I had the full ceremony. I remember, the night before, how dark and ghostly the chapel was. I wouldn't have dared set foot beyond the circle of light from the candles.'

Oddeyes had never seen a chapel. When the conscientious priest visited the Dale, he set up a portable altar in Bjorn's hall. The crucifix which Maria had kept in the private quarters was still there, since Estrith had been not only dominated by her mother-in-law but also devoted to her and had several times resisted domestic change because 'the old lady wouldn't have liked it', a phrase spoken in a hushed voice with a quick glance over the shoulder as though Maria might suddenly appear and wrest back her authority. It was still, however, the only permanent recognition of Chris-tianity in the entire Dale.

Baths he knew about, because Bjorn and his kinsmen followed the old Viking custom of taking a bath each week. It was an enormous and har-assing business. Water had to be heated in a huge cauldron and then scooped into large vessels and carried, one vessel to two staggering thralls, to the wooden tub set up near the fire. For the menfolk, that was. The women would take the tub afterwards and put it in the private room. They usually had a long wait because Bjorn liked to soak in his tub for an hour or more, with refreshments and someone to entertain him by singing, and thrall-girls (to Estrith's distress, he insisted on girls) running backwards and forwards with the food and drink. Estrith would wash his back and bring fresh clothes for him and keep a jealous eye on his serving maids. Even the other men sometimes grew restless, awaiting their turn for the tub.

The bondfolk, of course, had no baths unless they took a dip in the river or went to the trouble of heating well-water over their own small fires. Mostly, they went grimy and that was another difference between them and their masters.

'You had a bath?' Oddeyes said now, round-eyed. 'Like Master Bjorn does?'

'I had a bath a month in those days.' His grandfather laid down the bridle he was mending and glared at him. 'And I wore good clothes. I never thought to be dirty as I am now and to wear this patched-up rubbish.' He gripped the edge of his old brown tunic between finger and thumb and shook it at Oddeyes like an accusation. 'And I never thought to see my own flesh and blood going grubby and barefoot and wearing clothes fit for a swineherd, either.'

'I have boots for winter, Granddad.'

'Bah! Old common things! You should have deerskin boots, fit for riding in. You'll never even learn to ride. Nor did your father before you.'

'But, Granddad, I ride on the donkeys when you fetch them from the meadow.'

'*Donkeys!*' For a moment Oddeyes thought that a clout was coming and drew quickly back out of reach. But his grandfather's outraged expression softened. 'I forget. You're too young to know. But you'll grow and if I keep on saying it, you'll maybe remember. Your family is noble. We were made thralls when I was taken prisoner, after a man great enough to know better betrayed my leader. Remember that. Be ready to seize any chance that comes, of breaking free again, of getting back home to Clairpont and declaring yourself. Look.' He fished under his tunic and brought out what looked like a piece of bone on a string. 'I took this from a robber when I was young. I carved our family device into it – these markings here, see? Look well. Learn those markings, boy. Knowing our device and carrying that dagger-hilt – that and your eyes – will tell people who you are. All my children had my eyes; very likely you have odd-eyed cousins now in Normandy. If the chance ever comes, boy, *find* them. I'll give you this dagger-hilt to keep when you're older. I doubt I'll ever get free now, but you might.' His gaze fixed itself fiercely on Oddeyes, and suddenly he leant forward and gripped the boy's shoulders. 'Your grandmother can see the future. She says my descendants won't be bondfolk for ever. The one who wins our freedom back *may be you.*'

'What nonsense,' grumbled Dreda when her small nephew repeated some of this to her later. 'Here we were born and here we'll die unless one of us upsets the master so that he sells us off and that could happen, mark my words.' She shook a finger at Oddeyes and her small, pinched features were anxious. 'It could happen if the master heard you chattering about being free and going to Normandy. So you keep quiet and keep away from that old man. We'll find you some more jobs to keep you busy. You're getting a big boy now. Your grandmother Gunnor should have kept her foretelling to herself. Maybe she did it to comfort your granddad but she did a lot of harm. Kept him thinking about freedom when there's no sense in thinking about it. Thralls we are and thralls we'll stay. Things don't change.'

But the following year, when Oddeyes was seven, a number of things did.

He was too young at the time to recognise the significance of more than a little of what he heard and saw in the year 1066, but much of it impressed him enough to linger in his memory. Later, looking back, he understood.

In the spring of that year, Bjorn and his cousins, as usual at that season, rode to the town they called Jorvik. They went to sell the iron goods made by the old smith Halfdan, the cloth woven by the women and a few cheeses from the first worthwhile milking of the year, to buy salt and footwear, dyestuffs for the womenfolk and raw iron for Halfdan, and to bargain for fine fur rugs from Scandinavia where the animals grew such magnificent winter pelts. They also went to catch up on the news.

They were always behind with the latter, for in winter when the valley was either snowbound or liable to be at any moment, few people came to the farmstead, or left it. From December to February it was better to stay under cover, gather round the fire and tell stories. Few could be spared, either, when the weather first began to improve, for then there was the planting to see to, and the repair of winter storm damage to thatched roofs and longhouse walls.

By the time April arrived, therefore, Bjorn and his kinsmen, every year, were wild for information about the world outside, and wild also with an inborn craving for new horizons. A few generations ago, their Viking forebears had at this season regularly sailed off to raid or trade as the fancy took them. Their descendants sallied to Jorvik impelled by the same instinct, and regarded the event as a landmark.

But this time, they had a special purpose.

They were gone longer than usual and returned in a downpour, announcing their arrival with much blowing of horns, which caused the household to run out with shawls and rugs thrown over their heads, to welcome them and see what, or whom, they had brought.

There were three strange men riding with Bjorn. There was also a low cart dragged by two mules harnessed tandem fashion. On it, enthroned on the familiar hide-wrapped lump which was Halfdan's annual iron ingot, swathed and hooded against the weather as tenderly as though she might melt, was a young woman. Bjorn would not let her walk through the mud but carried her up to the longhouse. Another girl, evidently her personal thrall, who had been riding on a pony, dismounted and squelched after her mistress, carrying a small hooped chest.

Inside his longhouse, Bjorn put his burden down and beckoned to his cousin Sven. A few older men had stayed behind and so had three others: Bjorn's son Leif and his cousin Niall the Younger because they had been ill, and Niall's brother Sven because alone of all the males in the clan, the broad, stolid Sven disliked journeys and never left the Dale if he could help it.

'Here she is,' said Bjorn, helping the newcomer to remove her voluminous mantle. 'This is your bride, Sven. This is Signy.'

The three strangers had also dismounted and come inside. They came forward and he introduced them. 'Signy's father . . . her elder brother . . . her father's cousin . . . her mother is lying-in and couldn't come.'

There were understanding murmurs from the women. Bjorn's wife Estrith came to take Signy's hands and bid her welcome. With an arm round the girl, she led her right up to Sven.

'So you're called Signy? I'm Sven. I hope they've told you all about me.

38

I hope to make you happy here . . . we have a very good life here . . . you're so beautiful,' said Sven.

His square, blunt face had turned scarlet. Signy was clearly shy and unused to being the centre of attention, but her prospective bridegroom's embarrassment appeared to give her courage. She smiled at him and said: 'I am glad to be here after such a long journey. But your kinsmen have looked after us very well. I'm sure I shall be happy.'

She had a small clear voice ('Silvery!' said Sven to Bjorn ecstatically later) and this was all of a piece with the rest of her. She was a slender girl who carried her head well on a long, graceful neck and, now that her hood was off, they could see that the hair which was plaited like a crown was ash-fair, so pale that it too was almost silver.

The expressions of those watching the couple were now a mixture of the relieved and the fatuous. These moments were always fraught. First impressions were so important, and couples had been known to take a dislike to each other on sight, causing wedding preparations to dissolve forthwith into acrimonious cancellation and even into brawling.

This time, it was going to be all right. Oddeyes, hovering inquisitively as near to the principals as he could (he was good at finding jobs to do in places where something interesting was happening), saw Signy taken off by the women to wash and put on fresh clothes, was sent out then to help rub down muddy ponies, but came back inside in time to hear Sven saying urgently to Bjorn: 'Did you remember to bring back something for me to give her as a morning-gift?'

'Yes, you lazy sod. We even did that for you. We found an amethyst necklace for you to give her. It's supposed to come from Byzantium and to be very old and very lucky. It's in my saddle-bag. It'll suit her colouring.'

'The dowry's far more than I expected,' said Sven seriously, 'and Signy . . . I never dreamed you'd bring me such a pretty wife . . . how did you manage it, Bjorn?'

Bjorn also became serious. 'You've heard the news. Her parents wanted to get her married as soon as possible, before anything happens, as they put it, and they believe that lonely places like this are safer than the towns that invaders make for. And on our side,' said Bjorn, his grave tone acquiring a sardonic tinge, 'we told them that if any man could be trusted to keep out of trouble, you could.'

The marriage feast took place the next day, amid a welter of cooking and laughter.

Signy's maid, Inge, was introduced to the other thrall-women and went with them to fetch evergreens and spring flowers with which to make garlands for the big longhouse, and the hall was decorated and set for the feast, with Signy's dowry on show. On the principal table, placed there reverently by an impressed Estrith, was a set of six amber-glazed earthenware bowls. Except for one small jug, the survivor of a pair Estrith had bought on a rare visit to Jorvik, there was no earthenware at the Dale. The other jug of the original pair had been broken within a few weeks and Bjorn had said: 'Waste of money. Leather jugs and wooden bowls and a few silver things for feast-days, that's all we need. That's all our forefathers had and if you ask me, they showed sense.'

'But it's fashionable now,' Estrith said as the other women gathered admiringly round. 'Everyone in Jorvik has some, Signy says. It comes from East Anglia, where people have been making it for more than a hundred years. The way we live here is behind the times. This is beautiful. We must treat it with great care.'

Treating it with great care meant chasing Oddeyes away. Attracted by the gathering round the table, he had come to see what they were looking at and instantly reached out to touch one of the gleaming bowls. Estrith hurriedly pushed him away. 'Now be off with you. Those aren't wooden bowls that you can play at quoits with. Go and help carry something you can drop!'

Oddeyes considered this remark unfair, since he was not clumsy and rarely dropped anything. He was in fact showing signs of dexterity with his hands and sometimes now helped Old Ivon at repairing furniture or saddlery. But he presently forgot his disappointment in marvelling at the bride herself.

The chest which Inge had carried in proved to be her mistress's trinket box. When Signy was dressed for her marriage, some of its contents were brought out. She wore blue – the most costly of all dyes, and in all the Dale only Estrith had even a blue shawl – and she had silver arm-rings and a girdle with mussel-pearls strung into the tassels, and a pendant, by contrast, of gold and garnets. Her hair was combed out loose except for an embroidered headband. Sven looked as if he had been stunned with a mallet and Bjorn's son Leif, who was just sixteen, had to be kicked under the table during the feast, because he kept on gazing at her with his mouth open.

As usual in the Dale, no one had troubled about fetching the priest from Trygg's Thorpe. Signy's father laid her hand in Sven's and Sven promised to protect and maintain her and any children that she gave him, and with that, amid delighted cheers and whistles, the marriage was made.

Sven was one of those with his own small longhouse, and when the feast was done, the couple were raucously escorted thither. In the morning, rather a lot of people had headaches and the day was quiet. The bridal pair did not appear until midday and when they did, had a highly contented air at which the rest of the household grinned openly. Signy was wearing a very fine antique amethyst necklace.

The next day, she said goodbye to her family and cried a little as they rode away, but then wiped her eyes, smiled apologetically at Estrith and said: 'What should I be doing?'

'We have some weaving under way,' Estrith said. 'And a good fire to warm us while we work. It's a cold, raw day. Come and help.'

The men thought it a raw day, too. Old Ivon settled down beside the fire-trench in the hall to plait leather thongs into reins for a new bridle and Oddeyes joined him at it, while on the other side of the fire Bjorn and his

40

kinsmen gathered, taking the opportunity to groom their dogs and talk.

Mainly, it appeared, to talk. It was as though they had been waiting for Signy's menfolk to go before they could hammer out the Dale's own private response to the news which Bjorn and his companions had brought back from Jorvik along with Signy.

To begin with, the talk was too quiet to follow. Then Sven raised his voice. 'I can't see that it's any affair of ours. What's this southron king, Harold, to do with us here in the Danelaw? We're not obliged to draw sword for *him*.'

His relatives instantly raised their own voices in an indignant chorus, berating him for lack of spirit. 'I knew you'd say that!' Bjorn bellowed, drowning the rest. 'I told Signy's father you would!'

'I can't agree with Sven,' Niall the Younger declared. 'Earl Morcar acknowledges King Harold and we can trust Morcar; he's not like that madman Tostig that was earl before him. He doesn't murder men for disagreeing with him. I fancy he'll call us to arms if Harold summons him and then it'll be our duty to go whether you like it or not, Sven, and whatever Bjorn told your father-in-law. Besides, it'll be fun! When did we last have a chance of any fighting?'

'Think of it. We didn't even know the old Confessor king was dead. I wish we could get to Jorvik sometimes in winter. Why can't we?' That was Rolf, one of the younger and most restless men in the clan. He had been one of the Jorvik party. 'People must have come and gone across the channel down south,' he said, 'or no one would know about this Norman duke and his plotting.'

It's warmer in the south,' said Sven phlegmatically but loudly. 'And all of you go to Jorvik too damned often as it is. Half a dozen trips you made between you last summer. The work here gets neglected and I have to see to it all while you're off junketing . . .'

'You miserable stick-in-the-mud! You were glad enough to send us off this time. We were running your errands for you. You ought to get off your behind and leave the Dale now and again yourself! Odin's Beard!' Rolf let out an exasperated snort. 'We've just had to fetch a bride from Jorvik for you. You couldn't be bothered to climb into the saddle even to go courting! Are you telling us that if there's a fight going, you don't want to get into it?'

'If it's away south then no, I don't.' Sven was not easy to provoke and took it for granted anyway that no one would accuse him of timidity in so many words. They had all seen him handle a recalcitrant bull, and knew better. 'If enemies come to the Dale, I'll fight. Go looking for trouble away from home, no.'

Oddeyes listened with interest, as half a dozen voices protested simultaneously, earnestly praising adventure, the chance of booty and their duty to the unknown entity called Earl Morcar. 'You're outnumbered, Sven,' said Bjorn at last. He paused, thoughtfully. 'I think,' he added 'that we'd best look our blades over. Just in case.'

*   *   *

So, for the very first time in his life, Oddeyes saw all the mail and wea-
ponry taken down from the wall at one time, leaving an array of bare hooks
behind. Intrigued, he followed as the war gear was carried outside. The
cold grey weather no longer mattered; the men needed space and daylight.
Oddeyes watched round-eyed as edges were tested, and their owners set
about cleaning and sharpening swords and axes.

'So. They are preparing for battle,' said Old Ivon's voice harshly beside
him. His grandfather had followed him out of the longhouse and was
standing near, leaning on the walking-stick he used to help out his lameness. The hands folded on its carved head were quivering so that the whole
stick trembled. Old Ivon was not looking at Oddeyes but seemed to be
seeing some remote vision. 'The old king is dead,' he said, talking as much
to himself as to Oddeyes. 'Him they called the Confessor, that was brother
to the man I followed to England and to captivity. The old king has no son.
The Council have given the crown to his wife's brother, this man Harold.
But the Duke of Normandy is kin to the old king and he says that the
crown was promised to him and that Harold has sworn allegiance to him.'
He turned his head and focused on Oddeyes at last. 'Listen to me, boy. Try
to understand what I'm saying. The Norman duke, *our* duke, has said he
will invade.'

'Our duke?'

'We're Normans, boy. I've told you before. Duke William is our leader.
May God send him the victory.'

'Norman dukes, indeed! God help us all if the master hears that kind of
talk!' snorted Dreda, after Old Ivon had repeated these remarks ten days
running. She yanked crossly at the chain as she hauled the bucket out of
the well. Some of the women had formed a sociable habit of gathering at
the well at the end of the day. It was a fairly new well, dug when the old one
went dry during the hot summer which went before the great pestilence
and Eric offered a reward to anyone who could find a source of water
nearer than the river, which was itself down to a trickle. Ymme immediately volunteered and, with the entire community on her heels, wandered
round the longhouses with a forked hazel twig, and even hopefully
prowled inside them. Gunnor watched her with a smile of cynical amusement and Eric stood with his hands on his hips when she invaded the
private quarters, and enquired if she expected him to dig a well under his
own bed.

When Ymme had had quite a long walk and the twig remained inert,
Gunnor took it away from her and in ten minutes had found them water in
a good position at one side of the yard in front of the big longhouse. It was
far better placed than the old well had been, inside the palisade which
embraced both longhouses and huts, instead of in the secondary enclosure
which encircled the vegetable patch and a small meadow and was quite a
long trudge from the habitations.

This one never failed and the evening gathering there, to draw water ready for the morning porridge and provide drinks in the night for crying children, was now a pleasant, gossipy ritual.

'My sister Elfgiva,' Dreda said irritably to the others now, 'thinks that all the men'll have to go if it comes to it, maybe bond as well as free. So we'll have to manage alone. Very nice that'll be. As if we hadn't enough to do as it is.'

'You'll hardly miss Orm,' said Ymme with a sniff. 'He spends half the year out on the hills with the sheep even now.'

'If he goes, I'll probably be out on the hills with them myself!' snapped Dreda.

'If the bondmen go to war,' said Ymme, crouching to fill her pitcher from the bucket, 'that'll likely be the last we'll see of 'em. All the mess and muddle there'll be round a battle, with strangers everywhere, a man'll only have to rob a body and vanish into the handiest burgh. If he can buy a bed and a meal, who's to ask questions? He'll be just one more strange face among scores. Next day, he'll get work and the day after that he'll take a wife - or another wife if he's left one here - and that'll be that.' Ymme, safely widowed for years, favoured them all with a sly smile. 'Your men'll run off and set up as freemen and you'll be forgotten. Maybe you'll be sorry the old custom of branding thralls isn't kept up. More than one woman's been grateful for it in times gone by.'

'Well, don't go saying that where Bjorn can hear you.' Gunnor had joined them, with Elfgiva beside her. 'Or he'll likely decide to start the custom up again and the men won't thank you for that.'

'Gunnor's right.' Elfgiva had a whining voice very like her sister Dreda's. 'The master likes to keep us in our place. He makes me tired. Merry enough among his own but there's never a smile or a thank you for the likes of us. Unless we're pretty young things, of course.'

Inge, Signy's thrall, was one of the pretty young things and knew that this remark was meant for her. She was standing back, waiting for the older women to claim their water first. She blushed and looked away. Inge was timid and did not feel at all at home in the Dale, which was very unlike the town dwelling in Jorvik from which she and her mistress came. Signy, who, although already attached to Sven, was still shy and also found the Dale strange, clung to her maid somewhat and made a pet of her, which had not helped because it made the other women look askance at Inge.

She tried hard not to give them offence or let them have any lever to use against her, but unfortunately Inge's fresh skin and rare combination of honey-coloured hair and soft brown eyes were very pleasing and Bjorn had noticed. He had promptly commandeered her services as a bathmaid. Elfgiva's giggling twin daughters, who had had that honour previously, were jealous, Signy was too gentle to protest, and Estrith, recognising a certain, unusual heat in Bjorn's eyes when they rested on Inge, had taken to staring at her with unmistakable hatred. Inge, in fact, was wretched.

'If it'll stop the men running off, we'd best tell Bjorn all the same.' Wynflaed was Ymme's grown daughter. Unlike her sparely made mother, she was as broad-built as one of the oxen, but had an unbovine fame as the female wag of the Dale. 'Whoever pulls the short straw has to sidle up to him and . . .'

'Inge can tell him when he's in his bath,' said Ymme, with a lewd chuckle.

Inge shrank away from their laughing faces, not sure if they meant it or not. 'No, I couldn't!'

'Let her alone,' said Dreda good-naturedly. 'It's not her fault Bjorn's got his eye on her.'

'She'll have to face up to it sooner or later.' Ymme grinned, showing an array of brown teeth. 'I reckon he'll have her before he lets anyone else near her.'

Inge, biting her lip, moved without speaking to take her turn with the bucket. Dreda made a kindly attempt to change the subject. 'It's nearly dark. Time we went in.' She looked up at the sky. 'Wind's swinging south. Stars're out tonight, look, there . . .' said Dreda, and dropped her pitcher and fell to her knees with a scream.

They had been longer than usual at the well and the dusk was fading swiftly. The outlines of the hills were dark masses against a sky which was scarcely lighter, except in the west where a faint glow edged the nearest clouds with pink. The clouds were moving, blowing away northwards, with dim stars, as Dreda had said, making a fitful appearance between them. Even as she spoke, the sky to the south had been suddenly swept clear, laying bare the horror in the heavens which the clouds till now had hidden.

Bright stars they had seen before, but never one as bright as this, least of all before it was full dark, and never, never, with a trailing tail like luminous hair, streaming out across the sky – 'And not even lying with the wind!' wailed Ymme, as though this, somehow, were a final distortion of nature.

'It's an omen!' gasped Wynflaed, and crossed herself.

Elfgiva fell to her knees beside her sister and Inge, after one horrified upward glance, let the bucket fall down the well with a slither and a splash and stood trembling. Gunnor too gasped aloud, but then remained motionless, holding her shawl tightly round her, her face upturned. 'It is a sign from God,' she said. 'But I cannot see what it portends.'

'What does it matter?' sobbed Elfgiva. 'It's bound to mean something terrible, death or . . . or . . . oh I can't bear to look at it!' She buried her face in Dreda's shoulder.

'I can't bear it either!' said Inge, and ran for the shelter of Sven's longhouse, and Signy.

Dreda's scream had brought people from the longhouses. They too stood transfixed, staring upwards. From the huts a hundred paces away came a babble of voices and several shrieks.

Oddeyes had been sleeping and it was a shriek that woke him. He scrambled off his bed of piled heather and darted inquisitively to the door of his grandparents' hut, to see a panicky cluster of people pointing at the sky. He followed the nearest stabbing forefinger and gaped.

The women from the well ran up, babbling. Dreda rushed into the hut where her three children were sleeping and could be heard waking them up and frightening them with cries of relief because the monstrosity in the sky hadn't eaten them, while her sister Elfgiva, plunging into the hut next to it, similarly scared her own two girls from their beds by hysterical crying.

Her husband Snorri, whose pointing finger had shown Oddeyes the star, uttered an impatient noise and plunged after her. A moment later, they heard him trying to calm his terror-stricken family by shouting at them and hitting someone.

'What fools some people are,' said Gunnor austerely, coming up last of all and less breathlessly than the others. She picked Oddeyes up. 'It's only a strange star. It won't hurt you.'

'What makes you so sure?' Ymme lived in the longhouse with Estrith but she had scuttled towards them along with the rest of the women. 'How do you know? With that thing looking down on us all night, how do we know we'll ever wake in the morning?'

'You'll wake.' Old Ivon, leaning on his stick, limped out of the near-darkness. He had an old hooded cloak round him, the hood pulled up against the evening chill, shadowing his eyes and hiding the brand-scar on his brow. There were several sharply indrawn breaths. They all knew the tales of the Norse gods at least as well as they knew the gospel stories and there was a legend that Odin the Skyfather sometimes wandered the world disguised as an old man, leaning on a staff and wrapped in a hooded mantle. Just for a moment, Old Ivon, materialising from the shadows and addressing them in that tone of croaking authority, blended in their minds with that ancient tale. They all, except Gunnor, drew back from him.

'You'll wake,' he said again. 'It won't harm you, just by shining in the sky. It's a comet. I've heard of such things before. But yes, it's a sign and harm's coming to someone. That thing's the warning of God to King Harold, to give up his throne to his rightful lord the Norman duke, or wait for the duke to come and take it. The Normans are coming, my friends. My people are coming, to set me free at last.'

Afterwards, Oddeyes remembered the curious, tense quality of that summer very clearly. All through the months of waiting, the air shivered and sparkled with a fearful expectancy which even a child like himself could feel.

Bjorn went several times to Jorvik ('But we call it York, boy. Jorvik's *their* name, not ours,' Old Ivon insisted), and after his third trip, some new names began to be tossed about in the hall, not only those of King Harold and Duke William. The ogre-like Earl Tostig, who murdered people for quarrelling with him, and had been thrown out of Northumbria in favour of the better-behaved Earl Morcar, was apparently taking advantage of the troubled times. He had joined forces with the King of Norway, Harald Hardrada. 'They're planning to invade Northumbria – to invade *us*,' Bjorn said. He had arrived just before dinner and sat down to it at once. Round the tables, there was a stir.

They were eating, as usual, all together in Bjorn's hall. The aged Halfdan, always perverse and ill-tempered, now raised his voice on Earl Tostig's behalf. 'Well, he's the rightful earl, you can't get away from it. *And* he's brother to King Harold.'

This unfashionable opinion, however, was swiftly quashed.

'You must have short memories.' Rolf never had any respect for his elders. 'Tostig's a nithing, a man of no honour. He's had people killed who came to him under safe-conduct. He was thrown out of Northumbria and out of England long ago, and what's it matter if King Harold's his brother? It's King Harold he's going to make war on. He's come here with an invading army! Harold can't afford brotherly feelings for the likes of Tostig and Tostig's got precious little love for Harold. As for this Hardrada, he has no rights over here at all.'

The women sat together at their own table but were quite near enough for cross-conversation. 'Hardrada's name tells us all we need to know about him. Who wants a man called Harald the Ruthless as a foe?' Estrith demanded.

'Then maybe we'd better make him a friend!' said Halfdan.

'I doubt if Earl Morcar will give us the chance,' Bjorn said. The thralls shifted uneasily on their benches, wondering what part if any they would have in the dangerous events which threatened, but Bjorn, as usual, ignored them. 'We'd better put the palisade in good repair,' he said, 'and get the harvest in. It's ready to cut, in spite of all the rough weather we've had. Let's hope we live long enough to see the grain made into bread, and eat it.'

The messengers from Earl Morcar, three men on good horses, one man carrying a banner with a huge black raven on it, rode into the Dale ten days later. They did not dismount, and the household gathered round them out of doors to hear the summons recited. Every ablebodied man that could bear arms was to muster at Jorvik and join Earl Morcar. Tostig and Hardrada had landed. The earl was calling out his Northumbrians to defend its chief city against them.

For two days the Dale was full of a controlled fury, as Bjorn and his kinsmen set about finishing the harvest, putting final edges on their axes and on the massive two-handed swords, and packing for the expedition. Most of the younger and stronger bondmen were to go too. Bjorn took for granted his ability to control his thralls wherever he and they might be. Those he left behind were those the Dale needed most, such as Orm the Shepherd and Snorri the Cowman, and those, like Old Ivon and Halfdan, who were past fighting age. Leif, to his intense annoyance, was to stay at home because he was young. 'If I'm killed, I want to know I leave my heir alive,' said Bjorn.

The morning of departure was a little like the times when a party was setting off for York, with saddled ponies stamping in front of the long-houses, and women running out with last-minute gifts: extra cloaks, a bag of honeycakes.

But this time the men were setting out on a journey from which some might not return. Oddeyes heard Estrith, as senior lady, telling all the other women that they must not weep at parting, 'The men must go off feeling strong and happy. That will bring them luck in war.' Estrith herself then gave in and dissolved on Bjorn's shoulder at the last moment and it was Sven's wife, the gentle Signy, her own face stiff but tearless, who drew her away and wished Bjorn good fortune and then held Estrith's face against her, so that she need not watch the men ride off.

After that, an extraordinary stillness covered the Dale. People got up in the morning as usual and there was work in plenty, with so few hands to do it. People talked to each other. But every word, every movement, seemed to take place within a vast emptiness. No one ever said: 'I wonder what is happening at Jorvik?' But many times, Oddeyes saw folk pause from whatever tasks they were doing and glance south-east, at the hills beyond which the city of Jorvik lay.

On the fourth day, in the afternoon, he stole away from the business of bundling firewood and went to find his grandfather. The day was warm and mellow and Old Ivon was on his accustomed bench in the open air. He had a piece of leatherwork in his hands but he had stopped attending to it. He was looking up at the sky.

'What is it, Granddad?'

'Ravens,' said Old Ivon. 'Flying east. Look, see them? And I've seen crows and eagles too, this last half-hour.' He glanced down at the boy. 'You know what that means?'

'No.' Oddeyes was bewildered.

'It means battle. The birds of prey always gather to a battlefield when the fighting's over, to feast on the dead. There's been a great fight over there to the east, my boy. But who's won? That's the question.'

Two days later, Sven, riding painfully one-handed, his broken left arm strapped across his chest, rode in alone. It was Oddeyes who saw him first and he ran about shouting until everyone who had been within earshot gathered round to help Sven to dismount.

'But,' said Estrith fearfully, looking past Sven as though Bjorn must surely be there, and she had unaccountably failed to see him, 'where are the others?'

'Bjorn's alive,' said Sven. He was holding Signy to him with his good arm and Signy was weeping for gladness, shedding the tears she had held back when he rode away. 'So is Rolf,' Sven said. 'They're going south.'

'Going south?' Estrith sounded as though she were saying: 'Going to the moon?'

'We lost the fight at Jorvik,' said Sven wearily as Signy began to help him indoors. 'Earl Morcar tried to defend the city but we were defeated.

47

The men of Jorvik surrendered. Worse! There was a lot of support for Hardrada and Tostig in Jorvik; once they were in, the city fairly welcomed them. We heard all about it. Earl Morcar had his spies. He gave up then and disbanded us . . .'

'Sit here,' said Signy, pulling a settle forward for him. 'Gunnor – where's Gunnor? – you must look at his arm. You fought well for Jorvik, at least, my Sven.'

'I wasn't wounded defending Jorvik,' said Sven. 'Wait. There were terms agreed between the city and Hardrada. Jorvik was going to give hostages. There was to be a meeting, at a place called Stamford Bridge, to the north-east.'

'And due east of here?' said Old Ivon, from the outskirts of the gathering.

Sven glanced towards him. 'You know where it is, then?'

'No. But I saw the ravens flying east. They always take the straightest line. So the parley turned into a battle?'

'King Harold arrived from the south,' said Sven. 'We – Bjorn and Rolf and all the rest of us – were on our way home; we'd been disbanded, as I said. But we fell in with Harold's army and were swept into it. Yes, there was a battle at Stamford Bridge and that's where I got my broken arm. I was lucky. You never saw such slaughter.' He was silent for a moment. Then he said: 'King Harold won. Tostig is dead and so is Hardrada. King Harold had to fight his own brother to drive off the invasion. God pity the woman that's mother to them both. But the Norman duke's expected to land any minute. King Harold's going back south again as soon as he's buried his brother Tostig decently, and all of his men who are still on their feet are going with him. I'm not able to, but Bjorn and Rolf have gone with Harold's army . . .'

'But the others?' Niall the Younger's wife cried out. 'What about the others?' Behind her, other women, thrall and free alike, had drawn closer together, and the same question, concerning their own husbands and sons, was written on their faces.

Sven did not answer. His broad, weatherbeaten face was full of misery. It was Ymme who said it for him. 'Dead. They're all dead, ain't they?'

Slowly, Sven nodded. 'I didn't want to say. I've been putting off saying. I didn't know how to tell you all. The ravens didn't touch them,' he said painfully. 'Bjorn and Rolf saw to everything, saw to burying them.' He added, wretchedly, because it was the only consolation he could bring and it was no consolation at all: 'I've got some of their things in my saddle-bag.'

The gathering broke up in grief, as men and women, according to their various natures, wailed or shouted or shook clenched fists or demanded details or crept away with averted faces to mourn in some private corner. Oddeyes stayed beside his grandfather, and presently found that he was following the old man outside, and that the two of them were alone. Timidly, he said: 'I wonder if the master and Rolf will ever come back?'

'It's nothing to us whether they do or they don't,' said Old Ivon. 'Don't you know that yet? We're nothing to do with them. The Normans are coming, didn't you hear? And Harold's going to meet our Norman duke with a tired army!' Oddeyes had never seen his grandfather's hard, immobile face look like that before; as though its harsh lines were softening, losing their sharp edges. 'If they come soon, I'll see Clairpont yet before I die. I've dreamed of it, night after night, ever since I heard the duke was on his way.'

His hand came down on Oddeyes' shoulder, grasping it so fiercely that Oddeyes gasped and tried to jerk himself away. 'My son or my grandson will be the lord there now.' Old Ivon was lost in the world of his own memories. 'I don't want to put him out. All I want is a seat by my own hearth and to hear my own tongue spoken and to be with my own people. That's all. I'd take your grandmother Gunnor with me if she'd come. I think she would. She's never been out of the Dale but there's a strong spirit in her; she has good blood somewhere. Other well-born men besides me have been sold as slaves in the past. Oh God,' said Old Ivon, 'it's been more than twenty-five years but I haven't forgotten, not one detail. If I close my eyes I can see Clairpont there in front of me. It's built like a little castle; stone wall all round, crenellations . . . oh God,' said Old Ivon once again, 'send the Duke of Normandy a fair wind. Let him come in time!'

Chapter Four

The End of the World

Old Ivon kept his promise to give Oddeyes the dagger-hilt keepsake, on the freezing winter day when Sven the Peaceloving, as the Dale folk had come to call him, startled the whole household by not only claiming leadership of it, but enforcing the same with brute strength.

What was particularly amazing about it was that it was the first time for more than two years that anyone in the Dale had been roused to anything like an attempt to control the household's destiny. Even to Oddeyes, not ten years old until February, the Dale was not what it had been.

For neither Bjorn nor Rolf had returned from the south. News filtered back in the end, of a terrible battle in which King Harold and hundreds of his men had been killed; of the Norman duke's crowning in London the next December. There was more mourning in the Dale. There was also, for a time, something different about Old Ivon, who went about with a light in his eyes and a hobble almost brisk.

But no Norman ever showed his face in Eric's Dale and gradually the old man's new vitality faded again and meanwhile, all around them, bereft of two-thirds of its menfolk, the Dale began to shrink.

There was no need now for more than the one longhouse. The others were abandoned or used as byres and storehouses. Some of the fields went back to grass for lack of hands to till them. The taxes rose and Sven, cursing the new Norman ruler, sold some cows to pay them. Presently, some of the widows, Niall the Younger's wife among them, found new husbands elsewhere and went away. After that, the Dale seemed more denuded still.

'It's like it was after the pestilence,' Gunnor said when, entering Wynflaed's hut on an iron-grey January morning, she found Ymme's big daughter crouched on the floor, hugging her shoulders, rocking and wailing while a pot of beans boiled dry on the fire. Calmly, Gunnor found spoon and water jug and attended to the beans. 'Things will get better,' she said. 'They did then and they will now.'

'I'd like to see it!' The wail acquired words. 'What's going to become of us all, Gunnor? No men for Elfgiva's girls to marry; no men for us while we're still fit for having children. There's nothing ahead for us! Work, yes, any amount of that. But I'd like someone to keep me warm in the night and I'd like my sons back . . . my *sons!*' And Wynflaed, who had once, when she still had a husband and two sons, been the humorist of the Dale, put her head down on her knees and burst into a noisy bawling which seemed to come from the very pit of her stomach.

Gunnor stirred the pot and waited for the storm to pass. When the crying subsided and Wynflaed raised her wet face, she said, as if continuing an established conversation: 'Leif Bjornsen is quarrelling with our Sven again. I wonder if they'll ever get it clear which of them is master here? It ought to be Leif by rights and Sven himself would say so, only Leif's so wild; always wanting to rush off to war.'

'I know what you're saying. All the wailing in the world won't bring back the dead or get me new children so best look ahead and not back. I know. I don't give way so often now; I haven't in months. But on days like this when the whole world seems dead . . .' Wynflaed wiped her eyes and got to her feet with an ungainly heave. She took the spoon from Gunnor and said, over a meaty shoulder: 'What's the quarrel about this time? Is it Leif wanting to sell his little sister to pay the taxes, like it was last time they fell out? Reckon he'll do it one of these days, whatever Sven says.'

'If Estrith don't drown her first,' said Gunnor caustically.

Bjorn, before departing for war, had left the hapless Inge with child. Signy, who looked after Inge when her time came, had encouraged the reluctant mother to call the child after a saint and Sven, invited to inspect the infant, said she was as beautiful as the Mother of God and should be called Mary, which was the fashionable rendering of the name according to people in Jorvik. 'She's Bjorn's daughter. I'll see she marries a freeman,' he said. Bjorn's son Leif, not in the least pleased with this backhanded compliment to his father, was furious and Estrith had first threatened to strangle both mother and child, and then locked herself away weeping for a week.

'This time,' said Gunnor, after a pause to see if Wynflaed would smile, which she did not, 'what they're squabbling about is Leif wanting to go to Jorvik oftener. Too much to do here and no point going to the city when we've nothing spare that we can sell so there's nothing we can afford to buy, that's what Sven says. But Leif says he's sick of always being behind with the news.'

She was rewarded at last, as Wynflaed gave the fleeting smile which had replaced her once-ready laughter. 'Poor Leif. Thinks of nothing but war and defying the Normans. The way he went on the last time the taxes rose, I reckon if Hardrada came back to life, Leif would be off to join him. And he never has any luck getting to any battles. First he goes off to join that rising against the taxes, a few months back, and it's all over before he gets there, and the next rising he never hears a word about until it's too late! No wonder he wants to go to Jorvik oftener! Well, it'll give Estrith something else to think about besides Bjorn's by-blow, if Leif manages to turn himself into a dead hero.' She paused, spoon raised. 'Is that someone riding in? In weather like this? I looked at that sky this morning and I thought: Snow any minute. But that's hooves for sure.'

The door was pushed open, letting in a bitter blast. With it came Oddeyes. 'Grandmother! There are strangers in the yard! A man and two women, on ponies, with a pack-donkey!'

Oddeyes, too curious to be conscientious, loitered behind as Wynflaed and his grandmother made for the longhouse, so that somebody else would have to rub the ponies down. Behind Wynflaed's broad back, he dodged into the hall. It was shadowy on this dull morning, lit mainly by the fire in the central trench and a few torches stuck into brackets on the roof supports. It was easy for a small boy to escape notice. Old Ivon was sitting on his usual bench, waiting for the cause of the excitement to be brought to him instead of the other way about, and Oddeyes squatted down beside him. Most of the household seemed to be there. Gunnor and Wynflaed had gone dutifully to busy themselves at the hearth because these half-frozen guests would need hot food and drink quickly, though Oddeyes noticed that they had placed themselves as near as possible to the settle where Sven and Signy had put the new arrivals.

These were not strangers, apparently, for Signy greeted them delightedly as cousins. The two women were clearly mother and daughter. They responded to Signy's greeting in muted tones and then sat down close together, holding their mantles round them, trying not to let their teeth chatter and looking avidly at the ale Wynflaed was mulling. They had curiously faraway, stricken expressions. The man, who was short and sandybearded, was equally unsmiling but in better physical shape. He threw off his mantle, accepted a beaker of mead straight from the barrel and said to Sven: 'I'm sorry to descend on you like this. You may remember me. I'm Signy's cousin Grimkel – I came here with her marriage party. That's how I knew the way from Jorvik. I fancy you're behind with the news out here . . .'

'Very,' said Leif Bjornsen loudly from where he had sat down on the far side of Sven.

'. . . but you'll know,' said Grimkel, 'that the king appointed a Norman earl for Northumbria, after all the trouble there was earlier this year?'

'Yes, we heard that. And we weren't pleased. We don't want Normans up here. We'd have done better with Hardrada. The Norwegians are nearer kin,' said Leif.

'There's a good few in Jorvik who think as you do,' said Grimkel. 'The chief men of our city tried to support Hardrada when he came, if you recall. Well, there's been trouble. The new Norman earl's dead; he was besieged in Durham and burned in his own fort. Then the rebels shifted to Jorvik and besieged the Norman castle there. And Waltheof's with them!'

This was a new name to Oddeyes, but he wasn't alone in this and an explanation was forthcoming, because half a dozen puzzled voices at once said: 'Who?'

'Waltheof!' said Grimkel, the town-dweller from the centre of things, with a touch of impatience. 'The son of the old earl, that had Northumbria before Tostig did. He was too young to inherit when his father died. He's one of the rebel leaders. I've seen him in Jorvik. A fine-looking man, tall and fair, and a bold sword-wielder. Men are flocking to him. He's got none of the Norman's stark reputation.'

'King William has a reputation rather too stark for most tastes,' said Sven. 'There's a story or two about that gentleman. Lost his temper once, after a siege on his own side of the channel, and chopped the hands and feet off all the garrison, didn't he? And blinded a hostage outside the gates of Exeter, down in the south-west, when the city tried to stand against him. This Waltheof and his rebels may be gambling with more than just their lives.'

Leif interrupted. 'You mean the whole north is up? And we're out of it? The castle in Jorvik's under attack?' He sprang up. 'While we just sit here like . . . like peasants?' His eyes went to the swords and axes on the wall.

'Wait,' said Sven's voice, deep by comparison with Leif's light, excited tones. 'Let the man finish. He has more to say. Am I right, Grimkel?'

'Quite right,' said Grimkel. His face was pale and hard. 'The siege is over now. King William came. Out of nowhere; no one was expecting him. He and his army arrived in a sleet storm and the city look-out never saw them coming until it was too late. They crashed straight through the town to relieve the castle. I had two daughters once. One of them's dead, trampled underfoot by a Norman war-horse when she was buying gloves at a street booth. I saw it happen. I didn't waste any time. The besiegers round the castle are caught between the defenders inside it and William coming up behind and they haven't got a chance. He will mop them up and then sack the town. I say *are* caught, *will* mop them up; but he's probably done it by now. I collected my family and what we could carry on the donkey and we got out of the city, then and there. We couldn't think where to go that was far enough away and then . . .'

'We thought of you,' said his wife. She was staring into the fire. In one hand she held the ale mug Wynflaed had just given her; her other arm was tightly clasped round her surviving daughter. 'Out here,' she said. 'Well away from trouble. It's been a hard journey, in this weather, but the farmsteads on the way were hospitable.'

'You want to stay? You'll be welcome,' said Sven.

'We'd like to stay for a while, till it's safe to go home,' said Grimkel. 'It might be some time. I doubt the rising's over. The leaders have been in touch with the Danish king, or that's what was being said. There could be an invasion.'

'That settles it!' Leif's blue eyes were sparkling. 'Who comes with me?' He strode to the weapons and lifted down his axe. 'We'll find the leaders of the rising wherever they are and join them! They'll need an army to help the Danish king! Then we'll have a king who speaks our language and maybe an end to these monstrous taxes. We should have backed Tostig and Hardrada in the first place; Halfdan Smith was right!'

The old smith, who had come inside with the rest, to hear the arrivals' news, nodded and said, 'Aye!' Sven glared at him. Leif swept on.

'But Waltheof'll do for our earl, if he's really descended from the old earls of the past. Who comes with me? Who comes with Leif?'

'No one,' said Sven. 'Sit down, Leif! No one is going anywhere. Go chasing off into the middle of the winter to find the leaders of a broken rising? They're probably all dead by now, or hadn't you thought of that? They were at Jorvik, right in the grip of the Norman pincer! As for a Danish invasion, I'll believe it when I see it. It won't come in January anyhow. *Sit down*, I say, Leif! But put that axe back first. Go on. Put it back! Leif . . .' Sven had risen to his feet. 'Are you going to do as I say?'

'No,' said Leif, standing axe in hand and glowering at Sven. 'I am not. I am tired of you trying to keep me out of things and laughing at me as if I were a child. If I got the news too late, twice over, and twice set out too late to join in last year's risings, whose fault was that? Yours, Sven, for keeping us all mewed up here like prisoners in this damned valley. Our forefathers were Vikings, warriors! They'd have scorned to stay out of a fight like this. I am going to Jorvik to see if the leaders are alive or not and, if they are, to join them, and I'm taking with me every man in the Dale who can carry a weapon and is willing to come and—'

'You're taking no one. The Dale lost men enough in '66. We need every pair of hands here, to get the place going again, to bring the fallow land back under the plough, to rebuild and refill those longhouses. When the Dale is prosperous again and full of people, *then* we can spare men to go haring off on wild quests and not before. Leif, are you going to put that axe away or must I take it from you?'

'*Take* it from me? I'd like to see you try!' Leif had listened to Sven with mounting fury, his young features suffused.

'Very well.' Calmly, Sven advanced. Around him people hastily edged away, pushing stools and benches back. Grimkel quickly drew his wife and daughter away from the fireside and into a safe corner.

'Look,' said Leif, 'I warn you. I'm going to Jorvik. I'm taking anyone who's ready to come. And you're not going to take my axe off me. I don't want to hurt you but . . .'

'Give it here,' said Sven, holding out a persuasive palm as if to a pony which did not want to be caught. Leif stood still, gripping the axe and staring straight into Sven's eyes. Sven made a grab, Leif side-stepped and then, to the accompaniment of a scream from Signy, his eyes widened and he swung the axe back and struck.

Signy sprang up. Sven, in the brief second which Leif took to swing his weapon, snatched up a table and used it as a shield. The wicked steel-blue edge flashed in the firelight, embedded itself with a splintering thud in the table, and stuck. Sven hurled the table away from him. It took the axe with it, wrenching it from Leif's grasp. Sven, his speed astounding for a man who had always been bulky, moved in and seized Leif round the middle, hoisting him off his feet. Leif cursed and pummelled but Sven, carrying his young cousin like a puppy in need of house training, bore him to where

55

a pail of water stood ready for use in cooking, and sat him in it with a splash. 'Maybe that'll cool your bad temper,' said Sven, quite calmly.

The water was extremely cold. Signy sank back on to a settle and began to laugh as Leif, arms and legs flailing, overturned the pail and bounded up again with a yell. He hurled himself at Sven but by now others, including Grimkel, Halfdan and even Old Ivon, had recovered themselves and he found his arms caught by friendly but restraining hands.

'No, no, Leif, enough's enough . . .'

'Odin's Beard, you did try to kill him!'

'Best take it easy, young master; no one wants all this uproar.'

'Go and put on dry things,' said Sven, looking quite kindly at the boy. 'And then come back. No one will ever mention this again, I promise. It didn't happen. Hush, Signy. Don't laugh at him. Go on now, lad.'

Signy made her face serious again. She had in fact been badly frightened. Leif, however, red with rage and injured pride, gave her a bitter look as he left the hall. Sven sat down again. 'My apologies for that,' he said to the guests. 'Come back to the fire. These young hotheads! I know the north is full of them and that nearly everyone in it is supposed to be sworn to defy King William and bring in a Dane, but I don't want the Dale to join in. Leif will settle down again. He has a temper but it never lasts.'

Oddeyes, like nearly everyone else in the hall, was staring at Sven, astounded by what he had seen. His grandfather limped back to sit down again beside him. 'Young fool,' said Old Ivon, meaning Leif, and then appeared to become lost in thought, while his right hand, clenched, began, slowly and rhythmically, to pound his bony knees.

'The Norman king's in York,' he said softly. 'As near as that. If I could see *him*, speak to him in French, put my hands between his! If someone who represents him would only come to the Dale! But they never will.' The hand unclenched and rested wearily, flat on his thigh. 'Why should they? Here, boy, it's time you had this.' He reached inside his tunic and brought out the bone dagger-hilt. 'You're big enough now and it's never going to be any use to me. Take it and keep it safe; it could be your password for getting home, one day. Remember the story that goes with it. Your grandfather, Sir Ivon de Clairpont, took it from a robber on the way to Rome, nearly forty years before this day. Here you are. Put the cord over your head. Remember that the device on it is the device of Clairpont.'

'Perhaps Normans will come to the Dale one day, Granddad.' Oddeyes, feeling awkward, tried as best he could to comfort his grandfather.

'Why should they?' said Old Ivon bitterly. 'What is there here to bring them?'

The Danish army landed the next autumn. The people at Trygg's Thorpe, who went to Jorvik oftener than the folk from Eric's Dale (as it was still called at times, as though Eric still lived) brought them the news. Leif at once announced that he was going to join them and that no one should prevent him. Sven, who was now accepted as the head of the clan, despite

Leif's resentment, this time merely shrugged and made no protest, even though Leif took three thralls with him as well. They could be spared now, for Grimkel had made his home in the Dale, had bought a couple of bond-men, set about reclaiming some of the land, and suggested that his daughter should marry Leif. The girl was safely pregnant within two months of the wedding; there would be another generation. Sven had a small son of his own but he did not wish the other branches of the family to wither, he said. True, no one knew yet whether Leif's child would be a son who would stay in the Dale or a daughter who probably would not but Leif had done at least some of his duty; 'If you *must* go . . .' said Sven resignedly.

After that, once again, the silence of isolation descended on the Dale. Yuletide came and they held it as cheerfully as possible, although Estrith's smiles were forced. January began mild but wet and Halfdan, who was very frail now with age (and sullen because Old Ivon who was considerably his senior remained obstinately well, weathering rather than ageing), took a chill.

The mildness began to ebb from the air as the sun went down for the last time on the Eric's Dale most of them had known all their lives. Gunnor, called before daybreak to minister to a feverish and wheezing Halfdan, crossed the yard to the longhouse under stars like the points of needles and returned at first light beneath a sky of cold amethyst. Frost lay thick as a snowfall on thatched roofs and stiffened grass-blades. Inside their hut, Old Ivon was stirring. She knelt, shivering, to rouse the fire, keeping her face averted. Old Ivon glanced at the sibylline nutcracker profile, left his bed and came to her. 'What's the matter?' he asked.

'Halfdan won't come through.'

'That bad-tempered old devil? What of it?'

'I'm caring for him. I don't like it when I can't stop them dying.' Gunnor spoke as lightly as she could but Old Ivon, resting a hand on her shoulder, said: 'It isn't Halfdan. What is it?'

Gunnor looked up at him. They knew each other so well. These days they did not talk very much; they had heard each other's life histories a dozen times already and knew to a nicety what opinions the other would hold on any question that arose, and the strong, mellowed link between them had no need of small talk to sustain it.

But once in while, now, Old Ivon would read her mind as she had once read his, and then he would remark on what he sensed.

He had picked up the unreasonable, deadly sense of foreboding which had descended on her in the moment before dawn, when she saw those icy stars.

She attempted to deny it. 'Someone's walking over my grave,' she said, and forced herself to laugh.

The day began, under a clear, cold sky. Orm Shepherd eyed the frost, took his dog and set off to fetch the sheep nearer home. No one else moved far from the longhouses. The cattle in their winter byre were tended, the poultry fed, the corn ground. Gunnor went again to Halfdan, with a fever-reducing draught and a steam inhalation, and found him no better. Estrith and Signy met her in the doorway as she set off for her hut once more to fetch more medicines. 'How is he?'

'Not mending and that's a fact.'

'Do we need the priest?' asked Estrith. If Dale marriages were still mere contracts, baptisms and burials were now Christian, and the last rites offered to the dying when possible.

'Maybe. We'd best decide by noon.' Gunnor raised her shawled head and examined the sky. 'If it snows, we can't reach him.'

Automatically, Estrith and Signy looked at the weather too. In the windless sky above the hills between the Dale and Trygg's Thorpe, there was a drift of brown vapour, like smoke.

'Someone made their fire up too well last night, by the look of it,' said Gunnor. 'They've set their longhouse ablaze. Best wait a few hours before we send to them. They'll be in a right state if they've a bad fire. Halfdan'll last the day.'

The morning wore on. The frost melted and the temperature rose a little. The yard became muddy. Oddeyes, hauling a handcart-load of firewood across it, had to stop when the wheels caught in the sticky ruts. And saw, through the open gate, on the distant lower slopes of the hills where Orm was gathering the sheep, something he did not understand.

There seemed to be horsemen there, quite a lot of them, riding along the slopes towards the flock. He could see a dark dot which must be Orm's dog, and that must be Orm himself, lower down. The horsemen appeared to be bearing down on the flock. Then he saw two of them veer towards Orm. He stared, gaped, and then ran, shouting, to give the alarm.

People came pelting to look. 'Close the gate! At once!' Sven was there, taking charge. 'Fetch the big haycart to roll against it. Bring the weapons. Get that gate *shut*: what are you waiting for? Dreda, get out of the way!'

'Orm's still out there!' Dreda clung to the gate.

Sven dragged her away and kicked it shut himself. 'It's too late for Orm; you heard Oddeyes. He saw it.'

'No! It ain't true, Orm can't be . . . !'

'God help us all, it *is* true. Where are the bows? They're coming!'

Gunnor, from the moment that she saw the horsemen with the bright lances turn from the motionless specks which had been Orm and his animals and begin to stream down into the valley towards the homestead, understood that disaster was coming but it was beyond her to realise its scope. Her ordinary world, the people she knew, the thatched longhouses and clucking chickens, were still all round her and couldn't, said the prosaic voice of reason, simply be obliterated. Yet a deeper instinct, the one which had come awake as she knelt that morning by the fire, told her that here was such danger that she should lay hands at once on whatever means of survival she could find.

Her middle-aged joints were creaky now from long years of carrying sacks of flour and pails of water, but she hurried into her hut as fast as they would let her and snatched up a leather bag and stuffed into it a tinderbox, a knife, a loaf of bread and a jar of oatmeal. She slung the bag on her back under her heavy, blanket-like mantle, and then made a hasty bundle of rugs and cloaks and a hurried selection of clothing. She might never have a chance to use these things, but she must have them, said instinct, and would not be gainsaid.

Then she was out again, shouting for Oddeyes. Old Ivon was there in the yard, staring at the confusion and leaning on his stick. 'What's all the uproar?'

'Soldiers,' said Gunnor briefly. 'Coming here. They've killed Orm Shepherd and his sheep.'

Oddeyes ran up, gasping, his eyes shocked and huge. Gunnor pushed her bundle into his arms. 'You hang on to this.' She looked at Old Ivon and it was painful to have to say it. 'They've got long pointed shields like you've told me about and they kill from horseback. I think they're Normans.'

There were more than fifty of them, chainmail-clad, with tapering shields and conical helmets with cheekflaps and nosepieces that rendered their faces inhuman. The palisade on which the people of Eric's Dale had relied, did not hinder them. They knew all about palisades. They had bowmen among them carrying shafts primed with oil and tow. They also carried tinderboxes. Blazing arrows soared over the palisade to land in the thatched roofs within and that, as the Norman commander Messire Hugh Le Fort had known it would, had most of the defenders dropping their weapons and running for buckets.

Meanwhile, a dozen horsemen stood on their saddles to glance quickly over the palisade at various points and their reports told Le Fort what was inside. The enclosure was divided, apparently, with the dwellings in one part, and some grass and a vegetable patch in the other. Le Fort grinned and said: 'Strike for the heart,' and with the horses once more providing stepladders, his men swarmed over the palisade into the longhouse enclosure, while a squad of bowmen behind them poured arrows in over their heads by way of cover.

They were like a mailed flood. Suddenly the homely yard of Eric's Dale was full of them, striding about amid the terrified poultry and the yelping dogs and the people who were trying to form a human chain from the well to extinguish the blazing thatch of the longhouse and the storehouses. The smoke and the crackle were breeding panic. The byre was not yet on fire but inside it the ponies were kicking and neighing and the cows bellowing in alarm. Everywhere there were screams and curses entangled with coughs as the smoke rolled down.

Sven, trying to defend the bucket chain with his sword, was casually cut down with an axe. Gunnor, burdened with the leather bag and the mantle, tripped as she staggered across the yard with a pail and lay flat on her face, expecting a spear in her back. To her surprise, she was merely hauled up again by a steel gauntlet and with a shove set stumbling towards the gate. The Normans had dragged away the wagon which was blocking it and it was open.

More of them were surging through. She lurched out of their way, screaming for Old Ivon, for Oddeyes. Somehow, Oddeyes was there, clutching for her hand, his own poking out from under the bundle she had given him. Ymme appeared, being shoved by a spear butt, going backwards, because she was keeping her face towards the Norman on the other end of the spear, in order to curse him. He was laughing.

Out of nowhere, Inge crashed into them, wailing, her arms wrapped frantically round her baby. She had Signy's small son clinging to her shoulders. Signy was thrust after her, to slip in the mud and land on all fours. She scrambled up, pointing at the burning roof of the big longhouse and screaming: 'But Halfdan's in there!'

As if he had heard her shriek his name, Halfdan, bent double and coughing, staggered through the door. Smoke poured out round him. Gunnor, with the long sight of middle age, saw his smudged face with the fever-sweat making pale runnels in it. He lurched forward, his steps weaving. Then he fell on the ground and a passing Norman did what Gunnor had thought they would do to her, and drove a lance into him. He put a booted foot on Halfdan's body to hold it down while he pulled the lance out again, just as the flaring roof collapsed and all that was left of the longhouse went up into a furious conflagration.

From somewhere, the children and the other women had been herded to join them. Dreda was there with Elfgiva and their children, clinging together and screaming; Wynflaed was there, and Grimkel's womenfolk, and Estrith gripping a dagger stained with red; Estrith had evidently succeeded in doing some damage to the foe.

The smell of blood was in the air now. The Normans seemed to be sparing the women and children, but were spearing everything else that moved; smuts from the burning buildings floated down to land on the crimsoned heaps of fur and feathers which had been dogs and poultry. The neighing and bellowing from the byre was now ominously silent. From somewhere came the hideous squealing of a pig as its throat was cut.

They were killing the men. Gunnor caught sight at last of Old Ivon. He too was being pushed, despite his lameness; it seemed that the Normans were trying to drive the men apart from the women before spearing them. Old Ivon was gesticulating with his stick and shouting but in the din of the roar from the fire and the screams, he could not make himself heard.

But she knew, with a rage and pity powerful enough to overwhelm her own terror, that he was shouting in Norman French.

'He's Norman, he's one of you!' she shrieked into the nearest metal face but even if the man heard her, he did not understand and probably wouldn't have cared if he had. But Old Ivon, at that instant, used his stick to thrust away the man who was pushing him, and struggled towards the women, getting near enough momentarily to see Gunnor's face, for their eyes to meet.

The contact lasted only seconds and would be their last on earth and they both knew it. '*Ivon!*' Gunnor tried to get to him, as though the act of going into his arms would make a magic which could undo fire, raise a longhouse from ash, breathe back life into the dead, make fifty Norman soldiers not to be. A spearpoint drove her back but from beyond the man who held it, Old Ivon's voice reached her. 'Look after Oddeyes! Take care of Oddeyes!' Then he was wrenched away and Gunnor, turning, stumbling, let herself be driven out of the gate, away from the scorching waves of heat and the billowing smoke, and did not look back for fear that she would see him die.

In that final moment, the wife of Grimkel saw her own husband hurl himself on a Norman and be run through, and flung herself screaming towards him and straight on to a lance. His daughter, Leif's pregnant wife, would have followed her mother, except that Estrith and Signy caught hold of her and dragged her with them.

Oddeyes was still clutching Gunnor's hand. 'Grandmother, are they *Normans?* Did you say they were *Normans?*'

'I did. And they are,' said Gunnor. 'I know them by their shields and helms and speech. Your grandfather told me, long ago, how to know a Norman. And some of these,' she added as they blundered out into the empty world beyond the palisade, 'are those splendid and noble beings, Norman knights!'

Within the palisade, the last few men of the Dale, Old Ivon, two elderly thralls, Snorri the Cowman, three youths of Sven's kin whose fathers had fallen at Stamford Bridge and who had stayed at the Dale although their mothers had left it, were gathered, ringed by Normans, amid the rolling smoke and they all knew now what was to come.

Old Ivon had stopped trying to shout at the enemy that he was Sir Ivon de Clairpont and couldn't they hear he was using their tongue? These men were Normans and some were knights but they did not remind him of his home. They reminded him much more strongly of the savages who had butchered six hundred men (except for the seventeen they had sold) on the hillside above Gildenford long ago.

He was nearly seventy-five years old now and he had not feared death since that day at Gildenford. He had learned then that there were worse things than dying. To be rescued, hailed as a compatriot by the likes of these, was one of them.

But it was a bad joke, as though God had a twisted sense of humour, that he should die at last at the hands of his own people.

Chapter Five
The Long Walk

Messire Hugh Le Fort would have been extremely offended had he known that Old Ivon equated him with the butchers of Gildenford.

Hugh Le Fort was acquainted with the story of the Gildenford massacre and it had shocked him deeply. He considered the commander responsible to be the worst kind of barbarian. He held this view because according to the story, the man had arranged the atrocity for the personal amusement of himself and his followers.

Le Fort would never have done such a thing. Le Fort would order a large-scale killing only when acting under official orders, and he then carried out the task in accordance with a laid-down code of conduct. This could be imposed from above or imposed on oneself, but a code there must be. It made the deed legitimate.

He had arrived at Eric's Dale fully equipped with both orders and code.

The orders could hardly have been more official, since they emanated in the first place from King William the First of England, Duke William of Normandy, and had been passed down word for word through his chief barons to their followers.

Just before Christmas, William had driven the Danish army and their supporters out of the city of York where they had meant to spend Yuletide. He had them nicely penned up now at the mouth of the Humber, but all over the north, as he very well knew, in hamlets and small fortified burghs and isolated farms, were men of Danish descent who had already taken part in the earlier risings which had had him racing north to relieve York once before, and who might join the Danes in the future, if it looked worthwhile.

William considered himself to be a legal ruler who had overcome a usurper in battle. King Edward the Confessor, he said, had once promised that he should inherit England and Harold, King Edward's brother-in-law, had sworn to support this claim. Harold, taking the crown, was an oathbreaker; even the Pope had agreed and sent William a specially blessed banner to carry into battle.

That large proportions of England should persist in behaving as though Harold had been their rightful lord and William were the usurper, struck him as an intolerable insult, and the obstinate way that Northumbria in particular clung to this point of view and had even invited the Danish king to challenge him had finally caused him to lose his temper.

'Your task,' he said, addressing his leaders, 'is to sterilise the north. To destroy all rebel elements and then so ravage this land that no reservoir of rebellion can survive and no invading army find a crumb to live on. All winter crops, all granaries and stores of any sort are to be burned. All stock is to be slaughtered and incinerated. All houses and implements are to be destroyed. Slay every man old enough to carry a weapon. The women and the young children, you may let live.'

On top of that clear-cut mandate, Le Fort had imposed other rules on himself and on those he led. In the confusion when they first burst in on a community, anything could happen, but when it came to the dispassionate liquidation of those men who had not been killed in the first defence, he insisted that the women and children be driven away so that they should not see it done. He did not forbid rape, but he did not encourage it either and was pleased that, now that they had been at the work of harrying for nearly a week, his men had grown surfeited and were no longer bothering.

In addition, he usually advised the women on the shortest route to safety. Most of them wouldn't reach it, of course, but he had had no instructions to help them. He gave them directions and how they got there was their affair.

When the women of Eric's Dale had been thrust out of the palisade, he mounted and rode out after them with three of his men. Halting beside them, he studied the stricken little cluster carefully. He had no English but one of his men had. He pointed to Oddeyes. 'How old is that boy? The one clutching that bundle.'

When the question was translated and put to them, Oddeyes, head thrown back, opened his mouth to answer for himself but an old woman with a hump-like bulge under her cloak spoke first. 'He ain't ten yet!'

'Really?' Le Fort had seen the boy's startled glance at her. 'He looks older.'

'Well, he ain't,' said Gunnor flatly. She knew nothing of the king's orders but she knew the principles under which these men were acting. They had been set out often enough in the old fireside tales. War-leaders, when wiping out an enemy clan, always said: 'Kill every male old enough to bear arms.' Ten years old was, roughly, the dividing line. Oddeyes was just, but only just, over it.

The boy stared at the Normans with loathing but did not seem to realise that he should also be staring at them with fear. 'Where's my grandfather?' he demanded. The old woman put a hand on his arm as if to silence him but he shook it off. 'He was old, he was lame, *what have you done to him?*'

'Tell him the grown men are dead,' said Le Fort when this was relayed to him, 'as he would be himself if he were a very little older. He's a well-grown brat and pert on top of that and he looks quite capable of sticking a knife into someone even now. I'm not sure I shouldn't count him as grown.'

There was something about the boy which disturbed him. The brat

64

wore the coarse clothes of the lowest kind of churl, but the way he stood and stared at one was not in the least serf-like. He had extraordinary eyes, thought Le Fort. They didn't match. One was brown and the other more or less blue. But they were well set, the right distance apart, in almond-shaped, symmetrical sockets, and the boy's features and proportions, which were already well established (if he were under ten then Le Fort was Charlemagne), were in some way different from those of the dozens of other churls who had died at his orders in the last few days.

In build and feature, Oddeyes resembled his grandfather and Le Fort, without knowing it, was seeing the flat back and long thighs, the level shoulders and the high, sharp-edged cheekbones of the de Clairpont family, whose scions had been grafted into half the knightly families of Normandy and Boulogne. Boys like this had served him at dinner in more than one castle; the men they grew into had fought under William's banner at Hastings. He had one among his companions now.

He did not know what to make of Oddeyes and it annoyed him. He leaned out of his saddle and struck the boy across the face with a mailed hand. Oddeyes fell backwards, gasping, angry tears starting in his eyes.

'Tell him that I'll give him the benefit of the doubt and let him live,' said Le Fort. 'But all the rest of his life, I advise him to address Norman knights with courtesy.' While his interpreter put that across, he looked the rest of the group over. The women stared at him with terror and impotent hatred, huddling close together and holding their children to them as though they feared he would try to snatch them away. There were no youths older than the odd-eyed boy cringing here and hoping to escape the swords.

Behind him, the farmstead, buildings, palisade and all, was fully ablaze. 'Tell the women,' he said when the interpreter turned to him again, 'that their nearest place of safety is York. There'll be no farms or hamlets left standing in between. I suppose they know their own district, but tell them the way is that track leading south-east out of the valley. Tell them to start now. We'll camp close by tonight and they'd best be well on their way before the men start drinking. They may take with them,' he added, look-ing at the peculiar hump under Gunnor's heavy cloak and the bundle of cloth and fur which Oddeyes was still grimly embracing, 'whatever they're carrying.' Strictly speaking, he should seize the goods, such as they were, but he never did. Let the pathetic creatures keep them. Such oddments would hardly support the Danish army. The interpreter spoke. One or two of the women glanced over their shoulders towards the north.

'If they're thinking of the hamlet over there, tell them we fired it this morning and left a squad there to finish it.' Le Fort was tired of it all. 'Get them moving,' he said. 'Now! Use the flat of your swords.'

'But we can't . . . !' Elfgiva burst out as the horses and the swinging swords shoved them away from the flaring remains of what had been their home, to face the track that would lead them away for ever. 'We can't just *go* . . . our men . .!'

'No, that's right!' Signy too tried to resist, to turn back. 'Even if they're dead, we can't just . . .'

'They're dead and burned.' Gunnor put it brutally into speech. 'We can only save ourselves and the children.' As if the gulf between lady and thrall did not exist, she jerked Signy out of the way of Le Fort's horse and thrust her onwards. 'York's our only chance.'

'But if Leif is still alive and comes back for me . . . !' his wife wailed.

'Going to sit on the ruins and wait for him?' inquired Ymme, in this extremity supporting Gunnor.

'Or pass the time until he comes, by providing home comforts for this lot? Don't be a fool, Hildegarde. Gunnor's right. Come!' said Estrith, and turned her face towards the track and led the way.

It was against nature, when one's people had been killed and one's home destroyed, to walk away without ceremony, without as much as a pause for prayer, let alone for burials.

They did it.

Earlier in the day, the thin sunshine had melted the frost but the sky was dimming towards another night of bitter cold. The wind hissed. Trudging along the track beside the river, making their slow way out of the valley, the little band of refugees kept close together, as if for warmth.

They had sorted themselves out as they walked. Estrith and Signy, the chief women of the Dale and its leaders now that the men were gone, headed the procession. Signy had taken her small son from Inge, and perched him on her own shoulders. As they left the valley, she looked back once, at the smudge of smoke behind them. She turned away with a shudder. 'Don't look behind,' she said to Estrith, across the back of Hildegarde's head.

They had put Leif's pregnant wife between them where they could keep an eye on her. Hildegarde had not spoken since they made her set out, and her eyes were fixed on the distance with a sleepwalker's stare. Every now and then, she faltered and would have stopped short, if they had not urged her on.

Ymme and Inge, the two personal thralls, walked behind their mistresses, Inge carrying her little girl. Inge, with some care, kept a little distance between herself and the tall, angular figure of Estrith, of whom she was afraid.

Wynflaed, Elfgiva and Dreda marched next, Dreda trudging at one end of a string of children. Elfgiva's twin daughters followed their mother. They had been the first babies in the Dale to be baptised by the priest and he had suggested their names: Edith for the elder, after the queen of the time, King Edward's saintly wife, and for the second twin, whose arrival twenty minutes after her sister had come as a complete surprise to everybody, the gracefully appropriate name of Godgift. They were plump, brownhaired, rosy lasses with round faces meant for jollity. Now, their giggles extinguished and their complexions blanched, they were scarcely recognisable.

Three other women followed with their children and Gunnor brought up the rear with Oddeyes beside her. She still carried her leather shoulder-bag, but the clothes and rugs had been shared out as extra clothing. Everyone already had stout footwear, since in winter in Eric's Dale no one could do without it. The north-east wind which had now risen still cut through every single thing they wore.

They had yet to grasp the enormity of what had happened. Grief, like a foetus, needed time to grow. So did despair. As they went, they spoke of a future which they still imagined might exist.

'How far away is Jorvik?'

'Two to three days along our beck with ponies and then a few hours by barge down the great river. There's a burgh where the rivers meet, where we leave the ponies. We'll find help there, before we get to Jorvik.' Estrith spoke hopefully.

'They'll have been there too, for sure. That man said there was nothing left standing between here and Jorvik.' Ymme, as usual, sounded as though she almost enjoyed pessimism.

'Oh, be quiet. They can't have been everywhere!' snapped her mistress.

Signy was feeling the weight of her burden. But when Estrith made to take the child from her, she shook her head. 'I can manage.' Estrith looked slightly affronted. Inge said timidly: 'How long can we just go on walking?'

Their footsteps slowed. Realisation was coming now. They were out in the wilderness, in midwinter, without a roof to protect them and nightfall was not far away. In all their minds, the images of cheerful longhouse fires and friendly thatched roofs, of huts which might be cramped and squalid but nevertheless were *home*, were so clear that it was not yet possible to believe that they no longer existed.

'We must go on as long as we can,' said Estrith, trying to sound as sure of the right thing to do as her former mother-in-law Maria would surely have been. 'It will keep us warm and we'll gain ground. If we go on through the night, we'll be halfway to the big river that goes straight to Jorvik.'

'But I can't walk all night!' Hildegarde protested and stopped short once more, a hand pressed to her stomach. Her eyes were terrified.

From the rear, Gunnor said: 'I've been this far, after stray animals. There's a wood just round the shoulder of that hill. We can camp there and make a fire.'

'What do we light it with?' asked Dreda, with an hysterical laugh. 'Witchcraft?'

'A tinderbox might be more use,' said Gunnor. 'I've got one. I've even got some food.'

'And here's a flask of mead. Gunnor's not the only one to think of snatching up summat worthwhile.' Proudly, Wynflaed produced the prize from under her cloak. This caused them all to pause and take stock of whatever useful items they had between them. Several of them had small knives. Estrith had her dagger and Inge had a second tinderbox, complete with flint and steel and newly filled with wood shavings. 'Good girl,' said Gunnor approvingly.

They made a camp of sorts in a clearing surrounded by oak and ash. Here they were out of the worst of the wind and there was plenty of dead wood about; they could make a fire although much of the fuel was damp and the flames spluttered. Gunnor shared out the food. There was enough for one small meal each, with sufficient left for a bite next day. They drank from the river before they went into the wood, using their cupped hands, and handed round Wynflaed's flask after they had eaten. There was only a swallow each but it put some heart into them.

Into Estrith, a little too much. 'I think we should have saved more of the food. If I'd had charge of it, I'd have said so.'

'Too late now,' said Signy. 'At least we've got something in our stomachs to keep us going through the night. Anyway, Gunnor was the one who thought of bringing it and she's our wise-woman. It was right for her to decide when to eat it and how much to use.'

'Gunnor is a thrall. I was Bjorn's wife.'

'I was Sven's, come to that!'

'My mistress is right,' whispered Inge to Ymme.

Estrith heard her. 'Mind your tongue. You're a thrall too even if you did happen to bring a tinderbox with you!'

Gunnor intervened. 'Might be better if we don't squabble. Be grateful we had this meal, at least. It's near dark. We ought to set a watch.'

'Yes. We've got to keep the fire up.' Estrith took control again. 'Ymme, you'll watch first. Wake Gunnor when . . .' they had no means of judging time '. . . you think you should,' said Estrith.

'I want Snorri,' said Elfgiva suddenly. No one answered, until Gunnor at last said: 'If we give ourselves up to mourning now, we'll all die. Wait until York.' She said *York* and not *Jorvik* because Old Ivon had always called it York.

They settled as best they could, huddled close. The children whimpered. Few managed more than a half-doze, eyes repeatedly opening on the wavering, firelit trees.

Gunnor did not even doze. She took the watch over from Ymme before long and tended the fire until dawn, glad to be alone to think about Old Ivon. The moment he first appeared in the Dale, Gunnor had recognised in the lines of his hard brown face, and in his furious anger at his captivity and his refusal to accept it, a depth and strength of feeling which corresponded to some core of powerful feeling in herself. The man she then had was a shadow by comparison.

Perhaps that was because he was already ailing; she did not know. But he had died and she had fought for the right to mate with Ivon de Clairpont and won, and for nearly thirty years she had lived and slept and worked by his side. Throughout the long, bitter night in the clearing, she made her farewells.

In the morning, they roused to the ghastly reality. They had water, they had a small amount of food but there would be no more. They decided to save what there was and carry it with them. They warmed themselves as best they could by the fire, drank from the river and set out once again.

Away from the shelter of the wood, the wind was vicious. Their bodies wanted to shrink away from it, to cower within their clothing. Signy thought of sacrificing a shawl to make wrappings for people's hands, since only a few of them had chanced to be wearing gloves when the Normans struck. Dreda's youngest child, who was only four, was feverish and kept on crying in a thin voice. They were all ravenously hungry and light-headed and apt to double over suddenly as they walked, gripped by wind pains in the stomach. They had abandoned their tidy marching order now, but simply plodded along, indifferent to whether thrall walked ahead of freewoman, coaxing or dragging the children between them, first one and then another giving an arm or a shove to Hildegarde who otherwise might just have sat down and given up. After a few hours, they ate the last of the food.

They found a tiny cave, no more than a slit at the foot of a steep scree, and huddled there that night, with a fire of gorse twigs and dead bracken at the entrance to warm them. In the morning, slowly, they set out again. The cold had changed its nature; it was no longer crystalline but leaden and the sky was grey. Presently, it began to snow.

The flakes were small at first but quickly grew larger and soon they could no longer distinguish the track before their feet. 'But we *must not* stop,' said Estrith, leading the way doggedly, head down into the dizzying flakes.

Inge said suddenly: 'Have you thought that to stop might be the best thing? My father came from Norway. Winters are terrible there. He told me once, if you lie down in the snow you just go to sleep and never wake up again.'

'It might be best for you. Please yourself,' said Estrith.

'It ain't best for anyone!' said Gunnor fiercely. 'We got to fight to live. Do you want these children to die too, Inge? We're nowhere near done yet. Keep walking!'

In a scared voice, Hildegarde said: 'I'm getting pains.'

They all stopped, gathering round her in the falling snow.

'It's probably wind. You're not due for two months,' said Estrith.

'They're every few minutes. Ever since we started out this morning.'

'You can't lie down here.' Gunnor moved quickly forward. 'Someone help me with her. You've got to keep walking, my girl.'

'I can't!' Hildegarde wanted warmth and safety and Leif. She sagged between Gunnor and Estrith as they took her elbows.

'With one of us on either side of you, you can and you will. Come on,' said Gunnor. 'Left foot. Right foot. But *keep going*.'

'It's no use, we'll have to let her lie down.'

'In this? No, she mustn't!' Gunnor and Estrith were taking Hildegarde's full weight between them now, dragging her feet through the snow. She had been crying out continuously and struggling against them but now the cries had sunk to moans and her head had begun to loll. A red stream ran from under her skirts, fading to pink as it dissolved into the snow.

'She wants to crouch,' said Estrith. 'It's the best position to—'

'I know but we've got to find shelter first, even if it's only the lee of a rock.' Gunnor spoke in a slurred voice through lips that were slow with cold. 'I think the snow's slackening. I can see a little way. What's that over there?'

'Walls!' gasped Wynflaed, plodding behind them. 'Buildings. I'll help carry her. If only there's someone there.'

They veered to the right, where in a hollow on a moorland slope they had glimpsed, snow-shrouded but unmistakable, the line of a stone wall and the sharp triangle of a gable-end beyond. Under Hildegarde's weight, her helpers' feet slithered in the snow. 'If only,' said Estrith, 'we've come far enough. If only *they* haven't been here.'

'There's no smoke,' panted Gunnor.

Signy said bitterly: 'We're a little late. There was plenty of smoke here a few hours ago. The place is burned out. That Norman knew what he was saying. Nothing left standing between here and Jorvik, he said. So now we'd better believe him.'

There had been a surrounding stone wall with a gate. The gate was gone and, stumbling through, they stood in the midst of another desolation. The building whose gable end they had seen stood only because like the wall it was of stone and the fire could not destroy it. But it was a roofless shell. A few smaller stone buildings, similarly blackened and forlorn, jutted from the surrounding snow. One had a slate roof still half-intact.

In the middle of what had been the farmyard, was a dark mound where the snow hadn't settled because the mound was till warm. They could see the ash and the pieces of wood which had turned to charcoal, and the fire-scarred bones, human and animal, of those who had been cremated there. The remnants stank.

There were weary sobs of disappointment from half a dozen throats. Gunnor said firmly: 'Let's get into that barn. At least it has a bit of roof. Quickly, now.'

Hildegarde cried out anew as they set her down, twisting and drawing up her knees, fighting feebly as Gunnor, divesting herself of the hampering shoulder-bag and the torn pieces of cloth round her hands, tried to examine her. Signy knelt down to help. 'There's some wood on that pile out there, only part burnt, Get it, someone. We need a fire in here,' she said over her shoulder. 'Inge, get out your tinderbox.'

There was a rush of blood which steamed in the icy air, and Hildegarde collapsed into unconsciousness, her face waxen and her breath coming in intermittent rasps.

'The child's half out but it's dead,' said Gunnor. 'Hurry with that fire. She must have warmth. We all must!'

They tried to obey but, having once paused from their mechanical trudge, they found it hard to get moving again. Some of them whimpered, like children, as they stumbled to and fro with the wood. Inge's small daughter Mary began to cry on a dreary, persistent note and Estrith snapped at Inge to keep her quiet. Signy and Gunnor, crouched on either side of Hildegarde, trying to draw the child out and staunch the blood, exchanged glances. Gunnor shook her head, silently. Hildegarde's rasping breath had grown louder and slower. Suddenly it faltered.

'Hildegarde!' Estrith too came to crouch on the beaten-earth floor beside her. 'Hildegarde, wake up. You must try! There'll be a fire soon; when you're warm you'll feel better . . .'

The harsh breathing renewed itself and Hildegarde's body shuddered. There was another rush of blood. The rasping failed again and this time did not resume. Hildegarde's eyes opened and stared at the slate roof.

Inge whispered: 'Perhaps it's just as well. She couldn't have gone on walking, could she? I remember how I felt when . . .'

'Women and children should have teeth!' said Signy, suddenly furious. 'Why do we have no *power*? Men did this to us and there was nothing, nothing, we could do to frighten them. Whoever ordered those beasts to kill and burn . . .'

'The Norman king, I expect. Who else?' said Estrith bitterly.

'. . . then I'd like to do it to him and his! He's married, isn't he? Let his wife and family plod through the snow and starve on the moors! Let *him* wander and hunger and shiver, and see how he likes it. I want to make it be him; I want to make him know what he has done!' Signy shook a clenched, impotent fist in the air. 'We are so helpless. I *hate* us all for being helpless.'

'We're not quite helpless,' said Estrith. 'We can pray. God may hear us.'

'I doubt it. Where was he yesterday morning?' enquired Signy.

The twins had got a fire going and Oddeyes had found a dented iron cooking pot lying in the yard. It would do to melt snow in, for drinking water. Leaving Hildegarde, for whom they could do no more, they gathered round the warmth. 'But we need food,' said Dreda miserably, her arms round her children.

'We'd better search this place. We might find summat,' said Wynflaed.

'We'll die if we don't.' Inge's eyes were enormous in a face hollowed with famine and Mary, leaning against her mother, was still crying, in a series of whimpers and hiccups.

Estrith lost her temper. 'Will you keep that child quiet, slut!'

'I'm not a slut; I've never been a slut. I didn't steal your husband. He made me do as he wanted; how was I to say no to him? He was Master Bjorn, wasn't he? Anyhow, he's dead and gone now so . . .'

Estrith didn't answer. She was looking around her in bewilderment. In a frightened voice, she said: 'But where is Ymme?'

* * *

'But I ain't going on without my mother!' Wynflaed had stumbled about in the snow shouting her mother's name until she was exhausted, and now, despairingly, still hovered in the gateway, staring out across the whitened moorland.

'And we can't just leave Hildegarde lying! There could be wolves!' Elfgiva did not address Signy as *Mistress*. Such niceties were being rapidly wiped out.

'Wolves?' said Signy, leading them back to the barn. 'There are. I heard them last night. But we have no choice. Wyn, we've searched for your mother as far as we can. If she collapsed out in the snow, she's dead by now. We can put stones over Hildegarde. We can't bury her in this frozen ground. We'd better take her clothing. We need all the warmth we can get.'

'Rob her body? No, Signy, what are you doing?' Signy had knelt to pull at Hildegarde's garments and Estrith grabbed her arm. Signy threw her off. 'Why not? She doesn't need them now. We do.'

'But they're all over blood!' protested Estrith.

'Who cares? Inge, come and help me. My hands are so numb. Here, you can have the shawl.'

'I thought you were a sweet, gentle girl.'

'I was sweet and gentle when it was some use. Now it isn't, so I'm not.' Signy dragged off the last of Hildegarde's clothing, regardless of the grotesque and pitiful sight beneath. 'We need more bindings. We should wrap our feet as well as our hands, especially the children's. We don't want to risk frostbite.'

'Go on,' said Estrith bitterly. 'She was only my son's wife and that's only my grandchild down there, sticking out of her. Cut them up and cook them over the fire, why don't you?'

'It could come to that yet,' said Signy, shockingly. Her delicate features were set. 'We lost the path under the snow before we found this place. I know the way to Jorvik and it didn't go past a farmstead like this. I don't know where we are or which way Jorvik lies. Does anyone?'

The day before yesterday Oddeyes had woken to the ordinary world of hut and longhouse, to the cackle of poultry and the clank of buckets and the usual morning bowl of porridge.

Before the morning was over, his world had ended and here he was, trudging away among the cold moors, going he didn't quite know where and, as he went, the thought that hammered loudest in his brain was: The people who did this were Norman knights.

They'd killed his grandfather. One of them had struck him; his ear and jaw throbbed where the mailed palm had bruised them. He'd been taught to admire Normans and knighthood. He'd been told he should properly have belonged to both. His grandfather *had* belonged to both . . .

His grandfather had been a murderer, then, too?

A chasm had opened suddenly between what he had experienced and what he had been told and Oddeyes, lost and dizzy, felt as though he were falling into the void.

There were the nights in the wood and the cave, and next day came the fresh horror of the falling snow, and he learned new things about hunger and cold: how the desire for food crescendoed and changed into belly cramps and weakness and chill; how the cold became an agonising pain, attacking one's bones like an iron saw. Then he saw Hildegarde fall ill.

He had seen lambs born and knew that human beings and sheep were much the same in this respect. He also knew that never in the normal world would he, a boy, have been allowed to see such a thing. Another law of life disintegrated like a wormeaten beam and no one except himself heard it go or saw the dust go up.

And presently, round the fire in the barn, with Hildegarde's rigid shape lying by the wall and drawing constant uneasy glances from them all, he saw another terrible change begin: in the women. Estrith, who had been Bjorn's wife, whom they had called the mistress, was losing her authority, while Signy, slender, silvery-fair Signy, who had been so shy and kind that even Halfdan had been very nearly protective of her, stood there with her eyes wolfish and her voice as cruel as ice, and said that they might end up eating Hildegarde. Beside her, the others seemed dwindled; not like grown-ups any more. .

Except for his grandmother Gunnor. Elderly and crone-like though she was, she was the only other woman to gain in stature. After Signy's ominous pronouncement, it was Gunnor who went, arms crossed and feet stamping, to look out of the gate at the snowbound moors and Gunnor who worked out that in the morning the course they should take should be still south-east but more easterly than before, and picked out landmarks to help them.

They slept as best they could, leaning against each other and taking turns to feed the fire. The mound outside still contained a useful amount of wood, partly turned to charcoal but no worse for that.

They used the wood freely but the barn had no door and the wind was sharp. Wynflaed said once: 'Suppose she isn't dead? Suppose she's still out there, wandering?' No one answered, but Gunnor put an arm round her and eventually Wynflaed dozed, though sometimes she sobbed in her sleep. The children cried on and off. Mary was quieter now but Dreda's youngest child took to whimpering and kept it up till dawn. Then she fell silent.

In the morning, she was dead, curled up and stiff, knees to chest. And Wynflaed, drained by exhaustion and grief, her once full face sagging in yellowed folds, could not stand.

Dreda sat with her head in her hands and the two remaining children crouched against her, while the others melted snow in the dented pot and gave Wynflaed hot water to drink. But although she at last managed to get to her feet, with Estrith and Gunnor helping her, her legs crumpled when she tried to walk. She crouched by the fire and pleaded: 'Don't leave me here to die alone.'

'You won't die. You just need rest,' said Estrith reassuringly. 'We'll wait with you. Don't be frightened.'

'But we can't wait,' said Signy.

Faces, white, sunken, charcoal-smudged, hollow-eyed, turned to her. Even Dreda lifted her head and said: 'What do you mean?'

'She only needs a little sleep!' said Estrith.

'If she goes to sleep now, she'll never wake up again,' said Signy dispassionately, regardless of Wynflaed's desperate eyes. 'She needs food and proper shelter. Well, so do we all and there's none here. The only ones who will live are those who can go on, because they're the only ones with a chance of finding them. It was you, Gunnor, who said that we couldn't lie down in the snow because we'd got to bring the children through. Well, this is what it means. We can't wait here. Wyn, make an effort. Say to yourself, I *will* stand, I *will* walk. Because if you don't, we'll have to make up the fire for you, leave you some water and go.'

'I can't walk! Don't leave me, *please!*'

'We can't leave her. It would be cruel. Suppose it were mother?' Edith, the elder of Elfgiva's twins, looked at Signy as though Signy had sprouted devil's horns.

'I really can't imagine, Signy, what makes you think you've the right to give these orders.' Estrith, brushing with jerky and fastidous movements at the charcoal on her clothes, still attempted to speak with the authority of the Dale's mistress.

'Somebody must give them and you're clearly not going to! I tell you that if we don't find help soon, none of us will come through. Are these children to be kept here in this weather, with this barn the only shelter and nothing to eat? How long will that pile of half-used fuel out there last?'

'This must stop,' said Gunnor sharply and was heeded. 'How much fuel *is* there outside? We ain't looked round properly. If the pack of Normans who were here meant to destroy everything, they didn't make too good a job of it. Left us all that charcoal, and an iron pot, didn't they? And these walls still standing. Someone go and take a good look round now. Meanwhile, Wynflaed, I'll try a bit of massage on you.'

Oddeyes, who had been crouching by the fire and trying to comfort his empty belly as best he could by huddling his arms across it, did not want to uncurl and go outside but a vague feeling that, as the oldest male present, he ought to do so, urged him to his feet. When three or four of the women went out to do Gunnor's bidding, he followed shakily and wandered about in the yard, wondering what exactly he was searching for.

His movements were feeble; he was frighteningly weak. The trampled snow was perilous, too. While he was poking about in a corner away from the rest, he slipped, shooting feet-first into a snowdrift against the wall of the barn. It gave way under him and for a frightful moment he thought he was falling into a well. Then he found himself up to his armpits in snow in a small pit and some wild flailing revealed that there was a more conventional way to reach the place where he stood, for there were four stone steps down into it. In front of him, fire-scarred but still intact, was a low door.

It was locked but the fire had weakened it. When he pushed at it, it splintered. He crept inside.

When he climbed out of the pit again, he pushed snow down into it to hide the door, before going back to Gunnor.

Gunnor's attempts at massage had evidently failed. Wynflaed was lying in a miserable heap, staring at the fire with hopeless eyes and a confused quarrel was in progress around her.

Oddeyes arrived in time to hear Estrith say: 'I don't want to be the next one: left to die on the hillside with wolves on the prowl, as likely as not!' and to see her attempt to give Signy a push. Estrith was already weak enough to justify her fears and the push was feeble. The open-handed blow with which Signy retaliated hadn't much force either, but it made Estrith sit down abruptly on the ground. In other circumstances, it would have been funny. Oddeyes looked at them with a mixture of amazement and contempt, and pulled at his grandmother's sleeve.

'There's enough fuel out there to last through another night with care – just. Grandmother, suppose the two of us stayed with Wynflaed and let the others go on ahead?'

Gunnor glanced towards Wynflaed. 'It wouldn't delay us much,' she said in a low voice. 'Though I can't say that where Wynflaed can hear. You want just us to stay? Why?'

She spoke to him as though he were an adult and he answered her as one. 'I don't trust Signy after what she said about eating Hildegarde. I think . . . if we go on with her and don't find food, she might kill someone.'

'Humph,' said Gunnor. She glanced towards Signy, who was again haranguing the others on the necessity of starting out at once. The women who had been searching the yard had come back empty-handed and were listening with expressions which showed that they were weakening. Estrith and the good-hearted twins were still protesting tearfully, but in the failing tones of foreordained losers. And Wynflaed, curled in a ball and moaning, had given up hope.

Wynflaed died an hour after the others had gone, relieved of fear by the feel of Gunnor's thigh under her head, turning thankfully towards the friendly peace of oblivion.

'That's that,' said Gunnor, laying her down. 'Now we can move on, ourselves. But first, my lad, what is it you know that you ain't telling? Because there's summat. I can feel it.'

'I found an underground room,' said Oddeyes. 'You were right, Grandmother, this set of Normans were careless. They missed it, or didn't bother to break in. It was a storeroom. I found some farm tools and a whole lot of earthenware bowls and things there, beautiful ones . . .' Oddeyes had been fascinated by earthenware ever since he had seen Signy's amber-glazed dowry bowls set out on the table for the marriage feast '. . . and some cooking pots. *And . . .*'

'And what?' said Gunnor, since Oddeyes had hesitated.

'Something to cook.' He spoke slowly, not sure how this would be received. In the underground room he had taken a decision which was not

75

only very adult, but quite as ruthless as anything Signy had said. 'There's a bag with some oatmeal in it. Not much. Spread it round all of us and it won't make even one reasonable meal. But between just you and me . . .'

Gunnor gazed at him in surprise, her witch-like face hard to read. 'Your grandfather,' she said at length, 'would have told you that it was unknightly to keep it to yourself.'

'I know.' Oddeyes shrugged. 'But then, I've seen Norman knights now.'

'If we keep following this stream, it must join the big river somewhere, the one that goes through York. It's flowing south-east, which is right,' said Gunnor. 'Doubt if it's our own beck; that must be farther east. But it'll do as a guide. Reckon the others thought the same, since we're following their tracks.'

'We only need to keep on walking,' Oddeyes said valiantly.

It was easier said than done. They had become very feeble. It had not snowed again and, mercifully, what had already fallen was not too deep for walking. But the cooking pot and oatmeal now seemed as heavy as stones, and although, without discussing the matter, they had taken Wynflaed's clothes, the wind still sliced like a razor, straight to the skin. In addition, there were other miseries.

'I've got to stop again,' said Oddeyes.

In their relief at finding the oatmeal, they had overlooked its limitations as a sole source of nourishment. It was far better than nothing at all but it lacked substance and was all too likely to slide straight through the system undigested.

Gunnor waited beside him and helped him up. They moved on again, leaning on each other.

'The tracks look fresher. We may be catching up,' she said. 'We've got along pretty briskly, in spite of everything.'

'There's something down there,' said Oddeyes. 'Beside that big boulder.'

They were in a narrow valley which was dropping steadily between steep, white hillsides. The stream raced beside them, black against the snow, too swift to freeze over, here and there purling noisily round the boulders which sat in its midst or jutted from its edges. One of these lay ahead, barring their way. They would have to scramble a little up the hillside in order to pass it. Reaching it, they saw that of those who had gone ahead, two had not been equal to the effort.

Elfgiva's twins were dead. They had not been stripped; very likely they had been alive when they were left. They were lying against the boulder wrapped in each other's arms. Gunnor crouched to look. The bindings were loose on one of Godgift's feet and the sole of the shoe beneath was worn almost through. 'Frostbite,' said Gunnor. 'She couldn't walk. Edith stayed with her twin, I expect. Come along, Oddeyes. There's nothing to be done. It could have been worse,' she added grimly.

Two hours later, it was worse.

Painfully, helping each other, they had negotiated the hillside round the boulder and continued slowly downstream. From a distance, the sight of a small clump of birch and alder cheered them. They could light a fire and rest. 'And we'll make some porridge, thicker this time,' Gunnor said with determined brightness.

But the others had been before them. The ashes of their fire were there and so was Elfgiva. Gunnor and Oddeyes stood and looked at her in unbelieving horror.

'Signy meant it,' said Oddeyes at last, in a whisper.

Elfgiva's dreadful remains lay in the midst of stained and trampled snow, on the edge of the trees. Plain to see were the tracks leading on out of the trees and back to the stream, where the party must have travelled on again. But one single set of footprints went off from where Elfgiva lay, slanting uphill. Gunnor, peering at them, said: 'Someone was *running.*'

Oddeyes stared up the hillside. 'Up there,' he said. 'Look. Can you see anything?'

They put their burdens down and managed, because the gradient was slight, to reach the dark hump that he had seen. Estrith had, it seemed, fled from what was happening by the wood. She lay curled up, as Dreda's child had been. She had piled up some snow at her back to make a windbreak and then, it seemed, had lain down to die as peacefully as possible.

'But if you had shared out the oatmeal,' said Gunnor, 'it would only have staved this off a bit.' She patted Oddeyes' shoulder with a cloth-wrapped hand. 'Find some firewood,' she said, and picked up the oatmeal bag. There was not much left now. The act of bending made her head swim and she had to pause, leaning against a tree. Her vision cleared, to show her Oddeyes squatting again, groaning as his body once more gave up the food it could no longer stomach.

It was Oddeyes, as he staggered to his feet a few moments later, who looked furtively towards what had been Elfgiva and said: 'I wonder . . . what it tastes like.'

'So do I,' said Gunnor. There was a silence. Then Gunnor said: 'I'd never tell you to do anything you shouldn't. You know that. This is the choice between life and death. No one can do anything for Elfgiva now but perhaps she can do something for us. I said, start the fire again. And take no notice of what I'm doing.'

They both cried and they both retched before the frightful meal was cooked and eaten, but when they had finished, warmth and strength had flowed into them. They were able to doze a little that night and in the morning they ate before they set off again. Shudder as they might, meat on the spit smelt like meat on the spit, whatever creature had provided it. Again, without discussing it, they took some with them when they left, ready-cooked for eating on the march.

They passed other burnt-out farms that day and from a distance saw what had once been a small village. It was now only an expanse of ash and a stench on the air. 'Have they slaughtered everyone in the world and burned everything?' Gunnor asked in despair.

They lost the trail of the others, which turned away from the stream at a place where the water itself veered west. 'But we're sticking to the river,' Gunnor said firmly. 'It's our only guide.' It justified her presently, by swinging east again. The sky stayed clear as the day wore on, but the temperature fell further. The sun sank, a swollen ball of red, down into a haze, staining the snowy hillsides crimson. As darkness fell, Gunnor said: 'We dare not stop. We can't make a fire; there ain't a tree or a bush for miles that I can see. We must keep on walking and eat as we go. We can see our way. There's a moon.'

There was, and it was full. At twilight, it hung like a faintly gleaming medallion just above the hills, opposite the sun. Later, shrinking and brightening as it climbed, it cast a still, cold light more than strong enough to walk by.

Oddeyes afterwards remembered that night as though it were a beautiful and horrible dream. They plodded beside the stream among moors like the waves of a gigantic, frozen sea. The stars glittered. They and the moon seemed to watch the two human creatures, the ageing woman and the young boy as they set one foot before another, creeping through a frozen world and dead night hours not meant for human journeying.

They did indeed eat as they went and without the food they would not have been still on their feet at dawn. Each of them fell several times, but whenever this happened, was dragged up again by the other. The stars had faded and the moon had gone down into a bank of fog when Gunnor raised a hand to point to a silvery tracery of twigs, showing beyond a high bank, and said: 'They're fruit trees. *They* would have burned them, wouldn't they? There must be people near.'

One foot and then another; right foot, left foot, bones made of aching ice, and what little strength they had, drawn from a source they dare not think about: slowly and still more slowly, they stumbled on.

Eight miles to the east, in a farmstead which the Norman strike had missed by barely two miles, Signy woke beside the farmer into whose house she had led all of her companions who remained alive: Inge and her child, Dreda and one of hers. The best she had been able to do.

Her own son was among the casualties but she was beyond mourning. She had saved what she could, by whatever means she could. If there were such things as souls, as the priests said, she had probably damned hers. If it wasn't damned, it was at least well and truly mortgaged.

The farmer looked like a troll, stocky and dour, and his wife was a poor scuttling thing who seemed to be mostly a pair of bent shoulders and a shawled head, while the three or four other members of the household – sons, daughters, thralls; in a place like this there wouldn't be much difference – had done no more than stare and wait for the farmer to decide whether the scarecrows on his threshhold could stay or should be driven out to limp on to death or the next chance of succour, whichever might come first.

But even exhausted, emaciated and filthy, she, Signy, still had saleable assets. She had never, throughout the whole journey, removed her headdress and, under it, her silver-fair hair was clean. When she pulled off the veiling and let that hair cascade to her waist, the farmer's slab-granite face had changed.

She had done a deal with him. He should feed them and give them some heated water in which to wash. In return, he should have three nights with her, and the legal possession of her thralls Inge and Dreda and their children. He should also have the dagger which Estrith had thrown down, sobbing, beside Elfgiva's body, after trying to threaten Inge with it and then losing her nerve. In the end, Inge, who had been the one who said that perhaps lying down to die in the snow might be the best thing to do, had fought passionately for life, for the sake of her child. She had stood protectively over her mistress Signy, keeping the outraged Estrith off while Signy did what must be done to Elfgiva's body to keep the breath in the rest of them.

It had been most obliging of Estrith to drop the dagger. It had been very useful, much more effective than the small knife Signy had been trying to work with at the time.

She had resolutely refused, however, to hand over the amethyst necklace which had been her morning-gift from Sven. 'You're getting quite enough,' she said to the farmer. 'When my thralls are well again, you can sell them for a handsome profit.' He respected hard bargainers and she had won, although neither of them knew if the two remaining children would survive. Both were badly feverish. But they had had warm goats' milk with bread soaked in it, and a tisane brewed by the scuttling wife who was sorry for them (although by the look of her she would happily have put deadly nightshade into one for Signy).

But she wouldn't have Signy here for long, not if Signy could help it. The farmer said that Jorvik was a good two days' walk away but there was a decent track, still passable despite the snow, and if it didn't snow again, Signy meant to leave as soon as she could and look for her parents in Jorvik.

She had been careful last night not to eat too much. Now, this morning, she was still hungry but much restored in strength. She prodded the bulk at her side. He half-woke and turned over, dumping an arm like an elm-log across her stomach. Signy set to work to wake him up properly. She didn't want him to try to keep her here. She would deal with that if she had to; if she could survive the last few days, there was little that would defeat her now. But it would be better to arrange for him, simply, to be glad to see the back of her.

He would be. He'd be tired.

The high bank led to the start of a stone wall. They could see hearth–smoke rising into the sky. It wasn't York. Gunnor had no idea where it was. But it was an inhabited place; it was hope. 'When we get there, you're not to say you

79

were ever a thrall. You're freeborn like your grandfather was and don't you forget it. You come from a line of Norman knights, whether you like it or not.'

The wall was endless, Gunnor thought. Was there no gate anywhere? Or was it just that she was moving so slowly? Oddeyes had hold of her arm, but she couldn't feel him. She couldn't feel the ground underfoot. She was so weak, so light, she seemed to be floating, and so cold that she might be about to dissolve into the freezing mist which drifted round them.

She wasn't walking at all, now. She was lying on the ground. She could see the base of the wall, and a pair of feet, and the hem of a brown woollen robe. There were voices above her: Oddeyes' voice saying something in a frightened tone, and a man's voice answering him.

'I've brought Ivon's grandson,' she said clearly. 'We've walked to freedom.'

Chapter Six

St Cuthbert's

Maurice de Doucecolline, the newly appointed abbot of St Cuthbert's Abbey, had been told that it lay forty miles west of York and that the track was good. The royal clerk who had given him his scroll of appointment and his travelling instructions had said he could do it in a day and a half.

The clerk was a Norman and his only visit to the north had been to the highly civilised archbishop's residence in York. He hadn't, Maurice thought, the faintest idea what travel in these remote parts was like. Forty miles measured as a line on a map was one thing. Forty miles across these endless up-and-down moorlands were more like seventy in practice, especially when encumbered by a mule-train laden among other things with his precious and breakable glassware, his silver tableware and his four-foot-high gold crucifix.

They had had to spend three nights on the way. Fortunately, the fifty-strong knight escort provided by the Archbishop of York carried tents and food on their pack-animals, sufficient for themselves and the serving men and for Maurice and his suite of secretary, chaplain and six other monks. They hadn't had to seek accommodation anywhere, which was just as well since the only habitations they had seen were a grim little burgh and the dirty farmhouse where Sir Guy FitzRichard, the captain of the escort, who like Maurice himself had been in England for three years but had picked up considerably more of the language, asked if they were on the right road. Guy had commented that the farmer looked like a troll.

Messire Guy, though very efficient, was not, in Maurice's opinion, altogether sound. Although his long face was solemn enough to do credit to the most grief-stricken funeral party, he possessed that irreverent and unpredictable thing, a sense of humour.

Guy was now riding back to him from the head of the line. 'We're about to overtake some travellers, sir. They seem to be leading a lame pack-animal. If they're in trouble, do you wish us to offer help?'

Maurice attempted to stand in his stirrups to see over the intervening heads but the conical helmets, bobbing up and down in front, foiled him. 'Certainly,' he said, a little testily, as he settled back into his saddle. 'What else?'

He came level with the little party a few moments later. One of the men was leading a pony along the soft grassy edge of the track, its head bobbing at every stride. The group stopped and drew warily together as the caval-cade caught up and the young man whom Maurice at once identified as the leader put a hand quickly on his sword-hilt.

Guy raised his own right hand, palm out, and said in English: 'I am captain of the escort for Abbot Maurice of St Cuthbert's; nothing more sinister. We see you are in difficulties. My lord abbot wishes to ask if we can help.'

'Not unless you've a travelling forge with you,' said the man whose hand was still hovering not too far from his sword-hilt. He was not much over twenty, well if plainly dressed, and looked as if he knew how to use that sword. 'The pony's lost a shoe. We've turned away from our path to reach the nearest blacksmith. There's one in Hawkshawe, below St Cuthbert's, we believe.'

'There is.' Maurice had understood some of this exchange and answered in his own poor English. Hawkshawe was held by the abbey and Maurice's secretary had the deeds in his saddle-bag. Maurice himself had studied them carefully before setting out. Hawkshawe had a forge, a water-mill and a regular market. It was satisfactory to know that his abbey, though small, was reasonably well-off. He ran a more attentive eye over the party and concluded that they consisted of a leader with three companions, and a wife with a small boy. The other two women and the skinny little girl were servants, probably bondwomen. The girl-child and the thin young woman with the frightened brown eyes and the look of ingrained dirt were definitely villein types.

The young leader's wife was regarding them all steadily; not rudely, but not as though she were in the least impressed by an abbot or a baggage train or even an escort of fifty fully accoutred knights. She too was young and sat very straight and he supposed that her small, delicate features were pretty; it wasn't the kind of thing he ever let himself think about. He caught Guy FitzRichard's eye. 'Offer what help we can.'

'We can't carry your lame pony,' said Guy to the young leader. 'But if you wish, one or two of you can stay to lead it and the rest can ride on with us. We're bound for St Cuthbert's. There is a guest-house there where the ladies . . .' he said afterwards that something about the straightbacked young woman made him use the term of respect '. . . can wash and rest until the pony is ready to travel on; perhaps till the morning. Where are you making for?'

'A place called Eric's Dale,' said the young man. 'I doubt if you've heard of it. We came from there, originally. It's two days' steady riding in that direction.' He nodded towards the north, while his eyes roamed expres-sively over Guy's helmet, shield and mail. So did his wife's. Guy did not pretend to misunderstand.

'*You* came from that way? You've been able to bear arms for a good few years. How do you come to be still alive?' His mournful eyes surveyed the rolling heather-clad hogbacks of the moor all around them. 'Were you hiding up a tree in one of these dense forests?'

'I was with the Danish army,' said the young man coldly, 'and later, when they joined the English leader Hereward the Wakeful in Ely, so did I. But they left Ely and went home before it fell and I left with them and tried to go home too. I knew what had happened here in the north but I hoped that somehow or other . . . Eric's Dale might have escaped. It hadn't. So I went back to Jorvik . . .'

'Jorvik . . . oh, York. Continue,' said Guy.

'. . . I have relatives there, some with influence. I'm not a hunted man, Messire. I have made my peace with those who now rule us. I have the right to Eric's Dale; I am to hold it of the new earl and I'm going there now, lawfully!'

The language barrier was a nuisance, Maurice thought. He had understood only a few words of this. But the tone had conveyed something. 'Does he think we're accusing him in some way? What's the matter with him?'

'He regards me as an enemy,' said Guy. 'I'm a Norman knight and though he says he has made peace – with the Normans, I think he means – I fancy he has a good deal against us.' He turned back to the young man. 'No one has challenged your right to travel anywhere you like. But a moment ago, on behalf of my lord abbot, I offered you the hospitality of St Cuthbert's guest-house. You didn't answer.'

It was the straightbacked young woman who did so, without even glancing at her husband. 'It would be discourteous not to thank you. So – thank you. But we would prefer to be left to ourselves. We'll go on to Hawkshawe as we are. We are prepared for camping out and it is summer. You must forgive us. I lived at Eric's Dale once, too. So did these.' She nodded towards the bondwoman with the child. 'We walked for five days through the snow, starving, to reach help after we had had a visit from men who looked like you, Messire.'

'Well said,' remarked her husband.

She had a very clear voice and she had spoken calmly. Maurice, once again, had managed to pick up the gist. He also picked up his reins. 'If they don't want our help, let us waste no more time on them. Lead on, Messire Guy.'

'Wait,' said the young man. He reached into a belt pouch and took out some silver. He held it out to Guy and said something, glancing sideways at the abbot.

'What is he saying?' demanded Maurice.

'He's offering money to St Cuthbert's, for Masses to be said for the souls of some of his family, who died during the harrying. In particular, I gather, for those of his mother who died before she could reach safety, and his wife's former husband, who died in front of his own hall. He must have had plenty of opportunity to arrange Masses for them in York,' Guy added. 'I rather think he is making this request *at* us, or at me, if you follow me, sir. Though no doubt he has his reasons.'

Abbot Maurice frowned. He was a royal appointee, but the church was not obliged to underwrite everything that princes did and furthermore, the church, a community as tightly and intricately linked as a chain-mail hauberk, knew all about the views which the new Archbishop Lanfranc of Canterbury held on the harrying of the north. William, having summoned him from Normandy to take office, had been taken to task on the subject before Lanfranc's unpacking was finished.

'Give him back his money. The Masses will be said. Ask the names of the people they're for, and his own name, too.'

Guy did as he was told. It seemed a surprisingly long conversation, and the grubby bondwoman with the frightened eyes took part. It didn't seem to be her present master and mistress who scared her. 'His name is Leif Bjornsen,' said Guy at length. 'His mother was Estrith and his wife's first husband was a man called Sven.'

Maurice glanced over his shoulder at his secretary. 'You heard that, Hubert? Remember it. When we reach St Cuthbert's, make a note of it.'

'There was more,' said Guy. 'It was hard to follow – their accents are so thick – but the grubby girl wanted us to include someone called Dreda. Seems their mistress sold her and this Dreda to a farm somewhere – by the sound of it, it could have been that place where we asked directions – in exchange for food, I suppose when they were escaping from the harrying. Then their mistress went on to York. A day or so ago, she returned with her new man – they're this couple, here – to buy them back again but Dreda, whoever she was, was dead of rough treatment. The man called the farmer a rude name; said he charged them much too high for the girl and the child.'

'Disgraceful,' said Maurice. 'The church has forbidden slavery. Those sales were illegal.'

Guy shrugged. 'Slaves or villeins, there isn't much difference. You're not supposed to sell villeins outright but they go with the land if that changes hands, like one of the barns. I'm glad I'm not a bondman, of any sort.'

'Quite,' said Maurice coldly. 'Very well, the name Dreda shall be included when the Mass is dedicated.' He observed a faintly quizzical expression on Guy's face. 'She may have been a villein but all souls are equal in the sight of God.' There would be villeins on St Cuthbert's lands and if any of them absconded, he would have them hunted down, brought back and beaten. But bodies did not matter. Souls did. 'I think,' said Maurice, 'that that is St Cuthbert's, just ahead.'

The Abbey of St Cuthbert was sheltered by hills to the north-east and had an agreeable prospect over the fields and meadows which sloped away south-west. Cattle flourished there of a type which didn't usually do well north of the Humber. The abbey's walled garden contained well-tended fruit trees and the brothers could eat apples well on into the spring. Prior Guthlac wasn't sure if this was according to the Rule of St Benedict, which specified 'fruit in season', but the old abbot had said it benefited his community's health, and attributed his long life to it.

Supported by rents from a number of farms and villages, especially

Hawkshawe down beyond the fields, St Cuthbert's went short of nothing it needed. Assured of its material security, it was under normal conditions a serene place.

Conditions on this June morning were neither normal nor serene. Brother Edwin, who was in charge of the abbey school, had let his pupils take turns in keeping watch from the squat church tower, with instructions to report any imminent arrivals straight to the prior. The last youthful sentry had just come scrambling excitedly down to announce 'A lot of horsemen are coming, sir, with knights. I can see the spears!'

Well, they're good boys, thought Guthlac, wiping a harassed forehead and sending the lad off to say that the abbey bell was to be rung. He'd had his doubts about the idea when old Father Abbot decided to start the school. 'We'll have children all over the place, shrieking, when we're trying to study,' he remembered saying. But the venture had gone ahead; his scholarly labours hadn't been interrupted by unruly noises very often, and after the terrible destruction to the north, they'd all been glad they had a school, with accommodation and a teacher in place, so that they could take in the orphans who were brought to them or, sometimes, came stumbling to the door for shelter.

Now, as the bell rang out to welcome the new abbot, Prior Guthlac hurried into the forecourt where the community was hastily assembling in response to it. They had been carefully rehearsed. A group of lay brothers waited to one side of the gate to lead away horses and unload baggage; the schoolboys and novices with their mentors were drawn up on the left of the forecourt, and the other 197 brethren were arranged in rows on the right. Regrettably, the system of putting office-holders and senior monks in front automatically precluded the system of putting tall men at the back so that the incoming abbot could see over his community at a glance. If only Maurice had arrived at a different time of day, when everyone was in church, this reception committee could have been cancelled, but as it was he felt it to be obligatory.

If only Abbot Maurice wasn't coming at all.

It was the Norman king's doing, thought Prior Guthlac distractedly, hurrying indoors again to take a final look at the arrangements in the abbot's private room. King William, who had laid waste the north and half of Mercia, had – possibly in an attempt to retrieve his spiritual credit – then brought in an archbishop of saintly reputation to take over Canterbury and to clean up the English church, which apparently wasn't virtuous enough for him. But he and Lanfranc were doing more than spring-clean the church; they were Normanising it. Whenever an English abbot died nowadays, a Norman from the king's scriptorium would be rewarded for his services by being handed the vacancy. The brethren could no longer elect their own abbot or promote their prior, anywhere in the realm, for York had fallen into line behind Lanfranc of Canterbury.

When their abbot died, Prior Guthlac had said in all sincerity that he was glad of the new ruling; he didn't want to be promoted. Even as prior, he had found the administration work which went with the office a nuisance. Guthlac was a scholar who specialised in translations from Latin to English and he preferred to concentrate on these. Furthermore, his middle-aged eyesight was now growing too blurred for reading or writing, and he had to have another monk to read to him and take dictation. It slowed the work down. No, he most certainly did not want to be made abbot . . . but there was a renegade part of him which still resented Maurice's coming, still whispered that it was wrong, after all his long experience as prior, that he should be passed over without a by-your-leave.

He hoped the abbot's room would do. They knew nothing about this Maurice. If he were part of the campaign to purify a church in which monasteries had become too comfortable and parish priests had even taken to getting married, then his quarters must contain no worldly luxuries. But on the other hand, he was presumably a man of some eminence, used to court ways and . . . he was a Norman. He would expect respect. Guthlac had compromised as well as he could. The table was plain, but it had been polished. The candlestick was plain too, but it was silver, as was the rood above the prie-dieu. On the latter a white cloth with a little silver embroidery had been placed. Guthlac paused and frowned, reminded of something else. The address of welcome which was to be presented to Maurice was ornately illuminated (amid a fine panic, as well, when they feared the pigments wouldn't be dry in time). But producing fine manuscripts was part of a monastery's proper business; no, the new abbot couldn't object to that. Could he? 'Well, what else could we do but guess?' Guthlac muttered and hastened back to the courtyard to find Brother Edwin standing in front of his pupils and counting heads with visible anxiety.

'Is something wrong, Brother Edwin?'

'Ivon's missing,' said the young monk.

'Oh no!' said Guthlac, and hoped he hadn't actually gone pale. Edwin's blue eyes were fixed on him worriedly, awaiting instructions. 'He must be found!' said Guthlac promptly. 'At once. You had better—'

It was too late. With a fanfare of trumpets, the new abbot's cavalcade was already clattering across the outer courtyard where the guest-house was, and here they came through the inner gate. Prior Guthlac signalled urgently to Brother Edwin to get back in line with his charges, breathed an inward prayer and, as Maurice and his suite dismounted, stepped briskly forward, followed by the brother who had been chosen, on account of his good speaking voice, to read and present the address.

'My lord abbot,' said Guthlac, kneeling to kiss the abbatial ring. Maurice's knight escort remained mounted, drawn up into a semicircle behind him, for all the world, thought Guthlac crossly as he came to his feet, as though they feared that he might assault Maurice or Maurice attempt to bolt out of the gate.

'I am Maurice de Doucecolline,' the new abbot was saying. 'Allow me to introduce my suite. Father Roger de Bois, my chaplain. Brother William, my secretary . . .'

During the introductions, Guthlac assessed the newcomer's calm, polished countenance and assured manner and the value of the very pretty chestnut mare he had been riding (Barbary blood there, no mistaking it), and recognised him as a type. Prelates like Maurice visualised God as a prince on a grand scale and themselves as noblemen in a realm whose capital city happened to be called Heaven. 'Competent, authoritative, probably touchy,' Guthlac said to himself. He wondered uneasily where that boy Ivon had got to, and what kind of impression he himself was making on the impassive Maurice, and to his further annoyance, heard himself stammering.

Maurice was thinking: Long face like a horse, but my mare's a better-looking one. Eyes like gooseberries, good forehead, probably intelligent – reputation as a scholar deserved, no doubt – may be jealous of me (natural), is not my equal (of course not; I'm Norman), scared of me . . . good, but why is he quite this nervous? I haven't bitten him yet. I've just finished the introductions and . . . oh God, now he's stammering over presenting a monk to read an address of welcome. The monk's more self-possessed than the prior. Good reading voice. I wonder what the standard of singing here is like . . . ?

Something clanged loudly on Guy FitzRichard's helmet and, at the same moment, Maurice's chestnut mare stood on her hind legs with an indignant squeal, jerking the lay brother who was holding her off the ground. Coming down, he landed with one foot on a loose stone which hadn't been there before, turned his ankle and sat down. He had hung on to the reins and jerked the mare's head down with him. She promptly let fly with her heels instead. Another knight spurred forward to seize the mare's bridle and a second stone struck his outstretched gauntlet, striking sparks.

From the massed half-circle of knights came further clangs, accompanied by loud exclamations and curvettings among the horses. Maurice and Guthlac both spun round to look at the scene in horror and then upwards at the short square tower of the church from which the stones seemed to be coming. On top, stooping to an invisible stockpile and rising to hurl missiles, in a regular and furious rhythm, was the missing boy Ivon.

Four knights sprang down and sprinted for the church. Guthlac, racing after them, observed that Brother Edwin had already disappeared. He caught up with the knights to find them angrily rattling the door to the tower stair. 'It's bolted inside!' one of them shouted at him in bad English.

'Come with me,' said Guthlac, taking, even at this embarrassing moment, a mild pleasure in the fact that he could speak excellent French. He led them out to the courtyard again. The shower of stones had ceased. On the roof, Brother Edwin, who had got there first and prudently bolted the door behind him, was standing with an arm around Ivon's shoulders and had opened shouted negotiations with Maurice, also in French.

'Bring Ivon down here at once!' Guthlac bellowed, interrupting. 'I'll

deal with this! I'm extremely sorry,' he added to Maurice. 'The boy has
. . . he has an unreasoning hatred of Norman knights. He did the same
thing when some knights came here escorting the Archbishop of York's
messenger, to announce your appointment. I thought I had given him an
adequate lesson on that occasion but . . . Brother Edwin! I said: bring him
down!'

'I'm sorry,' shouted Edwin from the roof, 'but no! Thrashing him
didn't work last time and . . .'

'May I remind you that you're bound by a vow of obedience to your
superiors and . . .'

'Then I'm also bound to do as Father Abbot told me when he put me in
charge of the school, and safeguard the welfare of these boys!'

'All right, Prior Guthlac.' Maurice moved firmly in front of Guthlac
and tilted his head back. 'Did you say you would bring the boy down as
long as you could bring him to me?'

'Yes, my lord, and if I can speak to you privately before you talk to him,
and if the knights, please . . . I'm sorry, but please could they go out of
sight?'

Guthlac opened his mouth to shout 'How dare you?' but Messire Guy,
who had ridden over to Maurice's side, said: 'He doesn't look like a very
dangerous enemy. I'll get my men dismounted and into their quarters if
you wish, my lord. You can call me if you need protection after all.'

'Protection? Rubbish.' Maurice chose not to recognise the dry humour.
On the roof, Ivon stood rigid and silent in the curve of Brother Edwin's
arm. 'Yes,' said Maurice. 'Get your men away. This situation is absurd
and must not be prolonged.' He turned back to the tower. 'Your wishes are
being met. I expect you and the boy to be on the threshold of my office in
five minutes.' He looked at Guthlac. 'Kindly show me there at once.'

'This wasn't quite the way I meant to begin my abbacy,' he said to Guthlac
as the latter, maintaining what dignity he could, opened the door of the
abbot's room and stood back to let Maurice enter first. 'I had intended to
interview every member of the community, beginning with yourself as
prior, and working my way down in due order. I certainly didn't intend to
start with an erring schoolboy. However . . . no.' He raised a hand as
Guthlac began once more to apologise. 'No need for that. An outrage has
been perpetrated which I must investigate at once but I never prejudge any
case, prior.' He glanced about the room and decided to smooth his prior's
badly ruffled plumage. 'This office has been well arranged. The appoint-
ments are very suitable. I shall have a few things to add. As an abbot,
naturally, I shall observe the ban on personal property. But as a clerk in the
royal scriptorium, I enjoyed a little latitude and I have a small collection of
glassware and plate which I propose to present to St Cuthbert's. It would
not be improper, I think, for one or two items to enhance the abbot's own
quarters. Ah. Here are the offenders, coming in from the cloister. Leave
us, Prior Guthlac.'

Guthlac, dismissed, could do nothing else. He glared at Brother Edwin as he passed him in the doorway and on encountering Ivon, the boy who was also known as Oddeyes, who was responsible for this débâcle, could not restrain himself from a menacing gesture. Ivon did not move, but stood firm and stared back at him. Guthlac, seething, swept off along the cloister.

'Stand there,' said Edwin to his pupil. 'And don't you dare move. I will do my best for you but I'm ashamed of you, do you hear? *Stand there*. And come in at once when you're called and try to look contrite.'

Entering the abbot's room, he closed the door behind him. Maurice, who had sat down behind his desk, raised patrician brows in silent comment. 'My lord abbot,' said Brother Edwin firmly, as he rose from briefly saluting the ring, 'I find it best to avoid discussing the young actually in their hearing. It gives them inflated ideas of themselves.'

'That young man has them already, it appears,' said Maurice. 'Well, Brother – Edwin, is it? I'm waiting for your explanation.'

'The boy comes from somewhere north of here. We took him in a little more than two years ago. He arrived as a refugee from the harrying. They were trying to reach York but missed their way. He was with a woman; he says she was his grandmother. They were both starving, exhausted and nearly frozen and they were both desperately ill after they arrived. The woman died within two days. But the boy was strong and we pulled him through. Only,' said Brother Edwin, looking very steadily at the new abbot, 'he had seen his home attacked and destroyed, and many of the people he had grown up with, slaughtered. He had seen others die in the attempt to reach safety. The killers were Norman knights. He saw no other knights until a few weeks ago when, as you heard, the messenger came to give us fore-warning of your arrival. We – that is, the boys and I – were tending the garden, through the little arch from the inner courtyard. We could see the knights as they rode in. He fled indoors, shouting that we were all going to be murdered. He was quite obviously,' said Brother Edwin, 'in terror for his life. I went after him and found him hiding in the dormer. I tried to reassure him, but he broke away from me and ran off again, only this time he rushed straight back to the arch between the courtyard and the garden and started snatching up stones from the garden and pelting the knights with them. I dragged him away and then Prior Guthlac came and he . . . well, he insisted on dealing with Ivon very sternly. But I,' said Edwin, 'thought he had been rather brave, considering. To attack such an enemy like that, all by himself, I mean. Especially an enemy of whom he was really so afraid.'

'You considered Prior Guthlac's action erroneous?'

'Yes, my lord. And also useless. As I said, Ivon is essentially brave.'

'You like the boy? What is his background?'

'We aren't sure. There's a mystery about him.'

'A mystery? Doesn't he know where he comes from? Or do you suspect him of telling lies? Does he make improbable claims to be of noble birth? That happens sometimes, with orphans.'

'No. It isn't that. But his grandmother, if she was his grandmother, kept on insisting, before she died, that he was the son, or grandson – she was very confused in her mind – of a Norman knight, and that he was freeborn and we were to remember that. He himself agrees that he is freeborn but he denies passionately that he has any connection with any Norman knight, although in view of the circumstances, that's understandable. Whatever the truth may be, the woman was certainly what is called a thrall in these parts. She had tricks of phrase, a way of looking at you . . . one can nearly always tell. If she really was his grandmother, then very likely he was born in bondage too. It makes no difference to me. I treat all my boys alike. But there's something about him . . . as I said, he is brave.'

There was something about Brother Edwin, too, thought Maurice. It was difficult to define; it lay in the pattern made by the few lines on his young face and in the way he had stood on the tower and drawn the boy close. Maurice would not have put him in charge of a school.

True, men like Edwin could make excellent teachers provided their proclivities remained latent. But the problem was to know when the latent had become the active.

But his defence of Ivon on the grounds of the boy's courage was itself valiant and this Maurice could appreciate. He would leave Brother Edwin in office for the time being. 'We'll have the boy in in a moment,' he said. 'But first fetch the captain of my escort, Sir Guy FitzRichard. He is an aggrieved party. I take it that the boy has little French? No matter; Guy speaks reasonable English and you can help translate if necessary.'

When they all stood before him, he took careful stock of Ivon. How old? Thirteen or thereabouts, probably, and going to be handsome (Brother Edwin had assuredly been influenced by that). He was both frightened and angry. He had started away from the mailed form of Guy FitzRichard but kept on darting glances of sheer hatred at him. In between, he met the abbot's gaze defiantly. His own eyes were remarkable. They didn't match. 'This,' said Brother Edwin appositely at this moment, 'is Ivon Oddeyes.' He turned to the boy. 'And this is . . .'

'My lord abbot. I know.' Ivon sketched a bow towards Maurice, and waited. He was now ignoring Guy.

Maurice, through his two interpreters, proceeded briskly. 'I've been hearing your instructor's apologies on your behalf. Now I'll hear yours. What have you to say for yourself?'

'I don't like Norman knights.'

'That is quite obvious. To such an extent that when given to understand that a number of them are expected here, you collect a supply of stones in readiness to throw at them. Your first exercise in this, so Brother Edwin tells me, was more innocent. That time, you seized a few stones from the garden and threw them on the spur of the moment. But this time there was clearly premeditation. While you were about it, you wrecked a reception ceremony which I have no doubt that Prior Guthlac and all the good brothers have worked hard and long to prepare. You achieved nothing, except that one of your stones left a cut on my mare's shoulder. What you did was stupid, useless and selfish. Have you any defence to make?'

Ivon spoke. Brother Edwin, glancing quickly at Guy, made to translate, but Guy got in first. 'He says that Norman knights destroyed his home and—'

Maurice cut him short. 'Yes, he was a refugee from the harrying. Tell him that I already know that much and that is why he is being treated with such forbearance now. Then ask him if he thinks he can bring the dead back to life by behaving like a street urchin.'

Guy spoke. Ivon listened and then poured out words in reply, addressing them, however, to Brother Edwin. Maurice nodded to Edwin to transmit them.

'He doesn't know what a street urchin is,' said Edwin. 'He's never seen even a small burgh. But he says that the first time he saw knights in the courtyard, he was afraid and ran away. But then I came after him and he was ashamed that I'd seen him trying to hide. So he ran back to stone the knights to prove – to himself rather than to me, I think – that he wasn't too terrified to fight them. He didn't care what anyone did to him for it and he still doesn't. When he realised that the new abbot would also arrive with a knight escort, he collected stones and put them ready on the tower and he isn't sorry. He says it's the only thing that it's possible for him to do to avenge his people, so he's doing it. For all he knows, he says, the knights who came here today and previously are the same men who burned his home. They all look alike, he says. When their helmets are on they might as well be made of metal.'

Guy waited for Edwin to finish. Then, on a note of command, he barked: 'Ivon!' The boy turned sharply towards him. 'As it happens, I was not in Northumbria during the harrying and nor was any other knight in the service of the Archbishop of York, from whose household we come. However . . .'

'You'd have pillaged my home if you'd been ordered to. If you weren't there, it's just chance.'

'Let me finish!' snapped Guy. 'You're right, we would. We should have had no choice. I was about to say so. A knight carries weapons, Ivon, but he is also little more than a weapon himself. He's a sword in the hand of a commander and acts under orders which he dare not disobey.' Guy appeared to be struck by an absurdity. 'If you want to blame anyone for destroying your home, my lad, blame the king. But you won't get the chance to throw stones at *him* and if you did, I wouldn't advise you to take it. Ivon, you can't attack the king nor will you ever know who the men were who attacked your home. For your own sake, let the dead rest.'

His English needed no help from Brother Edwin, but he left it to Edwin to relay the gist to Maurice, apparently as a form of courtesy. 'Ask the boy,' said Maurice, 'who his parents and grandparents were. Ask him if it's true that he is himself a child or grandchild of a man such as Messire Guy here.'

The thunderous expression on Ivon's face when he answered almost rendered translation superfluous. 'He says no,' said Edwin. 'He says that he was brought here by his grandmother to whom he owed his life, and that they were freeborn but had nothing to do with any kind of Norman. We always come up against this with him. If that woman was his grandmother, then it's doubtful if he's freeborn.'

'There was an old thrall at Eric's Dale who was supposed to be a Norman captive of some kind,' said Ivon. He put contempt into his voice. 'But he wasn't my father or my grandfather.'

'Eric's Dale?' said Maurice. 'Did he say Eric's Dale?'

'He did, my lord.' Guy also looked surprised. 'The place which our wayfarers mentioned.'

'I think,' said Maurice, 'that some enquiries might be put in hand. It would be interesting to get at the truth of this. For the moment, Brother Edwin, ask the boy if he is willing to give an undertaking never to behave in this manner again, and if he now understands that every Norman knight in the kingdom was not in Eric's Dale three winters ago.'

'Allow me to ask him,' said Guy. He addressed the boy briefly. Ivon regarded him for several moments and then, slowly, nodded. His face, which had throughout most of this interview looked curiously adult, suddenly reverted to youthfulness. He was obviously very tired. He had reached the end of his fighting spirit.

'Tell him to leave us and return to his classfellows,' said Maurice.

'What will happen to me?' asked Ivon of Brother Edwin. The fear he had said he did not feel, flickered in his eyes.

Maurice understood and answered directly, in his difficult English. 'We will tell you tomorrow. Now go.'

'He'll have a bad night,' said Edwin as, with dragging feet, Ivon went out.

'That was my intention. He can't expect to get away with it entirely,' said Maurice. 'An interesting boy,' he added thoughtfully.

'More than that!' said Guy. 'I wish I had him in my corps. I could make something of him. What do you intend doing to him, my lord abbot? Because,' said Guy. 'I would like to put in a plea for clemency. In his place, I think I should have run amók not with stones but with a knife.'

'That is generous of you, Messire Guy. In fact . . .' Maurice turned to Edwin. 'What is the boy good at, Brother? Is he gifted at his studies?'

'Not very, no. He likes to hang round the pottery.'

'Ah, yes. The abbey has one of its own, I believe? You have a brother here who started life as the son of a Thetford potter. Does the boy show any skill?'

'Yes. He can use the wheel and the brother concerned says that he is deft in handling clay and could be trained.'

'Then,' said Maurice, 'put him to it. The sooner he has a place of his own in the abbey and regular tasks to do, the better. He's ready to become a man, instead of a boy. There! Your plea for mercy has been heard, Messire Guy. The boy is to be treated kindly and apprenticed to the abbey potter.'

'A boy like that,' said Guy. 'A potter. It's enough to break one's heart. Perhaps I'll come one dark night and abduct him. Except that I suppose he'd kick my teeth in and anyway, it would break Brother Edwin's heart instead of mine.' His face, as usual, was as dismal as a burial ground, but Maurice supposed he was joking. He was evidently shrewd enough to have seen in Edwin what Maurice had seen, and had sufficient bad taste to think it amusing. A sense of humour, thought Maurice, was most certainly *not* a virtue.

Later, when his belongings had been unpacked, Maurice sat alone in his office and surveyed it. The big gold crucifix had replaced the silver one above the prie-dieu, and hanging on the wall at one side of the room, a curiosity and a conversation piece, was his favourite piece of glassware, an antique drinking-vessel made exactly in the shape of a small ox-horn. He liked the watery green of the glass and the elegant curl at the tapered end. The light was exactly right for it just there; he was pleased with it.

No doubt his introduction to St Cuthbert's hadn't been quite what he expected but really, thought Abbot Maurice, it hadn't gone badly either. He'd created the impression of a fair and just abbot; he'd made it clear that Prior Guthlac's reign was over; and he might quite well, while he was about it, have set that difficult but surely worthwhile boy on a safe path. Not a bad start, not at all.

In the dormer, Ivon was lying on his bed. Under the tunic which, since he was not actually a novice, he was still allowed to wear, he was clutching the carved bone dagger-hilt which his grandfather had given him and which still, as always, hung round his neck.

'I'm sorry, Grandfather,' he whispered. 'But I can't claim you. You were one of . . . those creatures.' How could you be one of those creatures?' In misery, from the betrayal of Old Ivon and from fear of what might happen tomorrow, he turned on to his face. 'That man Guy wasn't so bad,' he said. 'Oh, *Grandfather*! And Grandmother Gunnor. And . . . and . . .'

The monks of St Cuthbert's had been very kind to him when they took him in and he, instinctively aiming to please, because he had been reared a thrall and that was that thralls did, had tried – at least until conical helmets appeared in the forecourt – to behave well, to be cheerful, not to wallow too much in grief.

But grief didn't disappear, for all that.

'We have had visitors today,' said Leif as Signy ducked her head to enter the tent.

'So I see. They've brought the split logs from York for our longhouse. I hope they're the quality we ordered.'

'Yes. Stout seasoned wood and all they should be. But I didn't mean that. While you were roaming the hillsides like a shepherdess looking for stray sheep . . .'

'They'd be wild by now but if they'd bred, we'd have the makings of a flock,' said Signy. 'But those Norman bastards did their work too well.' She used the expletive without the slightest loss of dignity. 'There was nothing. I got a couple of coneys with my bow, though.'

'We'll have them for dinner. As I was saying, while you were out on the hill, two monks from a monastery called St Cuthbert's came here. They were asking questions about a young thrall we had here at one time. Ivon Oddeyes. Apparently they've got him in their monastery.'

'Are they going to send him back?'

'No. They wanted to know if he was freeborn or not, and if there was any truth in the story that he had a Norman knight for a grandfather.'

'What did you say?'

'No to both questions,' said Leif. 'We can do with more hands. I asked them to send him back to us, since we're his rightful owners. But they said they intended to keep him; they just wanted to know what they were keeping.'

Signy looked at him sharply. 'But he *was* old Ivon's grandson.'

Leif shrugged. 'What of it? Old Ivon was a thrall too. But I wanted to put the boy's thralldom beyond doubt because I was hoping to get an extra pair of hands for the Dale. I failed. That's all.'

'But you didn't tell the truth.'

Leif sat down on the chest which was the only seating in the tent which was their temporary home, until the walls of a new longhouse could be reared for Eric's Dale. 'Telling the truth,' he said softly, 'isn't always a virtue, my lovely Signy. And perhaps you had better not ask what I mean by that.'

'I've no need to ask.' Casually, Signy sat down on their pallet and began to loosen her pale hair. 'My dearly beloved Leif, I know very well why, when you found that I was alive in my father's house at Jorvik, you offered to marry me. It wasn't just to restore me to my place in the Dale, was it? Or even to give Sven's son his place, either.'

'If he is Sven's son.'

'Quite. I thought we had agreed not to discuss that.'

'It was you who mentioned his paternity just now. I won't refer to it again. I have not blamed you for what you did to survive or remarked on how very unlike Sven that stumping boy of yours is. But, no, I didn't offer you my hand in order to restore you as lady of the Dale. Since you say you know, we'll say it openly. I have wanted you since you first came to the Dale as Sven's wife, and I have hated you since the day you laughed at me for being defeated in a fight, by Sven. I brought you here, my dear wife, to make you my creature, my servant, my thrall.' He rose and came to her and suddenly shoved her backwards on to the pallet. 'And before I'm done, I swear I will. Before I'm done, my dear, cool Signy, my thrall you shall be, so hungry for me that you will kiss my feet if I order it, for the sake of my love. *When will you crawl to me, Signy?* How long before I can make you?'

His voice and face were angry, but his caresses were swift and practised.

Signy lay back, glorying in them, but her calm smile did not change. 'Leif, my dear. I was here when Eric's Dale was set on fire. I walked through the snow and ate human flesh and sold my body to a troll to live. Do you think anything can frighten me now or make me crawl? Oh no, my dear. If anyone's feet are kissed, they'll be mine, not yours.'

'Oh, will they, indeed?' said Leif and entered her, furiously, to fight another battle in this long campaign between them, this struggle for mastery which would last, unresolved, for as long as the two of them should live.

Chapter Seven

Aldith

There ought to be time, Ivon estimated. The trick had worked before, three times now. For the rest of the afternoon, until None, everyone in St Cuthbert's would suppose him to be cleaning and pounding raw clay behind the pottery where Brother Edgar, the monastery potter, would be spinning his wheel. Brother Edgar was good about giving Ivon time to practise on the wheel, but in these afternoon hours, he prepared the quality work for which his pupil was not yet qualified and just now he was very busy. Except for calls of nature, he wouldn't stop until the None bell. Ivon had already cleaned his clay, flat out, during Recreation today and yesterday. Moving quietly, keeping outbuildings, walls and fruit trees skilfully between himself and any enquiring eyes, he went into the orchard and across it, under its canopy of blossom, to where a gnarled apple tree provided a convenient ladder for anyone wishing to scale the wall.

The rough twigs caught at his novice's robe and there were green stains on the unbleached wool before he had reached the ground on the other side. Well, they wouldn't be subjected to any further abuse. Halfway down the sloping abbey meadows was an oak grove in which there was a hollow tree. Inside, stuffed high up into a natural crevice, were the tunic and hose which had once belonged to Aldith's brother. Ivon was sorry that her brother had died, but the clothes he didn't need any longer were unquestionably useful. Once changed, with the robe stowed where the clothes had been, he set off downhill to Hawkshawe, striding joyfully in the freedom of the hose, thinking how green the young corn was and wondering why he had never before noticed that apple blossom was like warm snow.

He was fifteen, healthy, physically adult, and one short month ago, the admiration in the eyes of a girl had told him he was handsome.

Ivon Oddeyes was in love.

It had happened one month, four short weeks, after the day he had first met Gilbert FitzSimon. Ivon and Brother Edgar were lifting a tray of fired pots out of the kiln and Ivon, whose back was to the door, heard footsteps approaching, Brother Edwin's voice telling someone that this was the pottery, that Brother Edgar was born in that great centre of his craft, Thetford in Suffolk, and had brought his skills as a gift to St Cuthbert's, and that his assistant was one of the children adopted by the monastery after what Brother Edwin referred to, tactfully, as the tragedy in Northumbria. 'We had eight of them altogether. Happily, we were able to find relatives for four, people living outside the affected area, who were willing to take them in. One didn't survive, alas. He was ill when he came – as they all were – but he pined too much for the parents and the home he had lost, and died. Whether the rest will stay with us or not, we can't say. But Ivon, as you see, wears the novice's robe and is working with Brother Edgar. He is to become one of our community, as a lay brother.'

'It would be the best future for you,' Abbot Maurice had said nearly a year ago, interviewing the young Ivon in his office. With any orphan in the abbey's care this day had to come, when it must be decided whether the boy should go back to the world or take the cowl. 'There is no nobler way of life than the monastic and for a stormy spirit such as yours, no safer one. You will in turn have much to give us. Brother Edgar tells me you may be gifted at his type of work. How spiritually gifted you are, remains to be seen, but even a craftsman's humble skill may be offered up as a prayer. I am not one of those who despise such skills,' said Maurice, patting the arm of the carved and polished walnut chair he had discovered in a storeroom and installed as his abbatial seat. 'I have great respect for the man who carved this. May the work of your hands be as good and as dedicated to heaven.'

There was no other way of life he wanted. He certainly did not wish to go back to being a thrall on a remote farmstead and he knew of no alternatives. Furthermore, the rituals of Mass and Office, to which Ivon from the semi-pagan Dale had come quite fresh, had stirred him. It was no hardship to agree. Brother Ivon, respectful young novice of eleven months' standing, set down his end of the tray and turned to see who had come in with Edwin.

'This,' said Edwin, 'is Messire Gilbert FitzSimon de Doucecolline. He is Father Abbot's brother, recently arrived from Brittany.' He said this with a slight emphasis and a fixed stare at Ivon, telling him obliquely that Messire Gilbert couldn't therefore have been in the north four years ago, any more than Guy FitzRichard had. But it was a measure of how well St Cuthbert's had tamed Ivon, that he said it in French.

'I'm not going to learn *their* language,' Ivon had said.

'Yes, you are. It's going to be the language of the future. Anyway,' said Brother Edwin shrewdly, 'even if you insist on regarding all Normans as enemies for ever, will you be the worse for being able to eavesdrop on them? Come on now, lad. Do it for me. I'll be in trouble with Father Abbot if you don't learn. It'll be my job to instruct you. I'm in charge of teaching French and Latin to the novices as well, these days. Father Abbot seems to think I should be kept busy.'

Ivon's French was adequate now. He greeted Messire Gilbert politely in the same language. Gilbert was looking with interest at the newly fired pots and at a similar batch on a shelf. He turned to Brother Edgar. 'How do you obtain that green tinge in the glaze? I've never seen such a finish before.'

He recommended himself to Ivon at this point, by looking Brother Edgar straight in the eye just as though the green-glazed earthenware was really the most remarkable sight in the workshop. Brother Edgar's vocation was founded less on religious fervour than on his enormous hooked nose, his loose, thick lower lip and his pox-scars. His desire to escape from the world which had jeered at him had been so great that it was responsible for the fact that he had come to St Cuthbert's instead of joining an abbey near his home town of Thetford. It was in Thetford that he had heard the jeers.

At St Cuthbert's too, of course, strangers who encountered him would stare. Ivon, who had now grown too used to him to notice it, and fond enough of him to be protective, always bristled when this happened. But Messire Gilbert's smooth, well-fed and carefully shaven face and cold grey eyes held nothing but courteous enquiry concerning glazing techniques.

'I use copper ore,' said Brother Edgar. 'I have experimented with various ores besides the usual lead, and I've achieved some interesting results. This is my latest discovery.'

Gilbert FitzSimon moved over to the shelf and picked up a pot, turning it round in thick hands which nevertheless understood the material they were handling. 'Hand-painted decoration, I see. A traditional English design, I think, with those wedge shapes and these interlinked lines.'

He put the pot carefully back in its place. Ivon watched him, intrigued by the way that this man, who was built like a warrior, strutting from the hip when he walked, his thickset shoulders straining the mulberry cloth of his tunic, seemed to understand matters artistic. It occurred to him that perhaps this was a characteristic of the abbot's family. Abbot Maurice quite clearly had a somewhat unecclesiastical love of fine things: witness his carved chair and his gold crucifix. Brother Edwin had noticed it too and had once remarked that he thought the abbot actually loved that pagan-looking glass drinking-horn which he kept on his office wall.

Gilbert was speaking to Edwin, who now turned to the others. 'Messire Gilbert serves the Earl of Norfolk and when he leaves us will return to Norfolk where his lord has granted him a manor. He is collecting goods to enhance it. We thought we might present him with some items of earthenware, but instead, he would like to offer us a commission.'

'Yes,' said FitzSimon. 'I spent only a week at Rushley – that's the name of my manor – after arriving in England but I used that time to decide on the things I wanted done before my wife comes over. The hall was in a very bad state and completely bare. The thane who held it was killed at Hastings and his wife went to a nunnery but I rather think she took the household effects with her, wallhangings, ironware, earthenware, plate, utensils, the lot. I'll have, if you please, a set of a dozen bowls with the green glaze and painted designs as on the pot I've just looked at. I want them to be big bowls – a foot across – there's a plain one over there of the

right size; you can use that as a model. And a dozen jugs to match, so big.'
He used his hands to shape the size in the air. 'I want to take them with me when I leave in five weeks' time.'

'I take it that that's in order, Brother Edgar?' said Edwin.

The request was from the abbot's brother so the answer was a foregone conclusion. 'Naturally,' said Edgar, and waited until they'd gone before turning to Ivon and saying: 'We haven't enough fine clay in stock. Ulf's about to leave to buy some but he'll have to fetch extra and we can't start until he comes back.' He banged his forehead with a fist. 'I must ask permission and go down to Hawkshawe to see him. We'll have to work in a rush when he gets back again. Would you like to come to Hawkshawe with me when I go to see Ulf?'

It would be the first time he had been outside the abbey walls in the months since he had put on his novice's robe. He had not consciously noticed how confined he was, but the prospect of even so modest an outing sent a thrill through him. 'Yes, please,' said Ivon.

Ulf was now a Hawkshawe institution. St Cuthbert's and its satellite farms and villages were isolated and all the more so since every community to the north of them had been obliterated. There was a whole list of goods and materials which had to come from York or even further away and fetching them was a continual nuisance. Ulf, the youngest son of a freeman farmer, wanting a better life for himself and his family than acting as his elder brothers' unpaid labourers, had taken to bringing things from a distance for commission plus travelling expenses. He now had a regular round and a sizeable clientele which included St Cuthbert's itself, and Brother Edgar in particular. Ulf went south twice a year to the midland counties where there were claypits, and brought back sacks of clay.

'We must go to him and change the order *today*,' said Brother Edgar, fussing, and darted out of the door. Ivon gave him a moment or two before following, because he knew the reason for the sudden exit. Brother Edgar, in addition to his unprepossessing face, had a weak bladder.

Having won permission, they set off, hurrying because the wind was sharp, across the meadows to where the houses of Hawkshawe clustered. The houses were built of timber or wattle and daub, stoutly thatched, but dark and smelly within. They varied as to size. The miller's house beside his mill was the biggest but the place that Ulf now rented was an index to his success for it ran the miller's close. 'It's even got a loft,' said Brother Edgar, enlivening the way by describing it. Sheltering his face with his cowl as he passed through the village, he led the way to Ulf's door and rapped on it with his knuckles.

And from within, in answer, came a girl.

She was nothing remarkable; Ivon's age or a little less, a wiry, whitefaced little thing, not over-clean, with fair hair, also wiry, twisted into bristling braids. Her sloe-blue eyes were tired. 'You looking for Dad? He's over to Brockyholt village. That's eight mile each way; he won't be back till dusk. Would it be about the abbey order for clay?'

'Yes. We need more than we told him. Can we come in?' Despite the pulled-forward cowl, Edgar had attracted attention from a couple of small children, who had come up to stare. 'I told you two to go and play only don't fall in the fishpond,' the girl said to them. 'They're my little brother and sister,' she explained. 'I'm Aldith Ulfschild. I've not seen you before but I know who you'd be. Come through.'

She at least had the manners not to stare. Her father perhaps had described Brother Edgar to her. She led them in. The place was gloomy and soot-stained but roomy, receding into shadows above the half-floor which comprised the loft Brother Edgar had mentioned. There was a table, with some half-made children's clothes on it, and a fire-pit over which something bubbled in a cauldron. Loaves were baking on the stone kerb. 'You'll take summat? We've got some mead.'

'You would be keeping house now?' said Brother Edgar. 'Of course, your mother died in the winter.'

'And my elder brother. There was a rheum with a fever and we all caught it. The kids pulled round better than some of the older ones. My mother went in three days . . .' Aldith whisked abruptly away and begun unasked to struggle with the stopper of a stone jar.

Brother Edgar, rejected by the world, had had little chance to learn empathy. He observed that what Aldith was unstopping was a mead-jar but failed to observe that she was fighting tears. He said: 'Well, it's an indulgence, but I think we could allow ourselves a little mead after walking in that cold wind,' and began to hum a tune in expectation of the treat.

Ivon had literally not set eyes on a female human being since his novitiate began and was feeling shy, but he understood the blind fumbling at the jar. He went over to take it from her and whispered, awkwardly: 'Please don't cry.' Aldith relinquished the jar with a muttered apology, averting her eyes and brushing them with a sleeve, and on impulse he added: 'It won't always feel so bad, honestly. I've lost people too, so I know,' and for the first time, she looked directly at him.

With surprise, and gratitude for the kindness but with something else as well. For an incredible moment, Ivon saw in her eyes how he appeared to her, saw the involuntary flash of a girl's admiration for a pleasing youth, and that single glance went through him as if it were a spear. He turned dizzy and almost dropped the jar. He gave it hurriedly back to Aldith and retreated to Brother Edgar's side.

They presumably drank the mead after that but, if so, he never recalled it. He surfaced into awareness again in time to hear Aldith repeating over to Brother Edgar the instructions he had been giving her for '. . . three sacks altogether of the fine clay and one of copper ore. That right? I'd best be sure or Dad gets that angry. He'll be sorry he missed you. Some of his orders are urgent or he'd have put off going south for a bit. It means he won't be here for the fair.'

'The fair?' said Ivon.

'Yes, lad, where are your wits?' said Brother Edgar. 'Spring and

101

autumn, the Hawkshawe fair! I can recall telling you all about it. Hawkshawe's the biggest of the six villages the abbey owns. People come from all of them and further afield, too. Why, we have a lay brother selling our apples and plums in October, and selling my wares every time. You helped me get ready last time! It starts next Monday and lasts three days.' He then set down his mead, muttered an embarrassed excuse and slid hastily out of a rear door. Ivon, left briefly alone with Aldith, seized his chance without even thinking about it.

'I've never seen a fair. I'd like to see this one but I'd have to slink out because I'll never get permission. If I did, would you show me round?'

'You won't slink far dressed like that,' said Aldith, with devastating practicality and no hesitation. 'Anyone'ud know you was playing truant. *And* there'll be brothers from the monastery running a booth. Tell you what, though. Know that copse o' trees halfway up between here and your place?'

'Yes, of course. It's the only one in the meadows.'

'There's a big old oak in the middle and it's hollow. You can climb up inside; I've done it. I'll leave some ordinary clothes pushed up there. They'll fit you. We've still got my brother's things; Dad won't get rid of them.'

'It'll have to be the afternoon,' he said. He could hear Brother Edgar coming back. Aldith turned away to stir her cooking pot. 'If I can't manage it on Monday, I might on Tuesday,' he breathed.

The Monday proved impossible; he was busy and under surveillance all day. But on the Tuesday afternoon, he succeeded. Dressed as Aldith's brother, he slipped down to Hawkshawe and found her waiting and together they went wandering through the fair.

This proved to be an anticlimax though it was interesting to begin with, so that for half an hour or so Ivon was engrossed by the raucous crowdedness of it. They threaded their way among booths selling ale and pies and sausages, cheeses and cured pork, jars of honey, fresh-baked honeycakes, salt, spices, gloves and shoes and whole oxhides, woollen cloth and lengths of linen, dyestuffs, thimbles, needles, thread, knives, belts, tools and rope. On a flat open space beyond the houses were pens of livestock and coops of clucking poultry, and men were trotting horses up and down to show their paces. There were intriguing tents whose proprietors stood outside urging them to come in and see a two-headed calf, or the ugliest man in the world. Ivon thought of Brother Edgar and was glad he had no money so that Aldith couldn't ask him to take her in to gape at the poor freak.

But the lack of money was a nuisance. He could not as much as buy her a honeycake; and he was sure he shouldn't let her pay for things herself. Also, her small brother and sister were tagging along. Every now and then they paused and stared at him. Between his empty pockets, the unnerving gaze of his companion's siblings, and the necessity of avoiding the corner of the fair where the monastery booth stood, the excitement rapidly faded.

But not the excitement of Aldith's presence at his side. He found excuses to take her arm or put his own round her, and the sensation was both utterly strange and utterly right, as though he had come to a house he had never seen before, but knew belonged to him.

'Can't we get rid of these two?' he whispered to Aldith at last. 'And go off on our own? There's a proper wood out beyond the village. We could walk in there and talk.'

'Suits me. They're always in my way. I never get free of 'em,' said Aldith candidly, and, without being hindered by Ivon, presented some silver to the children with a recommendation to 'go and see if there's any ginger at the spice stall, and buy yourselves some cakes or pies and I'll see you at home come dusk—.'

'Oh, why can't you come *with* us?' The small girl, Ivon concluded, was the sort that had no sense.

'Oh, get along with you!' Aldith gave her a push.

'Come on, Sis.' The boy had slightly more sense, but an uncomfortably knowing expression. 'Big Sis don't want us for a bit.' He leered before he departed, taking the girl with him, but Ivon forgot them after that. He and Aldith were making for the woods together, and when they got there, no one would be able to see them and no one in the world would know where they were.

It was grey weather, though milder than the week before. They walked about among the trees for a while as they had said they would, exchanging life histories.

'. . . you lost your home and all and had to walk through the snow? That happened to a couple of women in the village; they came here to find relatives. That must've bin awful,' said Aldith, quite unable to imagine it, but trying.

'. . . so you started life on a farm, the same as I did?'

'That's right. Till Dad started this fetch-and-carry business. Then my mam went and died . . .'

As before, talking of it broke her. The wound was still too raw for touching. 'Hush,' said Ivon, guiding her to a space between the roots of an ash tree and drawing her down beside him. 'It's over now. It really does get better, in time. You'll leave it behind . . .'

'I don't *want* to leave my mam behind!'

'No, I know. But,' said Ivon from the depths of a knowledge which had added a decade to the age of his mind, 'it's the way things are. And it's just as well.'

'Sorry. Mustn't cry, it'll spoil things for you. Took a risk, didn't you, sneaking out to come here? You're warm,' said Aldith, letting him draw her against him. 'It's nice.' She looked up at him. 'Your eyes are different, did you know? But I like them like that.'

'People used to call me Ivon Oddeyes. It's mostly Ivon now, though.' He did not say Brother Ivon. He could not, at this moment, imagine taking a full monk's vows. 'You're warm too,' he said.

Neither had had any previous experience but neither was ignorant, both having spent childhoods in farmsteads which lacked both privacy and inhibition. As they began to exchange caresses, gentle and enquiring at first and then feverish and eager, they awoke each other and knew to what they had awakened.

They hesitated for a while on the brink of final discovery but only for the sake of prolonging expectation. Then they were joined, an easy, natural union, climaxing effortlessly and unthinkingly, lying close afterwards with Aldith's cloak to cover them, her head on Ivon's chest and his hand a patch of warmth in the small of her back.

He had climbed out of the monastery orchard as a boy. He climbed back in as a man.

On this fourth occasion, a month later, he sauntered warily past Aldith's door to begin with, for her father had returned. Brother Edgar was at this moment furiously using the fine clay on FitzSimon's behalf. But Aldith was on the look-out for him and called him softly. He stepped quickly inside. 'Where's your dad?'

'Gone off collecting orders. He won't be back for hours. I've sent the kids off to play. Come on. We'll use the loft again.'

The loft was where the family slept. It was reached by a ladder and spread with straw, and there were rugs. 'It's a good bit more comfortable than the wood,' Aldith had said after the first time they used it. 'Nice and warm and no tree roots in your back.'

They made love, taking their time, experimenting.

'Aldith,' Ivon said when at last they lay spent. 'They'll never let me marry you. I'm going to be a monk. I don't want to be, any more, but I can't think how to get away from it.'

Aldith raised herself on an elbow. 'Rotten sort of monk you're going to make. *Why* can't you get out of it? You're only what they call a novice yet, ain't you? You can leave if you want; you're not their slave.'

'But where could I go? I'd have nothing to offer you, nowhere to take you.'

'You've got your craft.'

'I'm only half-trained yet.'

'There's potteries outside of St Cuthbert's. First thing to do,' said his practical lover, 'is find out if they'd let you go and if they'd give you anything to help you set up. We might even live here in Hawkshawe! Don't know what Dad'd say but as long as he don't know till you're free . . .'

Below them, suddenly, the door crashed open and there was a spatter of feet. 'Sis! Come quick!' Someone, below, coughed and retched. Aldith was up at once, peering over the edge of the outsize shelf which was the loft. 'What's the matter?'

Ivon, craning his neck from the shadows behind her, saw her eight-year-old brother standing at the foot of the ladder with his small sister in his arms. She was no more than five, and he could just carry her. Her head hung back over his arm as though her neck were broken and she was choking and dribbling water. Both she and her brother were dripping wet and her hair trailed over her soaked dress like weed. The boy's upturned face was white. 'She fell into the fishpond. I got her out; she's not drowned but . . .'

'Turn her face down, stupid; let her throw up and get the water out of her! Oh, you damned little nuisances!' Aldith dragged her gown over her head, grabbed a rug and slithered angrily down the ladder. Ivon hauled his own borrowed clothing on and followed more slowly. The boy surrendered his sister to Aldith and eyed Ivon with interest. 'Don't stand there gawping, help me!' snapped Aldith, already busy pounding the child's back to clear her lungs. 'I could kill the pair of you. Can't be left alone for ten minutes, can you? You've always got to come whining round me, Sis this and Sis that . . . I'm that sorry,' she added apologetically to Ivon. Between the three of them, they stripped the shivering child, rubbed her as dry as they could and rolled her in the rug. 'She'd best be put to bed,' said Aldith. 'Then I'll brew a hot tisane.'

'I'll carry her up,' Ivon said.

Her shivering had subsided, though she was still inclined to cling and cry. Aldith settled her carefully on the straw which a few moments ago had been the scene of their lovemaking, and covered her with another layer of rugs. She glanced at Ivon. 'You'd better go. Quickly.'

'When shall I come again?'

'Not at once. I'll have to do some explaining if Dad comes back while she's like this. I'm not supposed to send them off by themselves though I *do*, 'cos they get under my feet so. And I'll have to make sure my brother keeps his gob shut, now he's actually seen us up here. But when I get a chance I'll slip up to the orchard wall up there and chuck a big white stone over it. You haven't got a lot of big white stones lying about under your fruit trees at the abbey, have you?'

'No, certainly not.'

'Well, keep an eye out for one. When you see it,' said Aldith, 'come as quick as you can.' And with her back to the edge of the loft, because her brother was peering up from below, curious to know what they were saying in voices too low for him to hear, she made a kissing-face at Ivon, and gave him what he now knew was a street urchin's smile.

There was no chance of a message from Aldith until the next day at the earliest, of course. She would not even come to the abbey church on the excuse of attending Vespers, for the Hawkshawe people had a small timber church of their own and did not share the one at the abbey. Aldith, giggling, had once regretted that they couldn't exchange secret glances in church.

He could have gone to the orchard the next morning but refrained because it was still much too soon. The chances were against a message at all that day. But in the afternoon, he could restrain himself no longer and made an opportunity to slip away.

It was another sunlit day. The apple blossom was a filigree roof brighter than the glimpses of blue sky above it. When the breeze shook the boughs, petals showered on to the grass, and Ivon, prowling along beside the outer wall and scanning the ground, thought that even a large white stone might be hard to find among these scented drifts of white.

But he searched carefully, taking his time and oblivious to all but his purpose. He had no idea that anyone else was in the orchard until a hand descended on his shoulder. He turned quickly and found himself looking into the grave, compassionate eyes of Brother Edwin. 'We're looking for you; Father Abbot wants you. Oh my boy,' said Edwin, 'what have you done?'

Ivon went with Edwin without troubling to answer the question, since he was fairly sure that Edwin knew the answer already. He walked steadily, belying the shivering in the pit of his stomach. Edwin took him to the abbot's room. Abbot Maurice was there and with him were his brother Gilbert FitzSimon and Aldith's father Ulf, and on the desk in front of Maurice, spread out in an accusing display, were the clothes which had belonged to Aldith's brother, which he had left, yesterday, in the hollow tree.

'Close the door, Brother Edwin,' said Maurice. 'Brother Ivon, come here.'

He went forward, but not straight to the abbot's desk. Some instinct which he did not then understand, made him walk slantwise across the room and take his stand against the wall beneath the glass drinking-horn which hung there, opposite the window, where the light could fall pleasingly on it.

'These garments,' said Abbot Maurice, pointing with a forefinger from an upturned palm, 'do you recognise them?'

'They're just clothes.'

'That is not what I asked you. I'll say it again. Do you recognise them? By which I mean, do you know to whom they belong?'

'How could I? They're just ordinary.'

'You had better not play games with me, Brother Ivon.' Maurice sat back in his chair. His spatulate fingertips caressed the polished carving of the arms. 'Master Ulf,' he said, switching from French to his difficult English, 'I think you should tell your tale again, for Brother Ivon's benefit. Use your own language. With Brother Edwin's help, I have heard the story all through already.'

Ulf had the same wiry build and wiry fair hair as his daughter. When he called at the monastery for orders, he was always very polite but he smiled rarely and Brother Edwin had once said: 'That's an angry man, under that quiet surface.' Aldith too had been nervous of her father's temper. The anger in his voice was raw as he told, briefly, how he had come home the day before to find his small daughter in bed, tearful and still damp-haired after her plunge into the pond, and discovered that Aldith had sent the two children out to play unsupervised.

'The boy was there, but you don't expect a boy to play nurse. That was for Aldith to do. She said she was sorry, she'd been busy. But there was summat all wrong about the way Aldith and the boy kept looking at me and for the life of me I couldn't see what she'd been so busy *about* – no special food being cooked, no needlework or spindle out, and the wood-basket half-empty.'

Shrugging, Ulf said he had gone to fetch something extra to wrap the little girl in. 'She was still saying she was cold. I had a cloak in my chest, that used to belong to my elder son, that died in the winter. Well, it weren't there, nor any of his other clothes that I'd kept.' Ulf's face flushed. 'You can't just forget; you can't just do with no reminders, not all at once. So I called Aldith and said had she moved them? She turned the colour of a sunset. I got it out of her and the boy in the end. She'd had a fellow there in the afternoon.' He glared at Ivon. 'That was what she was so busy with that she couldn't look after her little sister, and she'd lent him the clothes because he couldn't come and go the way he was; he was from the monastery, if you please! She told me where she'd hidden the clothes for him so I went and found them, in the oak grove halfway down the meadow. That was this morning. I came straight on up here. She wouldn't give me his name.' Ulf shot another furious glance at Ivon. 'She *wouldn't* name him, the bitch. Kept saying he'd never told her his name. "You've been playing in the straw with a fellow and you don't know his name?" I said to her. I knocked the daylights out of her and the boy but I got nowhere. I reckon the boy really don't know the name, said she'd never spoken it when he could hear. But he did know one thing that he came across with. He knew that whoever it was had funny eyes. Not the same colour, he said.'

He rested his case, giving Ivon a last contemptuous scowl and turning towards the abbot.

'So he came to me,' said Maurice. 'And found me already a little concerned because Messire Gilbert had mentioned to me, casually, that he went to the pottery workshop yesterday morning and couldn't find either Brother Edgar or Brother Ivon there. Brother Edgar, I'd sent for myself, to discuss some new tableware for the guest-house with him. But Brother Ivon should have been there somewhere.'

'I looked in the yard behind the workshop,' said Messire Gilbert in assent.

'Well, we know where he was now. Brother Ivon, have you anything to say? Oh, before you speak . . . Brother Edwin, will you ask Master Ulf if there is any danger that his daughter is with child by this precocious boy.'

'I wouldn't know,' said Ulf in reply to this. 'She isn't now, at any rate. A good hiding can cure a lot of problems.'

There was a pause while this was transmitted to Maurice by Brother

Edwin, who turned an embarrassed pink as the significance of it slowly dawned on all of them. Then: 'You've hurt her!' Ivon shouted at Ulf. 'You . . . you . . .'

'Be quiet! Neither Aldith Ulfschild nor any other woman is any business of yours. You are a brother of this monastery. May I take it,' said Abbot Maurice, 'that you admit to this liaison?'

There was little point in doing anything else. Ivon's head went back. 'Yes.'

There was a silence, full of grim meaning. The fate of monks – or novices – caught out in carnal sin was in St Cuthbert's a matter of nightmare legend. Abbot Maurice shook his head with ominous sorrow. 'Is that all you have to say?'

'I . . .' Ivon swallowed. 'I'm not a brother of this abbey, not yet. I think . . .' well, there was a lifeline and he caught at it. '. . . perhaps I wouldn't make a monk. Perhaps I . . . I ought to leave St Cuthbert's.' He wondered anew, as he said it, what on earth he would do and where he would go. He wondered too whether he would ever see Aldith again. From the surrounding faces, there was no response. He noticed that Abbot Maurice and Messire Gilbert not only shared a love of fine objects, but had a physical resemblance as well. The abbot was more patrician, but they had the same spatulate fingers and thickset shoulders. And, at the moment, exactly the same watching expressions. For some reason, Messire Gilbert's scrutiny seemed the more intense of the two.

Ivon addressed Master Ulf. 'I'll marry Aldith,' he said. 'If you'll let me.'

'You?' said Ulf, and let out a disparaging snort. 'A boy your age, with no future? A no-good young tomcat that St Cuthbert's don't want? Aldith's of an age to be thinking of marriage, I grant you; thirteen's old enough. If she'd started walking out with some decent village lad, I'd not be raising all this to-do, even if she did let her little sister fall into a pond. But *you* . . . !'

'There is no question of Brother Ivon leaving the monastery,' said Abbot Maurice coldly. 'He isn't the first novice to misbehave in this way. Others have done it before him, and repented and made good monks in the end. St Cuthbert's, like other monasteries, knows the nature of young men and is prepared to deal with it. You owe St Cuthbert's something, Brother Ivon. This abbey took you in when you were destitute and has clothed, fed and educated you. I personally offered you the chance to become fully one of us; I saw something in you that was worth cultivating. I still see it, but by God you are a garden in need of weeding. No, Brother Ivon, you will not fling my charity in my face, or desert this abbey with your debt unpaid. Brother Edwin, I did not wish to disturb the novicemaster before. He has been giving instruction in theology. But he must be free by now. Will you fetch him, please.'

'No!' said Ivon.

Up went Abbot Maurice's patrician brows, almost to his tonsure line. 'What did you say?'

'I said *no* . . . please! I . . . I *am* grateful for being taken in and looked after but . . . but . . . when I said I'd be a novice, I didn't understand, I was a boy then . . .'

'And what are you now?' enquired the abbot.

The answer came, unforgivably, before Ivon could stop himself. 'I'm a man.' There was a shocked gasp from Brother Edwin and a distinctly knowing grin from Messire Gilbert. Ulf, since the exchange had been in French, hadn't understood and frowned. Ivon, ignoring all this, stared at the abbot with the wide eyes of aggression and also of fear. He knew what he had said, and his stomach was twisting. He had claimed manhood but he was in truth very young and very surrounded. He knew that, too.

And then, smoothly, quietly, he found that he knew something further: the reason why he had moved so quickly to stand within reach of Father Abbot's best-beloved work of art, although he did not know that the impulse came from his grandfather Sir Ivon de Clairpont, who was a knight, who would have been addressed as Messire Ivon, and who was bred from a long line of shrewd warriors, so that the instinct to exploit an enemy's weak point was in their descendant's blood. He reached up, snatched the glass drinking-horn from its book, and held it above his head. Abbot Maurice shot to his feet. 'What are you doing? Give that to me!'

'I'll leave the abbey today and never come back. I'll leave in what I stand up in. No one here need ever see or hear of me again.' It was more even than the terror of the whispered retribution which was driving him. He knew now that he could not, *could not*, stay all his life in this place; that the man he had become was going to need a mate and was not to be denied. 'If you won't let me, Father Abbot, if you won't agree, if anyone tries to lay a hand on me, I'll smash this precious glass thing of yours on the floor here, at your feet. Promise me I can go unharmed!'

Abbot Maurice had paled a little. He had not realised, for one thing, that the depth of his passion for his treasures was so widely known. He had certainly not expected this fifteen-year-old product of a thrall's hut on a common Northumbrian farm to grasp it. But he kept his head. Holding Ivon's eyes with his own, he sat slowly down again. 'Once you do smash it, of course, you will have destroyed your hostage. It's in your interest, Ivon, to put off irretrievable action as long as possible. In the meantime, let us discuss the moot point of whether a promise extracted by threats can be binding. What if I agree and then go back on it as soon as my wall decoration is safe again . . . ?'

While the abbot talked, his brother had moved. Ivon, concentrating on Maurice, failed to notice as Messire Gilbert slid sideways out of his line of vision, to move stealthily round the walls and come up from the rear. Only at the last moment did a shadow on the floor alert him so that he dodged, setting his back against the wall, looking huntedly from left to right, from Maurice to Gilbert and back. Across the room, Brother Edwin was watching with a face full of distress, and Ulf was starting round the desk to come to Gilbert's aid. 'Don't come any closer, any of you!' he said, and knew his voice was pitched too high for dignity.

109

'Ivon, hand that thing over,' said Gilbert. 'You're making things worse for yourself. You've lost the game. Come on. You made a mistake,' he added, 'in trying to control only one man in the room. You should have made have sure none of us was out or your sight or within arm's length.'

'Really, Gilbert, is there any need to instruct the boy in how to conduct this disgraceful scene?' demanded Maurice.

'I'm instructing him in how to end it. Ivon, you will gain nothing. Come along now.'

'I'll promise you this much,' said Maurice. 'You may save yourself a last fine edge of pain if you give in.'

But he and Gilbert had both spoken French. It was that which now stiffened Ivon's resolve. He had been cornered, was being condemned, by men who spoke the tongue of those who had destroyed Eric's Dale and since then had forced their language on him. It made him furious. 'I hate you!' Ivon yelled and hurled the glass horn to the floor where it smashed, scattering shards of glass. Abbot Maurice leapt up, lunged round the desk in a vain effort to catch it, slipped and fell on all fours, cutting his hands on the bright splinters. He stood up, dripping blood, and Gilbert, stepping forward, closed powerful hands round Ivon's wrists and jerked them down behind him.

Maurice, nursing his damaged hands in his sleeves, said: 'You shall have your wish. You shall leave the abbey in what you stand up in. Later, that is, when your debt is paid. The novicemaster, Brother Edwin, if you please.'

There had been a world which contained Aldith, and apple blossom like warm snow. But it could not comfort him now; to think of it only made him cry. He would never see Aldith again and dreadful things had happened to her, too, because of him. He grieved for her as though she were dead.

He had lost count of the time he had spent in this stone cell. But it was many days and nights, five at least, since he had been thrown in here, half-naked, his back a single huge bruise from the base of the neck to the base of the rib cage, and streaked with welts which he could feel when he moved, like lightning flashes of pain. There was nothing in the cell except one rug. He could hardly bear anything to touch him, but he sat on the rug all day and slept, as far as sleep was possible at all, lying on it all night.

There was nothing to do. He had been told to pray for repentance but he no longer believed in God. If God existed, then He had let *that* happen to Eric's Dale and now He had let this happen to Ivon. He now preferred a world without the deity.

The brother who brought his unsalted porridge and his bread and water kept his face shadowed by his cowl and Ivon didn't even know which brother it was. When the bolts were drawn, the unidentifiable brother was all the open door ever revealed and he had given up raising his head at the sound. But he raised it now, because the feet crossing the stone floor to him were different, shod with something heavier than a monk's sandal.

Gilbert FitzSimon stood looking down on him. 'Are you recovering?

I'm afraid my brother meant it when he said that he would send you off with only the clothes you had on at the time. But I really can't take you to Norfolk wearing bloodstained undergarments and a novice's robe.'

'Norfolk?' said Ivon in dull bewilderment.

'Norfolk. Well, you've got to go somewhere, haven't you? I can make use of you. I've brought you some clothes; you'd better see if they fit. You're healed enough by now, I hope. We ride in three days. Oh,' added FitzSimon, 'the abbot said you might have this back. You brought it with you into the abbey so it's yours, not theirs, and it's correct for you to take it out again. Here, catch.' And in the palm which Ivon automatically shot out to receive what Gilbert tossed to him, there landed an object on a chain, an old bone dagger-hilt, with the device of Clairpont carved into it.

'You're sure you want him?' Abbot Maurice said to his brother.

'Oh yes, just as I'm sure that you don't. My manor of Rushley is a fair size, Maurice, but it's underpopulated. Many of the men followed their lord to Hastings and never came back and others went to join that rebel thane Hereward in Ely and were killed when it fell. I need to bring in more people and get the place going again. One thing I need is a new generation of craftsmen. I've got a smith and a potter and a carpenter but they're all old. This boy can help the potter and take over from him one day and I fancy that with his tendencies,' said Gilbert with a grin, 'he'll breed some healthy sons and daughters for the future.'

'I find levity on that subject quite deplorable, as you know, Gilbert.'

'Or on any subject,' said Gilbert, unrepentantly. 'You always were a trifle po-faced. Except, as I recall, for the time when I quite accidentally knocked a beaker of ale all over that illuminated psalter Father gave you. I was too young then to appreciate art,' Gilbert said, 'but you knocked me flat, knelt on my chest and banged my head on the floor until your tutor hauled you off and when I showed you my bruises later you laughed out loud. Tell me something. Where does Ivon come from? Brother Edwin says he was a refugee from the harrying. Is that correct?'

Abbot Maurice considered. He had resented Ivon's rejection of St Cuthbert's charity, but after all, this had been partly given before he himself arrived. After what had been done to Ivon, he could call that debt cancelled. But nothing, ever, would cancel the debt for the destruction of his irreplaceable antique glass drinking-horn. That he would never forgive. Whoever struck at his beloved treasures, struck at Abbot Maurice's heart.

'Yes, Brother Edwin was right,' he said. And added a detail for which his brother had not precisely asked. 'We were able to check on his origins. He was born a thrall.'

Brother Edwin knelt by his abbot's chair, his face in his hands. But through his fingers, he said: 'I did not sin. Not with Ivon, not with anyone. I never *did* anything, Father Abbot. Please believe me.'

'I do believe you, my son. I had guessed at it already although I did not know that it concerned one person in particular.'

'I hardly knew myself, until I saw his face when the novicemaster came for him, and when he was led away. I didn't know how to bear it, that he, Ivon, my Ivon . . . and then I heard that he was leaving St Cuthbert's and I knew I would never see him again, and I didn't know how to bear that either. Father Abbot, I am not a suitable person to teach the young. Relieve me of my teaching duties, I beg you.'

'You perform them very well. That's why I allowed you to continue with them. But perhaps the time has come to move you. You are appreciative of our abbey treasures, are you not?' said the abbot. 'Brother Sacristan is overworked. You shall help him care for the chalices and manuscripts. I will put another brother in your place. It's time for a redistribution of offices. No one need notice the change too much. Come, Brother Edwin. On your feet. It isn't the end of the world, you know. No harm has been done.'

In this appointment as abbot, Maurice thought as Brother Edwin, stammering with gratitude, went out, he was proving himself a great success. Most of the brothers trusted him, some admired him, and there went one who would be for evermore his most devoted slave.

He was pleased too, with his handling of the Ivon affair. He had got rid of the boy to a new life outside the abbey, and had even, in the end, given back the silly keepsake which Ivon had brought to St Cuthbert's with him. At the same time, he had, well, not overdone the magnanimity. He, the abbot, had been generous and correct and also authoritarian.

Abbot Maurice de Doucecolline was very well satisfied with himself.

PART III

Ivon Oddeyes: Norfolk,
AD 1075-6

[Earl] Ralph meant to go forth also with his earldom, but the Norman castle-men in England and the folk of that land came against them and hindered them all so that they did nothing – so that he was glad to flee to his ships and left his wife behind in the castle. She held it until they made terms with her; she then journeyed out of England and all the men who would go with her.

The Anglo-Saxon Chronicle

Chapter Eight

Rushley

After Northumbria, Norfolk was a revelation.

Bred in Eric's Dale among the Northumbrian moorlands and then confined for years to St Cuthbert's on the edge of the same moorlands, it had never occurred to Ivon that any other landscape could exist. Jogging uncomfortably in Gilbert FitzSimon's train, on a pony stolid enough for a rider who didn't know how to ride (but straight enough in the shoulder, had he known it, to be hell even for a rider who did), amazed to find himself the employee of one Norman knight and riding in a cavalcade with several more plus ten Norman men-at-arms and two Norman archers, he had also been astonished to watch his surroundings change.

Hills sank into lowlands and rose again into gentler, greener contours. Water tasted different. He saw new flowers, grasses, crops. He was so bemused that his final weeks at St Cuthbert's, even that brutal imprisonment, even Aldith, became like long-ago memories. FitzSimon had told him, casually, that Aldith would be married before a month was out, to a boy from Brockyholt. But he had known already that she was gone from his life. He was beginning to leave her behind.

Riding made him stiff at first and he fell off his pony several times, despite its placidity. Most of his companions regarded him as free entertainment. But one of the men-at-arms was friendly and at length gave him some instruction in how to hold his reins and keep his heels down, after which he got on better.

They went via York and he gaped at his first city: its walls and bridge, the narrow streets among the close-set houses, the street traders, the crowds. They paused there for a day because FitzSimon wanted to call on some goldsmiths and silversmiths. Then they transferred to a ship and sailed downriver, and presently he saw the sea for the first time. They sailed in rough weather but he wasn't sick, which was more than could be said for a good many of the others and he derived private satisfaction from watching them become in turn free entertainment for him.

They spent one night at a manor on shore, and on the following afternoon steered for the coast again, but this time to enter a river. The friendly man-at-arms, whose name was Alan, said that it was called the River Wend. It made a serpentine way between beds of reeds and muddy islets, opening out now and then into wide, still meres. All around stretched acres of marshland, inhabited by birds he had never seen before, which rose in huge flocks if disturbed.

When they finally reached solid land, it was almost as flat as the marshes. The horizon was far away and a vast sky arched above it. He had never seen anything like it. The enormous sky made him feel like an ant. Far away on that remote horizon were the outlines of thatched roofs, and a few threads of hearth-smoke. Alan said: 'That's it. That's Rushley.'

Rushley had an English manor-house still, a thatched timber hall with satellite buildings round it inside the ditch and palisade put in hand by FitzSimon before he went to visit St Cuthbert's. 'But the whole thing's temporary,' Alan told Ivon. 'You ought to see the hall inside. The timber's so wormeaten that bits of wood shower down round you if you sneeze. He's going to have a proper fortified stone house built one of these days.'

The village was half a mile from the hall, with fields all round. There were a few outlying farmsteads held by tenants of some substance; those who occupied the wattle-and-daub cottages of the village tilled smaller holdings close at hand. Some of them grazed cows on the common pastures and there were vegetable plots and tethered goats behind the dwellings and a couple of community pigs in a pen. There were several abandoned cottages, falling into ruin, and some of the commonland had been cultivated once. Too many young men had gone to fight at Hastings and not returned. One of the outlying farms had been deserted when FitzSimon came but had been given to a former man-at-arms of his, now past his prime for fighting.

Ivon lived in the village with Cob, who was of unknown age but to Ivon looked about a hundred, and had been the Rushley potter as long as anyone there could recall. Half his cottage was for living in and the other half was a workshop and, as well as a connecting door, each possessed an outer one.

The workshop faced the track but as it was the last dwelling in the village and there was no cottage opposite, it also looked across the marshes and the river, and it faced east.

At cock-crow every morning, Ivon (who was not now called Oddeyes) had to prepare the workshop for the day's work, putting water, clay, glaze ingredients ready to hand and rousing up the kiln fire. Rubbing the sleep out of his eyes and shivering in the early chill, he would open the outer door for the sake of the light, and then the dawn would break across the marshland.

Dawns varied: steely cold between overcast sky and glinting mere; a flood of pearly light washing out the stars and softening into gold as the skylarks rose singing from the meadows; angry pink barred with black cloud, with V-formations of wild geese outlined against it as if against a conflagration.

Stumbling half-dead with cold and hunger through that last night of the walk from the Dale to St Cuthbert's, a part of Ivon had nevertheless registered that the frozen moonlit moors were beautiful. The same part of him now noticed the same thing about the fenland dawns but it was of course no use mentioning this to Cob.

'Like watching the sun rise?' Cob said disbelievingly, when Ivon, just once, offered this as an excuse for being slow. 'When you've seen all the sunrises I have, you 'on't notice them no more and you ain't seen a winter here yet, neether. Watching the sunrise, garn! Get on with it!'

Ivon, free of St Cuthbert's walls and vows, could have been very happy, had it not been for Cob.

Cob spoilt everything. Cob was disgusting.

He was short, skinny and knobbly, like a goblin. He and his hovel were dirty to an extent which even Ivon, born in a thrall's hut, had never seen before. His idea of laughter was a malevolent cackle accompanied by bubbles of spit. He had a bent back and suffered from joint-evil in his knees and corns on his feet. And although he should in Ivon's opinion have been past such things, he was lascivious.

He was also undiscriminating. Before Ivon had been there a week, Cob had remarked with one of his horrible cackles that he was a 'good-looking lad' and attempted to crawl on to Ivon's straw-stuffed pallet. Ivon promptly kicked him where it would do most damage and Cob rolled off the pallet to recover on the floor, from which he rose with his discarded belt in his hand. Ivon took it away from him and ran out of the cottage with it to throw it in the river.

After that Cob did not attempt to assault him in either way again, but he had his own methods of getting his revenge. In the nine months which had elapsed since then, Ivon had not been allowed to touch the potter's wheel. He had not shaped a single vessel. He swept the hut and cooked the meals, prepared the clay and set out the materials, a slave rather than the apprentice he was supposed to be.

Cob had another subtle way of making himself unpleasant, too. Having been rejected, he went back to his usual practice of ogling the Rushley women instead. Here again, he was undiscriminating. His salacious gazing and suggestive remarks were directed at anything female, regardless of her age or appearance, showing if anything a perverse preference for the ill-favoured. Most of the women avoided him, sending their menfolk to the workshop to order goods or collect them. There were a few among the younger girls, however, who braved the menace of Cob for the sake, these days, of exchanging a word with Ivon.

Especially Ragenhild.

Ragenhild, fortunately, wasn't an Rushley girl. If she had been, the shop would have been cluttered with her even more often than it was. She came from the adjoining manor of Oxfen, whose fields were separated from Rushley's only by a water channel and whose village was a bare two miles away. Oxfen had a Norman lord too; his English predecessor had been another Hastings casualty and Messire Walter had married the widow. Gilbert and Walter were slightly inclined to rivalry, since Oxfen boasted better cattle pastures while Rushley could be reached by river which Oxfen could not, because it was further upstream where the river frayed into thin, muddy threads. But it was rivalry without animosity, since they had more to gain from solidarity. The knights and soldiers they each housed were not there for show. No Norman had been murdered hereabouts, but it had happened elsewhere and it was as well to keep the native population under control with a show of strength and unity.

The root of the rivalry was an instinct to amalgamate the two manors, and this was sound, for they had once been a single manor, split up fifty years ago when the lord of the time died leaving only two daughters who had to share the inheritance. Rushley's inhabitants and Oxfen's were closely inter-related. Ivon knew all about Ragenhild's family because Cob had told him.

'Her father's one o' the Oxfen villeins . . .'

'What's a villein? A thrall?'

'Nah. Christ's Elbow, you're bloody ignorant, boy, for all the book-learning they're s'posed to've given you in that abbey you was chucked out of. Thralls, they're owned by men. But Ragenhild's old man, he's owned by the land. He's got a share of it, but it's got *him*, just as much. He can't sell it or leave it, and he's still got to work on his lord's land three days in the week for it. But he ain't poor. He's got seven cows what are really his and a bull – his lord don't like that; reckons that's getting above hisself – and his wife's cheesemaker to Walter and gets a hundred cheeses a year and she can sell 'em or eat 'em; pleases herself there. Ragenhild could have a good marriage, to a freeman even, if only . . .' and here Cob began to chuckle nastily, so that Ivon, who knew quite well what he meant, turned his back and busied himself with his work.

Ragenhild was fifteen and her marriage prospects could indeed have been good, if only she hadn't been scrawny and sallow, with a missing upper tooth. And perhaps – since shiny dark eyes and a dowry of a cow and a bag of silver coin could outweigh much worse defects than hers – afflicted with a blatant and embarrassing infatuation for Ivon.

'Here's your girlfriend again, acomin' down the street,' said Cob, lifting the latest of a succession of identical jugs off the wheel and providing it with a handle. He would sell the jugs soon in Norwich or Lynn, the nearest towns. Spring had come and the markets were getting under way again. 'Visitin' her auntie again, I 'spect,' said Cob. 'Funny thing: it weren't till you come that Ragenhild suddenly noticed her aunt Withy was gettin' on and might be the better of the odd cheese or half-dozen eggs. Bet Ragenhild's dad don't know what's made her into such a lovin' niece all of a sudden, though if so, he's the only one wot don't. No one's goin' to tell him,' said Cob with a leer. 'Might spoil your fun, boy.'

'Oh, shut up,' muttered Ivon under his breath, turning away and crouching low over the jugs he was packing in straw.

'See she's on her own,' said Cob, unabashed. 'You'll be able to have a nice long woo.'

There was no escape. Here she came, gap-toothed mouth open in a wide, ingratiating smile, and dark, dandruff-speckled hair trailing in skimpy braids over her brown wool overdress. She sidled into the shop, keeping well away from Cob, who had once tried to grab her breast. Even if Ivon had been interested in her, Cob wouldn't really have co-operated.

118

Resignedly, Ivon stood up. 'Well, good day. What brings you here?' he said gloomily.

The unprepossessing smile grew still wider. She had had a hand behind her back and now brought it out to jingle a small cloth bag importantly under his nose. 'I b'ain't just passing the time of day this time, Master Ivon.' The arch voice and the adoration in the brown eyes were painful. 'Got an order, believe it or not. We had a little accident at home. I slipped in the mud after all that rain last week and went and dropped our best bowl and broke it. So will you make us another? Dad says we'll pay half in advance, in silver. I got it here.'

'I'm the potter, not 'im,' said Cob from behind his wheel. 'Orders gets given to me, girl. What size bowl you want and what colour? Got some bowls on that there shelf. See anything you fancy? They're all bespoke but you show me what'll suit and I'll make another. How you come to be carrying your best bowl about outdoors in the mud, hey? Feeding the hens out of it, were you? Or did you drop it a'purpose so as you could come and see old Cobby?'

It was all too possible that she had dropped it a'purpose so as to come and see Ivon and highly likely, judging from the way she flushed and addressed herself very earnestly indeed to choosing a sample bowl.

'One like that'll do,' she said at length, after scrutinising the selection intently. 'With the zig-zags on.'

'Oh, ah, well, let's see the money, then. For all I know, you've nothing but pebbles in that there bag. Put it in your hand and show me. Come on over here. I shan't bite.'

Ragenhild wanted to talk to Ivon and gaze at him and she wanted to stay away from Cob. She did as she was told with evident unwillingness, and shuddered as Cob pawed over the money in her grubby palm. Cob saw the shudder and chuckled. 'What's the matter, pretty? Don't mind old Cob, do you? He won't hurt you. Here.' He closed a knotted hand round her wrist. 'You didn't know old Cobby could tell fortunes, did you? Let's have a close look at this little palm of yours. Put all the money on this shelf here. That's my payment and that's what's left, put separate, see? Now, what's in your hand? You'll want to know who you're going to marry, I 'spect. Now . . .'

'No,' said Ragenhild, tugging unavailingly at her hand. 'I don't want to know anything. I don't want my fortune told. It's wrong, it's witchcraft. Please let me go.'

'. . . I see a husband for you soon. Oh yes, clear as daylight. He'll be a Rushley man, how about that, now? You got your eye on anyone in Rushley?' Cob looked up at her with rheumy eyes full of malice. 'You really don't want to know his name? Really?'

'Well . . . I . . .' Ragenhild was going red, caught between shyness and longing to hear Ivon's name spoken, even in a hateful jest like this. 'I . . .'

'Course you want to know. All maidens do. Only the lines on your hand don't spell names . . . but I can *see* him . . . oh yes, he'll be older than you,

119

my pretty one, quite a lot older. But he loves you, oh yes, he fancies you and he'll be good to you. You'll have a home that looks across the marshes and there's clay on your man's old hands . . .'

'Let me *go*!' Ragenhild cried, and this time succeeded in wrenching her hand away. She obviously wanted to bolt out of the door but some of the money lying on the shelf was still hers. Ivon, indignantly, came over and retrieved it for her. The sooner she left the shop never to return, the better, in his opinion, but Cob was a beast. The sound of horses' hooves outside was a very welcome distraction.

'Oh,' said Ragenhild, gladly seizing the excuse to make for the door without actually fleeing to it. 'It's the lords, back from the wedding!'

Messire Gilbert and his neighbour Messire Walter had been away in Norwich for over a week for the marriage of their suzerain, the Earl of Norfolk. He was marrying the sister of the Earl of Hereford, amid great pomp so report said, and taking quite a risk, since King William had for some reason forbidden the match. 'But there,' Ragenhild's Auntie Withy, a sentimental old woman, had said, 'maybe they're in love.'

'Fat lot the king'll care for that, by all accounts,' retorted Cob.

The Oxfen and Rushley parties were coming back together. Gilbert FitzSimon had no doubt offered hospitality. He and Messire Walter rode side by side at the head of their knights and soldiers, cloaks trailing over the high cantles of their silver-studded saddles, brightly coloured, scalloped reins carving the nervous sweat from the necks of their expensive horses. Their wives and the young ladies, daughters of other Normans, who attended on them, rode in the middle of the cavalcade, where they would have maximum protection from the armed men fore and aft.

Ivon, these days, took little notice of knights. He had grown too used to them now to feel even a residual desire to throw stones at them. Sometimes he would think about this and feel ashamed but then he would remember what Messire Guy had said: that he would never know who the men were who had attacked the Dale, and that they were only weapons in the king's hand anyway. Then he would finger the bone dagger-hilt which his grandfather had given him and which he still wore round his neck, and remember who Old Ivon had really been, and decide that it was all too difficult and on the whole he'd do best to get on with being Ivon, budding potter, and concentrate on tricking or nagging Cob into letting him practise properly.

Standing now in the workshop doorway, he took more interest in the ladies, to whom he had never spoken and probably never would but who were intriguing just because of that, and were riding past just now, Messire Walter's English wife in polite conversation with Gilbert's Breton one.

Walter's lady was fairish, plumpish and sweetly smiling. The local grapevine knew a surprising amount about the local overlords, but no one had learned what she really thought of having to marry Walter, one of the Normans whom her first husband had died fighting. She was convent-educated and spoke French, which perhaps had helped her to adapt to Walter, and he was said to treat her well.

Gilbert's wife was of majestic proportions and her horse had to be of sturdy build. She wore her hair in thick, black, gleaming braids twined with gold cord and liked silk gowns, even for travelling. It was partly because of her, Cob said, that Messire Gilbert had had to spend such a fortune on costly goods for the house. She was even madder for them than he was. She liked living in style and had made a terrible fuss over the bad state of the hall, especially when a gable collapsed during one of the north-easterly gales for which the district was famous.

Ivon and Cob watched the cavalcade pass, forgetting Ragenhild who, after a yearning backward glance at Ivon, with whom she hadn't had the delicious conversation for which she longed, wandered sadly away. Then Cob shoved an elbow in Ivon's ribs and said: 'First thing in the morning, lad, you go up there and see if there's any work they want done. Bet what you like with a crowd like that to feed, something'll get broken or they'll suddenly decide they ain't got enough of something else. Never miss a chance, that's what I say.'

Cob must be mellowing towards him a little, Ivon thought, for this was the first time he had ever sent him up to the lord's hall. He wondered if he would find it difficult to get past the gate-guard, but the man recognised him as being from the village and waved him casually in. Searching for someone to whom he could explain his purpose, he wandered right into the main hall. And saw at once that the Oxfen party were still here, and that he had arrived squarely in the middle of an impassioned argument.

Furthermore, although Walter and Gilbert were mature men in their mid-thirties and therefore neither was brandishing an axe or sitting his opponent in a bucket of cold water, it was essentially the same argument that Leif had had with Sven in the Dale long ago.

With a shock of familiarity, he understood that Messire Gilbert wanted to go off and join a war, and Messire Walter didn't.

'It's unthinkable, Gilbert. What my private opinions are is neither here nor there.' Walter was tall and a little bent-shouldered, with deep, fastidious lines from his nostrils to the corners of his mouth and a slightly squeaky voice which detracted from his authority when he spoke.

He was standing up, leaning a hand on one of the timber supports which made a double line down the hall, making an aisle along each side of it. Distaste was even visible in the way his long fingers curved round it. 'I have put my hands between King William's and sworn direct fealty to him and that's that. He may have gone to fight a war in Maine. He may have been too long away from England. Perhaps he'll never come back in person. I accept all that. He is still my overlord and I am still his man and I'll have nothing to do with any insurrection.'

'I can't agree with you!' Gilbert FitzSimon scowled up at Walter from a settle. He sat with thick knees apart, and hammered on one of them with a

121

padded fist. The knights and men-at-arms of both households were lounging or standing about listening unashamedly, as were the two wives, who were sharing another settle close by.

'I was the sworn man of the de Gaels, Ralph of Norfolk's family, before I was ever William's vassal,' Gilbert said. 'It was Ralph gave me Rushley, not William. I was a younger son with my way to make. I went to Brittany and took service with the de Gaels and Earl Ralph gave me Rushley because I crossed the channel to him when he was made earl and called for more men for his household and because before that I'd served his family well. My first duty is to him and besides, I agree with him. The king's been too long away. He won't cede any land to his sons, and he tried to forbid Ralph to marry Hereford's sister because he's afraid of a power-bloc developing between two earls with strategically positioned earldoms; but what arrangements has he made for strong government while he's gone? None! You were there at the bride-ale in Norwich! You heard the complaints. The murder of Normans is on the increase, and there's a good few lords who reckoned they gave their best men and broke their best swords at Hastings for not much reward. If Waltheof—'

Unnoticed by the door, Ivon, eavesdropping on Normans in their own language, just as Brother Edwin had said he might one day do, wondered who Waltheof was and then remembered. He was descended from a former Earl of Northumbria, and – surely – he'd been a leader in the rising that took Leif away and then brought the Normans down on them.

The name had aroused strong feelings among the knights and men-at-arms in the hall.

'Waltheof! More like a weathercock than a man . . . !'

'. . . never a truer word. My God! He makes peace with William after Hastings, then he backs the Danish invasion in the north and makes a chum of that rebel Hereward, *then* he surrenders and makes peace again and the king even gives his niece to Waltheof for a wife, and now he thinks he'd like to be king instead!'

'Mind you, it has its points. He'd be accepted by the English and his and Judith's children would carry the blood of both houses . . .'

'It might have its points if the king he's trying to displace wasn't William! Can you see him letting them get away with it? He'll be back here so fast . . .'

'Probably take a running jump straight over the channel and land on Waltheof's surprised blond head . . . !'

'Or else dear Queen Matilda will poison Waltheof's soup. She's poisoned other people's, so it's said. Though come to think of it, that's as good a reason as any for backing Waltheof now. Judith could be queen instead.'

'There's no point in backing him, I keep telling you. He *can't win!*'

'That is not the criterion on which a knight decides whether or not to answer his lord's call!' FitzSimon made himself heard above the clamour, and answered the last-heard argument. 'The criterion is whether or not the oath of fealty he has taken obliges him to answer it or not. Personally, I think that my oath to Ralph de Gael does cover it, and that my oath to King William makes no difference, because he gave me nothing in return for it and because it was forced from me. Without it, I would have been forbidden to take possession of any lands in England. Whether Ralph de Gael of Norfolk is right or wrong in backing Waltheof's claim is not, for me, the point. Ralph has called for my sword and I shall give it to him. You think differently, Walter. Very well. I only hope we don't meet across the battlefield, that's all. I've a son and daughter still in Brittany. I'd thought to bring them over soon and maybe suggest betrothing my girl to your son, to make a bond between our two estates. But now . . .'

'There's no question of such a thing,' said Walter disdainfully. He let go of the pillar, looked disapprovingly at his palm and brushed it. 'Your timber's crumbling. If all your roof supports are as bad as this, your hall is about to fall down. I wouldn't dream of marrying my son to the daughter of a forsworn man.'

'Forsworn! Are you calling me forsworn? I might level the same charge at you, my friend!'

'I am prepared to agree to differ,' said Walter coldly, 'I was given Oxfen the year after the Conquest, when Norfolk was granted to Earl Ralph's father. I consider myself a loyal follower of both our present earl *and* his father, but my oath to them does *not* cover treason.'

'*Treason!*' shouted Gilbert.

'That's how it looks to me, but as I said, I'm prepared to agree to disagree. As *you* say, let us hope we don't come face to face on the field. I accept that you believe that you're doing right. It's a pity that we shall never blend Rushley with Oxfen in our descendants, but should you lose the fight, as you will,' said Messire Walter calmly, preparing to leave and beckoning to his wife to come with him, 'there is always the chance that I shall be granted your estate.'

Gilbert suddenly burst out laughing. 'It might be the other way about!'

'We shall see. My lady, are you coming?'

As Walter's fair, plump lady came to his side, Messire Gilbert was apparently seized with an urge for mischief. 'What does your wife think, Walter? After all, she's English. How do you fancy the English Earl Waltheof as king instead of William, madam?'

'My wife,' said Walter, 'has domestic tastes as a lady should. She has no knowledge of these masculine affairs.'

'Oh yes I have, Walter,' said his wife, amazingly.

There was a staggered silence throughout the hall, as though one of the dogs had sat up and made a comment. 'Indeed?' said Walter. 'Well, may we hear your views?'

'I know nothing of the rules governing a knight's fealty, that's true,' said his wife calmly. 'But I'm sure of this, that Waltheof would be a disaster as a king, and that King William would never let him become one. Our estate will be safer if you keep your oath to King William, my dear, and I want it to be safe, for our son's sake.'

123

There was another silence, this time emanating from Messire Walter but spreading all round him, stilling them all, like oil on water. Then, with an inflection that no one present could at first interpret, he said: 'And not for my sake?'

His wife considered. 'Not yet,' she said at last, smiling serenely up at him. 'You are not accountable for my first husband's death. You followed your overlord to England as was your duty. Most likely, you never even saw my husband, let alone killed him. If I have memories which are still green, they are not your fault. Perhaps one day . . . if we grow old together . . . yes, perhaps one day . . .'

They had had conversations like this before. Suddenly the whole hall knew it and knew in what circumstances of combined hatred and tenderness they usually conducted them. There were a few grins and stifled sniggers but for the most part the silence, of embarrassment and astonishment, mingled, held. In the midst of it, Walter and his lady, followed by their escort, took their leave with conventional courtesies, and departed.

'Well, really!' said Gilbert's wife, stepping statuesquely back into the hall after seeing them off. 'What a shocking lack of dignity. I always thought Messire Walter to be so well bred. They might as well,' she added, brushing imaginary dirt from her sanguine silk skirts, 'have taken off their clothes in the middle of the floor and done with it!'

'Mmm,' said Gilbert. 'You know, Bertrade, they're as hot as fire for one another, and getting hotter, whether they like it or not.' His voice was just a little wistful.

'So common,' said Bertrade disapprovingly. Gilbert sighed faintly. He then caught sight of Ivon and snapped: 'And what are you doing here? Why aren't you down at Cob's?'

Ivon hastily began an explanation but stopped in the middle, as if distracted. Gilbert FitzSimon gazed at him enquiringly. 'My lord,' said Ivon, 'are you going to war?'

'So you heard that. Yes, I am. Why?'

'My lord,' said Ivon, 'I want to come too.'

His grandfather had been a knight and war was in his blood. He certainly didn't want to be a knight himself but: 'I could learn to fight, if I could be your man, at least just for this campaign. I'm strong. I could carry a spear. *I want to come!*'

He had wanted it from the moment he realised that the war would be against King William. Messire Guy had said that the king was responsible for the slaughter at Eric's Dale and Guy had also said that he would never get a chance to attack the king. But here it was and eagerly, vengefully, he was reaching out for it.

'You?' said Gilbert, but eyed him consideringly all the same. 'You're my potter's apprentice. You want to fight?'

'Yes, sir,' said Ivon firmly.

Gilbert FitzSimon put thick fists on muscular hips and looked him over as though he were a horse. 'Well, well. But they say a willing volunteer's worth six conscripts. You're filling out. Going to have a good chest and shoulders. We could teach you to handle a spear. Do you mean it? Will you put your hands between mine and promise to be my follower?'

Ivon paused for a moment, briefly irresolute, the loathing and distrust he had once felt for all Norman knights flooding back. Messire Gilbert was a Norman knight.

But the real foe was the king. 'I will,' said Ivon.

Chapter Nine

Hawise

The world of war, of forced marches, battle and siege, was not wholly foreign to Ivon. In Eric's Dale, when songs were sung and tales told round the fire, they had been favourite themes.

But the songs and stories had glamorised them. War, he discovered, meant sweat-soaked hours of charging straw targets with a spear under the orders and thumps of a Breton bully, down in the wide bailey in front of Norwich Castle, followed by much trudging over endless squelching miles of fenland.

The trudging started in hot sunny weather which gradually became overcast and humid until it broke in a thunderstorm. He was on foot all the time; there were no mounts for the unimportant likes of him. He never knew where he was going or what was happening. Alan, the man-at-arms who had been friendly on the journey from St Cuthbert's, was there and knew more but his explanations meant little to Ivon. He recognised few of the place-names that Alan mentioned, nor any of the names he heard bandied about, of the various lords who were leaders among their own forces, or among the king's supporters, whom they would have to fight.

He grasped that Ralph de Gael of Norfolk was their own lord, and saw him once, when Ralph was inspecting his following. De Gael was a thin, dark man with greenish, sparkling, ice-water eyes and a swift and disconcerting grin which showed his molars. He spoke good English because his father, Alan said, had served King Edward; Ralph had spent much of his childhood in England. Ivon, thereafter, could recognise Ralph but it was a long time before his knowledge went much further.

They marched south-west and eventually arrived at a town called Cambridge. They camped overnight outside it. They were to continue west, Alan said. But they had hardly started in the morning before horsemen with spears and banners appeared in the distance. Emissaries from the two sides met in the middle and talked and then the emissaries rode back to their respective leaders to report and there was a pause. Then the Breton who was leading Ivon's section as well as having trained it, marshalled his charges into a line; trumpets sounded and arrows whistled; horses whinnied and men yelled war-cries, and a battle had begun.

What followed passed in an ugly blur. The Breton bellowed: '*Charge!*' and beckoned them on with enormous sweeps of his arm as though hauling

127

them on an invisible rope and, when they obeyed, they at once collided with some spear-brandishing men coming in the opposite direction. Ivon thrust his own spear into one of them but didn't see what effect it had.

Then, beside him, Alan went down with a blade in his guts and there was a dreadful split second, as long as eternity, in which Ivon heard him scream and saw his face and the blood and then he saw that this was real, that Alan was dying, that this was Eric's Dale all over again . . . except that this time he had a weapon, so he drove it into another enemy and this time observed with pleasure that the results were fatal. He did this several more times, dodging attempts to do it to him, remaining alive somehow in the midst of bloodstained chaos and the mingled screams of grating steel and human vocal cords. His companions seemed to thin out and the numbers of the foe to increase. He saw half a dozen of them surround one of his comrades and throw him to the ground. Then the Breton was in front of him, grabbing him, spinning him round, shouting: 'Are you bloody deaf? That's the retreat! Run, you fool, run, or they'll have your right foot off. That's what they're doing to anyone they catch!'

He ran. He fell into a water channel and crouched, hidden by the long grasses curving down from the bank, while a dozen pursuers crossed the waterway a few yards off. He scrambled out. He joined a straggle of fugitives squelching back across the fenland much faster than on the outward march. There were fifty miles of it to cross with death and mutilation on their heels. Only nightfall allowed any rest. There was only muddy water to scoop in one's palm, and no chance of any food at all.

Fortunately, he was young and fit and the fugitives had an advantage, since a number were local men who knew the treacherous fenland paths. They spent a night in a reedbed, moved on at daybreak and caught up with a bunch of men being led by Gilbert FitzSimon, also now on foot. They reached the castle and pounded across the drawbridge into the bailey one hour before the bridge was raised, shutting the castle against the attack which followed swiftly, as the king's forces came up behind the fugitives and flung themselves against the castle's surrounding ditch and earthworks as though they meant to dismantle them with sheer hatred.

Ivon, impelled by terror of what would happen if the enemy prevailed, found within himself the same reserves of strength which had kept him living on the walk to St Cuthbert's, able to fight on with little sustenance and no rest, manning the defences, helping to roll great rocks down on the enemy as they toiled below, attempting to put up scaling ladders from the deep ditch which surrounded the castle but was, unexpectedly, dry.

After many hours, by which time continual clamour had become a normal condition of life and he had long since ceased to think of the foe in the ditch as anything more than ants to be squashed, the enemy withdrew and the castle settled down to a state of siege.

Within forty-eight hours, he had made a new discovery about the nature of war: that sieges were boring.

*   *   *

The defence of Norwich Castle was not being conducted by Ralph de Gael. When the first crisis was over and the exhausted defenders had had their first food and sleep, they were gathered in the hall of the timber keep, and Ralph de Gael's bride, Emma, Countess of Norfolk, came down from the upper floor where she and her ladies had stayed throughout the onslaught, to address them. With the castellan beside her and four women at her back, she stood on the dais and faced them, and it was Emma, at whose wedding feast this whole disastrous campaign had been hatched, who told them that her husband had not returned to the castle after the battle and that, meantime, she was his representative.

She was very young and must have been a lovely bride. She wore her hair as Norman ladies often did, braided and emerging from her head-veil to fall in front of her shoulders. Her braids reminded Ivon of something and at first he couldn't think what, until he saw that they were sandy, only a little lighter than the fox-colour of his own hair.

Her face was drawn now and her voice shook as she said: 'I don't know what has happened to my husband. Nor do I know why my brother of Hereford hasn't come to our aid with his men, or why Earl Waltheof has struck no blow on his own behalf. We must wait for news and . . . eat sparingly meanwhile,' said Emma and with that, turned and almost fled from the dais, back to her quarters above, her women hurrying after her. She did not come down again for some time.

After that, there was little to do. The castellan, Messire Ivo, whose name Ivon couldn't help but notice was similar to his own, arranged for regular weapon practices, and for a rota of sentries on the outer defences. He referred to these as the walls, although the palisade which crowned the high bank was timber except in one place, where there was a length of masonry with crenellations and a paved path behind it, wide enough for three to walk abreast. Earl Ralph had just started on an improvement pro-gramme when he went to war, and the masonry represented the first phase. The master mason who had been in charge had in fact been trapped in the castle and was pointed out to Ivon: a middle-aged man, noticeable because he had a goatee beard and beards were out of fashion.

Ivon took his turn at watching from the walls, looking out at the enemy encampment. Men came from there to remove the corpses from the ditch. As though impelled by some strange desire for tidiness they also came with nets and oxen and removed the rocks which littered it. This was odd, but seemed harmless. There were plenty of spare rocks still in readiness within the walls. They had plenty of arrows too and the means to make more, but Messire Ivo disapproved of waste and would not let his men shoot the tidying-up squads. Then, for days, nothing happened.

There was a reasonable amount of space within the castle, which was in a sense a fortress within a fortress since, in addition to the outer defences which embraced keep and bailey alike, there was a complete second ditch and drawbridge round the seventy-foot mound on which the keep stood within a palisade of its own. The keep was roomy as well as comfortingly strong. Judging by the blackness and hardness of its oaken walls, a number of defunct ships had gone into its construction, and the exterior was plastered with fire-resistant mud. But both keep and bailey were extremely congested, the former because of the trestle dining-tables and the bedrolls of over a hundred men and the bailey because it was crammed with barns, stables, a pigsty, a cookhouse, a bakehouse, a forge and assorted workshops. Presently, Norwich Castle began to smell.

Morale was bad, too. The countess's ladies sometimes walked in the bailey, escorted by senior men and also by the master mason, who was said to be the father of one of them. But Emma was never with them and word filtered out that the countess had taken to her bed and wouldn't eat.

It seemed to Ivon that fear was in the very air he breathed, like a mist. He could obtain little support from the men around him. Many that he had known, like Alan, were dead and FitzSimon he glimpsed only in the distance, mingling with men of his own rank. Of Ivon's immediate companions, many were Bretons or fenlanders, both of whom had dialects so incomprehensible that he often couldn't follow conversations. But in between weapon drill and sentry duty, he had much freedom of movement. He took to prowling about by himself. Almost at once he discovered, tucked away behind the bakehouse, a small potter's workshop. Enquiry produced its proprietor, an anxious-faced villein who was part of the castle staff as a handyman. 'If there's a bit of carpentry to do, or a roof wants repairing, I see to it. I make a few pots and whatnot as well – simple things, not for my lord's table, of course. Yes, there's some clay in there, in the bin. You can play about with it if you like. I don't care. We'll all be dead soon, I expect. I'm just a villein with no choice about anything but I don't suppose that'll make any difference when it comes to it. I've no heart to be making things.'

After a year with the horrible Cob, he was out of practice, but before that he had had two years with Brother Edgar, who had been conscientious about teaching his apprentice. Rusty skills returned after a while. There was clay fit to use, with sand already mixed into it, and some ready-prepared lead glaze for a simple amber finish. He made a jug and a basin on the wheel and then worked with his hands for a while, rolling clay into a long sausage and building it up, coil by coil, into a bowl with a fluted surface. The feel of the clay on his hands, the shape developing under them, was good.

When he had finished, the jug and basin struck him as too plain but he couldn't find any paint or any makings for it. However, Brother Edgar had taught him how to cut decorations into soft clay. Edgar had had some standard patterns and he had made Ivon practise until he could almost draw them in his sleep. There was an interlaced design, like a loosely woven and complex rope, which was not, however, quite as complex as it looked, not once you knew the trick of it. He tried on a piece of spare clay first, thought for a moment that he had lost the knack, rediscovered it with relief and proceeded to band the two pieces at lip and middle.

He fired his creations lightly and returned later that day to glaze them and fire them again. Early the next morning, he was there again, to inspect his products and work some more clay ready for use. He began to hum, and then to whistle, and almost forgot where he was until two shadows fell across him from the doorway and he found that Gilbert FitzSimon had come in with another man, a dark, stocky individual whom he had noticed before in Gilbert's company.

'So here you are,' said FitzSimon. 'Someone said you'd been asking about the pottery, so when I heard whistling from in here, I said to Thane Brand here: that's him! What the devil are you doing, Ivon? We're all being called together for some sort of briefing and when I counted my followers, you were missing. I lost two-thirds of my men at Cambridge and I can't afford to mislay any more.' Ivon stared at him. 'It was a joke,' said FitzSimon impatiently. 'Not a very good one but there are times, in war, when you either make bad jokes or crawl whimpering into a corner for lack of any at all. This is going to be a hard siege, my lad. That is what we're going to be told this morning, I fancy. I've got someone looking for you. But since we've found you ourselves, you'd better come with us. Messire Ivo wants us all present and correct in roughly fifteen minutes from now.'

'One moment.' The dark man had been looking at Ivon's jug and basin, with obvious interest. 'You made these?' he said. He spoke in French, as FitzSimon had done, but from his accent as much as from his title of Thane, he was clearly English.

'Yes, sir.'

'It's good work,' said the dark man approvingly. His face was square and brown with good-natured brown eyes and his smile showed excellent teeth. 'You come here to get away from the miseries of war, do you?'

'Well . . . I enjoy my craft, sir. I like to work at it.'

'You've used your time with Cob very well,' FitzSimon agreed, picking up the basin and scrutinising it.

'Cob never lets me go near the wheel, sir. I learned most of what I know at St Cuthbert's.'

'What?' FitzSimon looked at him in surprise.

'It's true, sir.'

'Is it, indeed? Well, when and if we get back to Rushley – I did say *if*; you don't know what the miseries of war are, yet – I'll look into that. But meanwhile, our commander awaits.' He put the basin down. 'Follow us, Ivon. Come on, Brand.'

The gathering was in the bailey. Messire Ivo, using a cart as a platform, stood in front of them, four-square, helmet under arm, raised his voice to make himself heard because there was a strong wind blowing, and announced bluntly that there was no knowing how long they would be under siege but it would be as well to prepare for the worst. An inventory existed of all stores and all weapons in the castle, and here and now, he wished to count heads. 'In lines of twenty, if you will. We'll reckon you up by the score. Knights first . . .'

131

He had a young squire at his elbow, with a wooden board and a piece of chalk, to keep the tally. The count took some time and was conducted in an unsmiling, businesslike fashion which made a man standing next to Ivon remark gloomily: 'Looks like there are too many of us for comfort.'

At the end, Ivo addressed them again, still bluntly. 'We can last six weeks with a little care, eight weeks with a lot of it. Water supplies are all right; there's a well within the keep. But I have to warn you all—'

From the keep, trumpets sounded. They looked up. Down the steps, across the inner drawbridge and into the bailey, attended by her ladies and her armed escort, came Emma. She was in a hurry. When she reached the bailey she broke into a run. Countess Emma, transfigured, her companions breathless at her heels, came with a flurry of skirts and flying braids, to jump on to the cart beside Ivo and the squire, seize Ivo's elbow and whisper in his ear, and then turn to address them all, flourishing a piece of parchment.

'Look at this, look, *look*! Hawise found it!' She reached a hand to one of her girls, dragged her up on to the cart as well and kissed her, standing on tiptoe, because the girl was tall. 'Hawise found it lying in the bailey when she was walking there at dawn! It was wrapped round an arrow. It's news of my husband! He's safe! He had ships in the river here and he got away. He's sailed for Denmark to ask for help. We have only to hold the castle until that help comes but come it will, now that Ralph has gone himself to fetch it! And my brother of Hereford will *surely* come soon to relieve us!' Her joy was infectious. For all the world as though she had announced that Ralph's army was already in sight, tired, unshaven faces began to grin. 'Of course, we must be prudent,' said Emma, grinning back at them. 'Relief may not come *instantly*. We had better begin by rationing the food.'

'I had just completed a head-count, my lady,' said Ivo. 'With that intention in mind.'

'Then we will proceed with it,' said Emma. 'You and I will work out together what each man's – and woman's – daily ration ought to be and you can be sure that I shall keep the rules the same as any of you and so will all my girls.'

It seemed to Ivon that the castle had suddenly been awakened. Emma, hiding herself no longer, was everywhere, talking to the men, even the humblest of them, even himself, inspecting the defences twice a day, laughing, being witty, making others laugh as well, her certainty of approaching aid so strong that they caught it from her.

Meanwhile, as Ivon observed on his very next sentry-go, the enemy was up to something.

The land beyond the outer ditch was flat, like everywhere else in this East Anglian country. On one side, the keep overlooked the thatched roofs of Norwich town but on the other side, the tents of the besiegers made a wide semicircle in the distance, with thin threads of smoke here and there from the camp kitchens. Ivon's long sight was good, and he could see that oxen were dragging timbers to certain points a little closer to the castle than the tents were although he thought they were out of average bowshot. Tiny, industrious figures were assembling them into odd, angular structures.

He was watching this, wondering if anyone had reported it and how he could report it himself without leaving his post, when the countess and Messire Ivo arrived, on one of their rounds of the walls.

The countess, as always, had attendants. One was Hawise, the tall girl who had found Ralph's message. There were also two men: the master mason who had been caught in the siege by accident and the dark, stocky English thane who had come into the pottery with FitzSimon. Ivon, mildly inquisitive, had asked about him. 'He's a bit of a character,'he had been told. 'Got a chequered past.' The Englishman had been to Normandy long ago and been knighted there, 'by Duke William himself'. But he had come home to fight for King Harold at Hastings and later on joined Hereward in Ely. 'It was Harold made him a thane. Some call him that and some call him Messire Brand. He made peace of a kind with William after Ely fell – maybe William had a soft spot for him – but he'd still rather see the crown on Waltheof's head. Got a Norman son-in-law, though.'

Ivon thought that Brand's attitude towards Normans was probably rather like his own, which meant confused.

'Anything to report?' said Ivo.

'Yes, sir. There's something I don't understand.' He pointed. 'Those things out there. Look.'

They stood, shading their eyes as the sun came out from a passing cloud, and studied the strange timber structures in the distance. Thane Brand said: 'They have been noticed already. We don't know what they are but the enemy isn't going to all that trouble to pass the time. We should beware.'

'Not for the first time, I wish I'd been wise enough to make you leave the moment this conflict began, before the siege,' said the mason unexpectedly, addressing Hawise. 'As your father, I should have looked after you better.' Ivon looked at them curiously. So it was the tall girl who was the mason's daughter.

'I would have sent all my ladies away, had I known,' Emma said. 'But I'm glad Hawise stayed. That arrow might not have been found for hours otherwise. It was in shadow, close under the wall, and Hawise only saw it because she tripped and fell and there it was six inches in front of her nose.' She gave the bearded mason her dazzling smile. 'Hawise will be able to command the attention of whole banqueting tables with that story one day, when this is all over. *Then*, Hawise, you'll know you wouldn't have missed it for the world.'

'I'm sure that will be so, madam,' said Hawise. She was not only tall, but regal. She had a high-bridged nose, thin, upward-slanting brows, and eyes with a far-seeing expression, like those of a sailor. Indeed, they were sea-coloured, blue with a tinge of grey. Her braids were between red and

133

flaxen, not his own fox-colour; but nearer to a deep gold. He wondered whether she was always as pale as that. He tried to catch her eye to smile at her, but she was looking at the mason, who was frowning at the strange timber constructions. 'I've never seen anything like them, but I agree with Messire Brand. I don't like the look of them. My Lady Emma, it would be best if you and all the other ladies kept off the walls from now on.'

Emma shook her head. 'You mean well,' she said, 'and I take it kindly, but I am Earl Ralph's representative and I wish to be seen patrolling every inch of his castle, unafraid, to keep the men in good heart. I lost heart when I thought Ralph was dead and I'm ashamed of that now, but at least I know now how it feels, and I know that if that . . . that deadness once really invades the minds of a castle's defenders, we might as well open the gates and stand about dressed in sackcloth and ashes while the victors ride in. To send me that message, Ralph – or someone – slipped through the enemy lines in the dark. That was a brave thing to do. I must match it. It is essential, master mason, that I *don't* keep off the walls. What do you say, Hawise?'

'I'm sure you are right, madam,' said Hawise respectfully. Her glance crossed with Ivon's at last, and encountered the smile he was keeping in readiness, which was meant to reassure her and tell her, too, that she was a pleasing sight for a man on sentry-duty up here on these walls with nothing to look at beyond the ominous eccentricities of the foe. She couldn't be much older than he was. He hoped for a response.

Hawise stared through him and turned away.

Regal, was she? Haughty would be more like it. So she had found the arrow and its message by tripping over in the bailey, had she? Well, well. And suddenly, Ivon found that he sincerely hoped that she had fallen flat on her face in a large patch of mud.

The next day, they began to feel the privation of the rationing on which Emma and Ivo had decided. Countess Emma, however, kept her word. She and her ladies took meals alongside the men so that they should see for themselves that no one was being favoured. Messire Ivo kept the keys to the stores and never used them without witnesses drawn by lot.

Once, on that first day, Emma overheard a man grumble about the slender rations, and rounded on him with an indignation which took him aback.

The morning after that, an archer was caught trying to pilfer bread from the bakery and Emma revealed a further fact of her personality.

'While we are defending Norwich Castle, we can do without this hungry mouth,' she said, when the whole garrison had been summoned to the hall and the archer, shaking, and trying to smile ingratiatingly at the pretty young countess, was brought before her. 'There's a tree in the bailey,' said Emma, standing on the dais, fragile and unrelenting, like filigree steel. 'Take him out and hang him. The whole garrison, except for the sentries on duty, will watch. Ladies too.' The archer collapsed, ashen and babbling.

'Messire Ivo,' said Emma. 'Make sure he dies quickly. I shall watch as well and I don't want my stomach turned. I prefer to get the full benefit of my *legitimate* rations.'

Ivon had seen death many times, in many guises. But he had never seen it like this before, in cold blood and ritualised, with a garrison chaplain reciting prayers and a man's own friends lined up to see him put out of the world. No one had protested; there was no one there who didn't in honesty think that Emma was right. But there were men who averted their eyes and one of Emma's ladies ran away, hands clutched to her mouth.

Afterwards, as soon as he could get away, he went to the pottery, wanting wet clay on his fingers. He knew no better anodyne.

In the pottery, curled up in a corner on a pile of old sacks, knuckles in mouth, was Hawise.

She started up when she saw him, apparently frightened. 'It's all right,' Ivon said. 'But what are you . . . ?'

'Did my lady send you to find me?' She sounded angry as well as scared. She got up from the sacks, shaking out her skirts. 'All right, I'll go to her. Just let me compose myself. Oh, do stop staring!' Her voice shook.

'No one sent me,' said Ivon. 'I come here sometimes, that's all.' He had never before been alone with a Norman girl and did not know what to say or how to feel about her. He had already concluded that this one was both very beautiful and infuriatingly haughty, but although the beauty was still there, she did not at this moment look in the least haughty. She was clearly quite wretched and to his surprise, he felt sorry for her. He perched himself on the edge of the worktable and said: 'Was it you who ran out of the bailey just now? Did it upset you?' He tried to say what a monk of St Cuthbert's might have said. 'It's all over. He's at peace now and he died shriven, with all his sins forgiven.'

Hawise looked at him as though he were mad. 'That must have been a great comfort to him when he was . . .'

'Look, you shouldn't think about it. You ought to be with your mistress. It would be best for you, I mean. You need company and something to do.'

'I'll go in a minute. I said so. When I'm ready, when I'm sure they won't notice.'

'Notice what?'

'Oh *God*!' said Hawise furiously, through clenched teeth.

It didn't sound very much like a prayer. Ivon, partly through curiosity and partly because he really wanted to help, said: 'What is it?'

'It's all right. It's nothing to do with you!' Her hands gripped each other as though she wanted to break her own fingers. 'Oh!' Hawise burst out. 'I'm so ashamed!'

'Ashamed? What of? Have you done something wrong?'

'No!' She looked round irresolutely and Ivon said: 'Look, if we push those tools and things along that bench there, we can sit on it. There we are.'

Hawise allowed him to clear the bench for them and did not object when he took her elbow and steered her to sit beside him. 'Now tell me,' he said.

There was a pause and then: 'It isn't anything I've done, it's what I *am*!'

'What do you mean?'

'I mean I'm Oliver the Mason's daughter, not really one of the countess's usual ladies at all. Her ladies are the wives and daughters of knights. But I go about with my father and look after him and, well, we were here when the campaign began. We didn't expect to be besieged like this but still, Countess Emma sent some of her women away, those that were willing to leave her, just in case. My father wanted to send me away. He sent his team of masons home. But I . . . I said no, I wanted to stay with him, that I wasn't afraid. And then, since she had so few girls left, the countess said I'd better be one of them; I was sharing their quarters, anyway. I was so proud, so pleased to feel I was one of the brave ones who hadn't run away . . .'

'And?' said Ivon. 'Come on. You can tell me. I won't tell anyone, whatever it is, I promise, not even if you've been stealing snacks. You haven't, have you?'

'What? No, of course not! I *said*, it's nothing that I've done! All right, then, here it is. I'll tell you and then you can laugh if you want to. That's what the other girls would do. They don't like me. My father often goes round the walls with the countess – she likes him – and then she lets me attend her. It's just a kindness but the others make remarks about Emma's pet. If they knew this . . . ! I'm terrified,' said Hawise. 'That's all. *Terrified!* I didn't know it would be like this. We're shut in here for God knows how long, and if the castle falls, what will happen to us? I think about it in the night . . . Knights' daughters grow up used to war but I didn't know . . . When I said I'd stay . . .' Hawise's voice now held a savage bitterness. '. . . I think my head was full of noble warriors and great ladies. But when they were attacking us a few days ago, I thought I'd die of fear and the other girls made fun of me when the countess wasn't looking. Why aren't they scared too? And I'm hungry all the time and the keep stinks and we may all be killed and . . . it's too late now. I can't get out. I'd give anything to be just walking across those green fields on the other side of that ditch. I feel as though we're trapped in here for ever!' On the last sentence, her shaky control almost failed and she maintained it only by a colossal effort, her whole body rigid and her teeth biting into her lip. 'What am I going to do?'

'I can answer that,' said Ivon. He had forgotten his affrontedness on the walls. He put an arm round her shoulders, giving her what warmth and strength he could and when her stiff muscles relaxed a little, he stood up, pulling her up with him. 'You are going to wash your face – there's water here, in that tank affair in the corner – and then you're going back to the countess. She's brave enough for two; follow her example. Imitate her, the way she walks and smiles and speaks, and you'll be all right. Listen. When we ran, after the battle, because people were shouting that they were taking prisoners and chopping off their feet, I nearly shit myself with fright.

We're all afraid at times. Those other girls as well! I bet half of them cry themselves to sleep at night, under the rugs. We hide it because it's catching.' Until now, he hadn't known he knew this, but as soon as he said it, he realised that it was true. 'But the countess will see us through if anyone can. She's just like my grandmother was.'

'Your grandmother?'

'Yes. She saved my life once through sheer determination.'

'Did she?' Hawise turned her head to look at him, for the first time, he thought, seeing him as himself and not merely one of the sentries. Her face was still haunted, but some of its naturally rather lofty expression was reasserting itself. He found himself thinking how much had been going on, unseen, behind that dignified façade. And was then, without warning, filled with a wild desire to discover what else it might conceal: what unknown depths of feeling, what heights.

'I'll tell you about my grandmother sometime,' he said. 'Not now, because I think you should rejoin the other ladies and I must go on sentry-duty soon. But I might be in here early tomorrow. I can show you how a potter's wheel works, too.'

'Perhaps,' said Hawise with a faint smile, 'I may be here too, early tomorrow. We always come to walk in the bailey in the morning. I may lag behind the rest and . . . lose them for a time. Perhaps.'

They met in the pottery in the morning and Ivon told her a little about Gunnor and the long walk to St Cuthbert's. Since she was Norman, they spoke French together, but because she was not of knightly stock, the story of Eric's Dale aroused her uncomplicated indignation. In return, she told him her own story.

There was far more to her than there had been to Aldith. Hawise had travelled widely with her father. They had come from Rouen three years ago, after Hawise's mother died and her father wanted new places and people to help him forget. He had worked as a mason in London, on the new Tower which King William had ordered to be built, and on other castles too, all over England. They were sprouting everywhere, said Hawise. She had been educated. She could read and write and understand a mason's drawing. Her French accent was as elegant as that of the well-bred countess.

'You're just as much a lady as any of those knights' daughters up there in the keep,' Ivon said. And then, because although she was not of knightly status, she was still a lady which meant forbidden and therefore doubly fascinating to anyone born in a thrall's hut; and because he knew that there was a frightened girl inside the lady, and he wanted to comfort her; and because she had once looked haughtily through him and he had unfortunately missed seeing her measure her length in the bailey; and above all because she was beautiful and he was male, he put his arms round her, brought his mouth down hard on hers, and attempted to pull her down on to the floor of the pottery.

Hawise instantly tore herself free with an exclamation of horror and slapped him. They found themselves sitting on the floor, several feet apart, glaring at each other and panting. 'What do you think you're doing? What do you think I am? A serf you can just tumble in a hayfield?'

'I've never tumbled anyone in a hayfield,' said Ivon. 'Only,' he added, before he could stop himself, 'under a tree, and up in a loft.'

'Who was it? No, don't answer that, I don't want to hear. Whoever it was, I'm not like that.'

'I'm sorry. I thought . . .'

'It's quite obvious what you thought,' said Hawise furiously, getting to her feet. 'Oh, I shouldn't have come here, I don't know why I did. I'm going.'

'Hawise . . . !' Ivon too was on his feet.

'Well?' said Hawise but paused halfway to the door.

'I'm really sorry. I didn't mean to offend you.'

'Well, you have!'

'I won't do that again. But please . . . you ought to go now, you're right,' he said, 'but could I just have a kiss before you go, so that I can think we parted friends. You're so pretty.'

She hesitated, with one eye on the door. Ivon came to her and very cautiously put his hands on her shoulders, 'Just a kiss, nothing else. Beautiful Hawise, please.'

It was hardly a passionate salute. Hawise's dry, warm mouth never opened. But he took the kiss with him to his bedroll that night and instead of having nightmares about having his right foot chopped off by steel-faced fiends, he dreamed about Hawise.

In the morning, he was on duty on the walls when Messire Ivo and the countess came on their twice-daily circuit. Emma varied her escorts constantly, giving the privilege to the lesser men as often as to the senior lords. This time, Gilbert FitzSimon (who as lord of only one manor was decidedly a lesser man) was with her, and, as previously, Thane Brand (who was well known but nowadays landless) and Oliver the Mason. Hawise attended her, walking a pace behind the countess. Her eyes met Ivon's from beyond her mistress's shoulder. She looked away at first, but then she gave him a shy glimmer of a smile which made his inside feel as though it were melting. He had to jerk himself back to reality as FitzSimon said: 'What *is* going on round those timber affairs out there?'

As once before, they stared out between the crenellations towards the enemy lines. The weather, which had been bright and windy since the thunderstorm, had changed in the night. The wind had fallen away and a mist had stolen in from the sea, fifteen miles or so away across the marshes. The surrounding encampment was hidden and the timber structures were barely visible. But there was a suggestion of movement close to them.

What it meant, however, they could not tell. 'What these lads are up to is a puzzle,' Messire Ivo admitted.

'Provided they go on getting up to it away over there,' said Emma, 'they're no trouble to us. My brother may arrive from Hereford at any moment. He was going to raise an army of Welsh mercenaries. They're magnificent fighters; even if he's been held up somewhere, he'll break through. And Ralph must have reached Denmark by now. He'll have had a fair wind. He'll never leave me here without help; he'll make the Danish king or at least some of his jarls come to the rescue, even if he has to sell all our lands in Brittany or offer the King of Denmark the English crown instead of that pitiful creature Waltheof. *He* ought to have relieved us,' said Emma with scorn. 'He just wants a foot in each camp.' She had turned her back on the crenellations and was talking to them all impartially, to Ivon and Hawise as much as to her more senior companions. 'Waltheof wants us to win the crown for him, but if it goes wrong, he wants to be able to say to the king: it was nothing to do with me; why, I didn't even leave my home.'

'Quite true,' Messire Ivo growled. 'The last we heard, he was quaking on his Northampton estate and hadn't even—'

He died in mid-sentence, cut off without time even to cry out, as a chunk of rock, too heavy for a man to lift, hurtled over the walls, missing Emma only by a few feet, and smashed him to the ground with his skull crushed in.

'*Down!*' shouted Thane Brand, grabbing Emma's arm and yanking her to the ground. 'Hard against the crenellations! Don't try to get down to the bailey yet!' Three more rocks arced overhead to bounce on the paved walk nearby and a series of crashes in the distance told them that missiles were coming in from other angles and hitting the buildings in the bailey. Hawise and her father were crouching beside Emma, the whites of their eyes glinting as they peered fearfully upwards. Gilbert FitzSimon hesitated, peering over the crenellations. 'What the devil are they . . . my God, I see! Those timber things are like giant catapults! They're—'

'Get *down*, sir!' said Ivon. He grabbed his lord's belt and jerked him to the ground in the nick of time, as a rock tore through the air where Gilbert's head had been. Another landed in the ditch below them. The earth shook. Hawise let out a sob. 'They've hit either the forge or the bakery,' said Thane Brand. 'Something's on fire; see the smoke?'

'We're as safe here as anywhere,' said the mason, with his arm round his daughter. 'As long as we keep hard against this wall. It's stout enough.'

The bombardment ceased, suddenly. They looked at each other. Carefully, no one looked at Ivo or the red mess which had been his head. 'We've got to get across to the far side of the bailey,' said the thane. 'Quickly! You too, my lad,' he added to Ivon. 'We can't afford to waste anyone's life. No wonder they wanted to collect all those rocks! What we need,' he added, 'is archers. I'd say those things are out of bowshot but it's our only hope. Can you use a bow? If not, you're about to learn.'

They tried the archers, shooting from crouched positions along the outer defences. Ivon acquired the basic skill quickly, after some brief instruction, but his shafts like everyone else's fell hopelessly short. The monster catapults had been placed by a shrewd planner. They were just out of reach, and their bombardment, resuming quickly after what had probably been an experimental first attempt, went on all day.

The aim of the machines was erratic and a good many of their missiles fell short, but dozens on dozens of the rocks which the defenders of Norwich had originally rolled from the walls on to the heads of the enemy now crashed back into the bailey like a murderous hailstorm.

The defenders continued to send relays out to crouch on the walls and shoot but too many lives were lost, some simply while retrieving the bodies. Before long, the rocks had swept the archers from the walls and a further assault had started from the other side, where the keep had no wide bailey between it and the outer bank and ditch. Rocks aimed from machines set up among the houses of Norwich began to strike the palisade on top of the mound, breaching it in several places.

The council of war which gathered in the keep, was in a grim mood.

'They'll launch another attack and be into the bailey if we can't put a stop to this.' One of Earl Ralph's foremost lords spoke in tones of ominous warning. 'The walls are wide open.'

'They're like huge catapults,' FitzSimon said angrily. 'As if we were squirrels and they were stoning us.'

'Catapults?' said one of the Breton leaders. 'Colossal crossbows, that's what they remind me of.'

'The point,' said Emma, 'is not what they're like but how to fight against them. They've driven us into the keep!'

It was Thane Brand who said thoughtfully: 'Crossbows. Who mentioned crossbows? They're not a weapon in common use, they're cumbersome and none too accurate. But they have a long range and those things are within crossbow shot or I'm a paynim. Are there any crossbows in the castle?'

Emma's face lit up once again, in that astonishing way which roused up the heart of anyone who saw it. 'There are crossbows, yes! Down in the stores below this hall. My husband's father had them made. My husband thought they were inaccurate, as you've just said. But if they'll serve now . . . Ivo is dead. Thane Brand, if the other lords here present consent, I will make you castellan of Norwich. Command our defence.'

One of the lords scowled, but then shrugged and said: 'We'd best search the stores.' They did, and found both crossbows and a good supply of bolts and as it was the bakehouse, not the forge, which a falling rock had hit, they could make more.

In one direction, it was possible to shoot from within the keep; on the bailey side, volunteers were called for who would brave the walls. Ivon swallowed hard, and offered. A crossbow was more complicated to use than an ordinary bow and his part this time was to stand behind a bowman and hand him fresh bolts. It was not only desperately dangerous but grinding, for they kept it up all night, shooting at the torch flames as the besiegers tried to fit up shelters for their engine operators.

Next day, the enemy moved the machines back and tried a longer range.

More missiles began to fall short and the defenders, heartened and also feeling considerably safer, redoubled their efforts.

By the end of that day, the diabolical inventions had been dragged back too far to be of any use at all. Thane Brand called the garrison together in the keep, looked at them with eyes bloodshot from hours of shooting and no sleep and said: 'My friends, the walls are still ours,' and in the shouts and whistles of joy and the careless embraces, Ivon, who had to his own surprise come through alive, found his way to Hawise and caught hold of her and kissed her once again. This time her mouth opened under his and that was the moment when the world changed for him, when he ceased to be Ivon, a young man in his own right, and became Ivon half-a-man, needing another whole person, a woman, Hawise, not as mistress but as wife, to render him complete.

Only, he thought, as he drew back to look into her eyes, the siege wasn't over. No one had come from Hereford or Denmark. And despite the jubilation all round them, it was in a frightened whisper that Hawise said: 'If only someone would come to relieve us. I still keep dreaming about watching that man hanged, and seeing Messire Ivo die. How long will the food hold out?'

On the dais, Emma was clapping her hands for quiet. 'My gallant, splendid friends! Whatever happens now, we've made a defence to be proud of and even if no help ever reaches us, that is something that both King William and his lords respect. If it comes to making terms, we may have saved ourselves yet.'

'That's true!' Gilbert FitzSimon took her up. 'Oliver Mason, when we're out of here, will you come to Rushley and build me a stone hall? The timber affair I'm living in is about to fall down. What about it?'

'I accept!' the mason called across the hall.

'You'll come to Rushley with your father?' Ivon whispered to Hawise. 'I'll see you there?'

'Yes. Yes, of course. If it ever happens.'

'It must happen. Hawise . . .'

'No,' said Hawise, holding him off as he tried once more to pull her towards him. 'No, no, I don't want this. I don't want a hugger-mugger affair. I want . . . life to be back to normal before I . . . do anything irrevocable.'

She talked in abstract terms in a way which he found unfamiliar, but the meaning came across like a splash of cold water. He was sixteen, a potter's apprentice following his overlord as a man-at-arms. He had nothing yet to offer her; he could not go to her father and ask for her with the slightest chance of being heeded; and in any case she was not yet ready. The siege must be over and they must be back in their proper worlds before he could dream of carrying this a step further.

If the siege were ever over. If the food held out.

As time went on, days becoming weeks, and the enemy stayed obdurately encamped before the walls and the number of floursacks and salted meat barrels went down, hope dwindled again. The rations became shorter. The daily allowance of bread, which was now made in makeshift conditions in the keep, had to be cut, even though they had lost twenty men and a dozen more lay gravely injured at one end of the hall, tended by Emma and her ladies, who were as dirty, as bloodstained and as emaciated as any of the men. Only Emma's iridescent spirit, her conviction that Earl Ralph would come, kept total despair away.

Once, an emissary appeared below the walls, between two heralds, and asked if the defenders would make terms. Slender and proud, flanked by two of her lords, one from Norfolk and one from Brittany, Emma informed them that the castle had a year's supply of rocks, crossbow bolts and food. The first two statements were exaggerations and the last a blatant lie. Her garrison, listening, cheered them all.

Five weeks. Six. Four of the wounded died and a few staggered back on to their feet, but the spaces on the hospital pallets were soon filled. The enemy had a new sport. Archers would creep up under cover of such small bushes and hummocks as the surrounding ground afforded and snipe at anything they saw moving on the walls. The keep smelt worse and worse, reeking of sweat, of blood, of gangrene, of death.

In all this time Ivon spoke to Hawise only once or twice and that briefly. But he saw her often as she went about her work of tending the wounded. Her far-seeing eyes looked as though a vision of hell constantly hovered before them. But she staunched and sponged, bandaged and comforted, helped her charges to eat and drink and relieve themselves, unfaltering; whatever her fears, she was enduring them. Ivon was proud of her.

Seven weeks. Eight.

'This is not defeat!' said Emma, standing on the dais, flanked by Thane Brand and the two lords. She was half their size but she dominated the hall. 'It is victory! It is true that help from Denmark cannot reach us in time and if yesterday's herald from the king's earls spoke the truth, my brother has been driven out of the country. In which case, we can give up hope that Waltheof will move for us. But I have negotiated for our lives and limbs. We will walk out of here sure of both, and I tell you, my friends, we have made a defence that will be remembered in song a thousand years hence. We must be out of England within forty days and what of it? I shall send word to my husband and he will meet me in Brittany. We shall have a place for every one of you, for when I call you my friends, I mean it. For that is what you have been to me, friends and comrades, and I thank you all. You are not to be downcast. I'm not!'

She certainly wasn't. Ivon thought he had never seen a face or heard a voice so joyous. Emma was going to rejoin her husband and she faced her hungry, exhausted garrison in the fetid, bedroll-littered keep, looking as though she were a bride again.

'There are a few exceptions to the terms of exile,' she announced. She was holding a parchment, and now read aloud from it. Such humble

142

people as the castle servants, like the villein who was handyman and potter, could stay because they went with the castle. As if they were part of the furnishings, Ivon thought, like the dais and the well. Oliver the Mason was free to stay in England since he had been, in the eyes of the enemy, 'a tradesman who chanced to be in the castle when the gates were closed'.

Ivon's head jerked up at that. He was glad that Hawise's father and therefore, presumably, Hawise, would be safe. But Gilbert FitzSimon would not go home to Rushley now, or build his house, and Ivon would, he supposed, have to follow his lord to this unknown place, Brittany. Unless Hawise chose to leave her father and go on serving the countess, in the company of the girls she disliked so much, he and she would be jerked apart.

'. . . also exempt,' said Emma's voice, still calmly reading, 'are certain individuals among the lesser lords whose kinfolk have ransomed them. First is Sir Gilbert FitzSimon and those of his followers who have survived. His brother Abbot Maurice of St Cuthbert's Abbey in Northumbria has bargained for his freedom and redeemed his land.'

'All the earls know that the king's heart is in his treasury,' remarked Thane Brand, somewhat sardonically. 'But you'll owe your brother a heavy debt, I'm afraid, Gilbert.'

'I know,' said FitzSimon gloomily.

He would be going back to Rushley after all, then, and for that Ivon was surprisingly glad. He had had enough of being forced out of places: Eric's Dale first, and then St Cuthbert's. But FitzSimon wouldn't be building his house, all the same. In Rushley or Brittany alike, there would be no Hawise.

When Emma had finished he waited for Hawise to come down from the dais where she had been standing behind her mistress. He moved swiftly, catching her arm as she was about to go back to her duty of tending the wounded. In his hand, her elbow felt like nothing but skin and bone, filling him with pity and a fierce desire to look after her. 'Hawise!'

'Ivon?' Hawise's voice was flat and her eyes were sunken. 'Oh, Ivon. We shall never come to Rushley now.'

'Can't you try?' To think that he might never see her again was unbearable. He must have hope of some kind to hold on to. 'You go all over the place with your father, don't you? He might come to somewhere close by, one day. You're not going to Brittany with the countess? A moment ago, I was praying you would. But now I know that I'm going back to Rushley after all . . . Hawise, find a way to come. If you don't, I shall come and find you! Promise me that we shall meet again!'

'You'd better not run away from your lord. He might reward you for your services here, you know. Ask him for some land.'

'If I do, and he says yes . . .'

'I'll try to come to Rushley,' said Hawise. 'Somehow.'

'You won't forget? You won't forget me?'

'No, no. Never.'

'I shall never forget you, either. I shall be in Rushley, waiting,' Ivon said, and, for the third time, they kissed.

On the day when he marched out of Norwich Castle, Ivon, to his surprise, did so with something close to regret.

In Norwich he had known fear and discomfort, but mingled with these had been other things which he now knew were precious. He had walked the walls on sentry-duty and handled a bow; he had withstood that gruelling night, handing bolt after bolt to a crossbowman and seen, in the morning, the fruits of their efforts as the foe withdrew. He had formed, eventually, a rough-and-ready comradeship with the men around him, even though they were mostly professional soldiers and he was not. He had been tested and had not failed.

Above all, in Norwich he had found Hawise. For that alone, the castle was very nearly hallowed.

The enemy was drawn up in ranks outside the castle and there were jeers and abusive shouts. But Ivon marched across the outer drawbridge behind Gilbert FitzSimon with pride in every line of his long back and straight shoulders. He had forgotten completely that marching with him were several of those fearsome and odious creatures, the knights that King William had imported into Engand. He felt at one with his companions, as though he were part of them, a limb of their body corporate.

When they returned to Rushley, it was to find that the last high wind had once more wrecked the hurriedly repaired gable of FitzSimon's hall, this time bringing a good deal of the rest of the hall down with it. His lady had done her best, sending the few men FitzSimon had left with her down to the village to conscript a workforce and have the place temporarily repaired, by putting up a new end-wall to cut the damaged structure off from the rest. The result was a hall half its original size, with a pile of broken timbers alongside it.

Gilbert FitzSimon, though up to his hairline in debt already, was still going to need a house to live in and no Norman ever built in timber if he could help it.

When he set eyes on the mess which had been his hall, FitzSimon was visibly near to bursting into tears. Ivon all but burst into song.

Chapter Ten

Lady Day

When Walter of Oxfen married his English widow, back in the year 1068, she had spent her wedding night with her knees accommodatingly apart, her lips compressed together and her eyes firmly shut. It had upset him.

Walter was a fastidious and civilised man. His fellow Norman lords didn't all merit that description, by any means. Years later, he heard of one in Sussex who took offence because his English wife hadn't given him any children and invited his followers to try their luck with her instead. And at the time of Walter's marriage, the Norman who had taken over Redesmarsh manor, which lay south-west of Oxfen, was reputed to be finding the thirty-five-year-old widow rather long in the tooth, and to have ejected her from his bed, installing her two young daughters, aged fourteen and sixteen, in it instead. Both, said report (and Robert of Redesmarsh hadn't denied it), at the same time.

Walter was not that kind of man. He had married this Englishwoman honourably. He couldn't get his tongue round her name, which was Ethelflaed, but he had said he would call her Mald instead, and meant it kindly, because it was his mother's name. He was going to have to live with her for a long time; he hoped for children. He wanted to make friends.

She spoke French, so it was possible to talk to her. Over the succeeding weeks, he talked to her continually, and in the course of this he told her a great deal about himself and his family; about how, as a younger son, he, like Gilbert FitzSimon, his neighbour to the east, had gone to Brittany and taken service with the de Gael family. 'They sent some men over with Duke William, as he was then, to fight at Hastings; that's how I came to be there. Then I said I'd stay on to serve the de Gael who was here already; that's now Earl of Norfolk.'

He told her about his birthplace in central Normandy, about the forests full of game where the stags grew bigger antlers than they did in England. He told her of his family customs, which included a pleasant if slightly ridiculous habit of giving people gifts on the anniversary of their birth.

Ethelflaed-Mald listened politely and commented little. She did not respond with confidences about her own past life, which might have been tact, considering that her husband had been killed at Hastings, in which battle Walter had fought on the opposing side. But she did gradually thaw to the point where she occasionally, without being asked, told him this and that about the customs of Oxfen.

When the matter arose of arrangements for the monthly manor courts, which every man on Oxfen manor and some of the women too must attend in order to keep the manor running smoothly, she said: 'We hold them in the hall in bad weather. But otherwise, we hold them in the home pasture. My . . . my husband used to set up his chair under the hoar oak.'

'Out of doors?' said Walter.

'Yes. Don't people do that in Normandy?'

'Yes, but my father never did after the day when one of his serfs was accused of something or other and just upped and ran for it, straight out of the meeting. There were no walls or guards to stop him and he got clean away. We never found out what happened to him, but we lost him, anyhow. After that, manorial sittings always took place between four walls. I'd prefer to do the same thing here.'

Mald said nothing more at the time, but two days before the first manorial gathering was due, she said: 'I liked the custom you described to me, of giving people birthday gifts. When is your birthday?'

'November,' said Walter, touched because she had remembered. 'On the twentieth. When is yours?'

'In two days' time,' said Mald mildly. 'On the day of the manor court. You'll be settling the date of the harvest this time.'

'Is there anything particular you'd like as a gift? I'd like to give you something,' Walter said, and added, stiffly: 'I hope, in time, you'll come to see me as not too bad a bargain. Because I think that in you, I have a good one.'

'Do you? Thank you. There is something, a favour, which I would like to ask.'

'And what is it?'

'Please,' said Mald, 'if the weather allows, let the Oxfen people have their manor court where they've always had it, under the hoar oak in the home pasture. It means something to them, keeping the customs they're used to.'

'Now that,' said Walter, 'is being almost too clever.'

But he indulged her and, weather permitting, the Oxfen folk had met under the hoar oak every few weeks thereafter. Eight years later, he still hadn't got used to it. No one had tried to run away and if they had done, he always had mounted men at hand to fetch them back, but it wasn't the way his father had gone about things and Walter was a loyal son; and besides, in the open air he had difficulty in making his voice carry. Messire Gilbert at Rushley had a fine, resonant voice, and the man at Redesmarsh an effortless roar but Walter's voice was what he himself described as light and dry.

He wouldn't go back on his word to Mald, for there was a strong bond between them now, but he was always delighted when it rained, especially on Lady Day. On that day, the twenty-fifth of March, the Annunciation of the Virgin Mary, every year, the principal manor sitting was held. Most of the annual dues in cash or kind were paid then and if any tenant's dues or

146

grazing rights or boundary demarcations needed renegotiation it was done. In this part of the country, he had discovered, the otherwise widespread system by which great fields were held communally and divided into strips for which tenants drew lots annually, did not hold good. Every tenant here had his own plot or smallholding and only the pasture was common. The tenants, all of them, down to the meanest cottager, guarded their cultivations like dragons and would arrive at the Lady Day court seething with righteous wrath if a neighbour had encroached by as little as six inches. The formalities usually ran over into the next day, and by the end he was invariably hoarse.

Mald could have spoken for him, of course, or transmitted his wishes to a steward, and, to begin with, he had had to do it that way. But he soon developed a strong suspicion that on occasion, the steward and possibly Mald were slightly amending the things he had told them to say. To put a stop to that without directly challenging them, Walter had been at pains to learn a little English (Robert of Redesmarsh sneered at this, but the king was said to be trying to learn English too and if it was good enough for King William, it was good enough for Walter). Once he was sufficiently equipped with the language, he used it and spoke to his human dependants directly as a lord should and as his father had done.

His voice did not grow stronger with time. By 1076, the year after the fall of Norwich, Walter of Oxfen had reached the point of not only hoping but actually praying for rain, preferably with an icy east wind to back it up and no treacherous breaks visible in the cloud. But Lady Day 1076 let him down badly. A warmer, more sparkling spring day could hardly have been imagined. The lord of Oxfen went out resignedly, over the movable bridge across the ditch which now surrounded the timber hall (Oxfen's hall, unlike Rushley's, was still in sound condition) and across a hundred yards of field, to comply with tradition and imperil his vocal cords again.

Under the gnarled and ancient oak, preparations had been made. There was a chair for Walter and one for Mald (the steward had to stand). There were a couple of benches where old or lame folk could sit. The rest, like the steward, were supposed to stand respectfully although it was quite likely that they wouldn't. In Normandy or Brittany, even a free tenant wouldn't dare to plonk himself down and relax on the grass in front of his overlord. But the English were different. The very villeins seemed to have no idea that their overlord was a superior form of life. He was merely a more wealthy and powerful one.

On one embarrassing occasion, Walter had been ill. The limited diet of Lent often upset his stomach and on this occasion he had had to bolt to relieve himself. 'Poor old bugger,' he had heard someone say on his return. 'Got a wonky stomach just like Granddad.'

If they wanted to sit, they'd sit. He had decided that it didn't matter, as long as the trestle table set up in readiness was shortly laden with the customary dues. A few items, like grain and honey, were collected at the end of summer, but the rest were presented now: matured mead and ale, woven cloth, six pairs of boots, seed corn, live hens and ducks and pigeons, dried fish, fresh fish, fresh eels and a newly baked, gigantic eel pie. Lent or not, dinner in the hall was always excellent on Lady Day. He had that to look forward to, at least.

Most of the Oxfen people were already there as he and Mald took their seats. The priest of Oxfen Church, who acted as his chaplain, as usual inaugurated the proceedings with a brief prayer. The two knights and six men-at-arms who represented his own dues to the Earl of Norfolk (two months' attendance on the earl per annum plus service on demand in emergency, though he'd withheld them from Earl Ralph's rebellion last year), waited close at hand, the knights mounted. The sun-reddened, bucolic faces of the Oxfen people had shown alarm the first time they saw this show of strength at a manorial meeting, but they were used to it now. He supposed that he was lucky in them; they were at least an ordinary lot. Despite the marshy nature of the district, and the manor's name, Oxfen was not in the true fen country, which lay further south. The inhabitants of the true fens, that land of peat islands amid bottomless bogs, were said to be barely human. They had a dialect all their own, stalked about on stilts and were reputedly born with webbed feet.

'We will proceed,' he said when the prayer was concluded. 'First things first. The dues.'

There were the usual defaulters, who hadn't brought all they were supposed to bring, or had brought something else instead, or wouldn't be ready with it until next week, or month, or Michaelmas. Nowadays, he knew who was honest and who wasn't, which ones merited leniency and which should be told to bring what they owed by tomorrow morning or lose their homes.

Then came a moment to which both he and his tenants were rather looking forward. He had done well for himself by refusing to join the Earl of Norfolk's rebellion. He hadn't quite got his hands on Rushley, but he had acquired some of it. Poor FitzSimon was still on his manor but it was mortgaged now to his brother and he was trying to repay. He wasn't paying interest (the Abbot of St Cuthbert's was a good churchman) but his house had unfortunately fallen down and needed rebuilding. He was recouping as best he could. He had raised the dues of all his tenants drastically, sold more than half his cattle, and leased a broad stretch of his home pasture to Oxfen.

There were few manors in the land which hadn't gone down in value since Hastings killed so many men. Acres of good farmland everywhere had had to go back to the wild for lack of hands to till it. But Oxfen, to his intense satisfaction, was one of the few that were growing and today Walter intended to auction the new grazing rights.

A quarter of an hour later, he was less complacent. The highest bidder, offering payment in kind in the form of his wife's cheeses, or their equivalent in silver, was the villein Haesta and Walter of Oxfen didn't like him.

It was not that he had anything serious against Haesta. The man's wife was a first-class cheesemaker while Haesta himself was the cleverest man with cattle in the county. He could look at a motley herd and pick out the best milker apparently by instinct, and he thought nothing of sitting up all night patiently working a cow's teats to clear her of mastitis. He looked after Walter's cattle as well as his own and did it well.

But five years ago, Walter had sent Haesta and his expertise to a Norwich fair to buy new cows for Walter's own herd, and Haesta came back not only with the cows, but also with a handsome bullcalf for himself, which he had proceeded to rear. Up to then, Oxfen's lord had had the only bull for miles; with Rushley and Redesmarsh both dependent on it. Every time he heard Haesta's rival concern bellow, Walter felt angry. In Normandy, a villein would never be allowed to get above himself like this and . . .

His thoughts had drifted this far when he realised that Haesta's bid wasn't the only reason why bulls were on his mind just now. He cocked his head. 'Mald, is that our bull I can hear?'

The two bulls were kept penned, separately, out of sight from where he sat because a barn was in the way, but not actually far distant. Mald also cocked her head. 'I think it is. He has a very deep bellow. Haesta's animal is younger and sounds it.'

'Well, what's the matter with him?' He waved impatiently at the nearest man-at-arms. 'Go and find out what all that noise is about. Some of the village lads have found a new sport lately,' he said to Mald. 'They let one of the bulls chase them across the pen and then vault the fence. Unfortunately, none of them have been gored yet. When they are, they'll no doubt learn better. I don't approve of it; a bull's energies shouldn't be wasted. Not my bull's energies, certainly. He sires better calves in my opinion than Haesta's nuisance. Gilbert's no judge of cattle. He's sending his cows to Haesta this year, did I tell you?'

'Perhaps,' suggested Mald, in the sweet, intriguing way she had, which always left him wondering whether she were joking or not, 'he was afraid you'd refuse him Thunder's services, after he came back from Norwich.'

'He shouldn't have come back,' said Walter virtuously. 'He ought to be in exile.'

'And we,' said Mald with a sigh, 'ought to be lord and lady of Rushley.'

Her husband looked at her sharply, but her habitual smiling calm hadn't altered and he still couldn't tell whether she was teasing him.

'It would be both improper and unwise of me to make difficulties for any neighbour, and quite disgraceful if I did so because I want his land,' said Walter. 'I may consider that he should by now be in Brittany, but the king's earls have pardoned him and that's the end of the matter. I'm only sorry if he thought I would be so short-sighted. Men in our position should hold together.' At his elbow, the steward coughed. Walter turned. 'The bidding seems to be over, sir. The man Haesta . . .'

'What? Oh, yes.' Walter raised his voice. 'Haesta has outbid his rivals and I therefore declare the rights of grazing on the land between the Upper

149

Wend and the Eelditch to north and south, and the Narrow Wood and the Green Dyke to east and west, are Haesta's until next Lady Day.' He nodded at the chaplain, whose duties on these occasions were also secretarial. 'Write it down.' He turned to the steward. 'What's next?'

'A case of a villein girl who wants to marry a man on Redesmarsh, sir. But her father is willing to pay the fine for marrying her off the manor so there should be no difficulty.'

'Good. A petitioner who presents no difficulties is a rarity. Tell those concerned to come forward and—' He stopped short. 'What on earth . . . ?'

The man-at-arms who had gone to investigate the bellowing bull, had reappeared. He did so with extreme rapidity, rounding the corner of the barn at a pace which spoke clearly of panic. He then came across a tree, leaped, grabbed a lower branch and, in a remarkable feat of agility, scrambled astride it.

'Sweet Christ!' yelled someone in the crowd. 'The bull's after him!'

From beyond the barn, horns lowered and hooves drumming, came Thunder. He had too much momentum to swing round the corner as his quarry had done, even if he had had enough sense. He pounded straight on across the thirty yards of meadow between the barn and the manor court. They watched his approach in brief stupefaction and then scattered with cries of alarm. One mighty bovine shoulder heaved the trestle table over, spilling fish and honeycakes and coops of frantically cackling poultry. Barrels of mead and ale went rolling, catching up with the fleeing personnel, crashing into the backs of knees and felling people like skittles. The gigantic eel pie bowled away like an errant cartwheel and disintegrated on the grass and a couple of dogs, which had been sitting beside their masters, delightedly pounced. Messire Walter grabbed his wife and dodged with her to the safe side of the oak tree. The two knights spurred their horses after the bull, spears levelled. 'Don't hurt him!' shouted Walter, knowing that his voice wouldn't reach them.

Then they saw where the chase was bound, and all of them who could, all who had not been knocked down by rolling barrels or somersaulting hen coops – Walter and his lady, steward, villeins, the remaining men-at-arms – began to run.

The mounted knights almost caught up. But the shouting and the hoofbeats had either frightened the bull or enraged him still more. He blundered on wildly, straight for the water-filled ditch which encircled the hall. There was a loud splash and a furious bellow, suddenly cut short.

The man-at-arms who had taken refuge up the tree had slid down and was running with the rest. He appeared suddenly beside Walter. 'Those bloody boys set him on me! I was telling them to behave and they opened the gate and *set him on me!*'

'Bull's gone mighty quiet,' said Haesta, running on Walter's other side.

With the rest of the crowd they covered the distance to the edge of the ditch and joined the two knights who were already there, looking down from their horses. Thunder lay half-submerged, a silent and unmoving bulk. One of the knights said: 'I think he broke his neck when he went in.'

Walter swore. He glared round him, discovered Haesta looking down on the dead bull with an expression which could only be described as a smirk and found himself so angry that words were all but useless. He wanted to terrify these rustic louts, run a few of them through, to teach them good manners.

Instead, he said coldly: 'The Lady Day manor court has been too much disturbed to continue now. The sitting will resume tomorrow. Will someone clear up the confusion under the hoar oak and bring what dues can be retrieved to the hall. And will someone also get that beef carcase out of my ditch? The meat will be tough but it shouldn't be wasted, and there'll be some good leather on him.' He swung round to face his villeins. At the back of the crowd, he observed some frightened-looking boys. 'When the court resumes, I expect everyone to be present, *young and old*. There will be a reckoning for this. The animal lying here dead is your lord's property. Your lord's *valuable* property.'

The boys looked even more frightened, which was excellent. He noticed that an ill-favoured girl who, he was dimly aware, was Haesta's daughter, was now smiling back at her self-satisfied father.

And was suddenly inspired. What a good thing he hadn't quarrelled irreparably with his neighbour Gilbert of Rushley. Neighbours should help one another. He might yet come out of this well. His solution wasn't only satisfactory; it was elegant. He could come out of it so well that he might even regard himself as having made a profit. Thunder was getting on in years, anyway. The standard of his progeny would soon have begun to drop. Walter looked round for the steward and beckoned.

'Get my man-at-arms to identify the boys and see that they're locked up. He can have the pleasure of personally taking the skin off their backs when the court resumes. But announce, if you please, that the sitting won't resume tomorrow, but the day after, instead. I have business at Rushley tomorrow.'

'You sick or summat?' said Cob, scowling down at Ivon, who was lying on his pallet with his hands locked behind his head. 'Sun's been up for hours. You go to FitzSimon behind my old back, you do, so I get him chucking out orders at me: you're to use my wheel when you want – garn! – and he's going to *give* you one of your own any minute, so what do you do in the morning when you ought to be settin' up the workshop and gettin' down to summat on that wheel you're so keen about? Lounge about in your bed! Though if you're ill, 'course, I'll get Biddy Alfricsdaughter to look at you.'

This was more of a threat than a promise. Beadohild, daughter of Alfric, was the Rushley wise-woman, but a more dubious one even than Ymme had been at the Dale. She had buried three husbands, who were popularly believed to have been poisoned by her well-meant ministrations. 'If you really can't get up, we'd better call Biddy,' was a magic charm which had cured far more patients than her repulsive brews ever had.

'I'm not ill,' said Ivon contentedly. 'I'm happy.'

'You'll get your reward next Lady Day,' FitzSimon had said to him, on the way back to Rushley, when Ivon, obliquely but determinedly, had reminded him of services rendered. 'I had it in mind. You saved my life when you dragged me down, the day they started hurling rocks. I shan't forget.' And he hadn't.

Ivon would never, all his life, forget Lady Day 1076, at Rushley, when FitzSimon had made him holder of two acres in return for 'yearly, ten great bowls, each to be one foot across and twenty small bowls each to be six inches across, to be provided for the lord's house or sold on his behalf as the steward shall direct, and two days' work on the lord's demesne, apart from harvest time when all must work on the lord's fields first, until his corn is in.' In addition, he might make goods 'of his own will' in his own time and sell them for silver, except that a tithe of such proceeds must be paid to his lord.

He had put his hands between FitzSimon's and promised to accept the conditions and faithfully to carry out his duties, and Gilbert FitzSimon had promised on his side to abide by the bargain, and added: 'I intend to present you with a new potter's wheel. I'm having it made in Norwich.'

Everyone had been there – *everyone*; and by that, of course, he meant Hawise and her father. For they had come to Rushley. FitzSimon, after much frantic arithmetic and gloomy wandering round his damaged home, had sent for them. Ivon had seen them ride on their ponies, with half a dozen men and a couple of servants and five pack-mules following, through Rushley to the truncated hall, the day before Lady Day, and they had been present at the manor session, and Hawise had caught his eye and smiled.

Everyone in Rushley hadn't enjoyed Lady Day as Ivon had. There had been scowling faces and even a few angry outbursts when the new, raised annual dues were announced and Cob had muttered in his ear: 'You look pleased now; just wait till you're trying to till your fields *and* do your two days on his *and* make enough pottery to please FitzSimon and pay for the clay and have some over. Tired, that's what you're goin' to be.'

Ivon didn't care. Hawise was here in Rushley and Hawise had heard him receive his reward for saving FitzSimon's skull from that catapulted rock. He was seventeen years of age, a young man with land to till and a craft to follow. He was more than ready to marry. Hawise, Hawise!

'Well, if bein' happy makes you laze about like this, I'd be glad to see you miserable,' Cob observed, still glowering.

Ivon sat up, ran his fingers through the thick hair from which all trace of the tonsure had long since vanished, laughed and gave Cob a friendly punch in the chest, which sent the old man staggering. 'I'm getting up now and I'll put the workroom to rights. But you can have it today, all day. Today,' said Ivon grandiloquently, 'I have business up at the hall.'

He took pains over his grooming. He washed from head to foot, including his hair, using hot water and the soap of wood ash and animal fat which was made regularly up at the hall and sometimes given in part payment for goods. 'You're barmy!' said Cob in horror, watching Ivon now. 'You'll 'urt your skin, a 'scrapin' of it like that!'

Ivon, ignoring him, dried himself on a piece of sacking and proceeded to give himself a clean and careful shave. He combed his hair neatly and dressed in his best clothes. They didn't fit too well any more, for he had grown taller and filled out even in the last few months. But he had bought the cloth for this outfit and had it made up with his pay as a man-at-arms; it had hardly been worn and it was good-quality wool; dark red tunic, belt to show off his narrow hips, stout brown hose, boots. He was fit to be seen. And the next time he had new clothes, Hawise would make them.

He walked to the hall through the bright early spring morning, enjoying the mares'-tail clouds which a steady breeze had brushed across the sky. Love did things to you, he thought. He even felt tender towards Cob today; before leaving, he had mulled some ale for him because Cob was complaining about his rheumatics. Some minstrels who had visited the village lately had said that Earl Waltheof, who had tried to support both sides at once and protect his neck by not fighting at Norwich, had been tried for treason and was to die. How terrible, when the sun was in the sky and summer lay ahead, to know you were going to die.

His only regret was that he could not ride up on a splendid horse to claim his bride. He was obliged to walk instead, and to tell his business to a gatekeeper. Or open his mouth to do so, at least. The gatekeeper as it happened forestalled him.

'You're Ivon. Know you by those odd eyes of yours. That's lucky; someone was coming down soon with a message for you. Messire Gilbert wants you.'

'Now? I've come to see Haw . . . Oliver the Mason.'

'One of the masons? You'll have to walk right round outside the palisade to find him. They're surveying the new site, as they call it. You've time before you see Messire Gilbert,' the gatekeeper added amiably. 'He's not expecting you till a bit later. The steward's with him now.'

The gatekeeper was right. On a stretch of firm, level land beyond the wooden hall, Oliver and his team of lesser masons were prowling purposefully about, dragging sticks through the turf to make lines. Ivon came within hail, but hesitated to call Oliver's name. The mason appeared to be very preoccupied and it seemed inadvisable to irritate his future father-in-law before he'd agreed to the marriage.

Oliver, however, caught sight of him and came over. 'Are you looking for me? I remember seeing you on sentry-duty at Norwich and I saw you yesterday at the manor court, of course. My congratulations on your land grant. You've a message from Messire Gilbert?'

'No, sir. I . . .' Ivon swallowed, remembered that his errand was very much a grown man's business, decided to behave accordingly and said: 'I'm here on my own behalf. I want to ask you something important. If this is the wrong time, could I come back when your day's work is over?'

It would be anguish to wait; it would make nonsense of his careful toilet, his jaunty expectation as he walked from Cob's. But he must not, dared not, make a mistake.

Oliver was studying his face. 'If it's that important, we can talk now. I have my own guest-chamber; we can go there.'

Like most English manor-houses, Rushley had sleeping accommodation for its master and mistress and guests of status, in the form of a few small separate buildings set close to the main hall. Most of these were still in a reasonable state of repair. The mason opened the door and held back the curtain which hung across it so that his visitor could pass in first, and Ivon, who had never entered any of the Rushley guest-chambers before, looked with interest at what he saw.

The hangings were actually better than those in the hall, which bore only woven patterns. These were embroidered with colourful scenes: huntsmen pursuing a white hart on one wall and a Nativity scene opposite.

Three tall, narrow, glazed windows were let into another wall, which was uncurtained. They threw lances of sunlight across the furniture: two big curtained beds and a pile of humbler affairs stacked for the day with their pallets piled on top and, in the centre of the room, a table with some silver candlesticks and goblets on it and settles at each side. The floor was thick with fresh rushes (in this district no one ever went short of rushes) and under a roof louvre was a brazier, not lit but ready filled with charcoal. It was the most comfortable place Ivon had ever seen in his life.

Oliver came in after him and dropped the door-curtain. Suddenly shy, Ivon cleared his throat before he said: 'Your daughter is not here, sir?'

'Hawise? No, why should she be? She'd hardly want to sit in here all day by herself. She is with Lady Bertrade and her girls, gossiping away no doubt, while they do their needlework. Hawise makes all my shirts; I'll miss her when she's married. Have a seat.' Oliver himself relaxed into one of the settles. 'What can I do for you?'

Now that he was being invited to come to the point, he couldn't find the words. Oliver studied him in surprised silence and then said: 'I did say, have a seat. What's the matter?'

Still on his feet, and quite incapable of sounding like an adult who was Oliver's equal, Ivon said: 'You spoke, sir, of your daughter's marriage?'

'I did. How does that concern you?'

Ivon swallowed hard and then said baldly: 'I'm asking if she can marry me.'

Oliver continued to gaze at him. Hawise inherited her far-seeing, sea-blue eyes from her father, Ivon noticed distractedly, but she must take her long limbs and her fair complexion from her mother. Oliver was stocky, his arms and legs a little short, his skin a little swarthy. His silence went on and on, and Ivon, at last remembering the words he had been rehearsing inside his head for two days, uttered them.

'I have been granted land here at Rushley; quite enough to support two people, and I shall make more with the pottery I produce. I hope in time to become truly prosperous. I suppose . . . I'm not a mason so the life Hawise would have with me might be different from the one she has had with you, but I'd do my best to make her a good husband. Of course, I'll ask permission to build a separate house for her. I live with Cob the potter at the moment but I don't expect her to put up with that. I'll take good care of her. We met at Norwich and I know she likes me. She was expecting me to speak to you.'

'Was she?' said Oliver, with a curious inflection. 'Look, do stop standing there like that. For the third time, sit down.'

Slowly, Ivon sank into the settle opposite his host. Oliver reached under the table and produced a leather flask. 'I wouldn't like to seem inhospitable. This is good wine from the Loire valley; let me give you some.' He filled the goblets and pushed one across to Ivon. 'There you are. Now, drink that and tell me something. How old are you?'

'Seventeen. Quite old enough to marry.'

'Yes, very likely. But also young enough not to. Listen, Ivon. I was your age once. I too fell in love, not once but several times. There were a few years,' said Oliver reminiscently, 'during which I thought of little else but girls. I was an apprentice in those days, with no chance of marrying until I was qualified and not many opportunities even then of getting together with a lass. I still had to work with an older mason's eye on me, and I used to make it look as if I had nothing on my mind but finding a shape in a lump of Caen stone, but all the time I'd be scheming how to get to close quarters with my latest love, imagining what it would be like . . . funny,' said Oliver, tugging thoughtfully at his beard. 'I think I put the yearning, all that sweet, aching turmoil into the work I did and it made my carving better. But in the end, after I'd become full-fledged and saved some silver, a man who'd been an apprentice alongside me, whose father was a mason too, suggested I marry his sister. I'd hardly seen my wife until I wedded her. I'd talked to her once or twice in her brother's presence; that was all. I knew she wasn't ugly and I hoped she didn't think I was, no more. I didn't have any longing dreams about her before my wedding day. But we were happy, as I hope you will one day be, and the reason, Ivon, was that we were the same kind of people from the same kind of families. We understood each other's lives. You and Hawise are not the same kind of people, and that would be true even if you were not a villein while she is free, but—'

'I'm not a villein!' Ivon shouted. He had listened to Oliver with rising outrage, seeing almost at once that this was the prelude to a refusal. He had taken only one sip from his goblet before rejecting Oliver's wine along with his arguments, and putting the drink decisively back on the table. 'What makes you think I'm a villein?' he demanded.

'Come, come, Ivon . . .'

'I'm a freeman! As free as Hawise herself!'

'Oh no, you're not,' said Oliver. 'And well you know it, or you should.

155

You hold your land – a couple of acres, a villein's portion – on the understanding that you'll render customary service every week on Messire Gilbert's home demesne. Those are villein terms and you accepted them formally; I heard you yesterday. Now go and ask your lord if you can give your land up and go away to live elsewhere, to work for another lord. See what he says. You're a villein, lad. Not that it would matter if you weren't. Look at this room we're sitting in. Messire Gilbert treats his guests well but not quite as well as this. I brought those hangings here with me, and the goblets and that wine you're so affrontedly not touching. These are the things that Hawise is used to as part of her daily life. Could you provide them for her? I know you mean well and I know you're serious. But Hawise herself wouldn't—'

'She would! She was expecting me to come, I told you! In Norwich, I said to her that I'd be waiting for her if only she could come to Rushley!'

'And what did she say to you?'

'She promised not to forget me! I've thought of nothing but Hawise, all winter. I haven't, I wouldn't, look at any other girl. Hawise loves me! She kissed me!'

'Ah, well. I'm glad to hear it. She's my only daughter and I love her but I've thought once or twice that she was a little too dignified for her own good. I sent her to a nunnery for her education and they taught her some haughty ways. But she's kind at heart and I'm glad to know the kindness is surfacing again.'

'*Kindness?*' Ivon was on his feet. 'She loves me, I tell you! *She'll* tell you! She . . .'

'Sit down and drink your wine,' said Oliver good-humouredly. 'Why waste it? I understand your feelings, believe me, and I'm not angry but—'

'*You're* not angry? Well, I *am*!' He was more than angry. He wanted to weep, to scream, to bang his head on the timber wall around the windows, to kill the mason. He had lived with Hawise in his mind since last year. She was part of him; she could not be torn away from him without leaving a huge, ragged wound in him. With a sweep of his arm he sent his goblet hurtling to the floor. The crimson wine splashed the rushes like blood. He wished that it were really blood, Oliver's for preference.

Or FitzSimon's. FitzSimon, the gatekeeper had said, wanted to see him. Well, it was mutual! 'A villein, am I? We'll see about that!' He leant over the table to shake a fist under Oliver's nose. Oliver did not move. The sympathetic smile on his bearded face was the most offensive sight Ivon had ever seen. It was too much. He could not bear this, not compassion as well as the loss of Hawise, the loss – oh God, no, let it not be true! – the loss of his freedom too. He let out a single expletive, the most foul of all the words he had learned from the Bretons in Norwich Castle and tore out of the guest-house, wrenching back the door-curtain and hating the latch because it didn't resist him and gave him no excuse to kick the door.

Outside, without pausing to think, driven by a rage which blinded him to the world, he made straight for the hall. He wanted someone or something to attack and hoped the doorward would obstruct him. But the doorward knew who he was and that FitzSimon had intended sending for him, and let him in with a casual: 'You're prompt. But the steward's gone now, so go along in.' He plunged into the dimness of the hall and discovered FitzSimon at the other end of it, sitting at a table on the dais and dictating to a clerk. He looked up. 'Oh, there you are, Ivon. Excellent. Come up here, will you? I've some news for you.'

To reach the dais, and the muscular figure of Gilbert, facing him across the table, he had to march the length of the hall and by the time he was on the dais, in spite of himself, some of the heat had gone out of him. Even through his haze of fury, he could see that Gilbert, tawny wool tunic stretched taut across his bull-like shoulders and thick, hairy forearms protruding from his embroidered sleeves, was not something to trifle with. Ivon was suddenly aware of himself as being only a boy, of no status, no power, in the presence of a man possessed of both. He halted in front of FitzSimon and stared at him, feeling the misery of hopelessness begin to sap his fury.

But he owed it to himself, and to Hawise, to speak up. 'My lord, I wish to ask you about something!'

'What? Oh, on your own account? Well, certainly. What is it?'

Ivon clenched his fists at his sides. 'It concerns the terms under which I . . . I hold land from you, sir!'

'Indeed? If you had any questions, you should have asked them yesterday. However . . . what is it you want to say?'

He wasn't sure. The scalding and abusive words which had burned in his brain as he ran from the guest-house wouldn't come out, not in Messire Gilbert's hall, in Messire Gilbert's presence. Instead, he blurted out the question at the heart of it all. 'I'm to work your land two days each week in part return for mine. Does that make me a villein? Am I villein or free?'

'Villein, of course. What on earth's the matter, Ivon? You're getting your two acres on very favourable terms; you're young and strong and should easily have time to cultivate it as well as carrying out your other duties. I could have driven a much harder bargain, had I wished. But I didn't wish, of course. I wanted to reward you, for a service I much appreciated; after all, but for you, I wouldn't be here. I'm presenting you with your own potter's wheel, as a gift. Why should being a villein worry you? You were born a thrall, after all. Well, Norman law doesn't allow that kind of thralldom, but without land you wouldn't have been much better off. Land gives you status. You've nothing to complain about. I assume that this is a complaint? Your tone of voice and your thunderous expression suggest it.'

'I was not born a thrall! Who said I was a thrall?'

Messire Gilbert's eyebrows rose. 'Are you questioning me? Not that it matters. My brother, Abbot Maurice of St Cuthbert's, did. He made some enquiries about you, apparently. He assured me that you were bondborn.'

Involuntarily, Ivon's hand went to his chest where, under his tunic, he could feel the knobbly outline of the carved dagger-hilt which his grandfather had given him. 'But my grandfather . . .' He stopped.

FitzSimon looked slightly puzzled. 'My brother did not mention your grandfather. Who was he?'

In Ivon's mind, at once, there was a check.

Momentarily, he stood silent, trying to frame words but balking at them like a horse confronted by a ditch too wide to leap.

As a boy at St Cuthbert's, after Gunnor's death, he had declared that he was free but indignantly denied that this was due to any kinship with those foul creatures, Norman knights.

He was older now and he knew more about knights. He knew that they came in all shapes. He was talking to one now.

Yes, indeed he was. And this one in all seriousness believed that his land grant and its terms were for him a coming-up in the world. Messire Gilbert in all seriousness believed that he, Ivon, should be content to be a villein and grateful to be one! Grateful to be, once again, a piece of property at his lord's beck and call. Grateful to be too far down the social scale even to look towards Hawise.

The attitude he had adopted in muddled fashion in St Cuthbert's, when he was ill and grieving for Gunnor and still very young, now crystallised within him. He saw it in his head as though it were written there in the elegant Carolingian hand which the novicemaster had taught him.

In claiming to be freeborn by right of a freeman grandfather, he was telling the truth and he could legitimately tell it as loudly and as often as he chose.

But although he might – because he must – endure the company of Norman knights, although he might even occasionally find one likeable, such as Messire Guy, never, never would he claim one as a kinsman, not even to obtain his freedom. Not even to save his life. He owed that to the dead of Eric's Dale.

As for the carved bone dagger-hilt that Old Ivon had given him, he would wear it in memory of the grandfather he had once loved. But under his tunic, hidden, a secret, private thing.

It did not occur to him that he was still very young to make a choice so final. Had he stayed at St Cuthbert's, he would have been bound by even graver vows by now. His integrity seemed bonded into this decision. He did not know that his instinctive need to maintain his integrity came from the de Clairponts and that they had cultivated it as part of knighthood.

'My grandfather was free,' he said sullenly. He was going to lose the contest. Anyone could say his grandfather was anything. Even a knight. FitzSimon would probably just have laughed at that, anyway.

'My brother didn't mention that,' FitzSimon said. 'But what of it? A child born out of wedlock takes the mother's status. Your grandfather may have been free but your grandmother . . . well.' He shrugged. 'These casual liaisons in out-of-the-way places . . . if you've been building on that idea, I'm sorry, but I couldn't afford to grant you your freedom even if I

158

wanted to or felt it was best for you, which I don't. I'm in debt, Ivon. I'm only here, you're only here, because my brother paid to save us from exile. I need men to work the Rushley land and get the corn out of it, and I can't afford to pay freemen to do it. I shall be straitened for cash for years and years to come. Which brings me to the reason why I wanted to see you today. This may please you. You may take a seat; there's a settle just beside you. *Raoul!* He raised his voice to a shout and a very young page came hurriedly through the door which led off the dais. 'Fetch some ale, Raoul. Three beakers, for me and the clerk and Ivon here, or, no, make it four and have a small one yourself.' He turned back to Ivon and said with a smile: 'Villein or not, you're a man of means now. Perhaps you can guess what I wanted you for.'

'No, sir,' said Ivon bemusedly. His lord could hardly want to borrow money from him. Man of means or not, he had no cash. He took the settle. Somewhere, beyond the partition which divided the back of the dais from another room beyond, he could hear women's voices, and one of them was that of Hawise. He knew it instantly, even though he had not heard it for months, even though it was beyond a wall and mingled with others. He couldn't live without Hawise. Would she agree to run away with him? Or would she wait? If he said: I'll work, make pots all night, by candlelight, sell them in Norwich, save and save and save till I can buy all the hangings and goblets and fine gowns your father thinks you ought to have, would she wait? Would her father let her? Oliver would probably say: Can you afford the candles?

'. . . you'll be helping me to do a favour,' said Messire Gilbert, as the page arrived with the ale and the beakers on a tray and began to serve it. 'But you'll be doing yourself one as well. You're a lusty youth; you ought to get some healthy sons to follow you in your workshop and on the land and the sooner you set about it, the better. And meanwhile, you'll have two cows of your own – you can graze them on the common pasture – and five pounds of silver . . .'

Ivon dragged his mind away from the elusive, will-o'-the-wisp of sound which was Hawise's voice. 'My lord? I don't understand.'

'I'm talking,' said Gilbert FitzSimon, 'and we are about to drink a beaker of ale to, the happy and immediate prospect, Ivon, of your marriage.'

'There is no question whatever of you marrying that boy Ivon,' said Oliver the Mason to his daughter, 'that must be understood. But tell me – did you want to?'

He had brought her back from the hall as soon as dinner was over, telling their two servants not to follow for a while. They were alone in the guest-house, sharing a settle. The evening was cool and the brazier had been lit. Hawise, who had been gazing at the pierced pattern round the top, through which light and heat flowed towards her, glanced thoughtfully up.

159

Since the death of Oliver's wife, father and daughter had grown close. They had abandoned much of the formality usual between fathers and daughters. They treated one another as friends.

With a candour which would have been beyond most girls when talking to their fathers, above all on such a subject. Hawise said: 'I thought, after so long, that he'd forget, or at least that he would see it wouldn't do. I encouraged him at Norwich, I know, but . . . in that castle, nothing seemed to be real. It was like being in another world. Whether people were villeins or freemen didn't matter, because we might all be dead by the next day . . . and even if we ever escaped back to everyday life, I felt that nothing I said or did in Norwich could carry over. He was kind one day when I was . . . upset about something; that's how we began to talk to each other. He showed me the pottery workshop there.' She stopped.

'I won't ask if you actually did anything which might have carried its consequences over. Clearly there weren't any, anyway.'

'I didn't,' said Hawise. 'Please believe me. It never went so far.'

'When did you realise that it wouldn't do?'

Hawise sighed. 'The other girls – the countess's girls – they didn't like me. Eventually, they noticed that Ivon was . . . was paying me attention. Once, one of them said to another: "She's got a lover among the men-at-arms," rather nastily, looking slantwise at me. And then one of the others – one of the nicer ones! – turned to me and said, "Well, good luck to you; he's one of your own kind," I think not meaning to be rude, but it seemed rude to me. It put me on Ivon's level and I felt that as insulting. I didn't see what that meant at first. But after we'd left Norwich . . . well, gradually, I realised. That girl was wrong. He isn't my kind, and if I could be angry because someone thought I was . . . then he's not the man I should marry. But I did catch his eye at the Lady Day court yesterday. I smiled at him. Well, I had to; I couldn't cut him, not after encouraging him as I had, though that was only because I was so miserable and lost. I'm sorry, Father. I suppose I did give him cause to think it worthwhile to speak to you. I wish I hadn't. I wish I hadn't smiled at him yesterday!'

'A smile isn't a crime. But he's badly smitten, Hawise, and I don't think I want you and Ivon in the same locality henceforth. I'm going to take you back to Rouen, my dear. My head mason can look after the laying of the foundations for Messire Gilbert's house, while I take you to your uncle, your mother's brother. You'll be very welcome there and your uncle can look out for a husband for you; someone from a mason's family. It's time you stopped roaming about the countryside with me.'

'I've enjoyed it,' said Hawise. 'Most of the time, at least. I didn't enjoy Norwich. If I hadn't been so terrified during the siege, none of this would have happened. I'd never even have noticed Ivon was there. He was very kind, Father. But he's a villein. I understand that.'

'Once or twice,' said Oliver, 'I've thought that those nuns we sent you to as a child gave you too many notions of your own dignity. But I see now that they were right. People need to know their worth. You're a good girl, Hawise.'

'You've done *what*?' said Mald to her husband Walter of Oxfen, jolted for once out of her smiling serenity.

'I have settled with Gilbert FitzSimon that Haesta's daughter Ragenhild should marry a Rushley boy. FitzSimon is quite willing to co-operate. But for his brother's intervention, he'd be in exile and he knows very well that he'll be looked at askance by his more respectable neighbours for a long, long time. He's, shall we say, anxious to get on well with us . . .'

'But the *bull*!'

'As it happens,' said Walter, smoothly overriding her, 'there's little difficulty, because the girl apparently wants to marry into Rushley anyway. Gilbert's wife Bertrade likes to keep apprised of what goes on in the village, at least as far as women's affairs are concerned. She was there when I went to see Gilbert and she told us straight away. The girl likes a Rushley lad called Ivon and it so happens that Gilbert wants to reward this lad for something or other and what better than a marriage with a good dowry? Haesta's been having trouble finding someone for his daughter and he's giving two cows with her now and increasing the amount of silver. So FitzSimon will request the marriage, I'll agree, Haesta will get his daughter married . . .'

'And he'll still have to hand over his best animal to you in compensation for letting his girl marry off the manor because that's the law! You'll force him to agree and then fine him for it! You're going to seize his bull!'

'Haesta has no business to have a bull anyway.'

'Then why not just seize it anyway, without all this rigmarole of a marriage? You might as well!'

'I prefer to act under the law where possible. And this way, a number of people gain. The young couple get each other and neighbourly relations are improved between FitzSimon and myself.'

'It's outrageous!' Mald, sitting up in the marital bed, positively glared at her husband in the candlelight.

Walter smiled lazily, leaning on an elbow. 'Are you angry, my Mald?'

'Angry! It's . . . it's cheating! Poor Haesta! He was a freeman until you came here and now you're stealing from him because he's a villein – who made him one, I'd like to know?'

'Dear me,' said Walter. 'What's this? Passion?' He moved closer and Mald moved away. He laughed, and his hand closed on her hair, not roughly but firmly, drawing her averted head towards him. His other hand slid warmly round her body.

'*No!*' said Mald.

'Yes,' said Walter. 'Yes, yes, yes. No mere, damned villein can come between *us*, my love.'

'You think not? My first husband would never have done a thing like this, never!'

'Your first husband,' said Walter, sure of himself, feeling the response in

161

her, knowing that it was against her will and amused by this, 'was no doubt a paragon of justice and kindness in his dealings with his tenants and maybe announced his so-humane judgements in a louder voice than mine but he never made love to you as I do.'

'You'll do as I bid,' FitzSimon had said, 'or I'll take away your land and still force you to work on mine just for the right to share Cob's cottage and make pots to earn your bread with. Don't make any mistake, Ivon. I mean it. What's wrong with you? I offer you a girl with a dowry to make your mouth water and you look at me as though I'd attacked you with an axe. Learn sense, boy, before it's too late.'

In Cob's house, Ivon lay face-down on the pallet where, that morning, he had lain with his hands behind his head and said that he was happy. It was a new straw pallet; he'd paid Biddy to make it for him and he had hoped to share it with Hawise. He pressed his face into it, trying to lose himself and his wretchedness in the friendly darkness.

Ragenhild. What sort of substitute for Hawise was that plain, sallow, wide-eyed little fool going to be? Better live celibate until he died than that. He wished he'd stayed at St Cuthbert's.

He could have thrown his head back and said: 'All right, take my land away, make me work on yours and live on making pots or cadging from Cob. What of it? I've shared Cob's bread since I came here, and I haven't starved. I still saved your life once and you know it.'

He was proud enough to say that, but he wasn't cruel enough. He could have withstood the threats against himself but not the one which, before he had time to speak, Gilbert FitzSimon had made against someone else.

'If you won't marry Ragenhild,' FitzSimon said, 'I'll have to find her another man, for she's going to marry someone in Rushley, that's definite. I rather think, Ivon, that if you won't agree, I'll present her to Cob. He's got quite an eye for the girls and he envies the way Ragenhild looks at you, or so my wife tells me. I know he's not quite the sort of husband most girls would want but there it is. She's never done you any actual harm, has she, Ivon? *Surely,*' said FitzSimon, laughing as though this were an extremely funny joke which he actually expected Ivon to share, 'you're not unkind enough to abandon her to Cob?'

No, he wasn't. He wasn't unkind. He was a villein, that's what he was, a helpless, put-upon villein. He loved Hawise: her proud walk, her mer-queen's eyes, her warmth, her scent, her kiss, would be part of him until he died.

But he was going to marry Ragenhild.

PART IV

Ragenhild,
AD 1076–1103

1096 This was a very heavy time throughout all England, both in manifold taxes and also through disastrous famine, from which this country suffered greatly this year . . .

1098 This was a very grievous year . . . through the heavy rains which did not cease all year; nearly all the tilled land in low places was ruined . . .

1099 This year also at Martinmas, the great sea-flood came up and did so much harm that no man remembered its like before . . .

1103 This was a very grievous year in this land . . . in death of cattle and perished crops, both corn and all fruit; also . . . the wind did more harm than any man ever remembered before.

The Anglo-Saxon Chronicle

Chapter Eleven

Alone in Company

Ragenhild of Oxfen finally knew how alone she was on the day that her son Edric was born.

Rushley's inefficient wise-woman Biddy was also Rushley's fairly competent midwife and she had been worried about Ragenhild from the start of the pregnancy. 'Too skinny, that's your trouble. Pity they didn't let you wait a year or two an' grow a little more. Girls ain't all the same. Some don't breed to start with and some do but shouldn't. You'd best eat hearty and watch what you do when you're working. No bending or lifting. I seen you heaving they bags of clay about; well don't, not no more. I'll be ready when your time comes and let's just hope you widen a bit round the hips between now and then. You're still growin', so you might.'

But she hadn't, and knew it as she crouched, terrified, on a pallet in Biddy's cottage. Ivon, who would have built a home for that other girl, Hawise, that he'd told her about in one of his bitter moments, had never built one for her and in Cob's cottage there was hardly room for the three of them at the best of times.

She had once, during the autumn, been forced to stay in bed for four days with a cough and a fever and Cob had called her a nuisance to her face. But whichever cottage she was in, the fact remained that her pelvis was too narrow for childbirth.

She had lost track, now, of the passing of time, but it was two nights, surely, since this horror began and struggle and cry as she might, sometimes crouching on all fours and sometimes lying on her back, clutching and dragging at a piece of hide rope attached to a roof beam, there was no result. Biddy was droning charms and doing something or other with hot cloths but nothing made any difference . . .

Another dawn must have come; the cottage door was ajar and sunlight made a glittering line at the edge of it. There was a world out there, full of light and air and everyday things, and people walked about out there who were not in pain and not in danger. Biddy, now, was stirring a potion over the fire and a cloying, sweetish smell drifted from it.

'Summat to ease the pain a bit,' Biddy said, seeing Ragenhild's frightened eyes on her. 'Best we can do; try to get you some rest an' save your strength.'

'I'm going to die, aren't I?' She got the words out before another convulsion seized her. It was unbelievable, that the meaningless, trivial thing that

Ivon had so reluctantly done to her had led to this. It was unbelievable, too, that she, Ragenhild, barely seventeen, should be here on this bed, trapped in the narrowness of her own tormented body, facing death and almost too exhausted to resist. Yet another clenching contraction seized upon her and she screamed, despairingly.

'Here,' said Biddy, arriving with the potion. 'Take this.'

'I don't want to die! Do something, help me . . . I can't believe this is happening. I don't want it to be happening. I want to go to sleep!'

'Drink, I said. Come on. That's right. And no more talk about dyin'.'

'Ugh! It tastes horrible! I want my mother!'

'Ah, well, things bein' as they are, you'll have to put up with old Biddy. You're young, that ought to help you through.'

Other village women had come from time to time, to assist Biddy or relieve her. The cottage brightened momentarily as two of them pushed the door open and entered. 'How is she?'

'Still fightin'.' Biddy tilted the cup ruthlessly against Ragenhild's mouth while Ragenhild choked and gagged. 'One of you, get some chicken broth hot; it's in that pot there. She's got to take summat.'

'Her husband's outside, wanting to know how things are.' One of the women, rolling up her sleeves, came across to examine Ragenhild.

'Is he now? Well, well, not before time,' said Biddy. 'Come on, girl, drink up; keep tellin' you, it'll do you good . . .'

Once again, an enormous pain seized upon Ragenhild, arching her body into the air. It was as though she were trying to give birth to the pain itself; it was like a solid thing distending her and fighting to be free, hurling itself against the too-narrow door between her sweat-drenched thighs. She swept Biddy aside with her arm, sending the cup to the floor. Women crowded round her, strong hands gripped hers; someone commanded: 'Now, bear down, go on, push, *push!*'

She couldn't push. She was too tired. She was dimly aware of the door being opened again and a figure appearing in the entrance, and of one of Biddy's helpers moving quickly to stand in the way. She heard her husband's voice. 'Is there any chance of saving either of them?'

The woman spoke, in low tones. She couldn't hear what was said. But Ivon's voice, replying, came to her clearly, cutting like a sharp blade through her anguish and exhaustion. 'If neither of them live, it might be a blessing.'

And it had all begun so differently, so much like a dream come true.

'I'm to marry Ivon?' she said when her father, who had been summoned to the hall for an interview with Godric the Steward, came back and told her. 'I'm to *marry Ivon?*'

'Aye, you are,' said Haesta grimly. 'Your mooning round the potter's shop got you noticed, seemingly. If I'd had the good sense to make you marry last year when Wulfric Cowherd was interested in you and your dowry, this wouldn't have happened. But no, you must needs go whining that you don't like Wulfric, he's too old, and like a fool I give in to you. If you'd been wed, Walter couldn't use you against me. It's my bull he's after. Hah! It's a favour asked by the lord at Rushley, Godric says to me. They're short of young girls and FitzSimon wants to see this Ivon with a wife. And since it's been seen that you're keen, he's made so bold as to send word on your behalf to Messire Walter. Pack of lies! Godric was shuffling his feet; he don't like being made a party to this sort of thing. "Messire Walter's disposed to agree," says he, "and it's true enough you're having a job fixing your girl up, so it's doin' you a favour in a way. But the law's the law; if your daughter weds off the manor Messire Walter claims your best beast. Can't waive the rules; it 'ud cause resentment." *Walter* dreamed this up, not anyone at Rushley, mark my words. "You don't really have a choice," says Godric. "It's a goodwill thing between Oxfen and Rushley, but still, you *are* gettin' Ragen off. Best just accept it; Messire Walter don't like folk causing trouble. Your tenancy could be at risk if you argue," says he. Well, you'd not have argued over marrying Wulfric, if it hadn't been that you were too busy makin' a fool of yourself over Cob's boy.' He raised a clenched fist and Ragenhild dodged, taking cover behind her mother.

'You're being a bit too hard,' said her mother mildly. She was standing at her well-scrubbed pine worktable, packing cheese into round moulds. 'Who could have foreseen this? We all reckoned Ragen would grow out of her nonsense . . .'

'It isn't nonsense!' said Ragenhild defiantly, with a wary eye on her father. 'I *do* want to marry Ivon!'

'What you want's not important,' her mother told her sharply. 'But we were prepared to be patient with you for a bit and it's plain now we made a mistake. Still, as I said, no one could guess this would happen so it's not right to blame you. Only I wouldn't be too sure you're going to be happy ever after, my girl. Ivon's not the one who asked for you.'

'I saved for years to buy that bullcalf,' Haesta said. 'I'll never afford another. I'd like to kill Walter. An arrow in the back, that's what he's asking for.'

'Now, don't talk like that!' His wife's hands, usually so sure, began to tremble. She stopped working on the cheese. 'You know what happens to people as do things like that. We can rear one of this year's bullcalves, can't we?'

'It'd take years and then he'd only be half-bred, Hildi, you know that. Our bull's a different breed from our cows, better. Anyhow, what's the betting Messire Clever-Clever Walter'd find a way of grabbing that one as well?'

There were tears in his eyes. He blundered out of the cottage. Hildi wiped still-tremulous hands on her apron and sat down, fumbling to put back the yellow plaits which were sliding loose from her linen cap. Her hard-featured face was anxious. 'I'm all of a shake. You didn't mean it, Ragen; it's our fault for being soft with you, but if you hadn't been such a naughty, silly girl, this wouldn't have happened.'

Ragenhild didn't care. Her parents were always fussing over what they called 'building up,' and 'not acting like villeins whatever Messire Walter calls us'. None of it meant much to her.

Adults were peculiar; they never seemed to understand what was important and what wasn't. Didn't they know, hadn't they ever known, what it was like to be in love? Hadn't they ever walked round a corner and simply come face to face with someone and known, from that moment on, that this was the person whose face would be henceforth pictured in one's mind unceasingly, the person to whom one belonged? Hadn't they ever lain awake at night planning how long to wait before walking again in a certain direction?

She had been very careful. Her mooning about had been noticed, they said, but she had tried not to moon; she had rationed herself rigidly, so that Ivon should not tire of seeing her. No oftener than every three weeks, unless an errand arose that was not of her making. Whenever one of these self-imposed deserts of time drew towards its end, her excitement and expectation would rise to unbearable heights. She would hug herself secretly and invent for herself wonderful conversations she would have with Ivon the next time she – oh, so casually – drifted into the Rushley pottery.

When she did actually see him, however commonplace the conversation, she would watch every movement that he made, remember every word he said, so as to take them away with her as memories to live on until next time. On the days when she hoped to meet him, her feet always wanted to dance and everything in the world, the flames in the hearth-fire, leaves in the wind, sunlight on the rippling waterways, seemed to dance with her. On those days, even raindrops in a puddle were like the footprints of merrymaking sprites.

Her parents might dismiss all this as silliness; Ragenhild knew better. And now the miracle had happened, which she had longed for but could not by herself bring into being. She had hoped, desperately, that one day Ivon would look past the thinness of her body and the sallowness of her face and the gaps in her teeth, and see the truth of the adoring heart they concealed, and ask for her. If Ivon, who had travelled, who had been, now, to war and back, could once be brought to fight to get her, surely he would win.

Now there would be no fighting required. The lords who controlled their two manors were in agreement and wished them to be married. Let her parents grumble and disapprove. Ragenhild was in heaven.

She hoped Ivon would come to see her but he didn't and she wasn't allowed to visit him. She couldn't even use the excuse of going to see Aunt Withy, because her aunt had died that winter. But meanwhile, there was work to do. Her mother unlocked her personal chest and took from it a length of yellow cloth which she said she had had put by for years, against Ragenhild's wedding day. It had to be made up into a dress. There were other clothes to make as well and, later on, much cooking of pastries and cakes for the marriage feast. 'We'll do it properly,' she heard her mother say to Haesta. 'No call to have folk sniggering because we've been put upon. I've told them she begged so hard to marry Ivon that we ended up asking Messire Walter for his consent.'

'That's daft. Everyone for miles knows better than that,' Haesta said.

'Maybe, but if we hold up our heads and keep on saying what I've just told you, they just might get to wondering whose story's true,' said his wife.

The wedding day came, one month later. Ivon came with it, accompanied by Cob and a good selection of Rushley villagers, dressed in his best dark red tunic, which went unexpectedly well with his hair; punctual, unsmiling and so handsome that Ragenhild felt faint at the sight of him.

They stood before the altar in the little church which belonged strictly speaking to Oxfen but actually served both villages, and the priest united them in marriage. It was one of the few occasions on which Ivon had ever come to church. He hadn't even attended to hear his forthcoming marriage announced. Rooks cawed in the elms behind the church and the sun shone through the small, arrow-shaped windows. Messire Walter attended, standing at the back. Ivon made his responses in a resonant voice which was already deep for a boy of his age but he never looked at her and when he took her hand, his felt cold.

After they were pronounced man and wife, everyone shouted: 'Go on, kiss her!' and he complied but impersonally, as though she were an elderly relation. She did not know that at the time, lacking enough experience. She understood it later.

The feast was held out of doors because the weather was good, and there was dancing, to drum and pipe and lute, on the green patch at one end of Oxfen, where the old men always gathered to gossip on summer evenings. Messire Walter joined in and danced with her.

Then she walked to Rushley with Ivon and his chattering escort of villagers. Her personal goods – her clothes in a little walnut chest, some household utensils, and her mother's gifts of a spinning wheel, a small hand-loom and an enormous cheese – were carried on a borrowed donkey. Cob, who had come to the wedding looking unrecognisable because someone had made him wash and get into a new russet jerkin, led the two cows which were part of her dowry, and Ragenhild carried the bag of silver which was the rest of it. Ivon did speak to her once or twice on the way, politely, as to a stranger. He commented that the feast her mother had provided had been very good, and said that it was fortunate that it hadn't rained.

At Rushley, the cows were put in their new byre and, amid a great deal of laughter, Cob was told that he'd better not sleep at home tonight, it might make him jealous and over-excitement wasn't good for a man his age. The donkey was unloaded and led away while Ivon and Ragenhild

169

carried her goods into Cob's dwelling. There was more noisy merriment and a number of the Rushley villagers crowded in after them to drink a toast to them in ale. Then Cob, who was being rather sullen, was firmly dragged out, Ivon was slapped heartily on the back and recommended to 'get to work; you've been idle all day', and then, suddenly, they were alone together.

It wasn't at all as she had imagined. When in her daydreams she and Ivon were alone like this, he had taken the lead, had talked to her, courted her. She had been able to toss her head and pretend reluctance, had been coaxed inch by inch on to the pallet where, with her heart thumping and her breath short, but her eyes held fast by his . . .

All Ivon said, once he was sure that the wedding guests had gone away, was: 'I don't want anything more to eat today. Do you?'

'No. Oh no. There was such a lot at the feast.'

'I'd better show you where things are, though, ready for tomorrow. We keep bread in that crock, and there's a ham hanging up over there. Those jars there are for flour, lard and honey, and the cooking gear is on that shelf. I'll put up another shelf tomorrow for the things you've brought and clear a space for your spinning wheel. I went to the well myself this morning and there's water in that pail in the corner. And you can put your chest at the foot of the pallet. This pallet's ours. Cob sleeps over there but I've rigged up a curtain. He won't be back tonight, anyway. That's the latrine bucket; in the morning, I'll show you which stream we empty it into. It's one the cattle don't drink from . . .'

'Yes, I know the one.'

'Oh, of course. You must know the village well.'

'Everyone does, in Oxfen, and the other way round, too,' said Ragenhild, sounding defensive before she could stop herself. 'There's always been plenty of coming and going.'

'Yes. Well. There are some turfs piled up over there; you'd better bank the fire and then I suppose we'd better go to bed.'

He said it as though it were nothing special, and turned away as he spoke. Although the evening was still light, it was dim in the cottage with the door shut and she couldn't at first see what he was doing. Then she realised that he was undressing. She paused in the middle of damping the turfs. He moved, to put his folded clothes on a stool, and stepped into the firelight.

He was as beautiful as she had thought he would be. The firelight picked him out, the shadows sliding between the strong ribs and the muscles of his back, finding a fugitive red-gold gleam from a dusting of hair on his chest and stomach. But he was also disconcertingly real, a solid piece of unpredictable masculinity, and he seemed utterly indifferent to her. He did not look towards her or tell her to hurry, or show the slightest interest in persuading her to undress. She must just get on with it, she supposed. Perhaps when they were in bed . . .

She already knew, at heart, that nothing was going to be as she had dreamed it would. She was also very tired, not only by the day just gone, but by the long month of living with the undercurrent of her father's anger, which had had more effect on her than she knew. To her horror, a few tears fell to help with damping the turfs. She brushed them angrily away. There was nothing to cry for. She was Ivon's wife as she had longed to be and this was their wedding night. She ought to be happy. She *was* happy. And she was going to see that Ivon became happy too. He didn't know her well yet, but when he did, everything would be all right.

She finished seeing to the fire. Ivon had already retired to the pallet. She took off her own clothes, rather shyly, although her bridegroom was lying with his head turned away. Copying what he had done, she folded her garments and put them on another stool before inserting herself timidly under the rugs alongside him.

She was at once aware of the heat of his body and wanted to draw close to the comfort of it but hesitated, waiting for him to make the first move. Eventually he sighed and edged towards her and at last the hands, the body, she had longed for, took possession of her. But they did so without affection or coaxing, and her own cautious attempts to explore him with her hands drew no response; she was like someone seeking a foothold on a completely perpendicular cliff.

There was no magic, no joy. She kept thinking: This is Ivon, this is my wonderful, handsome Ivon; I turn dizzy at the sight of his face. But even when, after his first, perfunctory touching, he pushed the rugs aside to give himself more room, she could hardly see him in the shadows and he could have been anyone.

He wasn't rough, but he was impersonal. He knelt up, tugged and pulled at her without speaking until she was in the position he wanted, and then proceeded briskly to a business which seemed to her extraordinarily clumsy and uncomfortable. She was bumped about for a considerable time in his grasp and there was pain, not very much, but enough to turn the whole process into an endurance exercise. It was like the times when she was a child and her mother had combed her hair too briskly.

Then it was all over and Ivon was saying, kindly enough: 'Thank you, Ragenhild. Here's a piece of cloth; you'll want to dry yourself.' She wiped away the sticky wetness which this uninspiring initiation had left behind and turned to Ivon to find that he had settled down with his back to her, pulled the rug over him and was apparently asleep. She went to sleep too, pressed against his back, wishing he would turn over and cuddle her but knowing, already, that he would not.

In the morning, he greeted her politely but uninterestedly and went at once into the workshop, leaving her to set about whatever domestic tasks presented themselves. She made up the fire, went to the well and tried to smile mysteriously when the other women met her there and said to her slyly that she was up very early, but having a good time took some people that way, came back again and made bread dough.

Later, she prepared food for Ivon and Cob and herself. Cob, who had now come back, combined surliness and sniggering in a way which made her shudder. The night was a repetition of the one before except that this time she knew that Cob was on the other side of the curtain.

Lying on the pallet afterwards, trying to fall asleep, she wished desperately to be home again in Oxfen and did not know how to bear her longing, or face the fact that she was here, with Ivon and Cob, for ever.

It was hard to believe that this man whose bed she shared, who scarcely spoke to her except on mundane matters to do with food and clothing, was *Ivon*, whose face had sent her reeling the very first time she saw it. There were the high cheekbones and the remarkable eyes, the difference between them not marked enough to look freakish, but noticeable enough to be fascinating. There was the thick hair which was unlike any she had seen before, warm red-brown like the sweet chestnuts her father brought back from Norwich every autumn, for them to eat. There was the fascinating, indefinable air of belonging to some higher form of life than herself.

But it had made no difference. He had given her nothing of himself, nor asked anything of her beyond compliance in a rough-and-ready night-time ritual, and attention to some everyday domestic duties.

By the time a month had gone, she had sunk into a dull acceptance of a life as humdrum as the one she had had in Oxfen except that now she was working harder since in this household she was the only woman.

She supposed that, after all, she had been just as silly as her parents said she was. On the first day of her fifth week as a wife, as she performed her morning tasks, livening up the fire, making oatcakes and frying strips of cured pork for breakfast, she made a decision.

There was no need for anyone else to know what a fool she had been. She would never admit it. It was time she paid a visit to her parents; she should have gone before. There would be questions her mother would want to ask. She would be very careful indeed about the answers.

Fortunately, she could return the right answer to the most important question of all. Her mother might not seek any further.

Ragenhild paused, suddenly smiling. Perhaps, after all, there might be something to look forward to.

When they had eaten, Ivon said: 'I'm working in FitzSimon's fields this morning.' She had already noticed the contempt with which he always spoke of his overlord. 'I'll be ditching,' he said, 'over on the west side of the hayfield. Can you make me a noon-piece? Bread and cheese and an onion or something, and a flask of ale. I'll be in the workshop meanwhile.' He glanced irritably towards Cob, who had woken up complaining of his rheumatics and was still on his bed. 'I shan't be in *his* way, evidently.'

Ragenhild nodded warily, knowing that on days when he was on duty in FitzSimon's fields, he was short-tempered. His heart was in the workshop. He sometimes swore because so much of the profits had to go to Fitz-Simon, but ignorant as she was, she could still see that to work with the clay gave him a deep pleasure that the lord's demands could not outweigh.

Even working on his own land didn't please him like that. Whenever she entered the workshop, she did so very respectfully, feeling as though she were intruding on some hallowed ritual.

When the noon-piece was ready, therefore, she went to fetch her husband a little nervously. He was arranging a row of small bowls on a shelf and Ragenhild, seeing them, could not forbear exclaiming at their colour.

'Those are lovely. Halfway between blue and green. I've never seen anything like that before.'

'I knew I could get a green tone with copper ore,' Ivon said. 'And in St Cuthbert's, where I learned that, the monk who taught me did say once that the tone could be changed by mixing in white sand and some kind of salt; he said one could buy them both in East Anglia. When I last went to Norwich, I found them for sale there, but the first try I made didn't work. The glaze cracked. But I've done it now!'

Ragenhild had made little of all this but was glad that he seemed pleased. 'They're as pretty as anything.'

'You can have a couple to use in the house if you like,' said Ivon. 'I take it that's my dinner you're holding?'

'Yes.'

He sighed and put a cloth over the turquoise-coloured bowls. 'I must be off, then.'

'Where you'll be is on the way to Oxfen, ain't it? I could walk with you. It's time I called on my mother. I could go today.'

'Eager to tell her all about it, are we, then?' Cob said when these plans were conveyed to him, but Ragenhild pretended not to hear and Ivon muttered something to Cob which sounded very like 'Leave off,' although she couldn't be sure.

But as they set off, Ivon suddenly remarked: 'Cob's a rude old man. I'm sorry.'

'I don't mind him,' Ragenhild said. 'He won't do anything he shouldn't, now that I'm married to you, and what he just says don't matter.'

'No, that's true enough,' said Ivon and she ventured to smile up at him. Without warning, her spirits soared. 'It's a good day for being out of doors,' she said.

It was. It was a May morning, still early enough for the dew to be lying. She was walking at Ivon's side and carrying his noon-piece in a shoulder-bag, and last night she had slept beside him. There was no other woman in the world with the right to do these things. And although he was on his way to FitzSimon's land, he had been pleasant to her. Perhaps it was nothing to do with her, but was only because he'd made the turquoise bowls so well, but it was enough.

Suffused with a joy she hadn't known since her wedding day, she began to chatter, talking about the haymaking – 'It's always fun, with everyone joining in' – and a ridiculous story she had heard from the women at the well, about one of Biddy's terrible potions. 'It cured Ham Eelfisher's headache but it made him sick, and when he complained, she said it was supposed to!' Ivon actually laughed once or twice. It's happening, she thought: We're starting to make friends. If I go on, serving him devotedly, day after day, he will love me. If what I think is going to happen next year is true, he *must* love me.

There were others abroad as well as themselves. Two Rushley men with spades over their shoulders were trudging along the path ahead of them, and far away ahead, the tip of a raft-pole showed intermittently as someone, perhaps the Ham Eelfisher who was Biddy's latest victim, set out along a waterway, no doubt in pursuit of the eels which gave his clan their name. They were a self-contained family of indeterminate status, who lived in a set of tumbledown shacks half a mile from Rushley and spent most of their time fishing but also worked a few acres in return for supplying Rushley with eels and other watery delicacies.

The path led past the Eelfishers' holding and past the fields worked by FitzSimon's man-at-arms. Rafe Gros-Nez kept himself to himself and most people knew his holding simply as the Norman's Land. Beyond it, the track led on across a meadow to the ditch where Ivon's work lay. She handed him his food bag, smiling, hoping he would kiss her goodbye. But he merely nodded, said: 'Give my respects to your parents,' hung up the bag on a bush and turned away to join the men who had been walking ahead of them and were already getting down to work. Ragenhild, the morning dimming a little, sighed, crossed the plank bridge over the ditch and went on her way.

Ahead, the track cut through the belt of trees called the Narrow Wood, followed the banks of the alder-hung Upper Wend along the edge of the pasture which had once belonged to Rushley but was now the property of Oxfen, and climbed the steep Green Dyke which had been built years ago to direct the river round the pasture instead of across it. There was another bridge, a stouter one, and then the path forked, the righthand track leading away towards Oxfen manor-house, which like the one at Rushley stood apart from its village and on slightly higher ground.

Ragenhild stopped at the fork, interested, because horsemen were riding towards her from the house. It must be Messire Walter with his usual knight escort; she could see the sunlight flashing on their helmets. She waited to watch them pass.

Ragenhild had been only eight when the new Norman lord first came to Oxfen and, to her childish and uncritical eyes, the knights on their fine horses, so much bigger than the ponies she was used to, were a splendid and heroic sight. She gathered soon enough that those around her did not see them in quite this light, but that first impression had never left her and she still enjoyed marvelling at them.

They went by at a brisk canter, going towards Rushley, oblivious of the small figure at the fork, and Ragenhild turned regretfully to go on down the lefthand track to the village. Then she saw that someone else besides the knights was in a hurry this morning. A woman, skirts and shawls flying, was running towards her. A moment later, Ragenhild saw who it

174

was and herself broke into a run. Her mother must have been out in the fields and seen her from a distance. How lovely, that her mother was so glad to see her. 'Mother . . . !'

'Ragen? What brings you here?' Hildi caught hold of Ragenhild's arm. Her face was dead white. 'Have you seen your father, did you meet him? Quickly!'

'No, why? Mother, I've come to—'

'Oh God, oh God! I was at the well and he was gone when I came back . . .'

'I haven't seen anyone.' Ragenhild was bewildered. 'Only Messire Walter and his men going off on the Rushley path.'

'What? Oh, dear God! Your father must have known!' Hildi jerked Ragenhild round and began to run once more, dragging her daughter after her. 'He'll have gone by the river bank, oh come *on* . . . sweet Mary be with us and let us be in time . . .'

'But what's happened, what's the matter?' Ragenhild, who was being towed at an angle of forty-five degrees, tripped over a stone but was ruthlessly yanked onwards.

'Your father's threatened to kill Messire Walter, that's what's the matter!' Hildi talked in gasps as they ran. They had left the fork behind and were tearing back towards the dyke. 'Ever since the lord's men took the bull away . . . he made a bow and shafts . . . we're not supposed to have them; it's trouble even if you've got them in the house . . . I quarrelled with him . . . hurry, hurry . . . should have taken and burned them; he'd have half-killed me but better that than . . . went to tidy the bed and they'd gone from under the pallet . . . He's taken them and he means mischief . . . mad, he is, out of his head . . . oh no!' sobbed Hildi, as they tore along, arriving at last in sight of the plank bridge over the ditch where Ivon and his companions had been working. 'We're too late!' Hildi wailed, and Ragenhild, finally understanding, broke from her mother's grasp and raced ahead, in terror.

The little knot of men and horses was still some way off. It seemed to take for ever to reach them. When they did, however, Ragenhild arriving first and her mother following with one hand clamped to a stitch, it was clear at once that nobody, least of all Messire Walter, was dead.

Walter, manifestly uninjured, was sitting tall in his saddle, controlling a restless mount with his left hand while his right rested aggressively on his hip. Two of his knights had dismounted, and one had his hauberk and shirt off so that the other could examine a dark red streak across his shoulder blade. The patient, however, was talking volubly; he was not perilously hurt. So much, Ragenhild and Hildi took in at a glance.

With their second glance, they saw others were there too: Ham Eelfisher, boat-pole in hand, and the ditching party, with Ivon among them. They were gathered in a cluster close to two knights who were sitting on their horses, and all of them were staring at something on the ground.

It was Haesta. He was lying on the grass. And, although he was alive, something was horribly wrong with him.

'Haesta!' Hildi screamed, as she and Ragenhild threw themselves on their knees beside him.

He didn't answer. He was snorting and jerking and his face was a suffused and unnatural crimson. One eye was distended and the other half-shut, and one side of his mouth was dragged down. He was also dripping wet. Hildi sprang to her feet again and shrieked: 'What have you done to him?' at Messire Walter.

'No one but God has done anything to him,' Messire Walter said. 'He shot at us – at me, I think – from those trees over there.' He pointed across the bridge, to the alders. 'He missed me but the shaft dug a furrow right through Messire Reginald's hauberk. It would have made a worse hole in me; I'm not wearing one. I sent two men to catch whoever had done it. They found a bow and shafts floating downstream and then they dragged this man of yours out from under the bank. He was trying that old trick of lying under water and breathing through a hollow reed. But the water wasn't muddy enough to hide him. They fetched him back. Naturally.'

'But how did he get like this?' Hildi cried. 'Haesta! Oh, Haesta, please answer me!'

'When I had him here,' said Walter coolly, 'I told him that even though no one had been killed, this was not a crime that could be allowed to pass. There's no doubt that his was the hand on the bowstring; innocent men don't hide at risk of drowning. He's been lucky, Mistress Hildi. I told him he would be blinded for this but God struck first. I had hardly finished speaking when he fell down in a fit. You can take him home. He's harmless now, and will be for the rest of his life. I fear it won't be a long one, but he has brought that on himself. You'll be fined most of your holding of course and you'll lose those grazing rights. But he's in no state to look after his holding, anyway.'

Ragenhild listened, numbed with shock but her mother took in only the first part of this horrific speech. 'You were going to *blind* him? First of all you steal his bull and then you meant to . . . !'

'God have mercy,' said Walter, 'on anyone who imagines that I and my men are roebuck and that they have a licence to hunt.' He smiled, feeling rather proud that his command of English had been equal to such an involved sentence and such an imaginative figure of speech.

Hildi stared at him in loathing. The full meaning of the things he had said was dawning on her. 'I must be on my way.' Messire Walter sounded impatient. 'I see you've got your shirt on again, Reginald. You'd best go back and get that wound tended properly . . . My good woman, it seems to me that you people don't know when you're well off. I'm a patient overlord compared to some and more tenderhearted than is good for me. Your husband complained because I took the bull I was legally entitled to, which he, a villein, should not have owned in the first place. For this day's work, a harsher man than I am would fine him every foot of land he holds and his

176

entire herd of cows, even now, in lieu of the blinding iron. I shan't, because your tears would distress me. I shall leave you a corn patch and a couple of cows to graze on the common. I repeat: I'm magnanimous. If I were FitzSimon of Rushley, you'd lose everything, I promise you; be glad he's not your lord. FitzSimon of Rushley,' said Walter coolly, collecting his horse and nodding to his men to get into formation round him, 'rode with King William's army for the scouring of the north. No tears would move him, believe me.'

From behind her, Ragenhild heard Ivon's voice saying, expressionlessly: 'Messire Gilbert wasn't in the north at the time of the harrying. It was over before he came to England.'

'Came back, you mean.' Messire Walter eyed this impertinent villein coldly. 'Are you contradicting me? For your information, although I can't think why you should care, Gilbert FitzSimon was at Hastings, with the men the de Gaels sent to the king. So was I; we were together. But I stayed in England and Messire Gilbert went home for a while after the fall of Ely, to see his wife. Then he came back to join Earl Ralph. Oh yes, FitzSimon's seen it all. He isn't one to play games with. But I give you fair warning; though I'm gentler than he is, neither am I. Well! We've wasted enough time. I've business at Rushley.'

'Somebody help me!' said Hildi, as the Normans spurred away, leaving a curious vacuum behind them. 'Somebody help me get Haesta home! No, no, not you, Ragenhild. I don't want you and your father won't, either. If you'd been a better daughter and married Wulfric, this wouldn't have happened. We'll be no better than cottagers, for the rest of our lives, and all because of you. Go back to Rushley; that's where you live now. Don't come near us again.'

'But, Mother . . . !'

'No! Go after your husband.' Hildi pushed her away and went to help as two of the ditching party came to lift Haesta between them. 'You wanted Ivon,' she said harshly. 'So go with him, go! It doesn't look as if he's got much time for you now, either, but that's for you to deal with!'

Ragenhild, suddenly aware that Ivon was no longer near her, got to her feet and looked wildly round.

Ivon was some distance off, walking away, back towards Rushley, as though he had no interest in her, or Haesta, or anything that lay behind him. Irresolute, she turned back and called: 'Mother!' but Hildi too was walking away, beside the men who were carrying Haesta, and she did not seem to hear.

Frightened, Ragenhild ran after Ivon. He was striding along with his eyes fixed straight ahead. She spoke to him but he did not seem to hear either, and it was as though she were alone, surrounded by an unseen wall which kept her voice from being heard by anyone.

She thought, all the way back to Rushley, as she ran and stumbled, trying to keep up with his relentless stride, that this was the worst and most

177

inexplicable thing that had ever happened to her. Her father might be dying and her mother had rejected her, and now Ivon himself seemed too angry to speak to her and she did not know why.

But when they reached home, worse was to come, for he made straight for the workshop, strode in, overturned the table, with both hands swept a row of pigment jars off a shelf, and then snatched off the cloth which covered the row of little turquoise-coloured bowls and heaved up the tray. Ragenhild cried: 'What are you doing?' but he took no notice. He hurled the pots against the wall. Some of them broke and some fell rolling, and these he caught up and smashed at his feet, one at a time. He picked up a lump of clay and plunged it into his water bucket and worked it frenziedly in his hands. When he had it soft, he hurled that at the wall too, where it splattered and stuck, sending runnels of dirty water down to the floor.

'Stop!' Ragenhild shrieked. 'Stop, stop . . . Cob! *Cob!*'

Cob had heard the noise and was there already and for once she was thankful to see him. They caught hold of an arm each and somehow dragged Ivon through into the living quarters, where he shook them off, flung himself on the bed and began to beat it with his fists and make a howling noise like a wolf, half-muffled in the pallet, but still horrible.

After a long time he became quiet and lay still, shuddering. Then, slowly, he sat up, looked at Cob's outraged face and Ragenhild's terrified one and said to Ragenhild: 'You'd better go home, back to your parents.'

'Back to my . . . ? I can't, my mother wouldn't have me, she says it's my fault Dad went and tried to kill Messire Walter . . . you didn't hear that because you walked away. And then you came back here and started smashing things.' To her own surprise, Ragenhild found that she was angry as well as terrified. 'Why? *Why?* You gone mad or something?'

'Gone mad,' echoed Cob. 'Must've.'

'Yes, maybe,' said Ivon. 'Maybe!' He pulled at a cord round his neck and dragged out the old pendant of yellowed bone which he always wore and stared at it. Then he looked at Ragenhild. She had an odd feeling that it was the first time he had ever really looked at her. Then he began to talk.

It was an attempt to explain but she couldn't understand more than one word in ten. He seemed to be talking about things which had happened to him long ago, before the abbey which she knew about, to do with a burnt farm and a long walk in the snow and people dying of cold and hunger, all of them things outside her imagination.

Then there was something about FitzSimon and the north which she didn't understand either, and then Ivon seemed to be saying that his workshop had been a private place, like a citadel or a shrine, and FitzSimon had got into it and thrown the filth of his body all over the walls.

She was frightened anew, because his angry eyes were demanding a response she didn't know how to give, and what he was saying was insane; the workshop was in a mess but Ivon had done it himself and it wasn't that kind of filth anyway.

Then she heard the last part of what he was saying.

178

Because of what FitzSimon had done, whatever it was . . .

'I can't create new things in my workshop any more, because *he'll* get profit from them. And I can't be your husband, Ragenhild. I can't be a husband to any woman. Wives have children and I couldn't look any son of mine in the face, and tell him I've let him be born in bondage to . . . to *that*. Oh God, to think I saved his bloody *life*! I pretended it was only the king that was guilty but it isn't true, it isn't true. I've tried not to be unkind to you . . . I don't want to be unkind . . . if you can't go home to Oxfen, stay here and keep house as my sister. That's all I can offer. Forgive me.'

'Excuse *me*,' said Ragenhild. She rose, walked with great dignity to the door, stepped outside and was sick. Then she walked back and sat down at the table. 'It's late for taking a vow like that,' she said. 'I'm already with child.'

'You're not going to die. I never heard such nonsense.' She swam up from black depths and found Biddy standing over her. 'Muttering in your sleep, you were. But you've had a good sleep and you've no fever. You made it, my girl. Young bodies like yours can stretch. Sit up . . . ah, sore, are we? That'll pass. Have a look at your son.'

Something was pushed into her arms, a warm bundle with a red, squashed-looking face. She said slowly: 'Ivon . . .'

'He's seen him. He sent good wishes,' said Biddy shortly.

'I know. I heard them.'

'And what might that mean?'

'What it sounds like!' She spoke with an acidity which surprised her. 'He hoped we'd both die. He doesn't want me or the baby.'

She had lived, all these months, with his bitterness. She had feared sometimes that it would freeze the very child within her. It had been in one of his fits of cold anger that he had told her about Hawise. It was the blessing of God, he said, that at least he had not been married to Hawise. He might not have been able to give up making love to Hawise, she supposed he meant. It clearly cost him nothing to reject Ragenhild.

'Has anyone told my mother?' she asked and then added, still in that tough, acid tone: 'Don't bother to answer that. She's still saying it was my fault my dad died. I know.'

'Lot of daft rubbish,' said Biddy, roughly commiserating. 'It weren't you as hid in the alders with a bow.'

'No. Well. Did Ivon suggest a name for him?'

'No, he didn't and what if he did, after what he said? You pick a name for yourself. Your father's father was called Edric, and that's a good plain name and he was a good man with more sense than some I could mention. I'm beginning to reckon, though,' said Biddy, regarding her with knowing eyes, 'that you might take after him. It's showing up, all of a sudden.'

'Is it? Oh, well. Edric'll do. Can you get word to the priest, about a baptism?'

Edric, she thought, holding him fast. Edric. A real person, her own flesh

179

and blood. He might be a friend, someone close. Bereft alike of parents and, to all intents and purposes, her husband, facing the long years at the side of an unresponsive Ivon who had wished her dead, she would need a friend.

Unless she could win him back. Biddy would say she was mad to try, mad to forgive Ivon now, but forgiveness, Ragenhild said to herself, thinking it out, trying to be a person of sense like her father's father, wasn't the point. She had no alternative except to face those long years at Ivon's side; she had nothing to lose by trying to sweeten them. She had a dogged nature, anyway. She had fallen in love with Ivon; she had ordered her life as a journey along that road and no other and she did not quite know how to give up.

Perhaps, when she was well again and when Ivon got to know his own son, he would soften and if so, she would be waiting.

Chapter Twelve
Echo of Times Gone By

It was half a day's ride from Norwich, where the man who had once been Thane Brand had spent the night, to Rushley. He had never been there before, but he had obtained directions in Norwich. Yes, here was the place where three paths met. The two to the left went off respectively to manors called Redesmarsh and Oxfen; the righthand way was his.

He pulled up, however, wondering whether, strictly speaking, he ought to be here at all. He was fifty miles out of his way, and his errand was such that he should ideally have made straight for the Monastery of Ely without glancing aside.

Brand, however, had never been a man who kept rules, not when the claims of friendship were pulling the other way. He urged his horse forward again. As the reed-thatched roofs of Rushley village came into sight, he suddenly laughed. It would be just his luck, after his long journey and his heartburning, to find that FitzSimon wasn't there.

But he knew as soon as he reached the hall that this was unlikely to be the case; the place was far too lively. Gilbert FitzSimon's slate-roofed stone manor-house was smallish – he'd been hard up when it was built, Brand remembered – and, when he had given his name at the gatehouse and ridden through into the courtyard, he found himself with hardly room to move.

Half a dozen horses, tied to stable doors, were being briskly wisped down; and a man who must be the steward was overseeing the business of unloading barrels from an ox-cart without knocking down a pile of trestle tables stacked under oxhide covers, while simultaneously fending off the importunities of two rival pedlars and directing a group of minstrels to take themselves and their instruments into the hall. Someone else went by, shouting to a minion that yes, splendid, all the mule loads were very neatly laid out ready but five loads for four mules wasn't too clever, now, was it? A groom came up and said: 'We've run out of stable space, sir. Can your horse go out in the meadow? The weather's still good; we've had a dry September.'

'Brand!' said FitzSimon, striding across the courtyard from the hall. He checked briefly, his eyes going to Brand's hair, which had been dark when they last met at Norwich and was now iron grey. Courteously, however, he refrained from comment. 'The gatekeeper sent his lad to say you were here. I didn't believe it and made him say your name twice. How do you come to be in England and how did you know to come here? You've come to the wedding, I take it?'

'No. What wedding? Yes, turn the horse out to grass. I'll take those saddle-bags first.' Brand dismounted and began unstrapping the bags. 'I've made my peace with King William, Gilbert. It's a long story, but the gist of it is that he knighted me in Normandy before '66, and he doesn't forget. He'd sooner men like me gave him their fealty than have us stay in exile. I've put my hands between his and now I'm free to go where I like. Who's getting married?'

'My daughter, to the son of my neighbour Walter of Oxfen. I wanted the betrothal long ago but then Earl Ralph sent for his followers to come to Norwich. Walter and I had words over that and the betrothal idea came to nothing. Then, that is. But the next year, after I'd been home for a while, and done him a small favour or two, to show the past was behind, he suddenly rode over to see me and said all right, what about it? I'll call someone to carry those bags.'

'I'd rather carry them myself. There are precious things inside although they aren't wedding presents because I didn't—'

'Never mind that; God's Teeth, we can hardly move inside the house for presents and women's clothes and whatnot; the hall looks like a market. That was a day to remember, when Walter came to offer for Adelisa. Some aggrieved peasant tried to shoot him on his way here. He said afterwards that that was what decided him. He'd set out intending just to sound me – about the dowry and so forth – but by the time he got here he'd made up his mind that solidarity between Norman neighbours was even more important than he'd thought. Here we are,' said FitzSimon, stepping briskly up the steps to the hall door and leading the way in. 'As you see,' he said apologetically, 'all we need are some booths with striped awnings.'

Brand laughed. In the hall there were more trestles, laden with new bolts of dyed woollen cloth, embroidered silk and bleached linen; silver bowls and candlesticks – 'They came from Redesmarsh; I couldn't afford them,' said FitzSimon – household gear of all kinds, jars of honey and mead and flour, a pony's saddle and bridle in red leather, with gilded studs and scalloped reins. Servants moved here and there, setting things out for display.

'My daughter in Sussex never had all this when she married her Norman,' Brand said. 'It seems a great to-do for a very simple matter.'

'When she married her Norman,' repeated Gilbert thoughtfully as he led them up to the dais, which was still reasonably uncluttered, and motioned Brand to take a settle. 'I always talk to you as though you were Norman too but that's absurd. You speak my language and you are a knight but when I met you, it was only four years since you'd been picked up half-killed after fighting on Hereward's side at Ely.' There was a table on the dais with wine and goblets. 'Have some of this. I'm keeping it out because people come calling all the time. All the ladies are shut up in the solar upstairs, trying on dresses; we'll see them presently. I don't annoy you, do I, when I talk about Normans as though you were one of us?'

'No,' said Brand, amused. 'I got used to it in Norwich.' He sipped his wine and scanned the hall. 'I shall have to think of a way to contribute something. When is the ceremony?'

'The day after tomorrow. You'll stay, I hope. Tell me, if you weren't coming for the wedding, what brought you?'

'I'm travelling to Ely Monastery,' said Brand. 'But I came out of my way to see you, because I thought you'd like a glimpse of these.' He had put his saddle-bags down on the floor and now bent to open one. 'When I was in Normandy, being sheltered by kinsfolk, the Monastery of St Evroul was close by and I visited it often. The abbot entrusted me with something to deliver to Ely. I think you'll appreciate this. You were always knowledgeable about artistic things.'

'It looks bulky,' said FitzSimon as Brand inserted his fingers with some difficulty between the saddle-bag and the felt-wrapped bundle it held.

'It is. I just had room for one spare shirt and my saddle-cleaning things . . . here we are.' Brand drew the bundle out and put it on the table. He then moved the wine flask and their two goblets aside. 'Whatever happens, nothing must be spilt on this.' Tenderly, he folded back the felt. 'There.'

'Sweet Mary!' said FitzSimon, awed.

His thick fingers, which when encountering works of art were also so reverent, came out to touch the gemmed covers of the two books now displayed. 'What are they called?' A fingertip traced the gilded lettering slowly. 'I learned my letters as a boy but I don't often have occasion to practise. The Gospel according to St John . . .'

'The other one is Matthew. The gospels of Luke and Mark are in the other saddle-bag. It's a full set.'

Gilbert was turning pages. 'I've never seen finer illumination. I had a small manuscript collection at one time, you know, but I sold it after Norwich. I've paid off most of my debt to my brother. Not that he was demanding it, but till it was paid, St Cuthbert's had a lien on Rushley. Are these new? The script is modern and they look new . . . but there's something in the design that reminds me of much older manuscripts that I've seen, from Lindisfarne.'

'You're right. The monk at St Evroul who designed it was trained at Lindisfarne and was sent to St Evroul to train others. He's famous. Ely commissioned this years ago.'

FitzSimon was touching the illustrations gingerly. 'Gold leaf, crushed malachite, powdered lapis . . . they've used the best pigments, I can tell. What beautiful vellum. These are worth a fortune.' He looked up. 'And you've been riding, on your own, through the countryside with these bumping about in your saddle-bags? You should have had a squadron of knights to escort you!'

'I had one in Normandy and on the ship coming over. But I have to admit that King William has made the rule of law strong here in England.

There are few robbers now. One elderly man on a not very impressive horse can ride about as safely as any armed squadron. All I had to do was not discuss the contents of my luggage. But I thought you'd enjoy seeing these, and since I was coming here to say goodbye to you in any case . . .'

'Goodbye?' Gilbert, who had once more been turning St John's exquisite leaves, stopped in surprise.

'Yes, my friend,' said Brand. 'I'm leaving the world. I became the Abbot of St Evroul's messenger because he knew I would be going to Ely after I had seen the king. I have a friend at Ely, a monk, who will speak for me and I am going there to present myself as a candidate for the tonsure.'

'But . . .' Gilbert heard Mass regularly and considered himself a pious man. He had even been comparatively faithful to his wife during the years when he was in England and she was on his knight's fee in Brittany. But the idea of taking even a technical vow of poverty like his brother Maurice appalled him. His debt to St Cuthbert's and his resultant straitened finances had been for him major disasters. He was still riding what he considered to be a second-rate horse and this house of his should be twice the size it was. 'What about your old home in Sussex, Fallowdene? Won't your daughter and son-in-law take you in?'

'Certainly they would but I don't wish to be taken in. I was master of my manor once. It was a long time ago, before the Conquest, but one doesn't forget these things. My daughter's widowed now, but if I went back there, I should still be no more than a caretaker for my grandson. I don't want that. I'm tired, Gilbert. I'm over sixty and my breath comes short when I hurry. Look at my hair. That's happened all in the last few years. Ely will be a haven, where I won't have to . . . oh, I don't know . . .'

'Be continually kicked in the guts by the past?'

'Yes.' Brand nodded. He looked away, down the hall where a young man had just come in, carrying a large osier hamper. 'More gifts, by the look of it. Yes, those are the words I couldn't find. I've had a complicated life, you know. I've been trapped between conflicting loyalties for almost all of it, it seems. Trapped between Normandy and England . . . it's no wonder you talked to me as though I were another Norman; I sometimes wonder myself. It hasn't been easy. Well, you know my story. I want to rest, to be quiet, and give my loyalty in just one direction for a change. I've decided to give it to God. It's a thoroughly peaceful prospect and at least I'll have a place to belong to. I shan't be just a tolerated guest at someone else's hearth. Surely,' said Brand, dismissing the subject and watching the young man with the hamper as he asked a maidservant where he should put whatever he had brought, 'surely, Gilbert, that's Ivon. He was with you at Norwich. He was there when the commander was killed by that flying rock and we came across him once making earthenware in the castle pottery. Making it rather well, too.'

'Yes, that's Ivon. I ordered some new tableware for the marriage feast. This wedding is costing me nearly everything I had left after repaying Maurice. You were lucky, my lad. You turned into an outlaw after

184

Hastings and you didn't have to bear the cost of your daughter's marriage.'

'Yes, I did,' said Brand. 'I told you; I paid with my manor. My son-in-law got it along with his bride. If I remember Ivon aright, he had an eye for shape and colour. Would he like to see the manuscripts?'

'My dear Brand. He's just a villein, you know.'

'Does it matter?'

Gilbert gazed at his guest and then laughed aloud, slapping his knees so that down in the hall, interested faces glanced his way. 'That's you all over! Does it matter, indeed? You've spent your whole life questioning whether things matter that everyone else takes for granted. All right!' He raised his voice. 'Ivon, come up here!'

Ivon had surrendered his burden and was about to leave. He turned back and came up to the dais. He had matured, Brand saw, into a tall and very well-made man, but he was not as good-looking as he had promised to be. His features were handsome enough but his red-brown hair was straggly and far from clean, and his eyes, which had once been striking not only for their colour but for their alertness, had a dull, withdrawn expression. Most people at Rushley nowadays wore bright clothes. On his way there Brand had seen woad and madder growing; cheerful garments would be easy to come by even for people who wore only homespuns and never bought made cloth from Lynn or Norwich. But Ivon, who had had an eye for colour, wore brown and dun, plentifully streaked with clay. 'My lord?'

'Ivon, this is Thane Brand. He met you at Norwich. He is delivering some books to Ely Monastery and thought you might like to see them. You can read, of course. You learned that at St Cuthbert's. So take a look.'

No one had asked him to sit down. Ivon greeted Brand with a respectful good day and leaned his fists on the table to examine the book which Brand now lifted and set before him, open. He raised a hand, noticed that it was grimy, and used the extreme tip of finger and thumb to turn the leaves. He looked for a long time at the tiny birds and beasts and fish and the patterns of precise geometry in azure and green and silver, scarlet and gold, which bordered each page of graceful script and from which each capital letter flowered.

Brand heard him breathe in sharply once and then breathe out on a sigh. He looked up and for a moment, in the sullen face of Ivon the man, he saw the bright eyes of Ivon the boy, who had sought out his craft in the midst of the siege of Norwich. Then the illusion was gone. The sulky villein was back. 'Thank you for showing me, sir. It was very kind of you. I remember seeing such things as a lad in St Cuthbert's. I've never seen anything as beautiful as this, though.' His eyes slid to FitzSimon. 'I have delivered your order, sir. Will there be anything else?'

'No, you can go. See the steward for your payment; the order was outside your terms of service.'

'So he's still here and working in Rushley as a potter?' said Brand as Ivon went out of the hall.

'Yes, although he hasn't fulfilled his promise. I used to think that in him, I'd got something really valuable. I had ideas of the Rushley pottery becoming well known, with customers coming from a distance and young men being sent here for training. But he never comes up with new ideas now and the everyday things he produces are sometimes careless – cracked glazes and handles coming off, that sort of thing. I rewarded him for saving my life, you know; I gave him land on good terms. But he turned crotchety because I didn't treat him as a freeman – I can't think why. He was born a slave; he's risen in the world. He's been a great disappointment,' said FitzSimon with annoyance. 'I fixed him up with a wife. I've been very anxious to repopulate Rushley, as I've told you. I need very badly to get it properly cultivated and making a profit. His wife produced a son six years ago and nothing since. I suppose it's no use expecting too much of the serf mentality, but it's usually possible to rely on their animal enthusiasms.'

Brand said: 'I must give your daughter a present on her marriage. I'll put some business Ivon's way. It won't be a costly gift, but my prayers for her happiness will be with it.'

'Happiness? Why should she be unhappy? She's getting the heir to the manor next to mine. She has everything to be grateful for, and she *is* grateful. She's a good, dutiful girl.'

'I'm sure of it,' said Brand. 'But I've seen a lot of life, Gilbert; probably more than you have. Between a man and a woman, there's more to happiness than that.'

'I used to think that, once,' said FitzSimon. 'But I've changed my mind. Walter of Oxfen and his wife used to have that something more. But not now, and Walter's far more miserable than if he'd never known it at all.'

There was no one in the workshop when Brand went in, although FitzSimon had said that Ivon would most likely be there; it wasn't one of his days for working on the demesne and he'd have little to do on his own land since the corn was in and the sheep were grazing in the stubble.

The place was untidy and depressing. There were two wheels but one of them was broken, and the row of bins had their lids on anyhow. Everything, walls, floor, bins, table, was splashed with clay and what must be spilt glaze materials. He banged on the table and called but no one answered although he thought there were voices beyond the inner door. This looked private, but he thought he had seen another outside entrance so he went out and round to the other side of the hovel-like building. This time his rather peremptory knocking produced results. A woman opened the door.

She was young, but it took about three glances to tell; she was so worn-looking, thin and sallow, with hunted dark eyes and lines in her face which had no business there yet. 'Yes?'

'I want to see Ivon the potter. Is he here?'

'Yes, but . . .'

'Who is it, Ragen?' Ivon appeared behind her. 'Oh, I'm sorry, sir.

186

I heard you call from the workshop but we were busy with old Cob.'

'Who's that out there?' demanded a cracked and ancient voice from within. 'Bring him in. Want to see him.'

'You'd better come in,' said Ivon in a resigned voice.

The place was dim inside and cluttered with hearth, table, loom, benches, stool, a stack of pallets and one low bed which had not been put away for the day. 'Come over 'ere; let me look. Don't often see a new face,' said the cracked voice, and Brand, peering, observed that the bed was occupied by an old man, who was beckoning to him.

'This is Cob,' said Ivon. 'He had the pottery before me, but he's bedridden with the joint-evil now. When you were in the workshop we were just, well, helping him. He can't get up by himself. Cob, this is Thane Brand, a friend of Messire Gilbert.'

Brand went to the bedside and allowed himself to be inspected. Ivon began to talk about the defence of Norwich Castle and how he had met the thane there. The old man listened, nodding his head, and peered through the gloom as though he were trying to memorise Brand's face. Then he seemed to grow tired, mumbled: 'Nice meeting you,' and turned his head away. 'Ragen, where's my supper?'

'Feed him,' said Ivon curtly to the woman and Brand followed him away from the bed, not sorry to do so, for the old man was shrunken and smelly, pitiful and repulsive at the same time. The woman came over with a bowl of porridge, sat down beside Cob and began to feed him with a spoon. He was obviously almost toothless. He reached an eager hand to the spoon and Brand saw that it was deformed, the knuckles knotted and the fingers fixed like claws, a terrible affliction for a former craftsman. Brand turned his back quickly, not wishing to stare, and almost tripped over a stool.

Ivon steadied his elbow. 'There isn't much room in here; we're a bit cramped.'

'I'd like to talk in the workshop,' said Brand, welcoming the excuse. 'I want to buy some of your work.'

'. . . That's settled, then. A set of three bowls, different sizes, jugs to match, and a big pot with lid and spout, all amber glazed with a little painted pattern round the edges.' Ivon recited his customer's requirements. 'There won't be time for anything more than that. You can collect them tomorrow, in the evening, so they'll be in time for the wedding the day after. Thank you, sir. That's a good order; bigger than I generally get. I have to work on my own, of course. Cob's been too ill to work for a long time now and my son's still too small to do more than help knead clay occasionally. It'll be just good, everyday ware for the kitchen; that's what I mostly do nowadays.'

'You showed promise of more than that, once,' Brand said. Perching a hip on the edge of the clay-smeared table, he gazed round the workshop and nodded towards a shelf of jugs. 'I've asked you for a painted pattern. I hope you still have the skill. There isn't a thing in here with as much as a few zig-zags marked on it.' Ivon bristled. As if he had not noticed, Brand said: 'What went wrong?'

'Wrong?' Ivon stared at him blankly. 'How do you mean?'

'You know what I mean. Listen,' said Brand. 'I'm on my way to Ely to enter the monastery there. I'm leaving the world. Very soon, as far as anyone outside the walls of Ely is concerned, I shall be as good as a dead man. So I can afford to be bold in talking to you; I shan't be passing this way again. I was impressed with you in Norwich; your skill, your love of it, the look in your eyes . . .'

'I'm sorry, sir. I don't want to be rude. But . . .'

'I've seen a man before, hurt himself as you're doing.'

Ivon, with an air of finality, stooped to straighten bin lids.

'It was my own son-in-law, as a matter of fact. He was in the north of England during the ravaging twelve or so years ago and when he came home, he had memories that made him ill. You needn't worry about being rude. You should have heard some of the things he called me when I was bullying him to talk to me and set himself free of it.'

'Your son-in-law was in the north?' Ivon stood up sharply.

'Yes. Why?'

It was there again, the flash in the eyes, a glimpse of the Ivon whom Brand remembered at Norwich, young and passionate and still innocent enough to think himself any man's equal. But instead of speaking, he picked up a lump of clay from a shelf, sat down on a stool and began to knead the clay violently between his hands.

'Say it,' said Brand encouragingly.

'I'm a villein. You're a man of rank. The likes of us can't speak plainly to the likes of you. Some of the things we're thinking would offend you, if we said them.'

'I told you, you're as good as whispering to my headstone. When I asked you what had gone wrong, I was guessing that there was a reason – I mean guessing that you, and the work you're doing, could be otherwise if you chose. But it isn't guessing now; I'm right, I can see it. Forget about rank, and forget about offending me. I daresay I'll survive it. Tell me what happened.'

'Why do you want to know?' Ivon, elbows on knees and eyes on what he was doing, worked his clay lump with fury.

'I suppose in case I could help.'

'You can't. I'm sorry, sir, but you can't.'

'All right, but still, I wish you'd tell me.'

'Listen,' said Ivon violently. 'Your son-in-law was in the north, you say, ravaging? Well, so was Gilbert FitzSimon.' The scorn in his voice was withering. 'And I was born on a Northumbrian farmstead.' Once again, as so often before, in words to other people and in the bitter privacy of his mind, he repeated the grim story of Eric's Dale.

'I didn't find out that Messire Gilbert was in it, not till later on. For all I know, he was the very man who killed my grandfather and stuck a torch into our thatch. Whether he was or wasn't doesn't matter, anyhow. He did it to *someone*, to people like us. But by the time I found that out, I'd saved his life and then . . .' He looked up. Yet again, his eyes had kindled, and this time the blaze did not die away but stayed in them, as an old, smouldering anger flared to new life. '. . . and *then*, would you believe it, he said he wanted to reward me and he turned me into one of his villeins. That man is my owner and he wants my work to feed his profits!'

'I see.'

'No, you don't. Sorry, sir, but you're a friend of Messire Gilbert. How can you see, as you put it? I'm sorry but . . .'

'Apologise to me once more,' said Brand mildly, 'and I shall probably brain you with that claybin over there. In some people's eyes, I'm a questionable character myself. I was in Ely with Hereward the Wakeful – you've heard of him?'

'Yes. Everyone has.' The clay in Ivon's hands was turning into the shape of a head. He refocused his attention on it and began to give it a face.

'When Ely fell, I was captured. Well, I'd been knocked out. I meant to fight to the death but in the end I didn't have any choice about it. Gilbert FitzSimon was put in charge of me. It sounds a peculiar way to start a friendship but that's how it began – when we were opponents and I was his prisoner. We still see the world differently, in half a hundred ways. He says he thinks of me as a Norman, as a matter of fact, but I'm not one and never will be. I can well understand why you feel as you do. But . . . look, Ivon, a knight . . .'

'I know.' Ivon was now providing his clay head with curly horns. 'I know what you're going to say. A knight is just a weapon in the hand of his lord. It was the king who did the ravaging. That's why I asked Gilbert FitzSimon if I could go to Norwich with him. I wanted to fight the king. Only it didn't make any difference, not when I knew that FitzSimon . . . when I knew that,' said Ivon, pinching ears viciously into shape, 'my work died inside me, because it didn't belong to me, only to him. Can you understand that? I don't suppose so; I hardly understand it myself. I *can't* make fine things, invent new patterns, find out new ways to glaze them. It's all been smeared, dirtied. I wish I'd let that rock take his head off! Then I wouldn't be so ashamed now.'

'You've nothing to be ashamed of,' said Brand. 'And what you believed when you asked to go to Norwich, was true. The men who ravaged the north were the king's tools. Whoever said that to you first – I doubt if you'd have arrived at it yourself – was right.'

'I hear what you say but it's only words. I don't care. We were the people who died, the people who walked through the snow into nowhere. The men who lit the fires and wielded the swords were responsible. Not just the king. The men, themselves. And I can't forgive them.'

'What exactly did you mean by saying you were ashamed?'

Ivon didn't answer. He put the clay head on the table. It was a gargoyle head, not only horned, but with a leer which stretched from one pointed animal ear to the other, and a suggestion of bared and feral teeth.

'Is that's a likeness of FitzSimon?' inquired Brand. 'He really isn't as bad as that, you know.'

'What he has done to me . . .' said Ivon, and stopped.

'In making you his villein?'

'More than that. When I knew he'd been in the north, I wanted to kill him. But I was there when someone tried to kill Walter of Oxfen – him that's the father of Lady Adelisa's bridegroom – and if the man hadn't been stricken with a fit, Messire Walter would have had him blinded. *Blinded.* I saw Haesta's face when Messire Walter said what he was going to do. I thought what it would mean. Messire Walter said it was the hand of God which struck Haesta down but it wasn't; it was terror. I would like to kill FitzSimon but I shan't because I'd be too afraid. Too damned afraid.'

'And that's what you're ashamed of? But there's no need. You're wise.'

'Wise? I hate myself. But most of all,' said Ivon violently, 'I hate *him*. I hate him for his part in the ravaging and I hate him for taking my work away from me. It was the thing he valued me for, the reason why he brought me here. If I'd known soon enough, I'd have made sure I had no children to grow up as his property. Every time I look at my son . . .'

The inner door from the living quarters was flung open. 'Ivon . . . oh, I'm sorry, it's been so long I thought you'd be alone . . . it's Cob, he's fallen out of bed again and made a mess in his pallet and on the floor and I need help.' The woman Ragen looked exhausted, brushing straggles of hair back from her face.

'Can't Edric help you? He's big enough now to lend a hand.'

'He's out somewhere, playing, as usual. I can never keep him by me; I wish I could. Oh, there's Cob groaning! He could move a bit if he wanted to but he says he can't be bothered. He'd rather lie in his filth . . .'

'Excuse me a moment,' said Ivon, moving after her as Ragen trailed back through the door.

'No need,' said Brand, following. 'I've cared for sick men in my time and the physician at Ely is a friend of mine; I daresay I'll care for more of them in time to come. I'll help you.'

'No, you can't, I couldn't ask . . .'

'You didn't,' said Brand, advancing across the cluttered room towards the grumbling, noisome heap which he had correctly identified as Cob. 'I offered. Mistress, if you'll put water to heat, we'll do the heavy work.'

Between them they stripped Cob of his tunic and washed him, washed the floor, threw out the stained pallet and rugs and substituted clean ones ('We keep fresh bedding in that hammock affair, slung from the roof beams; there's no room anywhere else,' said Ivon), put a clean tunic on the old man and put him back to bed.

When they had finished, Ragen at Brand's request heated more water so that they could all wash, and brought out food and drink. It was some time later, and dusk was falling, when Brand took his leave.

'I'll walk halfway with you,' Ivon said unexpectedly.

They strolled side by side in silence for some distance, before Ivon said: 'I was a long way from courteous. Only, this business goes deep.'

'I can see that.' Brand gave him a quick, sideways look. 'It's corroded everything, hasn't it? Your work, even your married life. You can't rejoice in your son, and both you and your wife lead hard deprived lives.' He paused but Ivon said nothing. Brand took a long breath, reminded himself that he would not pass this way again and that he would have no future link with Ivon that might be injured if he offended Ivon now, and took the risk. 'I'm very sorry for you both and I wish things were otherwise. Could some of them not be otherwise? If the heart has gone out of your work, need it go out of everything?'

Still Ivon said nothing. They paced on for a few yards and then Brand said: 'Tell me, when you were at Norwich, did anyone ever point me out to you as a man with a past?'

'Yes. But no one ever said much.'

'It's a long story,' said Brand, 'or it would be if I told you all of it. There's more to it than having been at Ely with Hereward. Did you ever hear of a place called Gildenford?'

'Gildenford? Yes. There was . . .' Ivon put a hand up to his shirt and fingered something under it. 'Where I was born,' he said slowly, 'there was an old slave who said he was once a Norman knight. He came to England with some great lord or other and the king of the time took it for an invasion and had the lord and his men all seized at a place called Gildenford. I don't know where it is. They were nearly all killed but a few were sold as slaves and he said he was one of them.'

'You have it quite right. I should think your old slave was telling the truth. When I was a boy,' said Brand, 'I served an earl called Godwin. It was he who met the men from Normandy when they landed, announced himself as their host and guide, led them to Gildenford and let them be seized. There was much argument afterwards, over whether or not he had known what the king was plotting, whether he had tricked his guests or whether it was as much a shock to him as to them when the king's men swooped. I wasn't there myself,' Brand said, 'and I'm glad of it. But I heard afterwards, every single one of the king's men was covered from head to foot in blood.'

He paused. Ivon walked along beside him in puzzled silence.

'I followed Earl Godwin for years,' said Brand. 'I loved him. I went on loving him even after I had learned, for sure, that he betrayed those men on purpose. But in the end, I betrayed him in my turn. I did that because someone else had been accused of the crime, someone who was far from being a saint, but was innocent of *that* crime, had never committed any wrong of that order, and was suffering. And so I lost my reputation and I was forced to leave England, until Godwin was dead and his son Harold brought me home. I am an oathbreaker. You know what that means?'

'Yes, sir.'

'Then you'll know that I have more to be ashamed of than you will ever have. But I've never felt ashamed. I think I did right. I shan't be sorry to leave the world behind, Ivon. I've seen too many people suffer for the wrongs done by others. At least I know that the one time I had the chance to defend just one person who'd been wrongly accused, I took it. I hate the sight of the wrong people being made to suffer . . .'

'The wrong ones suffered in Eric's Dale,' said Ivon.

'And perhaps now, too,' said Brand after a pause.

'You mean,' said Ivon, 'that in denying my children to FitzSimon, I am also denying them to my wife.' He sounded furious.

'I've said enough. Too much, perhaps. Let's leave it. That clay head you were making while we talked in the workshop; what will you do with it?'

'Roll it up and use the clay for something else.'

'Please finish it. Fire it and I'll buy it.'

Deliberately, Brand kept his voice warm and calm and Ivon unexpectedly responded with a snort of laughter. 'As part of the wedding present? It might frighten the bride. Have you seen her?'

'Yes. She's very gentle and pretty and it certainly wouldn't do as a gift for her. I want it for me.'

'In a monastery, sir?' *I'm willing to make polite conversation,* said Ivon's tone. *I'm even willing to make jokes, provided you keep off my private affairs.* 'But they won't let you have private property when you're a monk.'

'Then I'll present it to the common room as a warning about the nature of evil. You did it without thinking about it, but it's a grand piece of work.'

'It happened by itself,' said Ivon, and then returned of his own accord to the delicate subject of FitzSimon, although only, it seemed, to end it once and for all. 'Because it wasn't for *him*. He takes a tenth of what I earn as a potter, did you know? And when I think that my son will be his property . . . I know, Ragen gives much and gets little. But there are things I can't stomach any further.'

'It's for you to say,' said Brand. He added: 'Don't let FitzSimon know about that clay head. Keep what I pay you for it.'

Returning to FitzSimon's hall, he thought regretfully that his first campaign as a soldier of God had almost certainly been a sorry failure. Ivon had been civil, but there was a rampart in his mind and Brand had not scaled it.

He was very sorry for Ivon's wife. In Ely, he would pray for her.

FitzSimon's daughter Adelisa had been wedded in the chapel attached to her father's house. Dressed in blue with a cloak of white, eyes modestly downcast, she had made a shy and lovely bride. (Brand attempted conversation with her at the wedding breakfast and wondered if she were capable of whispering more than yes and no). She was then carried off to Oxfen by her bridegroom and parents-in-law, surrounded by spear-carrying knights in polished mail, for all the world as though they had kidnapped her, and once there, she had presumably been bedded.

192

The villagers of Rushley had been given a feast at the house, and most of them were present; even Cob had been carried there on a litter. Edric, the son of Ivon and Ragenhild, had not appeared until halfway through, however; he'd been off on some scheme of his own, as he so often was.

Edric had been company for a time, Ragenhild thought, lying on her pallet in the darkness, aware of his breathing beside her among the piled sheepskins. But that time was passing now. At rising six, he had become a curiously self-sufficient little boy with a liking for his own company. She didn't know where he was, half the time, but he never seemed to come to harm. Physically, he was going to resemble his father; build, red-brown hair, odd eyes and all.

He was old for his years. He had, Ragenhild thought, understood some of the risqué jokes at the wedding feast. It had been a rumbustious occasion; the very air had sung with sex and the sweet warming mead had tasted of it.

On the other side of her, she could just make out the dark humped shape of her husband on the separate pallet where he had lain every night for more than six years. Once or twice she had ventured to whisper an invitation to him to cross the space between them and he had pretended to be asleep although she knew he wasn't. And once, just once, she had tried to cross it herself. She did not like to remember that. He had picked her up bodily and dumped her back on to her own pallet. 'Do that again and I'll put you out in the road,' he said. Cob had still been his old self then. 'If he does, love, you can come in my bed,' he had called. Shivering with disgust, she had pulled her bedcoverings over her head and lain there all night, tightly curled, trying to cry silently, sleepless until morning.

Never again, she had said to herself afterwards.

But now she was going to risk it.

After the wedding, when they were on their way back to the village, staggering a little on account of the mead and because they had one end of the stertorously slumbering Cob's litter between them, Ivon, in a low voice which the friends on the other end of the litter couldn't hear, had suddenly said: 'That man Thane Brand, the one who bought pottery from me to give to the bride. He said you had a hard life. I suppose you do. I'm sorry about that. I wish I could make it easier.'

If it hadn't been for the mead, she would not have answered him as she did, but the rejoicings had made her candid. 'Yes,' she said softly. 'Sometimes it is hard. I'd like more children,' and this time it was Ivon who didn't answer.

Quietly, Ragenhild put back her rug and left her pallet. She moved silently across to his and stood looking down on him. His breathing was even and quiet. He was lying with his back to her. She lifted the edge of his rug and very softly slid in. She fitted herself to the curve of his back and let her arm slide over his ribs. Under her palm she felt the fuzz of hair in the centre of his chest. She lay still.

So did Ivon.

But after a time, he moved, turning from his side to his back. She let her hand move, stroking slowly down over his lean stomach. Her eyes were open and she saw the faint gleam of his; he was awake. He still did not protest. Her hand moved on, found the core of him and rested there. Presently, beneath her palm, she felt him stir.

Then, at last, his whole body moved towards her and over her. He put his face beside hers first, and pressed it there, before he gave her his mouth. They began to explore each other, tracing shape and texture, smelling and tasting, as they had never done in that first uneasy month of their marriage. Then, with a furious eagerness which told her plainly what his self-imposed famine had meant to him, all these years, he entered her and Ragenhild felt herself expand and soften as she had never done in that first month, so that when she received him, it was with joy and not with pain.

Neither of them spoke at all that night. But the next night, when she hesitated, Ivon held out his hand and she came to join him. 'If you wish for more children, it isn't right that I should deny them to you,' he said. 'But Edric nearly killed you. There's that, as well.'

'He didn't quite, though, and I wasn't full grown then.'

Later, when they were lying quiet and spent, he said: 'I'm your husband and I see now that I owe you something. I owe it to you to tell you who you've married. And why it is I hate FitzSimon so. I never did explain properly, did I? Look.' He stretched out an arm and picked up the carved dagger-hilt which lay on the clothes piled by his pallet. 'There's a story behind this.'

He lay beside her and began to talk about his past. She knew that he had once been a novice at St Cuthbert's, for this was common knowledge in Rushley. But for the first time since the Dale was burned, he told some-body not only the tale of that destruction, but the full truth about Old Ivon and himself.

'You mean your grandfather was a *knight*?' said Ragenhild. 'Like Messire Gilbert?'

'Yes. I'm not proud of it. I have told you only because you are my wife and Thane Brand made me see I'd wronged you. But you're never, never to repeat it to anyone else. *Never*, do you hear? I just want you to know you're the wife of a freeman though no one acknowledges it. But the only times I've claimed to be free, I just said my parents were freeborn. I'd sooner be dead and buried,' said Ivon fiercely, 'than admit to having Norman blood in me. I'm trusting you with the secret. But keep it.'

At Oxfen, Messire Walter stood in the solar and listened with disbelief while Adelisa, his daughter-in-law of two days' standing, read out the letter his wife Mald had left before leaving, with two men hired from among those who had crowded to their son's wedding, for Romsey Abbey in Hampshire.

'. . . our son is married now and the house will have a mistress. Adelisa is a sweet, sensible girl and will fill my place very well. I have loved you very much, Walter, but I have been unhappy all these last few years because there are burdens on my soul. In Romsey, I hope to be eased of them. So goodbye, Walter, and thank you for your kindness to me. Try to be a good lord to the people of whom I became mistress when I came to Oxfen with my first husband . . .'

'I don't understand,' said Walter. He thought about the marriage bed in the next room. He would have to lie there alone tonight. Mald was gone, as completely as though she were dead.

The enormity of his loss was not yet clear to him but he knew it was coming; it was rising over his sky like the anvil head of a great thunderstorm. He had not been reared to expect love within marriage. A man simply took a wife to control his home and satisfy lust and give him sons, or so he had thought. When unexpected passion blazed between himself and Mald, it had been an unlooked-for marvel; a lovely astonishment, and when it slowly faded, it was as if summer had inexplicably turned to winter in mid-June.

But at least Mald was still there; he could court her, try to get the warmth back. Now she had gone and he would never, never, cease to mourn her, or understand why she had fled.

Adelisa knew why, but Mald had told her not to tell him and in any case, it sounded quite unreasonable to her. Any peasant who was accustomed to pay rent for his land by working on his lord's farm was a villein, everyone knew that, and if one of his children married on to another manor, then of course his lord had the right to claim his best beast. This man Haesta, that her mother-in-law had been talking about, had been presumptuous to have a bull in the first place. Fancy a villein being in a position to charge his betters for a bull's services! And as for lying in wait with a bow and shafts and trying to murder Messire Walter – well, he was lucky if heaven had intervened to save him from the blinding iron, which he richly deserved. Why in the world such a story should make her mother-in-law say that it was a sin for her to go on living with Messire Walter as his wife, and that she had waited only to see her son married before departing to do penance, Adelisa couldn't understand. She could only conclude that my lady Mald had gone a little mad, as women sometimes did in middle age. In that case, then, it was best that she should withdraw to Romsey Abbey, for she would be a great nuisance about the house.

She placed a gentle hand on her stricken father-in-law's sleeve. 'Dear Father – I may call you that now, may I not? – if Mother Mald has been called to a life of religion, we ought not to try to prevent her. I am sure she will pray for us all, all her days.'

He had thought of ordering the horses and riding in pursuit, but Adelisa made him pause. It was not the way for a fastidious and civilised man to behave, to chase a woman bound for a nunnery and fetch her back in the midst of armed men.

'No,' he said dully. 'I shan't go after her.'

Adelisa made comforting noises to him as best she could and thought, with pleasure, about being sole mistress of Oxfen instead of merely hand-maid to My Lady Mald. It would be very pleasant, she thought. She would be able to stop pretending to be sweet and sensible (by which, she knew, people usually meant biddable), and be herself at last.

She had already inspected the kitchen and noticed a lack of certain spices. No cumin seed, no cardamom. Such things would be obtainable in Norwich; she would speak to the steward today and when the spices had been obtained, she would explain to the cook how to use them.

She would rule this house and enjoy it.

Mald of Oxfen kept looking over her shoulder all the way to Romsey, partly fearing but also longing to see Messire Walter and his knights thundering after her to take her home, but they didn't come.

Chapter Thirteen

The Keepsake

Some women said it was best not to tend the graves of dead children. 'It's easier in the end if you don't brood,' they said. The more pious would add: 'They're with God; what's in the grave doesn't matter.'

Ragenhild disagreed. She never made a show of it; she didn't approach the graves after going to church. But three or four times a year she made time to walk, on her own, to the church that Oxfen and Rushley still shared, in order to put wild flowers or evergreens on the five small mounds. Not to do so would have been to pretend they had never been and this she could not do.

Ivon did not comment except once when she remarked that she had tended her parents' graves as well. 'Your mother wouldn't even have you by her when she was dying.'

'Well, I hope she feels different now she's in heaven,' said Ragenhild.

In the thirteen years between the death of King William the Conqueror (as the result of an accident on campaign) and the death of his successor King William Rufus (as the result of an errant arrow while hunting and opinion was divided as to whether that was an accident), the land had seen trouble.

'Never known such weather,' Ham Eelfisher complained, when the third successive winter set in so hard that streams and marshes froze and landmarks vanished under a thick blanket of snow for weeks on end, and it was said that further south in the true fenland, the landscape was just a sheet of glass with frost-bitten reeds sticking through it like silver spears.

The summers had been as vile as the winters, afflicted with rain and terrible gales which drove the tides up river estuaries, backing up waterways which were already full to bursting. Huge areas of East Anglia had been flooded repeatedly. Four times during those years, the villagers of Oxfen and Rushley had had to take refuge in the halls of their respective lords. Both the manor-houses were on ground just barely high enough to escape and even at that, Rushley's manor-hall had had three feet of water in its undercroft more than once. Everyone had said, when King Rufus died, that perhaps things would improve now; he'd been a man given over to shocking vices and maybe the terrible weather was the wrath of God. But he'd been gone nearly three years now, and under his brother King Henry (who was also thoroughly amoral but in a more normal fashion), the climate was no better.

Bad weather meant bad harvests and the two together meant sickness.

197

Ragenhild and Ivon and their eldest son Edric had come through because all three of them were essentially strong and Edric had been well past his vulnerable childhood when the epidemics began. But five of those who followed him had not.

Two of them had fought so valiantly for their lives, choking slowly on the congestion in their lungs, that Ragenhild had found herself praying on her knees for them to die, to end their suffering. Only an essential toughness, the same toughness which had seen her through the long years of her estrangement from Ivon, kept her sane then.

She hadn't forgotten that. It was another reason for tending the graves. Those prayers had sprung from love and pity but she remembered them as a betrayal.

She hadn't been alone in her bereavement. The epidemics, which took a variety of forms, had robbed most households, the well-off as well as the poor.

Over at Oxfen, the Lady Adelisa, who reigned so despotically over the manor-house, hadn't been able to reign over smallpox or lung congestion or the terrible version of marsh ague which had come for five years in succession. Lady Adelisa too had buried five children although it was true she had three left, and might have had more except that after the first four she grew tired of it and took to talking seriously to her husband about his duty as a knight, whenever King William Rufus launched another of the campaigns which he seemed to regard as sporting events, and indulged in as often as possible. Packing her husband off to war at regular intervals had slowed Adelisa's rate of reproduction down.

Everyone in Oxfen and Rushley knew what Lady Adelisa was like; she was a constant source of amusement. She paid regular visits to her parents at Rushley and, as they aged, the daughter who had once said nothing but 'Yes, Mother' and 'Of course, dear Father,' now ruthlessly told them how to manage their finances and control their villeins. 'Though it's natural,' the villagers said. 'Her son'll inherit, since the marsh ague took her brother off. She's only guarding what'll be his.'

'If FitzSimon dies on us too soon, *we'll* be *hers*,' someone always said meaningly at that point, whereupon the company, resting on its spades or leaning its elbows on a meal table, would shudder, visualising doubled dues on Lady Day and an eight-day week on the home demesne. FitzSimon had piled burdens enough on their backs. His daughter, if she had the chance, would snap their spines like kindling.

FitzSimon and his lady, however, had survived so far and even Ivon now admitted that Rushley would be worse off without them. Ivon, at forty-four, had mellowed into a kind of acceptance although his work remained mostly commonplace. Of late years he had been seized by an occasional creative urge which would have him shut in his workshop for days together – even to the point, on occasion, of paying someone else to do his customary work on FitzSimon's land – while he experimented with shapes and glazes or new kinds of decoration. Ragenhild had some of the results in her home, and so had other villagers; Ivon would give them as wedding presents or in return for services rendered; to those who had done his farm work for him, or to Biddy for delivering Ragenhild.

But none ever found their way to the manor-house or to market. They were secrets, to be kept from FitzSimon.

Cob had died long since, before the epidemics started, but Biddy still lived. 'Been dosing herself with her tisanes since she were a young wench and if they can't kill her, what can?' said Ham Eelfisher.

And for Biddy, Ragenhild might still have work. Ragenhild was almost forty-four now herself and during her thirties had had no successful pregnancies, only a dismal succession of miscarriages and two stillbirths, and the grief of watching all but one of the children she had borne already, die. But at the age of forty-one, miraculously, she had been granted Britt and now, incredibly, she was with child again.

It was spring. The flowers she was putting on the graves were primrose and kingcup and the little wild daffodils which grew under the elms behind the church. She had put Britt, just turned three, to play at the edge of the churchyard, by the path. He had found a patch of mud and was industriously making mud pies, rather deftly, considering his tender age. It would be Britt, Ragenhild thought, not Edric, who one day took over the pottery.

She had put a cloak down on the grass to sit on while she worked because to kneel or crouch was uncomfortable in her condition. She paused from cutting daffodil stems in order to look fondly across at him. He was a delightful child, sturdy as a pony, with his father's red-brown hair in a deep, rich shade, but her own dark eyes instead of Ivon's odd ones. She was glad of that. In Ivon, she had found the oddity intriguing and attractive, but in Edric they just looked unpleasant. This was probably because Edric's habitual expression was one of stare-you-out resentment.

Once, she had thought that Edric might be company for her. He had been, in that respect as in most others, a sorry disappointment.

It was time to go. The morning had started well, but low cloud was blowing across the sky and a wind was getting up. She put her last flowers in place, and stood up carefully, tossing the cloak round her shoulders. 'Britt! We're going home now.'

It was much too far for a toddler to walk, so she had brought the donkey. They had one of their own now. If only Ivon hadn't so much grudged FitzSimon his ten per cent, they could have been better off than they were, because he would have made more goods and better for the market in Norwich. But things could have been worse. They had four cows and an ox, all bred from Ragenhild's original dowry cows, and a donkey which was a particular blessing. She would have had to leave Britt with someone, otherwise. 'Don't you go carrying that great boy any more,' Biddy had said. 'Must be crazy anyway, falling for another one at your age.'

'I couldn't help it. It just happened,' said Ragenhild reasonably.

'You should've come to me. I'd have made it un-happen,' said Biddy. 'I dunno what your husband's thinking of. After this one, you'd best let me dose '*im*, with a love philtre backwards, as you might say.'

'Don't you dare,' said Ragenhild. For most of the other women, sex was exciting in the first year or two of marriage; after that, it was one more chore to be wedged in between shutting up the hens at night and milking the cows in the morning, and when their husbands grew bored with them, they were relieved. But although, fearing disbelief or even scorn, Ragenhild never said it in so many words, she would rather die than not have Ivon's lovemaking, and she was proud of the fact that it was still forthcoming. With the passing of youth, she had unexpectedly come into her own. She still had a gap in her teeth but she had lost that one accidentally as a child, after climbing on the pigsty roof for a dare and falling off. She had kept the rest. She had also ceased to be scrawny and her skin, if still sallow, was not unduly lined. She was better-looking than most of her contemporaries.

As she settled herself and Britt on the donkey, the priest came jogging round the corner of the church, on his speckled mare. He waved and she stopped to wait for him. Father Gerald was a recent arrival, having taken over when his ageing predecessor retired to the care of a sister in Lynn. Gerald was half English and half Norman, young, active and an innovator.

He considered (and had said, frequently and in ringing tones) that since, epidemics notwithstanding, the Rushley population had grown, the place should have its own church and FitzSimon ought to take thought for the state of his soul and dedicate one. FitzSimon, who had barely cleared his debt to his brother before the era of bad harvests set in, was more concerned with the state of his coffers, and was said to avoid Father Gerald whenever possible.

He wasn't going to be able to avoid him today, though. 'Are you bound for Rushley, Mistress Ragenhild? I'm on my way up to the hall. I'll ride with you. I doubt you should be roaming so far from home just now; how long have you to go?'

'More than two months. I'll be all right.' There was no reason to think otherwise. Edric might have nearly killed her, as Ivon had once pointed out, but the barren years that followed had given her time to mature. She had had her children easily since; even Britt, the late arrival, had given little trouble.

'Well, the donkey's quiet enough, I suppose.' He held the mare back to her humbler mount's pace. 'There are guests from various abbeys staying with Messire Gilbert,' he said chattily. 'They're on their way to a meeting at Ely Monastery. I've been bidden to dinner. I must say I wish I were going to Ely with them. It ought to be interesting. There's to be a debate on whether minor orders should observe the rule of celibacy, and examples are to be shown of some remarkable new trends in manuscript illumination . . .'

Father Gerald always talked like that, racing away on whatever subject happened to be interesting him just then, oblivious to whether or not his

200

audience were interested too, or even understood him. Ragenhild sat on the donkey, holding Britt in front of her, resting a hand on her massive stomach, where the baby was kicking, and didn't listen.

By the time they reached Rushley, the wind was gusting strongly and it was beginning to rain. Father Gerald saw her to her door, pulled his hood over his head, said: 'I'm going to be drenched,' and departed at a canter. Ragenhild put the donkey in the shed Ivon had built next to their vegetable patch and hurried indoors with Britt. She was back in good time for getting dinner, but the weather would bring Ivon and Edric home early from the fields where they were working and they'd be glad to find food ready.

She was stirring stew by the light of rushdips and listening to the wind as it buffeted the cottage walls, when Ivon ducked in at the low door, slamming it quickly after him to keep out the gale. He stripped off a mantle black with wet, following it with the rest of his clothing. Ragenhild put down her spoon and went to help rub him dry.

'We all got caught in it,' he said. 'It's coming down in sheets. We were trying to deepen the drainage channels again – that stretch between my holding and Cynric the Smith's – but that's the end of that; all my land and his and Oswin the Freeman's holding as well will be under water in an hour.'

'Where's Edric?'

'I'd be very interested to know that myself,' said Ivon grimly, hauling a dry shirt over his head. 'Ham's grandsons were there and Cynric's boys; there were eight of us digging in a row, and then I glance round and there's only seven, because Edric's sloped off again. He could be any-where. He's probably,' said Ivon viciously, 'snug in a loft with a girl but I rather hope he went fishing and is now wet, cold and wretched.'

Ragenhild sighed and went back to her cauldron. 'Why is he so diffi-cult?'

'You know why as well as I do. I was a fool; I should never have told him who my grandfather was. I shouldn't have shown him that damned dagger-hilt and told him the story of it. I only did it because one day I was feeling soft about my granddad and I thought to myself: he'd want the story handed on. Stupid thing to do. Who wants to be descended from . . . well, I don't, but Edric just has to take hold of the story and start saying we ought to be freemen and why aren't we? Time and again I've said to him, yes, I know, but there's nothing to be done, and God help you if you go about saying – well, certain things just aren't to be mentioned again, and you know why.'

'I've never properly understood why,' said Ragenhild. 'What happened at that place – Eric's Dale, was it? – was so long ago. I never can under-stand why we can't talk about who your grandfather was.'

'I'm ashamed of what he was, and I reckon that when it came to the end, so was he, that's why! However much time passes, it won't make any difference. Bah!' Ivon, had he known it, sounded very like his grandfather.

201

'It isn't a right thing to be proud of and I said it's best forgotten and that's the end of it. Except to repeat that the time I was fool enough to talk about it to Edric is when he began all this business of avoiding his work and treating us as if we were nothing. He always had a sulky streak as a boy but it wouldn't have led to this if I hadn't been so stupid.'

'But I think he becomes sulky because he's not allowed to think or speak about something he knows. I think he feels he has a right to discuss it, to see if anything can be done with it to better ourselves . . .'

'There's no question of bettering ourselves anyhow. How could we? Who'd listen? Now, I'm not talking about it any more and you won't, either. I'll have some of whatever's in that pot while it's still hot.'

Ragenhild rose to serve him. 'There's an obstinate core in you,' she said over her shoulder. 'Like a stone.'

'Maybe. Better not bruise yourself on it,' said Ivon grimly.

The door opened again to admit another gust of wind, and Edric. He was as thoroughly wet as his father had hoped. 'Been fishing,' he said shortly. 'Didn't get anything, though,' He stripped and rubbed himself down, watched by his parents in silence as they sat at the table. Dried and changed, he joined them and stared at Ragenhild. 'Well, can't I have some food?'

Ragenhild automatically rose, picking up the bowl from Edric's place. 'Sit down,' said Ivon.

They both stared at him. 'Sit down,' Ivon said again. Puzzled, Ragenhild did so. 'Edric,' said his father, 'if you're hungry, take your bowl to the pot and fill it yourself. The bread and fried meat's in the middle of the table; you've the strength to stretch out for it, I suppose?'

'Look here . . .'

'Ivon . . .' Ragenhild began nervously. At twenty-six, Edric was a bigger man than his father, and the scowl on his face was alarming.

It didn't alarm Ivon, however. 'It's all right, Ragen. I've had enough, that's all. I've been left toiling while my son wanders off to enjoy himself, just once too often. You can eat this meal for nothing, this one last time, my boy. In future, if you don't work, you don't eat. We're not your servants.'

Edric's scowl intensified. He collected his share of stew as bidden but as he sat down again, he said venomously: 'I'm no man's servant, either. Digging fields and saying yes, sir, no, sir . . .'

'What else do you propose to do with your time?' enquired Ivon. 'No, it's all right, Ragen. It's time we had this out. Things have been getting worse for a long while now. You're useless in the pottery, Edric. What else is there but the farming?'

'There are towns,' said Edric. 'There's the sea. There's fighting and merchanting. I want to get away from Rushley.'

'Well, you can't!' snapped Ivon.

A sudden urgent hammering on the door cut Edric short as he was opening his mouth to argue. Ivon, ignoring his son, went to open it. Father

Gerald, hood over head and his mare's reins over his arm, was standing outside. He pushed back the mare who was nuzzling forward, trying to get through the door and out of the downpour, and said: 'The wind's backing round to the east and the tide will be coming up the river soon. We think there'll be flooding in the village again. My Lady Adelisa's at the house – she came to meet her father's guests – and she says everyone from the village is to come up there and drive the animals up too. There isn't much time to spare, so . . .'

It was not Lady Adelisa's business to give the orders in her father's house, which still had both a master and a mistress. It was, however, very typical.

It was typical too that the orders made good sense. All of them, Edric included, seized dry cloaks and went to it.

'Take Britt and the donkey and whatever clothes and things we'll need and go straight up. We'll bring the cattle,' Ivon said to Ragenhild. They both paused to glance round the cottage, with an eye to moving anything that might be harmed by water, to a high shelf or a hammock. Floods didn't always reach the village but they did so often enough to make people automatically prepare for the worst. The crops would probably be lost, anyway. Ivon stepped quickly to the chest beside the bed and pulled out the bag of silver it contained. 'We'd better keep this safe. Here, take charge of it.'

The donkey didn't want to go out in the rain and Ragenhild had almost to drag him the half-mile to the house. As they went, they met others similarly squelching through the downpour, carrying children or bundles of goods or pushing laden wheelbarrows. Somebody had rescued the Rushley sow, a valuable animal and the property of FitzSimon, loading her on to an ox-cart and restraining her under a net. Five men were trudging alongside the cart. It had probably taken all of them to get her aboard; she was huge, ill-tempered and in pig. The Eelfisher clan, with their belongings in sacks, were poling up the river in a couple of flat-bottomed boats and had collected two or three neighbours to take along with them to the landing-stage at the house.

The gates of Rushley manor-house were open and inside them was confusion. It was no use asking anyone where to go or what to do with the donkey. But it wasn't the first time they'd had to take refuge here. Ragenhild tied the donkey among FitzSimon's oxen in the undercroft; fed it by the simple expedient of taking some hay from the nearest ox-manger, heaved her bag of clothes and oddments over her shoulder, took Britt by the hand and made for the hall.

It was still daylight but the clouds were so heavy that the flambeaux had been lit. The confusion was less in the hall because the Lady Adelisa was standing in the middle of it, directing people. But although orderly after a fashion, it was an extraordinary spectacle. At one end of it, the rain-soaked villagers of Rushley, complete with children and bundles of belongings, were crowding in. But on the dais at the other end, like a palace next door to a slum, a formal dinner for well-dressed people of rank was determinedly in progress. Presided over – and even in the bad light, anyone could see it – by a very angry Gilbert FitzSimon.

This day had been in the planning since the previous autumn, when his brother Maurice had written from St Cuthbert's to say that he was attending a conference in Ely after Easter and intended to go to Norwich first to meet two abbots who would be travelling together from Normandy to the same conference. 'One of them is an old friend of mine; we trained for the priesthood together,' said Maurice's clerk, reading out his master's letter. 'If convenient, we could all spend a night at Rushley on our way to Ely. My friend, Denis de Moulinville, is an authority on manuscript illumination and will address the conference on this subject. You, like me, have a love for beautiful things. You will enjoy meeting him.'

And so here they all were: himself and Bertrade, their daughter Adelisa (unluckily without her husband Roger, who had gout, but had agreed that his wife should come on her own, as a courtesy) Father Gerald, his brother Abbot Maurice, and these two other ecclesiastical guests, men of eminence in Normandy and making their first-ever visit to England, and he had hoped, as Maurice's kinsman, to show them fitting hospitality. And what had happened?

Just as grace had been said and they were all sitting down to dinner at an elegantly white-draped table and he was thanking heaven that he had managed to replace the silver plate he had sold long ago for St Cuthbert's benefit, his bailiff had arrived. To step with diffidence but resolution on to the dais and announce that the river was lipping its banks even while the tide was still at ebb and the wind was backing east.

The bailiff, whom FitzSimon at that moment would willingly have killed, was only obeying orders. During the last ten years they had all learned to recognise the danger signs and agreed on how to act on them. If flooding seemed imminent, FitzSimon, or his representatives if he should be absent, must be informed at once, no matter what they were doing.

All the same. 'Is action essential *now*?' said FitzSimon protestingly, looking at the white napery and the silver and the raised eyebrows of his guests, and at his butler John standing there with a haunch of mutton on a serving platter and four minions lined up behind him with the supporting dishes.

'There will be no difficulty,' said his masterful daughter, rising to her feet. Eight pregnancies had made her stout and the curtsy which she gave the guests by way of excusing herself was more correct than graceful. However, it exuded presence. 'We are in a low-lying place here,' she said by way of explanation to the visitors. 'There is a risk that the village will be flooded out. We have a procedure. It is a pity that it has happened just at this moment but—'

'Sit down, Adelisa. We can't have them all taking shelter in this hall *now*.'

'They could use the solar,' said Bertrade, half-rising.

'They can't get into it without trooping up here,' said FitzSimon. The dais occupied one-third of the hall and the steps to the solar led from it. 'Adelisa, this is all unnecessary. It hasn't rained as much as all that. The village may well not be touched this time.'

'But it might be!' said Father Gerald, and locked eyes with his host.

'It is most creditable,' said Denis de Moulinville, 'to take thought for one's villeins. But in my experience they do very well if left to shift for themselves. They can be amazingly resourceful and often don't thank you for featherbedding them.' He accepted sliced mutton from a kneeling page – one of Adelisa's sons, learning manners and martial skills in his grandfather's house – arranged it on a piece of bread and dabbled long pale fingers in a bowl of the rose-water which Bertrade made every June from wild dog-roses.

The exchange had been entirely in French. The bailiff was half-Norman and had made his report in that language. And the second abbot had been listening with interest.

Abbot William was a spare, grey-tonsured man, not tall, possessed of calm eyes and a quiet voice. But the eyes missed very little and the voice commanded attention. 'If there is any danger,' he said now, 'then we can hardly put a desire for an uninterrupted dinner first. Messire Gilbert no doubt knows what conditions on his own manor are like and is in the habit of taking wise precautions in certain circumstances. A very responsible attitude, if I may say so. A good overlord does not leave even an ox in a flooded stall, after all. I feel sure that we can continue our dinner quietly up here, whatever else is going on in the hall. My people at the lower tables will give whatever help they can.' He nodded to where, off the dais, tables were occupied by the lesser household members and the considerable train of clerks and monks who had accompanied the guests.

Inside his best red tunic with silver embroidery, FitzSimon had stiffened. His shoulders were not as thick with muscle as they had been once, but they could still hunch aggressively and they were doing it now, of their own accord. He objected to being told what to do at his own dinner table, and Adelisa, Father Gerald and the two Norman abbots were all in their several ways doing precisely that.

He reclaimed his authority.

'I've no doubt that the Rushley people could shift for themselves if they had anywhere to shift to,' he said, 'but my hall happens to be their only refuge. After all, yes, I think they must come here. There isn't enough room in the undercroft for them along with all the animals and if the flooding should be severe after all, the undercroft's at risk too. Once when the river actually got into it, I had a ramp laid over the steps up to the hall and brought the animals in here. I wouldn't let oxen drown, quite right! Very well, make your arrangements, Adelisa. You'd better send a messenger to Oxfen as well; if the river backs up far enough they'll be in danger too. They may not have realised it yet. Father Gerald, you can go and round up your own flock.'

Father Gerald rose at once. Adelisa, who had been waiting impatiently to set things in hand, said briskly: 'The people at the lower tables must eat quickly so that the tables can be pushed out of the way. No, no, Mother, you stay here. I can manage. There had better be a serving of hot broth but don't you trouble. I'll see to everything,' said Adelisa and departed, aglow at the prospect of chivvying other people on a major scale.

FitzSimon sat back, simmering. True, he had maintained his position and the sight of Father Gerald leaving his dinner to go out in the rain was not unpleasant. The supercilious Abbot Denis had been put down too; expert on manuscript illumination or not, FitzSimon had found him supremely irritating from the moment they met. *But . . .*

And with the arrival of the first wet, windswept villagers with their babies and belongings and noise, that ominous *but* came into being.

They were continuing their dinner, under the pool of light from the flambeaux fixed high up on the walls. But the service was slow and fragmented, as servers and pages bore food and drink and napkins back and forth on a zig-zag course among the people who were taking over the hall. And what should have been informed and dignified discussions on the current market value of a well-produced modern manuscript or King Henry of England's new policy of allowing bishoprics to pay rent for their estates in money instead of knight service, were taking place in increasingly loud voices, while the sound of feet brushing across the rushes, the thump of deposited bundles, the rustic accents raised in enquiry or argument, and the wails of children grew more obtrusive every moment.

Whenever the door opened to let in another batch, wind gusted in and the sound of the downpour came with it. Adelisa had disappeared into the kitchen but Bertrade, defying her daughter, presently left the table clicking her tongue and saw to it that a length of rope was strung across a corner of the hall with an old curtain flung over it so that wet village women and wet offspring could change into dry clothes without outraging the sensibilities of the ecclesiastical gentlemen on the dais.

But discarded garments were being dumped in steaming heaps beside the central hearth and the smell of soaked and grimy humanity had begun to pervade the hall. There was also a faint smell of fish. The Eelfisher clan had brought a characteristic odour with them.

In addition, the racket in the hall was gradually being reinforced by an animal cacophony outside as lowing cattle and bleating sheep were driven through the courtyard to the undercroft. A loud squealing announced the arrival of the sow.

On the dais, the service suddenly appeared to evaporate altogether. FitzSimon, looking round in vain for the next course and some more wine, got up swearing and started across the dais to the kitchen himself, just as the hall door opened again, letting in a surge of wind so violent that the flambeaux streamed and the fire belched smoke and the rushes lifted from the floor. The wind snatched the door from the man who had opened it, and crashed it back against the wall, rising to a shriek so eldritch that cries of alarm broke out and a small child ran away from it, darting in fright towards the comforting bright light and the solid male presences on the dais. He toddled straight up its shallow steps and FitzSimon all but fell over him. He grabbed a pillar for support and looked down at the small being which had just collided with his knees. The colour of its hair was dimly familiar.

'Sorry, sir.' The child's father strode up the hall and on to the dais to retrieve his son. 'He's upset. My wife should have held on to him. Up you come, Britt' He straightened up with the child in his arms and his face came into the light.

'Surely I'm not mistaken,' said Abbot Maurice from behind FitzSimon. 'Gilbert – is this not Ivon whom you took with you from St Cuthbert's?'

Ivon turned to him. Across a space of nearly thirty years, they examined each other. Then Ivon, finally recognising his former abbot in this elderly man with the heavily lined face, shifted Britt on to his shoulder and bowed. 'Abbot Maurice. You remember me, then, sir? It's been a long time.'

'You wouldn't be easy to forget,' FitzSimon told him, 'quite apart from your eyes.'

Someone had shut the door and fastened it. Somewhere in the distance, Bertrade's voice, a little crackly with her years but nearly as incisive as in the days when her daughter had said 'Yes, Mother' instead of having to be shouted down, could be heard declaring that yes, Adelisa, certainly hot broth must be distributed but meanwhile the next course was due on the dais and John Butler, kindly get on with it.

John and his domestics appeared from the kitchen, red in the face and in no sort of order but bearing, at last, the expected flagons and the lark pie and pigeons in pastry for which the diners were waiting. The quiet abbot consented distractedly to be served with pie. His eyes had become fixed on Ivon's face, by which he appeared to be intrigued.

'You are a family man, I see,' Maurice was saying to Ivon.

'Yes, sir.' Ragenhild had come hastening up to take Britt and Ivon pushed her forward. 'This is my wife.' Ragenhild hurriedly curtsied.

'I hope he's given you satisfaction, Gilbert,' Maurice said. 'He was certainly out of place in my abbey.'

'He's done well enough,' said FitzSimon shortly. 'All right, Ivon, off you go.'

It was a dismissal. Ragenhild heard the tone of FitzSimon's voice and saw her husband's face acquire a sullen scowl worthy of Edric. Ivon nodded and went, turning his back abruptly. Ragenhild, feeling awkward, bobbed another curtsy, discovered that Britt had reached out to finger a shiny knife on the table nearby, and tried to detach him from it.

'But this is extraordinary.' Ignoring her, the quiet Abbot William addressed Maurice and FitzSimon. 'What unusual eyes that man has. 'I've never seen anything like them before except at home in Normandy. My abbey of St Simeon's has a manor called Clairpont which has been let for several generations to a family known as the de Clairponts. Those eyes occur among them quite commonly. And so does the name Ivon. The present tenant bears that name. Could there be a connection?'

'I wouldn't have thought so. But it's an extraordinary coincidence.' Maurice was also intrigued.

'The boy was once in your abbey, it seems. What was his history before he came to you?' Abbot William asked.

'He came to St Cuthbert's as a child, fleeing from the war in the north. He was brought by a woman who said she was his grandmother. Yes.' Maurice frowned. 'There was some tale or other about him having noble ancestry. But we investigated and there was no truth in the story. People who should have known said that the boy was just another thrall.'

Ragenhild had at last freed the knife from Britt's clutching fingers. She had not followed much of the conversation but she understood enough French to know that they were talking about Ivon. And she had heard the word *Clairpont*, twice. Ivon, long ago, telling her about his origins, had mentioned that name to her. She had not forgotten.

If she had stopped to think about what she was doing, she would never have done it. She had lived for twenty-seven years with Ivon. She knew his opinions all too well and she knew him. He had told her never to speak of his grandfather's identity and she knew how his core of stone could bruise. But her mind was full of the memory of Edric saying: 'I'm no man's servant' and 'I want to get away from Rushley'.

If he were free her son could be and do what he chose. On impulse, using the crude but quite efficient mixture of English and French which FitzSimon and his tenants had hammered out over the years as a means of communication, she said: 'Messire Gilbert, please, was the lord abbot saying something about Clairpont? A place in Normandy? Please tell me.'

FitzSimon looked at her and at the Abbot of St Simeon's. 'He was, as it happens. Why?'

Ragenhild took a deep breath. Out of the corner of her eye she could see that Ivon was waiting impatiently for her to join him. She almost decided to say 'No, it doesn't matter,' and hurry away. Then she thought of Edric again, and blurted: 'Please tell my lord abbot that my husband wears a dagger-hilt on a cord round his neck and that he says the device of Clairpont is carved on it.'

She then stood still, keeping Britt under control against her shoulder, and waited anxiously. FitzSimon frowned but the abbot was obviously asking him what she had said. FitzSimon answered. The abbot looked at her. She had gone halfway already and it was absurd to ignore a chance of freedom because of something over and done with half a lifetime ago. If time didn't make a difference, then it ought to. She dredged up a simple sentence all in French. 'My husband says, his grandfather was of Clairpont.' Well, she said to herself as she waited for their response, she hadn't actually used the word *knight*.

Maurice said: 'Now that is really very strange.' He spoke slowly and that too was a simple sentence, which she understood. Then he raised his voice and shouted: 'Ivon!'

Ivon came reluctantly back on to the dais. FitzSimon, glowering, sat down and folded his arms. Crisply, Maurice said: 'Are you wearing a pendant round your neck? Would it be the one I let you have back when you left us? Kindly show us.'

'What have you said to them?' said Ivon furiously to Ragenhild.

'They know you're something to do with Clairpont, I think,' said Ragenhild. She was holding Britt too tightly and he began to struggle. She shifted her grip and said, trying not to sound frightened, 'I just said about the device.'

'Come along. Let me see it!' Maurice barked.

'Do as the lord abbot says,' said FitzSimon shortly.

He had been doing what FitzSimon told him for too long to stop now. Unwillingly, he pulled the dagger-hilt out from his shirt and handed it over. Maurice turned it over in his hands, shook his head and passed it to the Abbot of St Simeon's. 'Your eyes are younger than mine, William. I can't see what's on it.'

Abbot Denis, who had been listening with an aloof smile, now unbent enough to lean forward and look as well. 'Wavy lines and curved lines over them,' he pronounced. 'I've seen that on a banner somewhere. It was in blue on a white ground.'

'Yes,' said Abbot William of St Simeon's. 'That would be right. That is the device of Clairpont. And this man has their eyes. Ivon! Abbot Maurice addressed you in French just now; presumably you understand me. How did you come by this?'

There was a silence, during which Ivon turned a cold, inimical stare on Ragenhild and then turned away again. She bit her lip and said nothing.

'Answer the lord abbot!' snapped Maurice.

Slowly, as though he were thinking out his words, Ivon said: 'An old man, at the place I come from, he gave it to me.'

'What old man? Who was he?'

The way Ivon was standing, with his chin raised, had an arrogance worthy of any Norman baron. 'Just an old thrall.'

'Was he Norman? Had he been a knight?'

'He said he'd been one. But it was knights that killed him in the end,' said Ivon shortly.

Abbot William chose not to notice the discourteous tone. 'Was he your grandfather? Or any kind of forebear?'

'No!'

'Yet he gave you what I should think was a precious keepsake and you have a Norman name. What was this old man, this former knight, doing on a northern farmstead?'

'He said he was enslaved at Gildenford. I know about Gildenford. There was a massacre there.'

'Indeed? Now that sounds quite a probable story,' said Abbot William thoughtfully.

'This Norman may well have been Ivon's grandfather,' said FitzSimon irritably. 'Ivon has claimed to be descended from a man of free birth, as a matter of fact. That the old man gave him the keepsake perhaps suggests the relationship. But what of it? So the man comforted himself with a thrall-woman and she named the brat for its father. Bondfolk everywhere carry their masters' blood in their veins, and sometimes bear their names as well. It means nothing.'

'Was this old Norman's name Ivon?' asked Abbot William.

'Perhaps. It was a long time ago. I can't remember. But he was not my grandfather,' said Ivon in an angry voice. 'I was born of a freeman in Eric's Dale but . . .'

'But, Ivon, you said—' Ragenhild began protestingly.

'You told them my secret,' muttered Ivon through his teeth, in English to Ragenhild.

'I never said he was a knight. I just said about the device. Anyhow, I did it for Edric.' Ragenhild muttered back. 'And for Britt and this one not born yet. Why shouldn't they be free if they've a right to be?'

The Normans had not been able to follow the muttering. But Abbot William was still pursuing the matter of Ivon's ancestry. 'This old Norman, who was possibly called Ivon. Was he also, possibly, called de Clairpont?'

'I don't know.'

'Did he have odd eyes?'

'No!'

Ragenhild's expression of despairing disappointment was not lost on the abbots.

'Your wife apparently thinks you *are* a de Clairpont descendant,' said Abbot William.

'She got it mixed up. I think the old man did say something about coming from a place called Clairpont. I told her that. She imagined the rest.'

Abbot William was eyeing him curiously. 'She didn't imagine that keepsake, or your name, or your eyes, and all three of them link you to de Clairpont. It's not an accusation, you know. You maintain you are the child of freeborn parents at your original homestead. Were your parents and their parents all lawfully married?'

'Yes!' said Ivon pugnaciously.

'Could the trouble be,' enquired Denis de Moulinville, 'that although the old man in question is his grandfather, he ought not to have been?'

Ivon turned puce. 'I know who my parents and grandparents were and they were properly handfasted according to the custom of Eric's Dale!'

'My reading,' said de Moulinville, 'is that he's a natural son or grandson of this enslaved Norman and that the Norman may well have been a de Clairpont. But as FitzSimon says, it's of no significance.'

210

'Ivon,' said Abbot Maurice, 'when you left St Cuthbert's with my brother, I informed him that you were bondborn. I believed it to be true.' He had also had the best part of thirty years' revenge out of it. This was an uncomfortable thought. A man of his age had to be prepared to face his maker at any moment and he did get headaches and attacks of dizziness at times. There was no doubt that an abbot who was too much attached to a piece of pagan glassware was in breach of his vows. Here, perhaps, was a chance to put himself in the right. 'Now,' he said, 'I'm wondering. You fled from Normans and you had a violent hatred of all things Norman when you came to St Cuthbert's. You threw stones at my men when we arrived. It strikes me that if you were in fact the descendant, legitimate or otherwise, of this de Clairpont, you might not want to admit it. Indeed, I thought something of the kind at the time. That was why I tried to find out the truth. Whether I did so or not now seems doubtful. There may have been injustice.'

'And if so,' said Abbot William, 'it should be put right.'

'I disagree,' said FitzSimon. 'Put right, you say. To what end? It will not benefit this man, who is no longer young, to disturb the way of life to which he is accustomed. It could cause trouble, if he goes to Normandy and importunes the people he may fancy are his kinsmen. It was all a long time ago. Best let things lie.'

He was talking as though Ivon were deaf or not there at all. Ivon himself stood rigid, expressionless. Denis de Moulinville was nodding in grave agreement. But Abbot William of St Simeon's was shaking his head.

'The massacre of Gildenford,' he said, 'was a most shocking event and of those who were enslaved instead of killed, most were later freed and sent home. If this man is indeed descended from a victim of Gildenford, and was acknowledged by him, then he has a right to be acknowledged now. The question of legitimacy may be irrelevant. King William the First was a natural son whose father had acknowledged him. I think that further enquiries should be made and, if such a thing is possible after such a lapse of time, that the facts should be established.'

'I entirely disagree,' said FitzSimon. 'And the man is, after all, one of my villeins.'

'But is he?' said Abbot William gently. He smiled at the unresponsive Ivon. 'I want to find out the truth,' he said. 'I have a besetting sin,' said Abbot William, shaking his head at himself but not with undue regret. 'I am inquisitive.'

Released from the dais, Ivon marched away without a word to Ragenhild. She followed him silently. Down in the hall, amid the bustle of people sorting out bundles and rugs, she put Britt down and said: 'Ivon . . .'

'Don't talk to me.' FitzSimon had handed his pendant back to him. He put it on again.

'Why not? What have I done? Don't you want to be free?'

'Yes. But not that way.'

211

'*What* way?' She noticed that Edric had come up and was listening, and was a little comforted. He would be on her side.

'Not,' said Ivon, 'by claiming to be descended from a Norman knight.'

'But why *not?*' demanded Ragenhild. 'After all this long time since—'

'Don't say it! I should never have told you or Edric my story, but afterwards I did warn you never to speak of it again. And now you've told *them!*'

Edric did not know how it had come about, but he had grasped what had happened. 'It isn't a crime to be a Norman knight,' he said.

'Yes, it is,' said Ivon, and walked away.

Ragenhild, with the tears standing in her eyes and her back suddenly aching horribly, watched the outline of his shoulders as he went and wondered how long it would be before he spoke to her again.

'I can't believe it. I can't believe it. What have you done to me? What have you done to us all?' Edric's body wasn't big enough to contain his rage and the cottage was hardly big enough to hold Edric, Ragenhild thought. He stamped round it as though it were a cage, as though he hated it and wished the floods two months ago had washed it away instead of stopping a furlong short. Once he actually pounded his forehead against the rough-daubed wall. 'I could be a free man today. That abbot – the St Simeon's one – went all the way to Northumbria to find things out and . . .'

Ivon sat at the table, stiffbacked, his forearms on the board in front of him. 'It was a pity you were with me when I was sent for, and a bigger pity that FitzSimon's messenger had to say, right out like that, that Abbot William and Abbot Maurice were up at the house waiting for me.'

'I knew what they'd come for. They wouldn't have come all this way back just to say we were all still villeins. I waited for you to come home and tell us we were freeborn. And all you say is that you . . . *you* . . . told FitzSimon that none of it matters, we're very well as we are; we don't want to change because we don't wish to claim Norman ancestry! To his face you go and tell FitzSimon that it was Normans that burned your home and that you'd sooner be an English villein! Well, *he* won't ram freedom down our throats!' snarled Edric. 'Not FitzSimon!'

Ragenhild was sitting on the bed, with Britt on her knee. Britt was frightened by all the shouting. His eyes were large and he was sucking his thumb. Her head ached and there was a nagging throb at the base of her spine. Her eyes were hot and dry. They were habitually dry now; she had given up crying because Ivon wouldn't speak to her. She had lived for the last two months with a man who came and went and ate his food in silence and slept with his back to her. Perhaps when the child was born, his silence would break. She prayed so.

Edric was still storming back and forth, shaking the room with his tread. 'You stupid old man! That's all you are, just a stupid old man, stuck in the past. Because some Norman knight long ago did something wicked, you won't admit we're of that breed ourselves, no matter what hangs on it! You can't see past the end of your nose! What's the matter with you, you old fool? What if they were wicked? It was war, wasn't it? I'd like to be a knight and go to war myself! Better be a knight than a stupid helpless peasant! *Anyone* might have had ancestors who did things like that and worse; who cares?'

Ivon said nothing, but only stared straight ahead of him. His spine, however, sagged a little. Edric's stride veered towards his father. He leaned over the table and shook his fist under Ivon's nose. 'You old *fool*!'

Ivon did not respond. Edric let out a sound halfway between a laugh and a sob. 'You're stupid, stupid about your grandfather. Why did you ever tell me about him? You can't forget him and yet we're not to talk about him! You won't let him go or admit to him either! Oh, *God . . .*!'

Abruptly, he flung away to the chest where he kept his clothes and belongings. He threw it open and began dragging out the contents. In a sparking silence, he stuffed garments, shoes and a small pouch of long-garnered silver into a bag, caught up a cloak and made for the door.

'Where are you going?' said Ragenhild.

'Where do you think? I'm going away. I *am* a freeman; those abbots said so, didn't they? Well, I'm going to live like one. I'm off.'

'If I'm an old fool, you're a young one.' Ivon got to his feet at last, and stepped in Edric's way. 'What do you know of the world outside Rushley? You'll be spotted as a runaway serf in five minutes, and FitzSimon'll have the word out for you, make no mistake.'

'And if he does, whose fault is that? Get out of my way. You'd better, or you'll be sorry.' Edric was two inches taller than his father, broader in the chest and seventeen years younger. He pushed Ivon aside and Ivon let him do it. A moment later he was gone.

Ivon came back to the table and sat down again, scowling. For the first time, Ragenhild noticed that the red-brown of his hair was streaked and speckled with grey. Edric had called his father old and Edric was right. The boy she had fallen so insanely in love with, the mature man whose desire she had been so proud to retain, had gone and she hadn't noticed them going. What was left was a sullen and ageing villein, too sunk in old habits and old hatreds to take the opportunity of a lifetime when it was offered to him, whose obstinacy had first of all twisted Edric and then driven him away.

She looked at her husband with new eyes and saw in him, to her horror, a fugitive resemblance to old Cob.

His silence towards her, which was part of his obstinacy and which even now he would not break, was hurting her bitterly. It was like a spear driven through her spirit.

And now, even through her body.

For an enormous pain like – no, not a spear, like a gigantic hand – had clutched her insides and was slowly, massively, squeezing. With it, her headache was mounting, to a blinding torment. In a moment she would scream. If this was the onset of labour, it was like no labour she had known before, not even that first time, with Edric. She put Britt aside and huddled together, shivering. 'Ivon,' she whispered. 'Call Biddy.'

Well, that was that, thought Abbot William as he boarded the ship which would take him down the river from Norwich and home to Normandy. Extraordinary. Fancy a man turning down the chance of putting villeinage behind him.

There was no doubt at all about Ivon's origins. Abbot William had found Eric's Dale. It was in the hands of the widow Signy, who ruled the place like a queen, lording it over a scowling but utterly cowed eldest son, a subservient daughter-in-law and a whole valleyful of obedient bondfolk, and she said she remembered perfectly. She was sorry her husband had once given inaccurate information about Ivon; he had hoped to get him back as a thrall. Leif had been inclined to seize questionable advantages if he could, she said with a casual, disdainful shrug.

She sat on the dais, opposite the abbot, in a chair made like a throne. She wore her hair in plaits round her head like a crown of silver. Her face was superb, its once delicate features sculptured by the years to the likeness of marble. Oh yes, she told him, Ivon Oddeyes, as he had been nicknamed, was, by the customs of the Dale, the lawful grandson of the man who had once been Sir Ivon de Clairpont, and had been taken prisoner at Gildenford. Ivon had been born before she came to the Dale but his story was known and she remembered it well. Indeed, lord abbot, Ivon Oddeyes possessed more claim to free status than William the Bastard had ever had to the dukedom of Normandy.

There she sat, her proud head tilted against the upright back of her chair, her arms in their pale green silk sleeves lying relaxed along the arm-rests, her thin, ivory-skinned fingers curving over the carved ends. She regarded all men with barely tolerant contempt: Abbot William, Leif her dead husband, the scowling son and William the Conqueror, all alike. She was undoubtedly telling the truth and she was undoubtedly remembering aright. She had a power and an authority which made Adelisa look like a bossy schoolgirl. She was the most terrifying woman he had ever seen in his life.

Edric had intended to go to Norwich and somehow or other get aboard a ship for another country. Any other country would do. But there was smallpox in Norwich and three weeks after he left home, he died in an outhouse behind an inn. The innkeeper had had the disease as a child and wasn't afraid of it; he had cared for the sick stranger with rough-and-ready competence and made him as comfortable as he could in the barn, where he wouldn't infect others. But the young man had taken the sickness violently.

In his last hours, he cried out for his mother, but no one knew who he was or where he came from and he was too delirious to tell them. The priest who buried him had to refer to him throughout the ceremony as 'our brother here departed' because no one even knew his name.

214

PART V

Margaret Brittschild,
AD 1140–4

I neither know nor can tell all the horrors they did to the unhappy people in this land, that lasted nineteen years while Stephen was king; and ever it was worse and worse . . .

Never yet was more wretchedness in the land, nor ever did heathen men do worse than they did, for against all custom they spared neither church nor churchyard, but seized all the goods therein . . .

Wherever the land was tilled, the earth bore no corn, for the land was all ruined with such deeds and men said openly that Christ slept, and his saints.

The Anglo-Saxon Chronicle

Chapter Fourteen
Matilda Go Home

'That's it!' said Meg Brittswife in a tone of angry triumph. 'Nail him down!' The neighbours had paid their respects and withdrawn while the coffin was closed; the funeral party was ready to set out for the church, and she had looked for the last time on Ivon's face and a good job too. As Alfred the Carpenter moved forward with hammer and nails, she added: 'It's no good looking shocked. You didn't have to live with my father-in-law! I've given him a decent coffin!'

'Aye, you have, that,' said Alfred. 'Reckon he weren't an easy man.'

'No,' said Meg in heartfelt tones. 'He wasn't.'

When it was all over and Meg and her small daughter were alone once more, Meg, still militant, marched to Ivon's private chest and began to empty it, muttering a commentary to which five-year-old Margaret Brittschild listened with interest. 'So-and-so can have this – that can be thrown out . . . this . . . here, Margaret,' said Meg, 'come here. You can have this, whatever it is. He set a lot of store by it, but you can do what you like with it. Wear it or play with it or chew it, if you like.'

She tossed over a piece of bone with a hole at one end and a worn leather thong through it. The bone was intriguingly carved. This meant nothing to Margaret, but it was interesting, if not exactly pretty. She put it round her neck.

Later that day, her mother sat her on her knee and said: 'Now, Margaret. I've something to tell you. Your father's been gone these three years, God rest his soul, and since then Adam has been learning the pottery work so as to take it over one day. It's been settled that I'm to marry him. So you and I will go on living here just as before, only Adam will live here with us. Adam's a few years younger than me but not many. You like him, so that'll be all right, won't it?'

Margaret nodded. She could hardly remember her father, and her grandfather had been an alarming figure, given to monologues over the table, during which he appeared to be blaming her or her mother, or anyone else who chanced to be there, such as Aunt Gytha or her son William, for various misfortunes.

If Adam was coming to replace him, that was all right. She knew who Adam was. He was the second son of the miller, the most prosperous

217

villein in Rushley. He laughed a lot, even when Grandfather Ivon was bullying him in the workshop.

And she knew how her mother had hated Grandfather Ivon.

'I'm glad he's gone. Glad!' Meg said without pretence to her sister-in-law Gytha the next morning. 'He made our lives a misery.' She had been pounding bread dough when Gytha walked in, and continued to pound it, furiously. 'He as good as killed Britt. Britt wanted to be a good craftsman, and all his father did was teach him the craft with one hand and stop him using it with the other. It was: "No, we don't want fancy stuff round here" and "No sense making quality things to sell, they'll only fill the lord's coffers." They might have put a bit of silver in our coffers too but that never seemed to strike him! I've not had a new dress since I was married.'

Gytha was considerably older than her sister-in-law. She had been widowed ten years, and sooner than take on another husband who might one day challenge her eight-year-old son William for his father's fields, had managed the work herself with whatever help William could give. Gytha had trudged behind plough-oxen and personally scythed wheat. Her dark hair had long since turned iron-grey. She was jerky of speech and lean of body. Her arms were corded with muscle from the weight of the plough-handles and her high-cheekboned face was both weatherbeaten and inexpressive.

But if Meg could not interpret Gytha's face, she understood her silence. 'All right, I know what you're thinking. Britt should have stood up to his father more. Maybe he should, but he couldn't. He was Britt, not anyone else. He thought his father must be right and he thought we ought to respect him. Britt was always kind to me.'

'I know. Ah, well,' said Gytha, 'you're free of the old man now.' She began helping to shape loaves. 'I hated him, let me tell you, more than you did. Never knew him much as a child; I was put out to nurse with the Eelfishers while I was small and Britt was there too for a while. But Britt went back to his father when he was eight, and I followed a while later. Idea was, I'd keep house. Then I found out what he was like. Hah! One minute, he'd be thumping the table and telling us we shouldn't just be villeins and how much he hated all Norman lords and the next he'd be cursing our mother's name because she once tried to prove that we weren't villeins! Never could make sense of that until in the end Father Gerald explained to me. You know about it?'

'A bit. Britt told me. Something to do with we could prove we weren't villeins but his father wouldn't because it meant proving we were Normans. Sounded quite mad to me. Who'd pass up a chance like that for any reason? Though maybe he'd be capable of it. There were times I reckoned he *was* touched in the head.' Meg snorted.

Gytha nodded. 'That's it. And he used to scowl at me and blame me for killing my mother when I was born. He'd contradict himself six times over across one meal. *And* gave himself plenty of chance! Never let anyone else speak. Britt used to say that before his brother Edric went away, his father'd never talk about his past. After Edric ran off, he wouldn't stop. You've had a lot to put up with, don't think I don't know it. I could keep away from him but you couldn't. You'll be better off with Adam.'

'Much better off, I hope.' Meg sighed. Britt had given her a little silver mirror as a morning-gift when they were married. She still had it and that morning she had consulted it. She was not yet thirty but her flaxen hair was already fading and her eyes, which Britt had once said reminded him of blue woodsmoke, were wary, with small lines round them. Well, perhaps Adam would give her a little prosperity. She hoped so. She nodded towards the corner where Margaret, still asleep, was a small curved bump under a fleece rug. There was a tumble of chestnut hair at the edge of it, and one little hand was closed round something from which trailed a worn leather thong.

'Margaret will be pretty,' she said. 'She's got Britt's looks, that nice-coloured hair and his dark eyes. I want her to have a good dowry and a good match, when the time comes. She'll have a chance now, thank the saints. *Oh!*' Suddenly enraged anew, she thumped her fist into the loaf she was moulding, driving a huge dent into it. 'Death isn't just nothing. Death's for ever. I'm not a wicked woman, Gytha, I'm not. I looked after my father-in-law when he was ill, I took care of him, I wouldn't have hurt him. I saw to it he died in a state of grace. Father Gerald and I had to *bully* him into taking the sacrament: horrible, irreligious old man that he was! I don't like being glad he's dead, it's not right that people should make you be glad when they die. He was so twisted in his mind that he twisted everyone else and every *thing* else that came near him. I hate myself for being so thankful . . .'

She stopped, wiping a floury hand across her forehead and trembling. Gytha hesitated for a moment, having almost forgotten how to be demonstrative. Her son William had long ago rejected maternal caresses as an affront to his male dignity, and one couldn't cuddle a plough-ox. Then she put an arm round Meg's shoulders. 'It's all right. I know. Know how well you looked after him. Let's talk of something else. You made something new to wear when you marry Adam?'

'Oh, yes!' Meg's laugh was slightly hysterical. 'I've got old Ivon's silver, now. Alfred Carpenter was going to Norwich and he fetched me some good cloth. Plum-coloured, but darkish. Won't shock anyone who thinks I ought to be mourning the old . . . !'

'We'll all be wishing you well,' said Gytha firmly. 'Lady Cicely's coming to the wedding feast as usual, I hear.'

'Aye, that's true.' Meg regained command of herself and set about reshaping the damaged loaf. 'Funny. She come down a time or two while Father-in-law was ill, the way she always does when someone's sick, and she said to me what you said. That I'd had a lot to put up with. She's all right, Lady Cis is. Even Father-in-law said that once. He said she was the only one of them up at the house he'd ever trust.'

'High praise, that was, coming from him,' said Gytha. 'Now, don't fret any more. You'll soon be settled down again.'

'We could all do with a bit of settling down,' Meg agreed. 'There's been too much disturbance, lately. That wasn't nice, having fighting in Ely. It was a lot too near. We never had all this trouble in King Henry's day.'

'It's a pity the Jongleurs aren't likely to come on their rounds at the time of your wedding,' Gytha said. 'They'd make a good addition to the fun, singing for us and that, *and* they'd bring us news.'

'Yes, news,' said Meg. 'Time was, when it didn't matter so much. I get scared sometimes, Gytha, thinking about Margaret and wondering what kind of world she'll have to grow up into. Since King Henry died and his daughter started fighting her cousin for the throne . . . well, I can't explain it but things just don't feel safe the way they did, not any more.'

Margaret Brittschild, in a new plum-coloured dress made of the same material as Meg's, saw her mother married to Adam Millerson in Rushley Church at the end of May 1140. The church was full. Weddings were occasions and everyone joined in who possibly could. Gytha was there, tall and angular, respecting both her father's recent death and the happy nature of Meg's marriage by wearing a dark-blue gown made of the best cloth she could afford. William, at her side, was less sober in russet. He had detested his grandfather and didn't care who knew it.

Alfred the Carpenter was there, with his two well-grown sons Peter and Ralph. Peter would be the next to be married, and he and his intended, Osbert the Shepherd's second daughter, kept on blowing kisses to each other across the church, incurring frowns from Father Gerald, who was an old man now but still possessed excellent long sight.

By far the largest family group in the church, however, were Adam's kin. Since FitzSimon's successor had established the water-mill, the family put in charge of it had prospered. Adam's mother was some years dead, but his father was there, resplendent in crimson, and there too were Adam's elder brother Siward and their two sisters, all with spouses and broods of their own. Between them all, the miller's family filled two well-dressed rows. The miller had in fact done more than prosper. Villein though he was, he was said to have savings in gold and to be well-off even by the standards of a freeman.

Adam had thought it would be a pleasing idea if Siward's eldest boy Philip were to walk hand in hand with Margaret behind the bride. Philip was a couple of years older than Margaret, but was much of a height with her; they made a good pair. The sight made the women in the congregation croon. Margaret and Philip themselves were inclined to giggle, because Margaret had new shoes which were too big, and kept on tripping her up.

It was the first wedding to be celebrated in the church at Rushley. Father Gerald had got his way at last but it had taken him the best part of a lifetime.

'I've no money for dedicating churches,' FitzSimon had protested, time and again, right to the end of his life. The truth was that after fighting his way out of the debt incurred at Norwich and surviving the series of disastrous harvests which followed, he had preferred to spend money on collecting fine manuscripts and gold and silver ware for his table.

His son-in-law Roger, with whom Rushley and Oxfen had come under the same lord, had also had a taste for silver plate if not for manuscripts, and additionally wished to invest in down-to-earth improvements to the manor, such as building the mill so that the housewives on the estate not only need not grind their own corn, but could be forbidden to grind it and compelled instead to send it in bulk to his mill and pay for the privilege.

Pleading that to share a church would help to bind the two communities together, he had resisted Father Gerald's blandishments as stoutly as FitzSimon.

And so, in turn had his eldest son, the second Roger.

But Sir Aubrey FitzRoger, inheriting young, was of a more pious turn of mind. 'Or maybe it's due to his lady,' said the people of the two villages. Because his forebears had built up their wealth, Aubrey had been able to make an advantageous marriage and Lady Cicely, convent-educated, was a religiously minded and charitable woman. The only person ever known not to like her was Sir Aubrey's mother. 'Taking medicines to the villagers when they're ill and attending their weddings, indeed. The girl's mad. She'll catch the pox and bring it home with her, mark my words.' The family, however, had taken to using the manor-house at Oxfen as a dower-house and Cicely did not have to live with her mother-in-law. She continued her charities unhindered.

Hitherto, the occupants of the manor-houses had been for the villagers simply 'them at the hall'. *They* had their uses occasionally. If the water-ways flooded, the lord's hall was a refuge which was never refused. But as that grumpy old man Ivon had frequently said: 'By God, we pay for it. Those Normans take our labour and our time; they claim the right to keep us here whether we like it or not; they grab every chance they can of snatching something off us. A son can't inherit from his father without he pays for it. Can't even marry on the same manor nowadays without paying up.'

But when he, or anyone else, used that disparaging *they*, it was not Lady Cicely they meant. And when her mother-in-law's forebodings were realised and Lady Cicely caught smallpox as a result of carrying a feverfew brew to a villein's gravely ill offspring and Father Gerald offered prayers for her, the villagers joined in with the utmost sincerity and did not even notice that they were praying for a Norman.

She recovered from the smallpox. Her forehead was pitted but that, said Lady Cis, was nothing compared to her life and her health. It was in gratitude for her recovery that she urged her husband to build the church that Father Gerald so much wanted. Sir Aubrey agreed, and did it thoroughly, importing stone, and hiring masons and painters with up-to-date ideas.

The church, though not large, was elegant. The days of plain round arches and heavy round pillars were beginning to pass. Churches were no longer being constructed as though they were fortresses. Rushley Church had modest taperings above its doorways, and pillars shaped to draw the eye up towards a roof of ribbed stone. It had a window depicting the healing of the lepers, and another illustrating the Day of Judgement, all in stained glass, crimson and amber and azure. It had a great silver crucifix and a silver communion cup, and a set of solid gold candlesticks. The bulk of Sir Aubrey's wealth had gone into it: 'But the land's good. As long as I can feed my family and fulfil my military duties, what more do I need?' he said. 'There's time to save up new dowries for my daughters.' The church was so fine that before the trouble broke out in Ely, a deputation even came from the monastery to admire it.

United under one lord, the two villages had grown over the years, new dwellings going up, new land coming under cultivation to support the extra mouths and areas of marsh being drained to provide it. Cattle grazed now where once there had been nothing but reeds and now that there were drier pastures, there were also more sheep. Wool fetched money and the same animals could provide fleeces over and over, which wasn't the case with calfskins and oxhides.

The process of growth and enlargement had gone on steadily for a long time, largely because on the whole the land had been peaceful. William the Conqueror's last son, King Henry, was far from being an angel but he was a very efficient ruler. He kept order. It had been a nerve-racking time for all his subjects when at his death he left behind over twenty illegitimate offspring but only one lawfully begotten child and that one a daughter.

The days when a bastard son could inherit a dukedom, as William the First had done in Normandy, were gone. To its considerable alarm, the realm confronted the prospect of a ruler called Matilda.

Aubrey's father Roger FitzRoger had still been alive then. 'I can't see what the fuss is about,' he said. 'I'm lord of Oxfen and Rushley and I got Rushley through my mother. Our new king'll be Matilda's husband.'

It was unfortunate that most of her father's barons had heartily disliked Matilda. It was more unfortunate still that the one opinion she and they had in common concerned her husband, Geoffrey of Anjou, and his family. Matilda and the barons unanimously detested the Anjou lords, who had been Normandy's hereditary foes for generations and were widely agreed to be violent, arrogant and probably descended from the devil. Matilda had objected passionately to the marriage with Geoffrey, which was her father's idea. 'We'll bring Anjou under Norman control at last,' King Henry had said, jaw taut, eyes hard and shining with the prospect of such a glorious triumph.

His subjects, including many who were humbler than his barons, commented gloomily that in his later years, King Henry had lost his judgement. It was no great surprise when the news went round, after Henry's death, that the barons had passed Matilda and her odious Anjou husband over and crowned her cousin Stephen, whose mother had been a daughter of the Conqueror, instead.

Only, not surprisingly, Matilda had not accepted this meekly. Much as most of the barons disliked her, there were exceptions, some of them powerful. The September before Ivon died, she had contacted her supporters, and invaded.

The ensuing conflict did not touch Norfolk until the Bishop of Ely unexpectedly took it into his head to declare for Matilda, collected a force and, as Hereward had done long before, put Ely into a state of defence, ready to offer Matilda a safe base there should she want one. King Stephen's army, arriving to winkle him out, were hungry, like most armies. They snatched sheep and cattle from the surrounding countryside including both Rushley and Oxfen and even the fact that Sir Aubrey was with the king's forces couldn't prevent it.

News of the royal conflict reached the two villages in various ways: through reports from passing travellers; by announcements made by Father Gerald and the priest who now ministered to Oxfen, who received information from their bishop; through gossip or proclamations heard in Norwich.

But there was another and far more enjoyable channel through which events were reported. How John and his Jolly Jongleurs managed to keep so up-to-date with their information, no one could guess, but they did. They were a group of roving minstrels who worked a circuit which took them twice a year from London to Essex, Suffolk and Norfolk and back to London via Cambridgeshire. John, who led them, played the lyre and put together most of the doggerel news stories which were the group's speciality. Howell, the second-in-command, was the son of a Welsh bard. He played a small harp, sang bass and created the tunes for the doggerel. They were melodious, irreverent and their information was reliable. Some of the sharper-minded villagers (including Meg, who was proud of the herd of cows which had grown considerably since Ragenhild's day) had kept their sheep and cattle from Stephen's men because the Jongleurs brought a warning in time for them to drive the animals to safety along the marsh causeways that only the local folk knew, to the island meadows which lay here and there among the reeds between Rushley and the sea.

Earlier, the Jongleurs had been the first with the tidings that Matilda had landed at Portsmouth, enshrined in a lyric with the refrain 'Go home, Matilda; Matilda dear, go home,' in which audiences joined with enthusiasm.

That particular tune was exceptionally catchy, and the guests even sang it during a sing-song at the wedding of Adam and Meg. But some of those who sang the loudest were apt to worry privately. Since the king's men came by and stole their animals, it hadn't been possible to think of the war as 'just the great lords' business' any longer.

* * *

Meg's marriage was celebrated without the Jongleurs, if not quite without their music. But the minstrels themselves arrived in June, two weeks after the wedding feast. They took up their usual stand under the elms near what was now exclusively Oxfen's church, and their audience came running, with Margaret and her stepcousin Philip (Meg said they spent too much time playing together) arriving first.

It was evening, with the sun just mellowing and the young corn brilliant green. The news was that peace had come again. Matilda was still in England, but she was 'far away, far in the west, where Bristol's palm's on Severn's breast, and if the king comes her to bind, the way to the sea is just behind,' sang the Jongleurs, grinning.

The church was to attempt a conciliation and Matilda's devil-descended husband Geoffrey, who appeared to loathe his wife as much as she loathed him, even to the point of ignoring the crown of England, had shown no signs of arriving to support her. 'All will be quiet and all will be well, and the devil's brood go home to hell,' declared the Jongleurs. 'Geoffrey won't give Mattie a hand. We'll never see Geoffrey in this land.'

The tune was sprightly and Margaret had a good ear for words. She remembered that doggerel afterwards.

The Jongleurs had been only half right. They had unfortunately assumed that there was only one Geoffrey.

'I get scared sometimes, Gytha, thinking about Margaret and wondering what kind of world she'll have to grow up into.' That's what Meg had said to Gytha, the day after Ivon's funeral. She continued intermittently to worry, and with reason. True, the next three years were quiet as far as Rushley was concerned. But while Meg settled into her new marriage and provided Margaret with two small half-brothers, while Adam flourished and built another room on to the cottage and Margaret herself grew and stretched in the uncritical atmosphere of a house where Adam had replaced Grandfather Ivon, the political storm still raged in the distance as the attempt to mediate between the royal cousins dissolved into new violence. In this uneasy time, the Jongleurs became more of a favourite source of news than ever.

For while the fortunes of the self-styled Empress Matilda and her cousin King Stephen swayed to and fro across the land, the Jongleurs did far more than simply tell their audiences what was afoot. They also mined the best stories, like amethysts from rock, and displayed them in settings of verse and music, thus extracting their maximum entertainment value, and simultaneously comforting the nervous by making it all seem, once more, far away and comical.

They made a sardonic tale of the failed mediation and a spirited one of Stephen's queen seizing the port of Dover for her husband. And then, on two successive occasions, they won the tribute of uproarious laughter with a couple of deplorable stories of great earls who in the confusion had seen a chance to build power bases for themselves.

224

It was disgraceful, but very funny, that two noble lords should decide to revolt against the king and grab the castle of Lincoln to do it in, and gain entrance by apparently escorting their wives on a friendly visit. 'The wives walked first,' chanted the Jongleurs, 'all womanly charm. The husbands followed as sheep the wether, side by side, in talk together, each with his lady's cloak on arm. Oh, how gentle, oh, how knightly; the flame of courtesy burneth brightly; each had his lady's cloak on arm!'

On, it transpired, to the delight of the audience, the sword arm. In strolled the two noble lords behind their wives, and an escort of their household knights sauntered after them, making demure conversation about the weather. Until such time as they were all inside, when the cloaks were tossed aside to reveal drawn swords and the hitherto charming escort held a dagger to the castellan's throat and a hand over his shrieking lady's mouth until the garrison had thrown down their weapons and allowed themselves to be locked up.

But more entertaining still was the frightful behaviour of one Geoffrey de Mandeville.

The name of Geoffrey de Mandeville was already vaguely known to most of the villagers, for he was Earl of the neighbouring county of Essex. He was also Constable of the Tower of London. But it seemed that these positions were not remunerative enough for him, and he had had the happy thought of kidnapping both Stephen's queen and their new daughter-in-law and imprisoning them both in the Tower until Stephen paid a ransom for their release.

'You've got to admit,' said Adam, grinning, as they talked it over that evening at home, 'that some people have enterprising ideas.'

'So had the Bishop of Ely, not so long ago,' said Meg warningly. 'He got away. He's with the empress now, according to those Jongleurs. But what of the folk as lost their cattle? Let's hope none of these enterprising ideas come close to us again.'

'Why should they?' Adam was an easygoing, optimistic young man. He saw Margaret looking at them round-eyed and put her on his knee. 'Nothing to be scared about, sweetheart. The great people aren't interested in the likes of us and in a lot of ways we're luckier than they are. We can live quiet and safe while they're out risking their lives because they've got to be loyal to their lords and all the rest of it. Now, don't fret, Meg. My, that was a grand story. Holding the queen and the young bride to ransom! Wonder whose side this Mandeville is really on?'

Subsequent reports from the Jongleurs and elsewhere suggested that he was on no one's side but his own. When Stephen was captured while fighting personally and magnificently in an attempt to regain Lincoln Castle, and the Empress Matilda gained the ascendancy, de Mandeville obligingly put the Tower into her hands, only to change his mind and reject her when the Londoners, annoyed by her arrogant manners, threw her out and obliged her to flee for shelter to Oxford.

She was reported to have had her imprisoned cousin put in chains by way of revenge for that, after which she set about winning over the support of the powerful Bishop of Winchester, who happened to be King Stephen's brother. She chose to recommend herself to him, said the Jongleurs acidly, by besieging him in his newly built palace, and in the uproar of that, Winchester was nearly burned to the ground.

It was Stephen's queen, at last, who drove away the empress, and it was the Bishop of Winchester, emerging from his damaged palace and stumbling across the smouldering ruins of his city, who succeeded in negotiating Stephen's release. The Jongleurs at this point had hard names and vicious rhymes for Empress Matilda. She was 'Henry's daughter and Queen of Slaughter'; she was 'Lucifer-proud and unwomanly loud'; she was urged to 'go home, Matilda; Geoffrey should have killed her'. They meant de Mandeville and it was he, now, who was always meant when the name Geoffrey was spoken.

'But no one saw ahead,' Margaret said, long afterwards. 'No one saw him . . . *growing* . . . until it was too late. Not even,' she added, 'the king.'

The empress's reputation went up somewhat after she took refuge once more in Oxford, was trapped there by Stephen, but escaped in the depths of winter 1142 by dressing herself and some of her men in white, climbing down a rope from a tower at night and escaping on foot over the snow to join supporters twenty miles away in Wallingford. One of the supporters, a man called Brian FitzCount, was believed to be in love with her.

'Well, it's a fact,' everyone said, 'it isn't every gently brought-up young woman would have the nerve to slide down a castle tower on a rope, or be tough enough to march all that way across country in the snow and the darkness. Haughty in her manners she may be, but most of the people she's been rude to probably couldn't do what she's done. And she must have something to her, or this Brian FitzCount wouldn't be so faithful. He's a decent, honourable body by all accounts.'

The same certainly could not be said of Geoffrey de Mandeville, who was presently revealed to have been conspiring with the empress again in secret, with an eye to what he could get out of it.

'But chivalrous Stephen, wise and brave, wouldn't be fooled by such a knave,' said the Jongleurs, somewhat overestimating his wisdom. No one had ever doubted Stephen's courage or his chivalry but it was quite clear that Geoffrey de Mandeville had been fooling both Stephen and the empress for his own ends for a considerable time. However: 'Into prison and for good reason, de Mandeville's been cast for treason,' the interested if detached inhabitants of Rushley and Oxfen were assured, after which John's Jolly Jongleurs, their current visit over, went on their way towards Cambridge.

Margaret, who loved them, pulled a sad face when they were gone. 'You silly chicken,' said Adam indulgently. 'You just like songs and tales – that's it, isn't it? Pity your grandfather's not still alive.'

'Whatever makes you say that?' Meg, just back from milking the cows and shutting them up for the night, came through the door with a milk pail

226

in each hand. In her household, cheese and butter had gradually begun to challenge pottery as a means of income. She exchanged them for eggs and fowls, sent them for sale at Norwich and at the small market which Oxfen was now licensed to hold three times a year and bought small favours with them here and there. She poured the contents of the pails into a large lidded tub, and said: 'I don't remember Ivon ever singing a note or dandling Margaret while he told her fairy-stories.'

'No, but he had some interesting memories. He'd had quite a life,' Adam said. 'When he was in a good mood, he used to talk to me, in the pottery.'

'Was he ever in a good mood?' enquired Meg, astonished.

'Now and then.' A grin broke across Adam's round and amiable countenance, always a little reddened from the field work which was as much part of his life as the pottery, and with a lock of flaxen hair always falling into his eyes. 'Not often, I grant you. But when he was, I liked hearing him. Did you ever hear him tell how the place he grew up in was attacked, and he and his grandmother had to walk for days through the snow to safety? They had a harder winter march than the Empress Matilda had. Want to hear about it, little Margaret?'

'Yes, please!' Margaret had not only watched the Jongleurs go; she had also been dragged indoors away from her playmate Philip. A story would be compensation.

'I *don't* want to hear about it,' declared Meg. 'I heard enough of his talking over the table when he was never-endingly going on about the way he shouldn't be a villein, and how he'd never forgive his wife for trying to prove he wasn't. Awful, stupid, obstinate old man!'

'You needn't listen,' said Adam, with a flash of temper. Meg was a good wife and he was fond of her but she could be waspish and he didn't see why Margaret, who was obviously longing for a story, shouldn't have one. Only, he was no good at inventing them and Ivon's life story was something he knew by heart. 'You can start the next batch of cheese and feed the baby. I'll amuse this one. Anyhow, she ought to know her own family history. She is old Ivon's granddaughter.'

'I want her to help me heat the milk with the rennet and get it strained once it's turned.'

'But I want to hear the story!' Margaret wailed.

'She can listen while she helps you, can't she?'

'I'll have to listen as well.'

'All right, then I'll tell it afterwards, quietly, just before she goes to sleep.'

'I sometimes think you care more about my daughter than you do about me.'

'Now, what's all this?' said Adam, annoyed. 'It's all right, Margaret. No one's cross. Your mother's tired. You help her with the milk and later on there'll be a bedtime story for a little girl with chestnut hair and blackberry eyes, see?'

'Oh, please yourself,' said Meg. 'Get on with your story, then!' and with irritated energy put the milk to heat and set about frying onions for supper. 'You never,' she muttered to the spitting lard, 'say anything nice about *my* hair.'

She said it, however, so that Adam, well launched in any case on the first story about Ivon, wouldn't hear. After all, her braids were so sadly faded now that she could hardly expect compliments on her hair and wouldn't believe them if they were offered.

The story-telling was a success. Adam's memory was good. He could recall not only everything Ivon had told him but the way it was divided up. Ivon, as they worked in the pottery, cleaning and wedging clay, spinning the wheel or patiently painting and glazing and applying slip clay patterns, had talked about his past in a series, so to speak, of chapters.

There was the one, for instance, about Eric's Dale, which always sounded to Adam like something out of the Nordic sagas which minstrels – though not the Jongleurs – still sometimes sang. There had been a hall, occupied by people with names like Sven and Bjorn, who swore by Odin and Thunor, where Ivon's grandfather had been a slave . . . on the subject of his grandfather, Ivon had sometimes contradicted himself but Adam was fairly sure that the first Ivon really had been a Norman. The name of Ivon was a strong indication.

Then there was the one about the mailed horsemen who rode into the valley one morning and killed all the men and set fire to the hall and turned the women and children out into the snow. The story of the trudge through the snow made a third.

There were two stories about St Cuthbert's, one about throwing stones at knights and one about Ivon smashing the abbot's favourite ornament because he'd fallen in love with a girl called Aldith and wanted to leave the abbey and get married, and how he had come to Rushley with the abbot's brother instead.

Next came a grim, exciting saga about Norwich Castle, and a gloomy tale about the lord of Rushley pretending to reward him and trapping him into bondage. And there was the tale of how Ivon had refused the chance of freedom, so that his son Edric ran off to be a freeman and was never heard of again.

In fact, there was a good week's worth of good-night stories for Margaret. Meg needn't listen if she didn't want to and she always had plenty to do, anyway.

Over the next week, after the final jobs of the day, he sat on the fleece rug while Margaret nestled beneath it, and he talked, while she listened, sometimes asking questions, and once or twice bringing out the old dagger-hilt her mother had tossed to her. Adam said that in an expansive moment Ivon had once shown it to him and hinted that part of the carving was a Norman emblem. 'Perhaps of his real family?' Margaret whispered.

The stumbling footsteps came to their door just as Adam was ending the last tale, by rushlight as an autumn dusk came down and a mist drifted across the wide flat fields outside, and Meg was by the fire, cutting rushes to make more wicks and determinedly not listening. Adam stopped short and Meg laid down her knife. Someone pounded, frantically but oddly, on the lower half of the door.

'Who's there?' said Adam.

A man's voice answered, but they couldn't make out what it said. It too seemed to come from ground level. Adam crossed the room and opened the door. Howell the half-Welsh minstrel from the Jongleurs half fell and half crawled in and collapsed on the floor. His travelling pack and his harp were still slung on his back but the harp hung in splinters from a smashed case, and the black hair on one side of his head was soaked in dark crimson blood from a deep wound in his scalp.

They pulled a pile of rugs in front of the fire, removed his harp and pack and gently washed his head. He moaned when they handled him and Adam, investigating further, found great black bruises on one shoulder and hip. They gave him warm milk and some broth with barley and beans in it from the stockpot which Meg, like any good housewife, always had at the ready.

'I'll do. I'll live,' he said at last. 'Sorry, I am. I was so tired. I lost my way. Mist and marshes, there's confusing they are. I never found a hearth all the way. I was making for Redesmarsh but I missed it and Oxfen too. Miles, I've come. But I'm not dying. Can't think why not. All the rest are dead!' said Howell, and put his broth spoon down, looking at the bowl as if he no longer knew what it was. He put his hands over his face and began to shudder.

'The Jongleurs?' said Adam. 'All *dead*? But . . .'

Meg sat down slowly beside them. Margaret had begun to sob. Howell drew his hands slowly down and raised his stricken face to them.

'Yes. All dead. We shouldn't have been there, even. We should have been at Cambridge, but we hadn't got so far as Ely when John got the marsh ague so we laid up for three days in a hamlet . . . we'd just taken the road again, bound for Ely, when we met these knights. We could see smoke in the distance, looked as if it was coming from Ely. I reckon they'd set fire to some building or other there. They had prisoners; two girls there were, crying their eyes out, poor things, sitting in front of the men who'd got them, and a man who looked half-dead, slung across the horse in front of another . . . when they saw us they just went for us, laughing. Sport, it was. We tried to dodge away and they just spun their horses this way and that, and came for us. John was run through at once. Two of them started batting me about between the flats of their swords. Then one took a swipe with a blade that did for my harp. Oh, my poor harp!' Howell saw the ruined instrument lying beside him and picked it up, cradling it as though it were a hurt child. 'I fell into a ditch and I suppose they thought I was dead . . . they just left the others lying. They killed them all, for nothing. Then they galloped off. I couldn't believe it. I still can't. I got up and ran and ran. And lost my bearings. It was yesterday, not today . . .'

229

'But who were they?' said Meg in alarm. 'And which way did they go?'

'Oh, back towards Ely. Not this way. They've not been here, that's plain. You'd have noticed if they had, indeed to goodness you would.'

'But *who* were they?' Did they carry any devices?' asked Adam.

'Oh yes, oh God yes, I knew them. I knew their leader. We've seen him in London. Sung about him too, the rat-faced bastard . . .'

'Who was he?' asked Adam quietly.

'Geoffrey,' said Howell. 'Geoffrey de Mandeville.'

The news arrived by official channels, through a proclamation in Norwich and one of Sir Aubrey's friends, who sent him a worried message of warning.

The king had made Geoffrey de Mandeville surrender his earldom of Essex and the keys of his castles, and let him go. He had made straight for Ely, that well-known malcontents' stronghold, and was now embattled there, building himself a new and unlicensed territory by force, a war-lord owing allegiance to no one but himself and the men he must feed and pay in order to command their swords.

In the spring, he came to Rushley.

Keeping the cows going through the winter was never easy. They had to manage on hay and by the time the first green grass showed in the meadows, they had hip bones like spade handles and the calves they carried were slung beneath their spines like bundles of washing. Taking them out into the meadows when the year turned in March was always a pleasure.

Many people in Oxfen and Rushley owned cows or oxen but there was a wider choice of pasture now. Apart from the reclaimed stretches of marshland, the Grosnez family who farmed Normansland, halfway between the two villages, and held one of the best tracts of grazing, were willing to let others use it for a consideration. The Grosnez family had grown wealthier since FitzSimon's day, taking over additional tracts of land. They still kept themselves to themselves and spoke French at home, but they were reasonably co-operative neighbours. Meg sent fresh cream cheese to Normansland every May and three matured cheeses every Christmas; the smith, who kept two cows on the side, now and then shod Grosnez horses for nothing and the Eelfishers, who did the same thing, sent an eel pie twice a year. In return, they could graze their animals on the Grosnez pastures for several weeks each year. It worked very well.

Margaret now had the task of driving her family's cows to pasture and bringing them back for milking, but occasionally Meg went with her, to keep an eye on the cows and their condition.

At nearly nine years old, Margaret, as well as the chestnut hair and blackberry eyes which Adam had admired, had acquired a chunky and pugnacious jaw and a firm way of walking which were perfectly accurate guides to her character. 'You have a mutinous streak,' her mother sometimes said. Things about which Margaret regularly felt mutinous included the eternal round of tasks Meg expected her to do in the house and Meg's disapproval of her friendship with Philip. Herding the cows was greatly to her taste because it took her outside the house and sometimes she encountered Philip while she was out, although he found it harder to get away since the old miller died and he had to help his father Siward in the mill more than before. He didn't appear when her mother was with her, either. She was glad that this occurred only rarely.

Meg accompanied her, however, at the end of the first week's grazing that spring. 'Daisy's going to be the first to drop her calf,' Meg said, looking critically at the cows as their muzzles went down eagerly to the fresh grass in the Normansland meadow halfway between Rushley village and the ditch close to the place where Ragenhild's father had once lain in wait for Messire Walter. 'They've all come through the winter well. So've we, considering.'

By that, she meant that all through the winter she hadn't had more aches in the joints than usual, the outbreaks of ague had been mild, and even her two small boys, who were still at a vulnerable age, had reached the spring with sound lungs and limbs although they did have cold sores.

Even now, thick mantles and sturdy boots and gloves were wise, but when the sun came out between the swift brown and white clouds, there were signs of warmth in it. As she and Margaret began to walk back to the village, Meg surveyed the landscape with a sense of better times coming. The distant ploughland was misted with green where the corn was beginning and it looked already like a promising crop, which would next year give ample work to the mill whose steep-pitched oak roof was a distinctive landmark on the edge of the village. There were buds on the alder trees which now grew along the River Wend, all the way from Oxfen to Rushley hall. And she was not yet old.

Adam always became more attentive in spring; they might have another child before next Christmas. She might try some kind of brightening wash to put the colour back in her hair.

She then clicked her tongue in mild disapproval at the sight of a small, familiar figure hurrying towards them along the path from Rushley. She could not have said why she so much disliked Margaret's friendship with Adam's nephew Philip. She would not have admitted to herself that Philip already looked amazingly like his uncle, and that she feared the attraction that seemed to lie between males of their type, and Margaret.

She thought only that the friendship was 'not a good thing, too much all in the family', and that Margaret should be married the moment she was old enough, and most definitely not to Philip.

Philip was in a very great hurry indeed. He saw them, waved wildly and broke from a trot into a sprint.

'Philip!' said Meg severely as he came up. 'What on earth's the matter?'

'Hide!' gasped Philip. 'Quick, quick, hide! Take cover! That's what Dad said to tell you! We saw you go past the mill with the cows . . . oh come on, quick, hurry!'

231

'Look, Philip, what do you mean? Who have we got to hide from? If this is some sort of game . . .'

'Of course it isn't a game! It's him, he's come, he's ridden into the village! He . . .'

'Who?'

'That de Mandeville man! Oh, quickly . . . !'

Margaret said, in a high voice: 'The mill . . .'

A mile away where the timber roof of the mill jutted up above the humbler reed-thatched roofs of the cottages, a thick column of black smoke was rising into the windy skies. Philip looked once, made a choking sound and would have begun at once to rush back home, but Meg caught hold of him. 'No, Philip, don't! You're right, we must get out of sight. Margaret . . .'

'But the cows! Our cows!'

'But, look!' Philip pointed urgently towards Rushley. 'There are horsemen coming!'

'The alders!' said Meg.

It was their only chance. The wide pastures under the arching East Anglian skies offered no other protection: no hillock or copse or blessed clump of bushes. Narrow Wood, which might have given some shelter, was too far off, on the other side of the ditch, and the ditch itself was useless, with nothing but a steep drop straight into muddy water. But the alder-hung river was fairly close. And de Mandeville's reputation was horrifying. Abandoning the cows, hustling the children before her, Meg ran. The grass caught at their feet and the open ground between them and shelter seemed endless, wide as infinity. They were all panting for breath before the ground sloped under their feet and they plunged down the river bank. If they had not been seen already, they would have a chance. If they had been seen . . . crouching with Philip and Margaret on the tiny ledge of earth between the bottom of the bank and the purling water, under the drooping alder branches which were not yet even in leaf, Meg shuddered.

Adam Millerson and Gytha's son William had been working in the beanfield near the manorhouse and ran to warn Lady Cicely, but with the invaders so close behind them that there was no time even to bar the gates. But the modest defences of the house could not in any case have kept this expert warlord out. Cicely summoned the other men of the household and told them to stand behind her at the entrance to the hall. The women she ordered up to the solar together with the three children she had at home. Her eldest son Gilles was training for knighthood in another household, which was as well, for he was a well-grown and hotheaded twelve years old. Then, arms folded, she awaited the invaders.

They consisted of two dozen men, including several knights, and their leader, whom she recognised instantly. She would have known him even if he had not had a standard-bearer at his side. The Jongleurs were gone but before their end they had described those small mean eyes and mouth and that retroussé, rodent-like nose in graphic and disparaging verse, and more than once.

'Good morning, Sir Geoffrey. It is Sir Geoffrey de Mandeville, is it not?' She stopped, unable to think what to say next.

De Mandeville looked at her. Lady Cicely looked steadily back at him. She knew very well what was going through his mind. He was probably aware that Sir Aubrey was away with his own overlord, among the king's forces, and that Rushley manor was defended only by the handful of men he could see before him now. He might also know that the bulk of Sir Aubrey's wealth was now tied up in masons' work, stained glass and gold and silver in the new church. He was wondering how much plunder he would find here, and he was also wondering whether or not to include Lady Cicely in his booty.

But she was no longer all that young and she had had the smallpox. Usually, she wore her veil drawn over her forehead to hide the scars but now she had pushed it back so that the damage should show to the best advantage. She waited.

Sir Geoffrey drew off his gauntlets and said: 'We want all the food you have in the house. And your treasure chest. Co-operate and no one will be hurt.' He glanced over his shoulder. Some of the men had already dismounted and were catching fowls and opening the stable. Behind her, Lady Cicely sensed the stable boy making a movement of protest. Without turning, she made a stay-there sign.

Still without looking round, she spoke to the steward immediately behind her. 'Gerbert, lead our visitors to the stores in the undercroft. The rest of you men, step back and stand along the wall. If you will come this way, Sir Geoffrey, I will show you our money chest.'

He followed her through the hall. Two knights and two men-at-arms came too. She had already had the chest brought out from the bedchamber where it was usually kept and placed on the dais table. Silently, she handed him the keys and watched him inspect the contents. 'Is this all there is?' he said. His voice was light and cold.

'Not quite.' Lady Cicely unclipped a pouch from her girdle. 'Here is my jewellery. There was, of course, more in the money chest than this at one time. My husband has the rest with him.'

'Ah yes. He's away on his knight service. An admirable man and an example to us all,' said de Mandeville. He snapped his fingers and the men-at-arms set about emptying the chest. The jewel pouch he attached to his own belt. Lady Cicely waited once more, and silently prayed.

'Does your husband always leave you alone here with only men as companions?' de Mandeville asked.

'No, Sir Geoffrey. I ordered my womenfolk to withdraw out of sight. I am sure your own lady would do the same in like circumstances.'

De Mandeville regarded her thoughtfully. She kept her chin up and her hands clasped over her girdle in the hope that he wouldn't see them shaking. She met his eyes squarely. His were a dark slate-blue, flat and opaque. He and she were both of knightly rank. From the moment of his arrival, she had maintained the conventions of an exchange between such people and she had done it with such conviction that those conventions were still restraining him. But the least provocation would break that cage of convention asunder and within it was a beast full of an ungovernable fury.

If she had never been told what kind of man he was, she would still know; she would smell it. He would murder as easily as he would step on an ant. He would watch torture while eating his dinner. He would rape as lightly as though he were passing water.

He was just three feet away.

He looked at the stairs that led to the upper floor. 'I take it that the women are up there. Some may be good-looking and some may have families who would pay for their safe return. Are you about to tell me that two of them are sick with a violent and contagious pestilence?'

Continuing to hold his eyes, she risked a response to the dangerous banter in his voice, and said: 'No. Three.'

De Mandeville laughed. It was an extraordinarily unpleasant sound. His men, whose very lack of facial expression conveyed menace, stood poised behind him, ready to climb the stairs at his order.

'You're lucky,' de Mandeville said. 'It's too early in the morning for rape and I have mouths enough to feed in Ely. I daresay my boys have picked up a few pretty but worthless extras in the village anyway. Good day to you.'

Fifteen minutes later, the intruders were gone. Lady Cicely sank down on a seat by the table and leaned her pitted forehead on her hands. The sweat of terror streamed down her temples and her back. Her hair was soaking, as if she had dipped it in a basin of water. She was shaking uncontrollably.

There was a not a scrap of food left in the house or a fowl left in the courtyard. They had taken everything away, on the ponies stolen from the stable. There wasn't likely to be much left in Oxfen or Rushley, either. She would have to send Gerbert to Norwich to buy provisions in a hurry. Fortunately, she had money. The money chest had indeed been somewhat depleted, but not because Sir Aubrey had taken it on knight service with him. As a precaution, as the news of de Mandeville's depredations grew worse and worse, he had put several pounds of silver in a bucket and dangled it down the well.

So far, so good. And the household were all safe. When she thought what might have happened, she wanted to be sick. It was difficult not to be as it was. She had protected the people in the manor-house, but she had been able to do nothing for the village.

And she had already caught sight of the smoke rising from the mill in Rushley.

In the village, the morning had been proceeding as usual. Most of the women had congregated at the well to collect water for the day, and Mary, the wife of Alfred Carpenter's son Peter, decided to wash her linen. It was a lengthy business and now was a good time because she hadn't to worry about feeding Peter. He was away in Norwich, buying timber for his father. Lady Cis wanted some new trestle tables made.

She and Peter had been married a fortnight after Meg and Adam, the second couple to celebrate their wedding in Rushley's new church. Their little boy was two years old and for the last few days, Mary had been thinking that it was just possible there was another on the way. She never took much account of time but she was fairly sure she was overdue. Also, she hadn't much fancied her breakfast that morning, and she usually had a hearty appetite.

She made a good fire out of doors in the space between the back of the cottage and the edge of the vegetable patch, and set the linen to boil. She put small Peterkin where she could keep an eye on him and gave him a toy, a wooden animal which Peter had made, to play with. She used a pole to push the fabric well down into the cauldron. Her mind was full of the work in hand, and with wondering whether the possible new baby would be a brother or a sister for Peterkin, and whether the thin patch she had lately noticed on top of her husband's head meant that he was going bald, when she heard the sound of hoofbeats and an outcry.

She couldn't at first make out which direction the sounds came from. Then she saw smoke pouring up from somewhere, and ran round the cottage in alarm.

The village street was full of confusion. People ran distractedly about, clutching belongings or small children, and mailed figures on horseback seemed to be chasing them, apparently for fun. Other mailed figures, on foot, were striding in and out of the houses, grabbing things: sacks of meal, casks of fish or ale; one man was catching fowls and tying their legs.

Another had hold of a screaming girl and was dragging her towards his horse. Mary wheeled, obeying the instinct which said *seize your baby and get out of sight.* But the armed strangers were everywhere; they had already invaded the space behind her cottage. Before she reached Peterkin, she heard him shriek. Rushing round the corner, she found that two of the invaders had caught hold of him and were playing ball with him, throwing him back and forth between them. They were laughing and as Mary hurled herself towards them, crying: 'Stop, stop it, leave him alone!' they deliberately let him fall and one of them kicked him.

He had seen her. He screamed for her to save him. There was blood on his face and on his hands and knees and as he tried to get up and run to her, another kick knocked him down.

It was all happening so quickly. A moment ago she had been boiling linen without a thought in her mind beyond the matters of everyday and now . . .

'Beast, beasts, stop it, let him be,' he's only a little boy!' Sobbing and raging, Mary ran and tried to pick Peterkin up. One of the men, still laughing, shouted something at her in French, drew his sword and made believe to be protecting himself from her, while all the time getting between her and Peterkin. The other man tried to catch hold of her.

She wanted Peter; she wanted to call his name, to bring him miraculously from Norwich to defend her and Peterkin, but even while she was thinking: *I want him*, she acted. The cauldron was still bubbling on the fire. She turned and seized it, heaving it up with more strength than she had known was in her and lurched round to throw it over the child's tormentors.

But it was heavy and she was too slow. They saw the danger. But Mary never saw the swinging blade which sliced her almost in two and left her butchered with her blood soaking into the steaming linen and the puddle of spilt water where she lay.

'It must have been quick,' people tried to console her husband Peter later. 'She can't have known anything about it. And you have your son. They just left him there. What a mercy he wasn't badly hurt. Maybe Mary died saving him.'

'I'm glad Peterkin is safe. But I want Mary,' said Peter dully.

The patch of thinning hair that Mary had noticed just before he went to Norwich, had before the year's end developed to full-scale baldness. Peter thought it was with grief, and then grieved afresh, because it was so absurd, so feeble an expression of a sorrow so tremendous.

Although there were no leaves yet on the alders, only buds and catkins, there was a twiggy undergrowth, sprouting from stumps where trees had been cut, usually by the Eelfisher clan, to make clogs and stilts and boat-poles from the water-resistant wood. As they crouched beneath the overhang of the bank, this tangle made a thin shelter above them.

'Keep still!' Meg panted. 'Quite, quite still.' She secretly thanked God that none of them happened to be wearing anything red or yellow. They were all in serviceable russet and green and would blend with their surroundings.

'But the *cows!*' said Margaret for approximately the sixth time.

'It's probably the cows they're after. Do you think you could stop them?' snapped Meg, with her face against a tree root and her knees driving into mud. 'Fancy being carried off to Ely and used for a pallet every night? For anyone who thinks you'd be warmer than straw? Now shut up!' With the flat of her hand, she pushed her daughter harder against the ground and held her there.

'I can hear hoofbeats,' whispered Philip.

'It's all right,' said Margaret. She slid out a hand to take one of his. 'They won't find us.'

'They found the mill.' He bit the last word off sharply on a sob.

The hooves were near now. There were voices, shouting to each other across the meadow. A horse went past so close that the alders above them quivered. Far off, cows lowed in alarm. More shouts, and hoofbeats receding at a gallop. Meg dared not lift her face from the tree roots but guessed that the horsemen were rounding up the cows. That's right, harry cows in calf. Stupid brutes. Oh dear God, was Adam safe? He'd gone off to Sir Aubrey's land that morning; they were planting vegetables and making new fowlhouses, he'd said. Had he had warning and been able to hide?

Only yards away, a horse snorted. All the intruders hadn't gone after the cows, then. She pressed herself yet harder against the earth and pressed Margaret with her. Terrifyingly close at hand, a man spoke, in French. She recognised a few words. He seemed to be saying that the cowherds must have run away.

Another man answered, saying something she couldn't hear. Then he laughed. The first one, whose voice was slower and carried more, said – again comprehensibly – 'They've more sense than that fool girl who went for us with a washtub!' They both laughed this time.

What was happening up at the manor-house? Meg wondered feverishly. Had Lady Cis been harmed? Rumour said that it was usually villeins and ordinary freemen whom de Mandeville and his men robbed and raped. The Grosnez household would be in danger. So would the two churches. De Mandeville had no respect for things sacred. He was said to have turned all the monks out of Ely Monastery and stabled his horses in the cloister. Oh God, oh dear saints, protect everyone. She must not tremble too much, or the twigs would crackle.

Above them, the horses fidgeted. What if the men brought them down to drink? No, the bank was too steep just here. But one of the horses was so close that it had brushed against the alders and rustled them. She could see Margaret's and Philip's hands pinkly clasped and would have covered them with a fold of russet skirt, but movement was dangerous. It might draw the eye. Her hand was still on Margaret's back and under her palm she could feel a shudder which might at any moment turn into a sob of fear. Her own heart was pounding so hard against the earth that surely, in a moment, the men above them would feel the vibration. Every sinew in her body was like a lyre-string. If anyone touched her even with a fingertip, she would give off a long quivering moan.

The men had fallen silent. Did they know someone was hiding here? Were they making signs to each other? Grinning, jabbing thumbs, preparing to dismount and inspect the bank?

She was seized by an unreasonable but incredibly powerful desire to spring up and surrender before they were all dragged out by force. Her head came up. But someone in the distance was shouting, and bridles chinked nearby as reins were gathered up. Meg's head sank again, the breath going out of her in a long, slow sigh as she heard hooves moving away, receding towards Rushley.

After a long time, a very long time, cold, cramped and frightened, they crept out from beneath the alders and timidly looked about them. There were no horsemen to be seen. There were no cows either. The smoke still poured from the place where the mill roof had been but the roof was no longer there. There was smoke also from the direction of the Grosnez farmhouse.

'We must go back,' said Meg. 'But carefully.' She wanted to run wildly to find Adam, to see if their small sons, whom she had left with Adam's sisters, were safe, but another part of her feared to leave the shelter of the alders and she had her daughter and Philip to protect. She began to lead them warily back along by the river, still under the trees, gnawing her lip in dread.

The columns of smoke were gradually dying down. The men wouldn't have hurt the little boys, surely. Meg kept on saying it to herself, over and over. But de Mandeville was a name of such darkness that anything was possible. Then Margaret said: 'Someone's coming!' and a figure running along the path from Rushley turned into Adam, and Meg, crying out with thankfulness, abandoning the alders, catching the children's hands, was running in turn, to meet him.

'Oh dear God, you're all right!' On Adam's face, the ruddy weathering of wind and sun lay in patches over the greyness of fear, but he was alive and on his feet and babbling with relief at finding them the same.

'Yes, we hid!' Meg gasped. 'The boys, Adam, our boys, are they all right?'

'The cows are gone,' said Margaret miserably.

'So's the mill,' said Adam. 'They . . . yes, our boys are all right, Meg. My sisters took them into the reeds across the river. But . . . Philip, I'm sorry . . . you'd best come home with us. I didn't get back to the village till it was all over but when I got there I found out . . . they've taken your parents away. Siward and your mother; they carried them off. They searched the mill for his gold and couldn't find it, so they fired the place . . . oh God, it's so horrible; they've taken three or four young girls away and . . . Gytha . . . they were searching houses. Seems she shouted at them and they ran her through, just drove a pike right through her . . . she wasn't the only one, either; young Mary's dead too . . . they ransacked Rushley Church and they killed poor old Father Gerald. He tried to stop them . . . Meg, oh Meg, I was so afraid for you.'

'And I for you.' She was in his arms, hungry for the security of the man's chest under her face and the strength of his arms round her. 'Where did you go? Where were you?'

'In the beanfield, with Gytha's William. We ran up to the manor-house, to warn Lady Cicely. She protected us. I see you've taken care of these children. You've kept Margaret safe. She's already so pretty,' said Adam, quite unaware of causing any hurt, 'child as she is, with men like that, anything could have happened.'

Over the next few days, they tried to realise what had been lost but could not yet take it in.

There had been a few lucky escapes. Someone had seen de Mandeville approaching, recognised his banner – Geoffrey de Mandeville never showed the slightest desire to hide his identity – and given the alarm just in time for a handful of villagers, such as Adam's sisters, to get away into the reeds on the other side of the Wend. Some people, too, had had cattle and sheep on the reclaimed pastures near the marshes and had succeeded in driving them away to the same marsh refuges which had proved such a blessing during the trouble at Ely. Rushley still had a few animals left, including about half of the plough-oxen.

But the two eldest Grosnez sons and their father had died defending their house and though their mother and the thirteen-year-old youngest boy had fled in time and hidden in Narrow Wood, the mother was ill with grief; she had been attacked by the marsh ague and might not live.

Rushley Church had been stripped and a second squadron of de Mandeville's men had attacked Oxfen, robbing the church there of gold and silver candlesticks and ornaments, while the dower-hall at Oxfen had been ransacked and the steward knocked unconscious in resentment because the family was not using the hall at the moment and there was so little there worth taking. From all the houses in the two villages, anything of the slightest value had been snatched. In one day, Rushley and Oxfen had become poor, as they had not been even when FitzSimon first came to Rushley.

De Mandeville's men came back a few days later, went straight to the byre where Siward the Miller housed his oxen and found the hoard of gold rings and silver coins which he had inherited from his father, hidden under the floor. They brought Siward back with them and dumped him unceremoniously in the byre.

He was wearing the clothes in which he had been taken. They were splashed and stained with blood, and blood was crusted on his hands and round his mouth and in long crimson streaks down his chin. He stumbled from the byre and into Adam's house, where Adam and his family found him when they returned from the hiding place in the reeds. He tried to speak to them and they saw that he had lost all the upper teeth on one side of his mouth.

'They pulled them out, one by one, till I told where the gold was,' he whispered. 'We've nothing now. No savings. No mill.'

Philip said tearfully: 'Where is Mother?'

His father, crying and pressing a palm to his mutilated jaw, said: 'She was still comely. She died. Don't ask how.'

Chapter Fifteen

Bid for Freedom

'Do my eyes deceive me,' said young Sir Gilles FitzAubrey, 'or is there a coffin dangling from that apple tree?' He reined his restive horse in and surveyed the spectacle with interest, one gauntleted hand on his hip.

'You're quite correct,' said his father's steward Gerbert. 'That is the coffin of Sir Geoffrey de Mandeville and this is a short cut through the orchard of the church to which his body was brought when he was killed. That coffin's been there for eight years.'

'You mean he's in it? You're talking about the de Mandeville who stopped an arrow in 1144?' Sir Gilles flexed his fingers and checked his stallion's apparent desire to take off from de Mandeville's proximity at a gallop.

'That's right, sir.'

'Took his helmet off on a hot day,' said Sir Gilles reminiscently. 'He was besieging a royal outpost in Cambridgeshire, wasn't he? I remember. I was only thirteen but there was a lot of laughter at his expense and the sergeant who was training us said we'd better take it as a warning. So they brought him all the way back to London for his funeral, did they? But what, pray, is he doing up there? Isn't it more customary for dead men to be buried? Why is he slung in an orchard? He really doesn't go with all that pretty blossom.'

'He was excommunicated,' said Gerbert. 'He'd despoiled the church. He threw the Ely monks out of their monastery, put his horses in the cloister and then went and plundered another abbey and burned it down. He can't be buried in consecrated ground and his sons won't let him be buried anywhere else.'

'He was the one who held the king's daughter-in-law to ransom as well,' said Gilles, grinning. 'Quite a man, wasn't he? You can see why his sons admired him.'

Gerbert looked sidelong at his master's eldest son and sighed, but was wise enough not to let Sir Gilles see it.

Young Sir Gilles, alas, was nothing like his father Aubrey.

Heredity was a funny thing. No one in the world could be sweeter or more fairspoken than Lady Cis, but her father, whom Gerbert had seen two or three times, was arrogant and sensual and all these characteristics had come out in her son. Even at the age of twenty, his type was fixed. It was there in the full hazel eyes with the thick, mobile brows above them, in the broad lips and the arch of the nostrils, in the intonation of the light, super-cilious voice and the way he was sitting his bay destrier now, deliberately annoying it with the spur and controlling it with one disdainful hand while the other lay idle on his hip.

Perhaps time would mellow him. He was raw, said Gerbert comfortingly to himself. He could make jests about coffins and death even though he had been summoned from his service to his lord because his father was ill. Neither life nor death had touched him yet.

Mildly, Gerbert said: 'Perhaps we should get on. We should be well clear of London today.'

'Quite, Gerbert, if you say so.' Sir Gilles was indulgent. He waved his escort forward. He had a squire of his own, and his father had sent three knights to lend him status. 'On our way!' he said and led the way across the orchard, with the stallion curvetting under him.

Lady Cis was waiting on the steps of the hall when they rode in. Sir Gilles dismounted, tossing his reins to his squire, and ran up the steps to kneel and kiss his mother's hand.

'Madam!'

'I'm glad to see you, Gilles. Very glad.' He had sent one of the knights galloping ahead to warn her of his approach and Lady Cis had taken the opportunity to put on a fresh gown and head-dress. But they could not disguise the tiredness of her face. 'Your father is waiting for you,' she said.

'How is he? Is he any better?'

'Come and see,' said his mother, and led the way inside.

When she brought him to the bedchamber where Aubrey FitzRoger lay, even the unsubtle Gilles saw at once that when she said 'Your father is waiting for you,' the words had more than their face value. The man who lay propped up on the pillows because he was too weak to sit up without their help, the man with the violet shadows under his over-bright eyes, and the yellowed skin stretched over bones from which the flesh had melted like wax, had done more than long for his son's return; he had held off death in order to see it.

Gilles came to the bedside. 'Father? What's wrong with you?'

'Who knows? I can't eat. I'm sick if I do. I've had terrible pains in my stomach. Not so much now, though.'

'Then you're mending, perhaps?'

'No,' said Sir Aubrey quietly. 'I think not. That's why I told your mother to send for you.'

There was something wrong with his voice. It was husky. There were curious knobs and bumps on his face, too. One hand lay outside his covers and when Gilles laid his own hand over it, it was hot to touch and very thin.

'What does your physician say?' Gilles asked. He glanced up at the brown-habited monk who had been on duty in the sickroom when Lady Cis brought him in. This, she had said, was the physician, loaned to them from Ely.

'He recommends prayer,' whispered Aubrey. 'Very wise. Nothing short of a miracle would work. But there isn't going to be a miracle. Now, listen to me. My head isn't always clear but I *made* it be clear when your mother came and said your banner was approaching . . . in a short time now, you will be lord of Oxfen and Rushley. You'll live here from now on. You understand?'

'Yes, Father.'

'Your younger brother is in service as a squire and will make his own way. Your sisters are betrothed and their dowries set by. Your mother has charge of that. There's some . . .'

His voice faded. The monk-physician moved forward with a cup of water and moistened the patient's mouth. Aubrey turned his head restlessly from side to side under the ministrations. The monk stepped back and Aubrey forced himself to resume, although his speech was fainter now. 'There's a little treasure for you. Not much. I tried to replace some of what that devil de Mandeville stole from our church and I had your sisters to consider. But there's something. And you'll have the lands. I want you . . . promise . . .'

Firmly, Gilles grasped the burning fingers beneath his. 'I'll promise whatever you wish, Father.'

'The lands. The church. The people. Look after them. They'll be in your power. Power means responsibility. Be . . . be . . .'

'It's all right, Father. Don't try to talk. I understand.'

'Remember the parable of the good shepherd,' whispered Sir Aubrey. 'You'll be a good lord to everyone that looks to you? I want . . . your . . . promise . . . promise?'

'I promise.'

'Thank God,' said Sir Aubrey and closed his eyes. In the quiet, his breathing was harsh.

The physician came to Gilles's side. 'He'll sleep, I hope. I shall remain with him. I have a draught for him in case the pain comes back. I am hoping that the end may come without that.'

The stone hall of Rushley manor had a buttress tower at one end. This contained the tiny chapel and two bedchambers above, one of them the room where his father lay. The roof of the tower was flat and surrounded by crenellations as though it were part of a miniature castle. On leaving his father, it was to this roof that Gilles immediately went. He went up in the first instance to get away from the bedchamber with its shadows and the odours of sickness and the cloying sweetness of the herbs which were being burned in a brazier in an attempt to dispel them. He wanted too to get away from the monkish prayers and the tears of his sisters, who had been waiting to come in as soon as he left.

But once there, he realised that the roof provided more than the fresh wind blowing across the marshes from the sea. It also provided a view of the lands that one day, one day very soon, would be his.

His.

It wasn't that he didn't love his father, he assured himself as he stood with his palms on two adjacent crenellations and looked out between them. But he had seen him only twice since being sent away at the age of ten to learn his knightly trade in another man's household. And besides . . .

Well, *of course* he loved his father. It was terrible to see the poor old man in such a pass as this. Really, it would be a mercy when God saw fit to take his soul away to heaven. But there was no denying that Aubrey wasn't the kind of father Gilles would have liked best to have. The kind of father he would have appreciated was more like, well, Geoffrey de Mandeville. De Mandeville had been a real man. In the midst of the civil war, he'd given King Stephen a second enemy to fight, one nearly as dangerous as the empress herself. Now that was a feat. He'd terrorised the whole of East Anglia too and that was another.

People had fled at the sight of him and frightened disobedient children with the sound of his name. He'd only died because of a moment's carelessness. He'd never been defeated. Geoffrey de Mandeville had been *someone*.

Of course, he understood what his father meant about looking after his people. Naturally, if you wanted your villeins to work for you, you had to see that they had enough to eat and all that sort of thing. Not too much, of course. Fat villeins were no good; they'd be too shortwinded to work well. But within reason, yes, he saw the point of looking after them. One would look after one's oxen in the same way.

He would be a perfectly good lord to the people of Oxfen and Rushley, provided that they behaved themselves.

But he wouldn't be soft. His father had been too soft; he'd seen that from simply riding through Rushley village on the way here. There'd been children playing who were old enough to be doing something more useful, and Gerbert had said that some very good cows which they'd noticed grazing, belonged to a villein family. Apparently, a few of the villagers had managed to drive their cattle into hiding at the time of de Mandeville's visitation and although Sir Aubrey had lost all his, it hadn't occurred to him to replace them by claiming the villeins' cows. Absurd. As if villeins could own anything outright apart from their ever-grumbling bellies. What was theirs was their lord's.

Lords who didn't claim their rights gave the bondfolk ideas and when they started having ideas, they were apt to start wanting to commute their traditional service on the land to money. He knew of places where this had happened, and the villeins in question had tried to claim that this gave them free status. Once let them do that, and they'd be up and off, leaving the land without hands to work it.

No, no. He had a great deal of leeway to make up. His mother was too given to charitable works and his father had been far too devoted to the church – from the look of him now, God hadn't been exactly grateful – and the treasure chest was obviously not as full as it ought to be. He'd want every possible ounce of work out of those smug villeins down there.

He'd better see his father's clerk – what was his name? Wilfrid, yes – who kept records of all rents and services owed and what they were for, and go through them with him. Oh yes, when he, Sir Gilles, was lord here, those folk were going to see some changes.

After a time, he went down again to the hall and found that food was ready, and that his mother was there to share it. 'How is my father now?' he enquired politely.

'Unconscious. The physician hopes he won't . . . won't wake up again. He only held on so long for your sake. You've promised him everything he wants?'

'Yes, Mother. Mother, what will you do if. . . ?'

'I shan't stay here to be a nuisance to you,' said Lady Cis lightly. 'The house at Oxfen has been kept in good order but none of us has lived there since your great-grandmother Adelisa died. I shall move over there. But this house will need a mistress and indeed, since you will be lord here, you should be thinking about your own heir. I have one or two young ladies in mind for you to consider, unless you have already . . .'

'By no means, Mother. I shall be happy to abide by your choice. I'm sure I can trust you to choose well.'

'You're a good son. We've been apart for a long time but perhaps, in time to come, we shall get to know each other better.'

He knew what she meant. She would live a couple of miles away at Oxfen and be riding over here every five minutes, advising his wife on how to bring up his children, trying to influence her so that she in turn would influence him, attempting at one remove to dilute his rule with piety and softness, just as she had very probably diluted his father's.

He'd keep his word to his father, but he'd be a good lord in his own way, not Sir Aubrey's way – or Lady Cis's way, either.

Get to know each other better? Not, thought Sir Gilles as he kissed his mother's hand, if he could help it.

'For the last time,' said Meg, 'you are not going to marry Philip. I'm sick of telling you. You deaf or stupid or something? Philip's got no more to offer you now than three years back when all this nonsense started.'

And I still wouldn't let you marry him if he had. I hardly know why, myself, but I don't care. Philip looks like Adam and you're not damned well having either of them.

'It isn't fair!' Margaret wailed. She crouched in the corner where Meg's backhander had thrown her, her arms protectively over her head. 'If only the mill had been rebuilt instead of them just making the Oxfen one bigger . . .'

'If only, if only. The world's full of if only's, my girl!'

If only looking after that horrible old man Ivon hadn't worn me out before my time; if only I'd had bright hair and no lines on my face when Adam married me, I'd be happier, I'd feel safer, I wouldn't hate my own daughter . . .

'Philip's doing all he can. He's got his father to look after. His father just sits by the fire all day and broods; he won't even *try* . . . Philip works and works; he does other people's demesne service for them; he's saving and putting things together. In a few more years . . .'

'You think you're going to clutter this house up for a few more years? You've another think coming, let me tell you. How old are you? Sixteen, seventeen in another month and still not married. I'd have got you married long since, except that you made such a fuss and said you didn't want to and Adam backed you up and then you started all this nonsense about Philip. Well, you just forget about Philip! What's wrong with Peter Brownpate? Anyone'ud think I was trying to fix you up with a hunchback or something. Brownpate's a good man; you're the envy of every girl in the village because he's offered for you. When Mary was alive there wasn't a happier wife in Rushley. Adam's in favour. He won't back you up this time, my lady!' said Meg. Margaret whimpered, knowing that it was true.

The day that Meg and Adam were married, she had seen for herself how Peter the carpenter's son had blown kisses to his own future wife, Mary, across the church. During the time that those two were married, she had been still too young to understand the comments that she heard. But she had heard them repeated later, many times over, after Mary's dreadful death. She understood well enough now about Peter the son of Alfred Carpenter, now called Peter Brownpate, and his young wife Mary.

Marriage was a part of life, unless one left the world behind altogether and entered religion, and few villeins did that, even in Rushley, where Sir Aubrey had been generally in favour and even willing to waive his right to charge for his consent. For the most part, as soon as a boy was capable of providing for a family and as soon as a girl was capable of having one, they were urged to get on with it. Life was uncertain and the sooner one made one's contribution to the next generation, the better.

The business of getting the next generation was the link between man and woman, and there wasn't much else. Young girls and boys sometimes took irrational fancies to this or that member of the opposite sex, and imagined that their union would take them into fairyland, but if they married, it wasn't long before the gruelling cycle of toil, daybreak to sunset, to keep the earth tilled and the animals tended, the roof repaired and the floor swept, the household fed and properly clothed, had battered romantic dreaming to death. Partnership might endure; there might still be possessiveness and clutching need. Meg knew all about that. But not romance.

Between some couples there was active dislike; where there was violence or unfaithfulness or somebody was too lazy to do their share. The rest, if they thought about the matter at all, considered themselves happy.

Except when confronted by a couple like Peter and his Mary.

Peter Brownpate had acquired his nickname only after Mary's death, when he suddenly went bald, and then developed a permanent tan on his scalp as a result of working in the fields, for as well as helping in the carpenter's workshop, he tilled his father's smallholding. Mary hadn't known him as Brownpate.

The man Mary had married was the short, strong young Peter with a head of dark hair, inherited (as Ragenhild's had been) from a strain of dark-haired Danes who had settled the district long ago and mingled with the flaxenhaired Saxons. He was good-tempered, quiet in his speech and sure in his movements, but until his marriage, there was nothing else about him that was remarkable.

Mary had been like many other girls: fairish, roundish, strong of body and uncomplicated of mind. Their wedding was well attended. They were both popular and the match was suitable in an ordinary kind of way. Sir Aubrey had let Peter build a small wattle-and-daub cottage of his own for them to live in and another ordinary villein couple set up house in Rushley.

It had taken a little time for the word to get round that there was something very slightly unusual about that household.

It was a good deal more than just happy.

Even after a year, and with the usual baby on its mother's hip, Peter was still more inclined to smile at his wife when he came back from the fields than to make brusque demands to be helped off with his boots and given his dinner. Mary would join the other women to draw water from the well and would gossip like the others or exchange obstetric confidences, but she never joined in when the other women were capping each other's tales of their husbands' bullying. She looked, on the contrary, slightly puzzled and occasionally shocked.

Then it began to get known that if one chanced to call at the Brownpate cottage when both he and Mary were there, there was, well, a feeling about it. A warm feeling, Adam had called it once, when talking to a group of cronies at the end of a summer day, and heads had nodded thoughtfully. They knew what he meant. One of them expanded on the theme. 'It's a sort of solid feeling, like.'

And solid it had remained, without wavering, until de Mandeville came.

Afterwards, it was clear from Peter's stricken face, from his unashamed tears at the graveside and the astonishingly rapid loss of his hair, that those who thought they had detected something remarkable in that marriage had not imagined it.

But he had strength of mind; he had pulled himself out of his grief, arranging for Mary's sister to take care of Peterkin, and hurling himself into an orgy of work on the grounds that he must make some recompense to his sister-in-law and her husband for their trouble.

He had made more out of his extra work than poor Philip had, since he had carpentry skills to sell. Now, since his father's death, he and his brother had decided to share the workshop and they'd done a deal with Sir Aubrey: extra carpentry work on the demesne in exchange for more land. There was no good land vacant at the time: 'But if you can drain that marshy strip over beyond Smith's Acres, you can have it,' said Sir Aubrey.

'You won't even have to look after his son,' Meg said furiously to her daughter. 'He's stopping with Mary's sister, he's growing up handy and he's welcome, she says. You'll have your own cottage and a man that can

247

give you anything you want within reason. Philip's nothing but a cottar; he hasn't a single acre to call his own and it's not much wonder. Even the jobs he does take on, he can't do properly. His thatching sticks up in tufts as if a cat's been clawing it and what happened when he tried to take to eelfishing? He puts all his odd-job earnings into buying a boat and gets it stuck in the mud and when he goes back for it, the river's risen with the high tide and floated it away! Brownpate's coming round here this evening to hear your answer and by God you'd better make sure it's the right one or I'll skin you alive. You hear me?'

'You've always hated Philip!' Margaret shot at her resentfully. 'He's never done you any harm but you've always hated him. You hated him being here after de Mandeville came; you almost pushed him out on to his other kinfolk. He used to come round of an evening to listen to Adam telling Ivon's tales, but then you stopped it, you told him not to come.'

'So how do you come to know about that, my lady?' Meg glared at her, standing in mid-floor with arms folded. 'I never said a word to him where you could hear as far as I know, mistress long-ears!'

'Because Philip told me,' said Margaret, as though this were some obscure kind of triumph.

'Been meeting him secretly, have you? I hope you've been up to nothing worse. Yes, I told Philip he was here too often. I told Adam the boy was getting too friendly with you.'

And I couldn't stand seeing the pair of you sitting so close, gazing at Adam, and getting all Adam's attention; you were like a magic circle and I was shut out.

'It wasn't *fair*!' Margaret shouted again. 'Philip hadn't *done* anything.'

'Did you hear what I said?' said Meg ominously. 'You're to be betrothed to Peter Brownpate this evening. Don't square that obstinate jaw of yours at me like that unless you want the flat of my hand across it again. You're nigh as obstinate as your grandfather!' Meg's loathing of Ivon had not diminished since his death. 'You're lucky to have such a worthwhile suitor. Pity you aren't more grateful. You go out now and take the cows back to the meadow. Then come straight home. There's all the cheese to make and we've got to get you nicely dressed for tonight. And I warn you, my girl, don't give me any trouble.'

Meg's cows were at present grazing one of the reclaimed marsh pastures. When Margaret arrived there with them, Philip, knee-deep in the thick green grass, was waiting for her.

It was still her task to take the cows out and to bring them home, and the meetings which had become a habit when she and Philip were children, were now their times of courtship. She never knew when or where to expect him for he had to find his moments in between his endless odd jobs for anyone who would pay him half a silver penny or a crock of beans. But she had the certainty that every day, at some point, she would see him and each morning she woke to warm anticipation even when the skies were bleak and the east wind was blowing across the pastures.

Summer mornings like this were usually magical; it was as though the dew on the meadow, the song of lark and blackbird and the call of the warblers in the reeds, were part of her secret excitement, as though the world were singing for her the song she was not gifted enough to make for herself. Today, because of the scene with her mother, the magic was spoiled. Her mother had spoiled it. Margaret, angry and miserable, tramped behind the cows and failed to notice the larks. But her eyes searched for Philip with even more than their usual intentness, and when she saw him, she ran straight into his arms.

It was no use for her mother to say that Philip had nothing to offer and to keep on about the virtues of Peter Brownpate. To Margaret, Philip was part of her life, part of herself. He had always been there, his open, windburned countenance better known to her than her own, his mind so close to hers that their verbal conversations were only the surface of their communication. The very smell of him was the smell of home.

'Philip!'

'What's the matter?' he said, instantly.

'Oh, *Philip!*' The cows were settling to graze and Margaret turned her back on them. 'Peter Brownpate is coming to see us tonight. Philip, it's awful. He wants to marry me and my mother's been on at me about him for a long time and now she says . . .'

She couldn't finish. Philip did it for her. 'She says you've got to agree?'

Speechlessly, Margaret nodded.

'Here,' said Philip.

He led them to a sheltered place, halfway down the bank of a waterway. They sat down, side by side. 'Now tell me,' he said. 'Tell me all about it.'

'I don't know what to do! My mother's so . . . but I shan't say yes to her, Philip, I promise! Only . . .'

'I know your mother. She doesn't like me, does she? Even if I could support you, she still wouldn't like me.'

They sat in silence. Presently Philip put out a hand and gently turned her face towards him. She was a little startled to notice that he was more grown-up than she had realised. His grave expression now gave him the look of an adult man. 'But I can't support you, can I?' he said. 'And it may be years before I can. I have no right to ask you to wait.'

'You're not asking me,' said Margaret. 'I *want* to. You know that.'

'What does Adam say?'

'Not very much. He tries to please my mother.'

'Everyone tries to please your mother,' said Philip ruefully. 'It isn't easy, is it?'

'Tonight's going to be awful. But it's all right, Philip. I shan't give in, no matter what.'

She expected him to respond, to smile or hug her, but he remained silent. 'Philip, what is it?'

'Your mother may be right,' he said. 'It's been on my mind for some time, to tell you the truth. It isn't a new thought, not to me. I can't marry you yet; I

249

don't know when I will be able to. I've still so much to learn before I can make myself into a man who can earn. I've scratched about doing this and that, a bit of boating, a bit of thatching; I can plough and sow all right but so can everyone else. I need a trade that everyone hasn't got and it'll take time. Meanwhile, time's going on. Brownpate's a good man; everyone knows that. Maybe you ought to say yes.'

'Philip!'

'It's true.'

'No! Oh no, Philip, I couldn't, you can't mean . . . !'

She couldn't grapple with it. Ever since she could remember, she had been going to marry Philip and no one else. Now he was looking at her, kindly but distantly, as though she were a separate person instead of an extension of himself. Her words faded out. She turned away and stared out over the pastures. They were verdant, beautiful. Why couldn't life be verdant and beautiful too?

'Margaret . . .'

'If you've changed your mind and you don't want to marry me, just say so. It would be kinder.'

'I'm not saying that! That *isn't* what I mean. Margaret, I want to be your husband more than anything else in the world. But I can see that perhaps it wouldn't be what's best for you.'

'It is! It is!'

There was another silence. Then Philip said slowly: 'I knew what your mother was planning. She's been talking to Brownpate on and off for some time. As I said, I've been thinking. I've done a lot of it. Margaret, there is one way. It would mean that you'd have to hold out for a year – well, a little more than that – but then, perhaps, I'd be able to offer you something worthwhile. But I'd have to go away.'

'What?' Startled, she turned back to him and scanned his face. 'Go away? But . . . you can't. There's your father . . .'

'I know there's my father,' said Philip grimly. 'Well, someone else'll have to look after him, that's all. Why shouldn't they? I've got two aunts. They do his washing and bake our bread as it is. They didn't want him muttering by their hearth-fires and made me build a hovel and take him to it, but they can lump it for a while. Why not? I'm sick of working in the lord's fields just for the right to one hovel and a cabbage patch! Or else he can move in with you! Your stepfather's my uncle, after all.'

'My mother wouldn't stand for it.'

'No, I daresay not. She's never let your stepfather help us more than a little bit, has she? Maybe I'd be in a better position now if my uncle Adam had been allowed to do more for us, as I think he wanted to. As it is,' he said in a grim tone which Margaret had never heard him use before, 'I've still got all my way to make, and as long as I'm here in Rushley, I've got to feed my father as well as myself. Well, what am I to do, put living my own life off till he dies? Sit about waiting for him to die? It could be years and I'd end up hating him. I hate him now, half the time. Reckon he could do his bit in the field if he'd rouse up. He's not crippled. But he won't try; he just hangs round my neck like a millstone . . .'

Margaret was looking at him in alarm. 'I've never heard you sound so angry.'

'No. Well, what I've said wasn't pretty; I couldn't say it if I weren't angry. But it's the truth.' Philip passed a hand across his forehead. 'Sorry, Margaret, but I've said what I felt, for once.'

Margaret bit her lip. It had been a bad moment, with Philip suddenly sounding like a much older and very bitter stranger. But he was smiling at her now and the old Philip, whom she knew and loved, was back. Only, he was threatening to go away again, in a long-term and entirely physical sense, and this was not only unbearable but as far as she could see, impossible as well. 'You can't leave Rushley,' she said. 'You belong to it. You wouldn't be allowed to go off anywhere.'

'Not if I asked permission. But they say that if a villein can get away and support himself as a freeman within a town – like Norwich, say – for a year and a day, then he can call himself free, lawfully. Isn't that what your uncle Edric did? I remember Adam telling us about him, round the fire, when I used to be welcome at your house.'

'No one ever knew what happened to him,' said Margaret soberly. 'He never came back, or so Adam says.' She fingered the bump where she wore the bone dagger-hilt under her dress. She didn't wear it outside because she didn't consider it ornamental but it had come down to her from her father's father and for this reason had meaning for her. She had little to remind her of her father Britt; she could scarcely even remember him. This keepsake at least came from his side of the family. She valued it for that.

'He may have made his way and have descendants who are now living as free men,' said Philip. 'Why suppose the worst?'

Unwillingly, Margaret said: 'My grandfather always maintained that we were of free descent. But my mother says it's all nonsense.'

'Oh, descent!' Philip brushed this aside. 'That's the past. I'm talking of the future. I think I should go to Norwich and find work. I can come back when the year and a day are up. I'll get whoever employs me to give me a parchment saying that I've worked for him for a year and a day and then I'll come to fetch you.'

'But what would you do in Norwich?'

'Learn a trade,' said Philip. 'Or at least find some sort of steady work. I'll live rough and save. There'll be more chances there than here; people have more money in towns. I'll come back with silver in my belt and free status to offer you, and I'll take you away to Norwich as my wife.'

'You'd have to pay the fine for me to marry off the manor. I don't suppose my mother would let Adam pay it.'

'No. We'd just go, before anyone knew I'd come back.'

'But . . .'

It sounded fine enough, but there would be the long, empty year during which she would be exposed to her mother's campaign to make her forget him and she would not have the sight of his face to strengthen her.

'If anything happened to you,' she said, 'how would I know?'

'You wouldn't.' Philip spoke soberly. 'But if I don't come back in one year and a half, then . . . take it that something has gone wrong, and . . .'

'I don't want you to go!'

'Nor do I. But it seems to be our only chance.'

'Suppose you're caught?'

'I know,' said Philip seriously. 'Sir Gilles isn't like his father.'

'He's already hanged two men for poaching. Just on the spot.'

'I know. I'll have to be careful to get clean away. I think I should go soon, maybe at night.'

It was becoming terrifyingly real. She had set out that morning alarmed and angry because of the quarrel with her mother, but at least into a world where Philip was *there*. Now even that reassurance was ebbing from her.

'It will be all right.' Philip ran a forefinger down the side of her face. 'Don't look so scared. Being scared's no good. I want to be frightened too but I mustn't. Be brave, darling. I will come back if I can, I swear it, Margaret. I won't forget you, or look at any other girl. I shall think of you every night as I go to sleep, and every morning when I wake, until the day I return to make you my wife. When you're going to sleep, or waking, think about me thinking of you. Margaret, wouldn't you like to be free? If you marry a freeman, you will be.'

'I've never thought about it before.'

'Think of it now.'

There was a new silence, while Margaret brooded, linking her hands round her knees and trying to bring these strange new ideas into focus in her imagination. A world without Philip. But then a life away from Rushley, as a freewoman, in Norwich. For a moment a crazy excitement possessed her. 'I could come with you!'

But even as she spoke, fear drowned the exhilaration. She was, and was aware of it, a curious mixture of the bold and the timid. She was brave enough when dealing with dangers she was used to. She could answer back when Meg was in a temper or deal with a cow that didn't want to be parted from its calf. But the unknown paralysed her with alarm. And Philip, who knew her so well, knew this too.

'You mustn't come,' he said. 'Not till I've made a life to take you to. It'ud only make things more difficult. There would be two of us to feed and find lodgings for. I want you to be safe, Margaret, whatever else happens.'

'I don't want to be safe if you're in danger,' said Margaret, trying hard to pretend that the cold quivering in her stomach was not there.

'I'd worry myself to pieces if you were put to any kind of risk. But, Margaret, I *swear* that if I can, I'll come back for you. We're plighted; that is, if you'll swear too.'

'We ought to go to the church,' said Margaret. 'But someone might see us. There's eyes and ears everywhere in Rushley, *and* wagging tongues. I wish we had something to swear on. Well, there's this.' She pulled at the cord round her neck and drew out the bone dagger-hilt. 'I've shown you this so you know what it is. It isn't a sacred relic, but my grandfather set great store by it and it's all I have to remind me of my father's family, so it isn't something to take lightly. Will it do?'

The dagger-hilt, dark yellow now with age and slightly cracked, was in Philip's eyes more like a bit of rubbish than a relic of any description but he knew Margaret would be hurt if he said so. He held one end and she held the other. Margaret looked at him. 'You first.'

'I, Philip, promise that if I win my freedom in Norwich, I will come back for you, Margaret, and that from this moment on I regard you as my wife and I will be faithful.'

'I, Margaret, swear that I will wait for your return and marry no other man.'

'You'd better add: Until I am as sure as I can be that Philip is not coming back. I could fall into a bog on the way to Norwich.'

'Until I am as sure as I can be that Philip is not coming back,' said Margaret obediently. 'But you must come back! Oh, Philip, no, please don't go. It's too risky.'

'You may have the hardest part,' said Philip lightly. 'You'll have to withstand your mother!'

It was the time of year when the cows had young calves at foot and produced so much milk that they could be milked three times a day. Margaret was bringing them back to the byre at noon, trying to keep a couple of frisky calves from darting sideways into the wheat, when Peter Brownpate stepped apparently out of nowhere, herded the unruly calves back into line with a few casual taps from the long stave he was carrying, and then fell quietly in beside her.

'Thank you,' said Margaret politely, of necessity.

'It's a pleasure. I was waiting for you,' said Brownpate calmly. 'I want to talk to you.'

'Yes?' Margaret stared straight ahead, at the brown and white rear ends of the cows. She had never noticed before how much they looked as though they were carved from wood.

Brownpate did not answer at once; he seemed to be collecting his thoughts and taking his time about it, which was typical of him. She knew him quite well, since he was a friend of Adam's. Quietness of movement and considered speech were Brownpate's trademarks. So also was that powerful but abstract characteristic, presence. She was intensely aware of him and found it hard to resist the urge to turn her head and look at him.

'I'm eating at your house tonight,' he said at length. 'And I fancy you know why. Your mother says you do.'

'Yes.' She would have to turn her head now. She did so, and found that his steady hazel eyes were watching her. 'There's something I'd better tell you,' she began. 'It's only fair. It's . . .'

'About Philip Siwardson?'

'Yes,' said Margaret, sounding unintentionally pugnacious. 'Yes, it is. I'm sorry, Master Brownpate. I don't want to hurt anyone's feelings and I . . . I'm grateful if you've asked for me, as my mother says you have. It's a compliment and I know that, but I'm promised and always have been, and that's that.'

'So your mother said,' said Peter Brownpate in his quiet, deep voice. He continued to pace steadily beside her, a strong, compact figure in a loose shirt – a very good one, of fine, bleached linen – and green, cross-gartered hose and calfskin shoes. He smiled slightly, thinking of what Meg had actually said.

'Margaret's a good girl but she's young enough to be a bit silly, still. She and Philip Siwardson have known each other all their lives and played at being sweethearts and she still thinks it's real. But sooner or later she's got to wake up and I'll see to it that she does. I wouldn't have mentioned it, only you mentioned it first.'

'Well, the whole village knows she and Philip are walking out,' said Brownpate mildly. 'Only, if you don't mind, I'd as soon you *didn't* try to wake her up, as you put it. I'll see what I can do about that, myself.'

Now he said: 'I've told your mother I don't want her pressing you against your will. I'm man enough to do my own courting, I should hope. But there's something I want to say to you. I don't want that you should answer me. I just want you to listen and maybe think over what I've said, later.'

Margaret returned her gaze to the tails of the cows and said stiffly: 'Naturally, I'll listen. But I mustn't linger. My mother was cross when I was late this morning, after taking the cows out first thing.'

'I don't mind if we canter the cows and run behind them all the way,' said Brownpate, apparently with real amusement. 'As long as you hear me, and don't stuff your fingers in your ears.'

'Please say whatever it is. I'm here, and my ears aren't blocked.'

'All right. Well, first of all, I'm a natural, healthy man and it goes against the grain with me to speak anything but ill of a rival, but I'm no liar either, and the fact of the matter is, I've no hard words to say of Philip Siwardson. He's a good lad who's had a deal of bad luck.'

'Yes, he is!' said Margaret violently. 'And I don't desert people because they've had bad luck!'

'You won't know how or why I first became interested in you,' said Brownpate. 'Your mother can't have told you, because I never told *her*. I've seen you about the village, and in church of a Sunday, since you were a child, and when it happened, it took me by surprise, I can tell you. Do you remember my Mary?'

'Yes, of course. I remember the day when . . .' Margaret stopped. No one in Rushley ever mentioned de Mandeville in Peter Brownpate's hearing.

'When Mary was killed?' said Brownpate quietly. 'Yes. No one who was here then is likely to forget it. Listen, Margaret. When I lost Mary, I was like a candle that had been blown out. There was just blackness and misery like dark smoke, where there'd been a bright, warm flame, and that's how

254

my world stayed, for years. I thought it would be for the rest of my life. Until one day, early this year, when I was looking across the church one Sunday. The sun had just come out and shone through one of the windows. I glanced that way and there you were, right in the shaft of the sunlight. I tell you, I'd seen you every week at least and sometimes oftener since you were small, but at that moment I felt I'd never seen you before. You were someone completely new and very beautiful and all of a sudden, the last thing I expected to happen had come about. My candle was lit again, with a new, clear flame and it will never go out, whether you ever say yes to me or not.'

Margaret was silent. They were passing the place where the mill had once been. The ash and the charred timbers had long since vanished and where they had been was a weedy patch of thistle and dandelion and marsh ragwort. The great millstones, which had of course not burned, had been dragged by ox-teams to the new mill at Oxfen. But the huge wheel, which was timber but being wet hadn't burned either, still rested in its deep and narrow channel, held by its rusting axle, and although the mill leat which had been diverted from the River Wend was choked with mud where once it had spilled over the wheel to turn it, it still sped through its old overflow channel on its way back to its parent river.

Once or twice, when Margaret encountered Philip as she went to and fro with the cows, this was the place where she had found him, and very often he was standing by the leat, looking sadly at the motionless wheel and the place below the mill where the leat, no longer harnessed, ran faster and deeper than it ever did when the wheel was turning.

Brownpate saw her glance at it. He did not comment directly, but said: 'There's something more that I must tell you. Part of your beauty was that steadfast air you have about you. It's written in your face, did you know? And that's why I'm not angry that you want to stand by Philip. Steadfastness is one of the great virtues. Only, Margaret, sometimes more than one person has a claim on your loyalty, and sometimes you can only hold to one by letting go of another. I won't annoy you by pointing out that you'd have an easier life with me than with Philip. You'll say that that doesn't weigh with you . . .'

'No,' said Margaret proudly. 'It doesn't.'

'I thought not. But whoever you marry, one day, God willing, you'll have children. What sort of a life do you want for them? They too have a right to your care and devotion. They have a right to the best you can give them. That's all, Margaret. I shall see you tonight but nothing will be settled. I've made that clear. I've seen your stepfather as well as your mother this morning and made myself plain, I hope. I'll be glad to sit at the same table with you and happy if you'd talk to me, just of ordinary things. And I'll be happy to eat of the cheese which your mother says you make so well. I shan't urge you to anything against your wishes, tonight or at any time. I only ask you to remember what I've said, and to think about it. Here's the byre. I'll leave you here,' said Brownpate and without as much as one single endearment, or the slightest attempt to touch her, he turned and went.

That evening, when she returned home after the third milking, she found the house in a state of obvious preparation for a guest. Since Adam had enlarged the cottage, their sleeping quarters were separate from the room used for cooking and eating. In the latter, the scarred table where they ate had been draped in a length of bleached linen that Meg had put by for making new underclothes, and on it had been set the best pewter goblets and some of the handsome bowls that Adam and Ivon before him had made. Cheese and fresh bread were arranged on a wooden platter and a fowl was roasting on a spit over the fire-trench, while, alongside it, something aromatic was stewing in a pot. Margaret eyed these preparations dubiously and went through into the second room. Adam had built it big, with a half-loft above where his two small sons could sleep, ample space for the curtained bed which he and Meg used, and space too for clothes chests and the spinning and weaving gear.

Meg was standing in the middle of the room, shaking out their best dresses.

'I've had these pressed flat under weights and then hung up for a while and most of the creases are out,' Meg said. Her voice was surprisingly quiet and friendly. Brownpate's doing, Margaret supposed. She took the dress her mother was holding out to her.

Margaret's best dress was of thin wool cloth, fresh green with yellow embroidery at the neck and round the wide cuffs. Adam had given it to her for her birthday last year and she hadn't grown much since; it still fitted her well. 'Birthday presents!' Meg had snorted. 'Most people have better things to do than remember their birthdate!'

'Well, you're the one who told me what it was,' said Adam, laughing. 'The last day of June, the year King Henry died, that's right, isn't it?'

Margaret liked the dress and had been grateful to Adam. She decided to make no trouble about putting it on.

Later, when Adam arrived with Brownpate and her half-brothers came in from the fields, she helped to serve the food and listened quietly to her elders' conversation, in which she was not referred to at all.

Brownpate had said that nothing would be settled, and he had apparently convinced Adam and Meg that this should be so. The question of betrothal was not so much as mentioned, even by her half-brothers, who would certainly have said something teasing, had they known what had been planned.

A hint that this was anything more than one neighbour inviting another for a well-arranged meal, only showed itself when Brownpate, as far as anyone knew for the first time since Mary's death, suddenly spoke of de Mandeville.

'De Mandeville's dead and gone but it doesn't seem that we're much better off now. The talk in Norwich is that there's still a possibility of fixing the succession on the empress's son Henry Plantagenet, but of course, King Stephen's son doesn't like it and we all know where that's led.'

'Aye. He's set himself up as a robber baron and taken de Mandeville for a model,' said Adam dryly. 'Where is he now? Still ravaging Suffolk?'

'Yes. Let's hope he stays there. We've been left in peace since de Mandeville's visit. We're off the main track. But times are still uncertain and God alone knows when they'll improve. It's a pity the king can't control his son but that's been the trouble with Stephen all along. He's a kindly, chivalrous man, or so everyone says, but he couldn't master the empress or check de Mandeville and now his own boy won't mind him. Now, my boy minds me. I'm seeing more of him now he's older and he's a good lad. I regret I've only the one but I'm lucky in him, so I won't complain. I'd take it kindly if I could have another slice of that excellent cheese, Mistress Meg.'

The air hummed with words not said, such as *Poor Peter Brownpate would like more children* and *In these uncertain times one ought to get on with life*. Margaret attended earnestly to the chicken wing she was eating. Brownpate must, she thought later, have impressed Meg very powerfully indeed with the importance of not saying certain things, for it seemed incredible that, after that, Meg would refrain from raising the subject of Margaret's marriage once the guest had gone but she did, and they all went to bed without a word being said on the matter.

Margaret lay under the single thin rug which was enough bedcovering on this warm night, and couldn't sleep.

She wanted Philip badly. The vista so suddenly presented to her, of a world from which Philip was absent but in which she was subjected to frequent encounters with Peter Brownpate, was too strange and distorted to be borne alone. If she could just see Philip, it would put itself straight again. There was no denying that for the first time ever, she had found herself imagining a future in which she had married Peter Brownpate instead of Philip.

She wasn't imagining it from choice, of course, and she didn't intend to go on imagining it. Peter Brownpate himself had said he admired her for being steadfast; well, steadfast she would be. She belonged to Philip and that was that.

They had never made love. He was too respectful and she was too wary. She had seen what befell girls who got into the family way to men who wouldn't or weren't able to marry them. There'd been the time when some important guest or other was staying at the big house and had a crowd of men-at-arms with him, and they'd come swaggering round the village looking for entertainment and one of them had sweet-talked a cousin of Philip's, a girl called Wilbertha, into having a cuddle with him in a haycock. He was long since gone on his way by the time Wilbertha knew what he had left with her and her parents were God-fearing people – rather too God-fearing, Adam had commented – and all they'd had to say was that she would have to confess and do penance in public and then she might get work up at the manor-house or with the Grosnez family, where one more serving girl and one more baby would hardly be noticed, but they couldn't give her a home any more and she needn't expect anyone to marry her.

Wilbertha had gone out of the house, straight to the place where the mill leat ran so fast and deep in what had once been its overflow channel, and flung herself in.

No, Margaret didn't intend to become another Wilbertha. But at least, she thought, turning over restlessly, if she were to go with Philip and there were – well, results – she didn't think Adam would let Meg throw her out or allow the priest to shame her (though the current incumbent of Rushley Church was a stern believer in morality and might well try), and it would bind her to Philip as powerfully as any wedding ring. It certainly ought to make Peter Brownpate withdraw and then Meg wouldn't be able to go on pressing her to marry him.

Perhaps it was a mistake to be so cautious. Yes, she decided, rolling on to her back and staring into the darkness. She could trust Philip; he was no fly-by-night soldier.

She would seek him out the very next day, she decided, before he had had time to think any more about running away to Norwich. They would be lovers. And if he still insisted on going to Norwich, well, she would face what came, trusting him to return and make her and any child she had borne him into free people.

Suddenly, Margaret sat up in the darkness. She had had no idea, until Philip held it out as a prospect, how much she wanted that. She had never thought herself envious, for instance, of the Grosnez boy, the youngest one, who had survived de Mandeville and had to set about reviving his fortunes as best he could. He'd been very successful but the process had involved endless hard work and a marriage with a gawky lame girl from Redesmarsh, whose family were willing to give her a good dowry just to get her off their hands. Yesterday, Margaret would have said that she was better off than he was.

But yesterday, Margaret had thought of free status as something for ever out of reach. Now Philip had brought it – almost – within reach after all and, since then, she had been slowly realising what it meant. Philip had said that when he came to fetch her, he would whisk her away and not pay the fine for depriving her lord of a villein. Adam had had to make two dozen big bowls with a fashionable new blue glaze, in order to marry Meg, even though he wasn't taking her away from Rushley. Free people didn't have to buy permission to marry. Free people didn't have to work their lord's fields, either.

The desire for freedom had featured largely in Adam's stories about Ivon, and their lack of it was now one of Meg's major grievances against her father-in-law.

Yes, because, according to Adam, the old story that Grandfather Ivon had once had the chance to become free, and refused it, was true. She could remember Adam telling that story, more than once. She had heard it when she was a little girl, before de Mandeville came, and again later, when Philip was with them. And she could remember her mother's face in the firelight, set hard with anger, as she listened to Adam's account of how Ivon had betrayed his descendants.

And it had been betrayal. She had never understood that before. How could he? How *could* he? From somewhere deep within Margaret, there

258

rose up an enormous longing for that splendid treasure which her grand-father had cast aside, a deed which now seemed to her as mad as burning one's own house down. She *wanted* freedom. And Brownpate couldn't give it to her. Only Philip had offered to try. Only Philip.

'Philip!' she whispered, and into her mind's eye, as plain as though he had actually appeared in the velvety darkness above her, she saw his dear face, the lock of straw-coloured hair that constantly fell over his brow, the broad, sun-reddened countenance of him, the good-humoured smile, his excellent teeth. And now, with astonishment, Margaret for the first time experienced physical desire, as though her entire body was opening and reaching out to him.

Tomorrow, first thing, she would go to him. One glimpse of his face would put the world back as it used to be, and somehow, before the day was out, she would have come together with him, or her name wasn't Margaret. In the attempt to win their freedom, he would be taking a terrifying risk; she must risk something too. She must give him something more than just an oath sworn on a dagger-hilt to take away with him.

If he had scruples, and being Philip he was sure to have, she would over-come them. Although she was not yet seventeen, she felt all of a sudden as though she were a woman as old as Eve and, although she did not realise it, her square little jaw was set like granite.

A decision taken could, she now discovered, be an instant answer to sleeplessness. Her eyes closed. She turned over again and curled up on her side. She did not awaken until dawn was breaking, and a persistent tapping on the outer door had roused not only herself but the rest of the household too. A touslehaired Adam with a tunic pulled on quickly and awry, appeared from beyond the bed-curtain and went through to the outer room to see who was at the door. They heard him exclaim: 'Siward!' and heard Siward's voice answer, though indistinctly for, ever since he had lost so many teeth at de Mandeville's hands, his speech had been unclear.

A few moments later, the boys came slithering inquisitively from their half-loft, and Meg and Margaret, having also pulled on clothes in a hurry, were out in the living-room too.

Adam was kneeling to rouse up the fire. His brother Siward was shivering on a settle close by. He was older than Adam by a good few years, but these days he looked so very much older that he could well have been Adam's father, if not his grandfather. He was sitting half-doubled, with one forearm pressed across his abdomen, so that Meg at once cried out: 'What is it, Siward? Are you ill?'

But Adam, blowing on the fire and feeding it with twigs from the wood-basket, shook his head and Siward, although he didn't stop cradling his middle, mumbled: 'No, no, it ain't that,' and raised his other hand to wipe away the spittle which in moments of stress always ran from the side of his mouth from which the teeth had been torn.

'Well, what is it, then?' demanded Meg impatiently.

'Philip,' said Siward. ' 'S Philip.'

'Philip?' Margaret ran forward to crouch beside him. 'What's happened?'

Adam raised his head. 'He's gone,' he said. 'Siward woke at first light and saw that the chest where he kept his clothes was open and empty. His bed hadn't been used and there was food missing. And there were things he was saying last night, it seems. It looks,' said Adam gravely, 'as though Philip has run away.'

'The answer,' said Sir Gilles of Rushley without even pausing to consider the matter, 'is no.' He spoke French as he always did, good, pure French, not the hybrid patois which his peasantry understood, and therefore addressed the steward Gerbert, who was half Norman and completely bilingual. The little crowd of supplicants standing humbly at the foot of the dais had put on their best clothes to enter his presence, but they had gone to a good deal of trouble for nothing, because he never spoke to them directly even once and scarcely even glanced their way.

Well, Sir Gilles would have said if queried on the matter, one didn't. They were only two-legged cattle and one didn't hold conversations with cattle. He despised men who talked to their hounds and their horses. Animals, however many legs they had, were simply there to be used, that was all.

Gerbert, standing beside his master's highbacked chair, had to do the talking for him. He did not much like what he had to say but his own employment and therefore the futures of his children depended on giving satisfaction to Sir Gilles.

'Sir Gilles does not feel that there is any need to waive or even reduce the dues of customary labour which Siward the former miller has always rendered in return for his holding. Indeed, he feels that the unlawful flight of Siward's son Philip must be partly Siward's fault, since a father should exercise authority over a son. He also notes that Siward is not yet past field work and that he has ablebodied relatives – yourselves. We observe that we see before us his brother and his two brothers-in-law, and we are aware that there are also growing nephews. If Siward refuses to do the work, you can do it between you. This matter is now closed, except that Sir Gilles reminds you all that anyone who has any knowledge of the whereabouts of the absconding villein Philip Siwardson, is duty bound to report such knowledge to us. Such persons should come to me and I will take the necessary action.'

Under his breath, one of Siward's brothers-in-law muttered: 'Hark at him. Where did he learn all those long words?'

There was a pause, while Gerbert searched the faces of the quartet in front of him and they stared sullenly back at him. Sir Gilles said something.

'You are dismissed,' said Gerbert. 'But my master wishes to remind you that if the absconding man is caught, he will suffer to the fullest extent of the law and that anyone found to be harbouring or comforting him will be considered equally to blame with him. As it is, his father must pay a pound

260

of silver to his lord, as an example to other fathers, to keep tight hold of their sons.'

'But I *can't*! I ain't got a pound's weight of silver!' Siward's voice was panic-stricken. He was trembling, as he always did when distressed, and the spittle was running from the corner of his mouth. 'And I shouldn't have to owe three days' labour a week,' he added resentfully. 'It's not right, that was for the mill. I ain't got the mill now and I ain't got any fields. All I've got now's a little bit of a cottage and a vegetable patch! Sir Aubrey brought my rent down to half a day a week after that de Mandeville came!' Adam put a fiercely protective arm round his brother's shoulders.

Sir Gilles apparently asked what had been said. Gerbert answered. Sir Gilles laughed and spoke a few short words.

'My lord says,' said Gerbert, giving his master a rank to which he was not strictly speaking entitled, 'that Siward may have time to pay. But the full amount must be in by Michaelmas. That's all. You may go.'

Sir Gilles made a waving-away gesture and a couple of the men-at-arms who were always about the hall, lounged forward, thumbs in belts, not too far from dagger-hilts.

Unhappily, the unsuccessful deputation went.

It was a grey and windy day, but most of Rushley was waiting for them in what had become the habitual meeting-place in front of the church. Meg looked at Adam's face as he came up to her and said: 'There's no need to say it. He turned you down.'

'Flat,' said Thurgar, the brother-in-law who had commented on Gerbert's vocabulary. He was a gnarled man with a permanent stoop from the hips. 'Thinks we can do the work between us if we rope in the lads. But we *can't*, not since that young bugger up there at the house put back Siward's rent to what it was before the mill was burned. Couldn't believe it, when he did that. Just looked up the old records and wiped out all the reductions after de Mandeville came, and never asked what damage had been restored and what hadn't.'

'In Sir Aubrey's day . . .' said Adam miserably.

'Aye.' Agmund, the second brother-in-law, younger than Thurgar, nodded. 'He was reasonable. But this young one . . . bah!' Lacking words with which to express an adequate opinion, he spat.

Siward said in a trembling voice: 'My little place that Philip fixed up for me, and my little patch, they're all I've got since the mill went. Philip's coped. We could never build things up again, somehow. I've not been the same man since we were attacked and my wife was . . . What I'll do now, I don't know. Maybe one of my nevvies . . .'

His voice trailed away as he sensed an unresponsiveness in the silence all round him.

That Sir Gilles, unlike his father, was demanding to the point of being frequently unreasonable, no one questioned. Sir Aubrey would let a holding to a man in return for three days' work on the home farm and make sure that he got his three days in full. Sir Gilles, through the medium of steward and bailiff, would name specific jobs which it was reckoned would take three days to do. If they took three and a half, or four, or worse, they still had to be done, and the sufferer would be told that he'd been unlucky but would make it up next time he did a job that didn't take as long as expected ('And pigs will fly afore that happens,' was the Rushley verdict on that one) or else that it was his own fault for not working faster.

Nor was there any question that the dues were often far too high. Both Agmund and Thurgar needed their sons to keep up with theirs and still care for their own land.

And that, just now, was precisely the point. Siward's 'nevvies' were already fully occupied.

It was Agmund who put it into words.

'You weren't the only one as lost someone or was hurt by de Mandeville. Look at Peter Brownpate there.' Brownpate, standing on the outskirts of the group, made an embarrassed gesture. 'And there's others, been hurt or lost people through accidents or illness. Thurgar here's got a bad back from heaving corn sacks and whatnot about. He has to manage. Maybe you'd have pulled round better if you hadn't had Philip to do it all for you!'

There was now a startled quality to the silence of the others, but not, on the whole, a disapproving one. In the nine years since de Mandeville's visitation this was not, of course, the only time someone had exasperatedly taken Siward to task. But the result was always the same; he shrank into himself and broke down into a pitiful, tremulous mumbling with the saliva oozing down his chin. They had largely given up, and taken to treating him as though he were genuinely crippled, helping out by giving Philip odd jobs, although sometimes he was exasperating too, for there was no denying that he wasn't as efficient as some.

Now, for the first time, Siward's distressed mutterings and scared, watery eyes, were being ignored. Agmund was surging ruthlessly on.

'De Mandeville pulled your teeth out; he didn't pull your arms or legs off. What you'd have done if the mill had still been standing, I can't think. Maybe if you'd got back to your field service, you'd be the better for it now. Maybe the old lord would have rebuilt your mill instead of sending all the work to Oxfen. Reckon he took one look at you and thought: Hopeless, he'll never work a mill again. You cut your own throat, or as good as. Pity you cut Philip's at the same time. He might have stood a chance if—'

'All right. That's enough, Agmund.' Adam spoke loyally in his brother's defence. 'Different things take people different ways. Folk can't always help themselves. Siward would have worked if he could.'

'No. Agmund's right,' said Thurgar. 'If you'd *had* to help yourself, Siward, you might have found you could. But first of all, we were there to lean on, and then Philip grew a bit and you took to leaning on him, and maybe if you hadn't leaned so hard, he wouldn't have run off now. I've been wanting for years to tell you you were putting upon him. Well, I tried once or twice, but you wouldn't listen. Time you did, that's all.'

'Stop it!' Siward whimpered. 'It's not fair. I thought you were on my side. You came with me to the manor-house.'

'We are on your side,' said Brownpate mildly, coming forward. 'But . . . well, since the thing's in the open now, I think we'd better say all of it. You've not set foot in the fields in years, but still, you've taken a hoe to your vegetable patch now and then. If you braced yourself up a bit, I think that even now . . .'

'It's not fair,' said Siward again. 'Three days' work a week for next to nothing and now a pound of silver. That's not lawful, that's not. He's got no right to ask for that.'

'Law!' snorted Thurgar. 'There's been no law in the world for twenty years. The lords make their own. Sir Aubrey made fair ones and Sir Gilles makes what suits him, but they're doing the making; there's no one above them.'

'If he wants that silver, he'll have it,' Agmund agreed, and appeared to take perverse pleasure in Siward's moist, pleading eyes and pitiful dribbling. 'And I'm not going to lend it to you. You get out and earn it, my friend, same as Philip would have done.'

Siward stared round at them and then collapsed, sinking into a broken heap on the ground. 'Now look what you've done!' said Adam angrily, and knelt at his brother's side. Siward pushed him away. 'If you'd let your girl marry my Philip, he wouldn't've run off. That's *why* he ran off; wanted to make something of hisself, get his freedom, and come back for her then. If she'd married him, he'd still be here and she'd've brought silver and a couple of cows and we could of built on that but you wouldn't have it, would you, you and that stuck-up wife of yours! Let me alone. I don't want you!'

'How dare you?' Meg ran forward. 'Oh, you disgusting old man, don't talk about my daughter as if she was nothing . . . nothing but a cow for you and Philip to milk! I'm glad Philip's gone, do you hear? Margaret's safe from him now, and from you!' She actually began to pummel Siward. Adam pulled her away from him. Siward, with surprising agility for a man who claimed to be incapable of any hard work, sprang up and fled. Adam stood up and glared after him but did not attempt to give chase. 'How dare he talk like that about Margaret?' Meg was still furious. 'And it's a pity she's at the cheesemaking. I wish she'd heard it. Then maybe she wouldn't go yearning after that Philip any more!'

'You don't want to worry about that. She'll forget, in time.' Adam was still staring after Siward. 'When I think of all we've done for him . . . well, he needn't expect me to lend him the silver. I was going to offer, but not now. Philip won't come back, Meg. Margaret's safe enough from him now. She's a lovely girl and believe me, I am – was – fond of Philip but I do realise that she's too good for him. But don't fret. If he ever sets foot in Rushley again, he'll be a fool.'

The law said that if a runaway villein could reach a chartered borough, such as Norwich, and live there free for a year and a day, he would have the right to his freedom.

But as Thurgar had said, law had had no backing now for nearly twenty years. Since the civil war between King Stephen and the Empress Matilda began, the lords, great and small, had made their own. Sir Gilles certainly made his and if he ever got his hands on Philip again, God help Philip.

'I made it very clear to them,' said Sir Gilles, sitting ankle over knee on a settle in the Oxfen manor-house, where in company with his new-wedded wife, he was calling on his mother Lady Cicely. 'They need a firm hand, you know, like horses. They'll drift off early from their work, leave fences half-mended, do all sorts of things unless they're watched, or so the bailiff says and I believe him. The man Siward is perfectly ablebodied, you know. He's spent years lazing by the fire or going into his garden once in a while, just because he could get away with it. Well, he'll have to work now, since his son's deserted him.' He grinned. 'Can't altogether blame the son for deserting his father, but of course, if I ever get him back, I'll deal with him for deserting me. Can't let that pass, or they'll all be off. As it is, they hid his disappearance; how long for, I don't know. When he was due to work in my fields, he didn't turn up and my bailiff was told that he was ill. Finally, shrewd man that he is, the bailiff made enquiries and found out that he'd vanished but by then he had God knows how big a start and by the time I put the hounds on his track, it had rained and washed the scent away. They're as slippery as eels. Once in a while, it's as well to make an example; it keeps the rest in order. They get above themselves very easily, you know. They even call their children after their betters, these days. The missing man's called Philip and I hear there are a couple of Margarets in the village, too. Hardly the right names for peasants.'

His bride Alicia was, he was pleased to see, gazing at him in silent admiration. His mother, less admiringly, drowned his last few words in a fit of coughing, added a few stitches to the embroidered wallhanging she was making (with large stitches and a large pattern because her eyesight wasn't what it used to be), handed her needle to one of her women with a murmur of: 'Would you thread that for me, please, Elinor?', turned to Gilles and said: 'What kind of example had you in mind?'

'Ah, well. You're tenderhearted, mother, as a woman should be. It's best you don't concern yourself with these things. Pray for the soul of the miscreant, if I catch him. I'll take the responsibility for the rest of him.'

Lady Cicely coughed, wishing she could shake off the cold she had caught – it must be two months ago now – and thought: 'It's no use asking myself where I went wrong. He was brought up far away from me most of the time, and in an age of such war and brutality that men said openly that God and His angels are asleep. I can't change him now. I'm very glad that foolish young villein's people kept his flight a secret while they could and I hope he has the good sense never to come back.

Chapter Sixteen

The Return

'It's for your own good, Siward, old friend,' said his brother-in-law Thurgar firmly. 'You'll be grateful to us one day . . .'

'You can't mean this. I can't go up to the fields. I'm not strong enough any more. All these years . . .'

'You've done nothing beyond lift a hoe for half an hour on a fine day,' said Agmund. 'You've saved your strength. Come on. The bailiff'll be waiting and there'll be trouble if we're late. They'll keep us after time.'

'But it's cold. There's a cold wind today.' Siward was cringing on his seat beside the hearth. The alleged cold wind was actually a light easterly breeze and refreshing in the summer weather. The hearth, however, was lit and the air in the dark hovel of a cottage was stifling.

'You can put an extra jerkin on. An hour of work and you'll be tearing it off again,' said Adam. He looked round for one, found it and advanced on his brother, holding it out. 'Come on. I'm sorry, Siward, but you've got to. We can't do it all. We work all the hours God made as it is, to please Sir Gilles and pay our taxes and feed ourselves. It's time you helped.'

'I can't. You must see I can't. No, stop it, leave me alone . . .'

His words became muffled as Adam, as though dealing with a difficult small boy, popped the extra jerkin over his brother's head. Thurgar and Agmund seized his arms and steered them into the sleeves. Siward struggled feebly, watery-eyed and quivering, but was relentlessly pulled to his feet and with a brother-in-law at each elbow and Adam behind, was marched out of the door. Peter Brownpate and his son joined the party as it set off to the fields. Siward's repeated wails of 'No, I can't, I'm not well enough, let me go, let me go, I say!' brought a number of people out of their homes. They observed Siward's reluctant progress towards a day's work on his lord's demesne with more enjoyment than compassion. Since Agmund's wife was ailing, Thurgar's wife and daughter were currently doing all the washing and breadmaking for Siward and Thurgar's wife in particular surveyed the scene with satisfaction, arms akimbo.

Meg was also pleased to see it. 'About time, too. Nothing but a lazy sod, that's what Siward is, and if you think, Margaret, that I'd no sympathy for young Philip, saddled with a father like that, you're mistaken. But sympathy's one thing and marrying's another. Now then. Thurgar's girl Joan's going to see to the cows today. It's time you and I had a talk.'

'What about?' said Margaret as her mother led her into the cottage.

'About a matter of importance. Sit down there. And listen.'

Reluctantly, Margaret sat on the stool to which Meg was pointing, opposite the settle on to which Meg sank with a sigh of tiredness. As the boys grew, Meg thought, there seemed more work to do every week, weaving and making clothes for them, keeping them fed. It was a mercy, really, that there hadn't been any more children, just miscarriages, although they were bad enough; left you all weepy and drained-like. Not that there was much risk of any more; Adam never bothered these days. But that was a poor consolation. Meg was not a happy woman and she could do without a daughter who seemed determined to be difficult.

Sitting on the stool with her hands clasped hard on her lap and her tough little chin defiantly raised, Margaret looked young and hard and vibrant. She was going to take a good deal of taming and Meg wasn't sure she was equal to it. She began the interview therefore, on a conciliatory note, the same that she had used to get Margaret into her best dress for Brownpate's benefit.

'I think you know what it is I want to talk to you about, Margaret. By the look of you you've already made up your mind you won't listen, but that isn't right. I'm your mother and believe me, I only want the best for you.'

'I suppose,' said Margaret, 'that you're talking about Peter Brownpate.'

She has her father's eyes, Meg thought, narrow and dark. But Britt's eyes were gentle, and there was something in Margaret's that made her mother think of Ivon. She'd rather do herself an injury than admit she was wrong, she thought ruefully.

'The fact is,' Meg said aloud, 'that Philip has run away. He's gone, Margaret. Sir Gilles sent men after him but they didn't find him and if they had, he'd be no use to you by now.'

'No. He'd probably be dead. But with luck,' said Margaret, 'he's safe in Norwich.'

'Oh, so you knew what he was planning and where he was going?'

'He spoke of it, yes.' Margaret hesitated and then decided on openness. 'I wasn't sure he meant it and I didn't think he'd go so soon. *But*,' said Margaret, 'I know what he wants to do next. He wants to make a living in Norwich for a year and a day and come back with proof of it, and fetch me away to be the wife of a freeman in the town. And I've promised to wait for him.'

'Oh, my dear girl!' said Meg, with almost genuine pity. 'You've promised to . . . Margaret, Margaret. He's a young man. If he did get safe to Norwich or any other town, and does find employment and lodgings, do you think he won't notice how many other girls there are in the world? He may well make his way in Norwich, without his father to hinder him and I wish him well. But if you're putting your faith in any promise he made to come back for you . . . if he makes a life in Norwich or anywhere else, he won't want to remember Rushley, much less come back to it. I'm sorry, Margaret, but it's time you awoke from your dreams and saw life as it is and people as they are.'

266

'You mean see Philip as he is,' said Margaret. 'But I know him and you don't. I'm going to wait for him. If he's not back in two years, then I'll believe that he isn't coming. But if he doesn't it'll be because he was unlucky and couldn't get work, or because something's happened to him, because he's ill or dead. Not because he's forgotten me. He meant what he said and he'll come if he can.'

'And so where,' said Meg, unable to keep the sharpness out of her voice, 'does that leave Peter Brownpate?'

'I'm sorry for Peter,' said Margaret. 'But I don't think he should waste his time on me. There must be others that would suit him better.'

'And meanwhile, you're prepared to go on living here unwed? For another two years? Oh no,' said Meg with resolution, 'oh no, my girl, you're not.'

'But why not?'

'Because . . .'

Because Adam's lost the urge with me and because I've had to talk to you when he's well out of the way for he'll jump to defend you if I even speak roughly to you. Because I've lost all the looks I ever had and you, for all your mulish ways, have a bloom on you that you've no idea of.

'Because I want to see you settled with a man who can look after you. Times are hard now, Margaret, and they could be worse at any minute. We've got the king's own son ravaging to the south of us, no better than de Mandeville: we could be back where we started, any day. I want you safe with a man of substance. Brownpate's got silver put by and if any man's shrewd enough to keep himself out of the hands of anyone with designs on it, Brownpate is. Margaret, I just want to know you're settled with a good man and—'

'No!' said Margaret.

She said it with more force than she meant, because her mother's arguments were horribly persuasive and it wasn't as though she hated Peter Brownpate. These things were like an undertow, to which it would have been all too easy to yield.

Strangest and most frightening of all was the extraordinary blankness which Philip had left behind him. He had just *gone*, and it was as though he had never been. Sometimes, in the depths of the night, Margaret herself had thought: What if he just forgets me, or finds when he's remade his life that he doesn't want to remember? It was less than three weeks since he fled but already his promise of winning their freedom seemed empty and meaningless, the idea of freedom only a glamorous impossibility, like becoming queen.

But she had given her word and she wasn't going back on it, and the very fact that she seemed to be considering just that, horrified her.

'Margaret,' said Meg on a warning note, 'I don't think you should say no to me in that tone of voice.'

'I can't help it. I'm promised to Philip and that's all there is to it. I'm sorry about Peter Brownpate, as I said, but . . .'

'You'll be sorrier still for yourself if you're not careful.'

Margaret clenched her hands tighter. 'I said, I can't help it. That's the way it is.'

'That's the way,' said Meg, rising, 'it isn't going to stay.'

She had been afraid all along that it would come to this. Her daughter's obstinacy couldn't be overcome by mere words. Something stronger would be needed. Margaret, watching her as she crossed the floor and went to the hook where Adam hung his belts, understood what was about to happen and was both afraid and, oddly, relieved. If she withstood this, she would know that she was not weak, not treacherous, that for Philip she could at will call the bold half of herself into play, and that he could trust her as she had sworn she would trust him.

On the demesne land, they were carting dung to the beanfield, with two ox-carts and three men and a boy to each, and another squad in the field to spread it between the rows of plants. It was a smelly, messy job but companionable. Peter Brownpate, Adam and Adam's elder son had formed an ox-cart team with Siward. He was far from being an ideal partner, but he was improving.

He had started the day by standing helplessly by, muttering that he wasn't up to it and didn't feel well, until Adam thrust a spade forcibly into his hands, and even then he merely stood there holding it until the bailiff came round and encouraged him by threatening to push him head-first into the midden if he didn't move himself. Hubert the Bailiff, descended from an offshoot branch of the Grosnez family, was a rough, harsh individual and a wholehearted lord's man. Siward, frightened, dug a few token spadefuls, and old habits, formed long ago when he did demesne work in return for his mill, slowly took over. He acquired a rhythm, slow but definite. Adam and Brownpate exchanged glances which said: 'Now we're getting somewhere.'

In the team which consisted of Thurgar, Agmund, another villein and Brownpate's son, Thurgar's contribution was limited by his bad back which prevented him from lifting a fully loaded spade. He was apologetic about this and, as he often did, said that to make up for it, he had asked his wife to bring out noon-pieces for all of them. Unlike his father, Sir Gilles never provided any midday dinner for his villeins.

When Thurgar's wife Helga came in sight, both ox-carts were unloading in the beanfield at the same time, and across the backs of their oxen Thurgar and Brownpate were holding a deliberately loud conversation on the subject of people they'd known who'd ailed for years – just like someone not a hundred miles away – but recovered and lived to be eighty. At the sight of Helga's stolidly plodding form, they broke off and Thurgar, dumping his spade, said: 'I'll meet her. Save her the rest of the trudge,' and set off towards her. Brownpate went with him.

'There's truth in what we were saying,' Brownpate remarked. 'Maybe if Siward gets himself going again, he really will live the longer for it. He's puffing now, but by the end of a month, he'll be surprising himself and us.'

'Let's hope so. We ought to have taken this line with him years back,' Thurgar said. 'Agmund wanted to, but there, I'm soft compared to him. Ah, thanks, Helga. What have you got for us today?'

'I've brought you new bread, cheese, onions, radishes and ale to wash it down with. The cheese is mine; I'd just got a batch ready. Just as well; I doubt I could have got any from Meg this morning. There's been such a to-do down there . . .'

'A to-do?' said Peter Brownpate sharply.

'Well, you'd best not tell Adam, maybe. It'll all have blown over before he gets home, I expect. When a man's been in the fields all day, he doesn't want to be bothered with the women's quarrels. But saints alive!' said Helga, her round face now acquiring round eyes and mouth to match as she remembered, 'I never heard such a din. Meg shouting at the top of her voice and Margaret crying and screaming fit to break your heart. I almost went in to see what was up and then I thought: No doubt there's a reason and if Margaret's misbehaved, her mother's got to deal with her. But I was sorry to hear such a carry-on and that's a fact.'

'Save my dinner for me,' said Brownpate brusquely to Thurgar, and was gone, at a sprint.

It was a good half-mile to the village and he covered the distance in a few minutes. There was no sound from Margaret's home as he ran up to it; the uproar was apparently over. The door was fast shut. He pounded on it and after a moment, Meg opened it. Her expression was annoyed. 'Master Brownpate! Whatever's the matter?'

'That's what I'd like to know,' said Peter Brownpate and pushed his way inside. He saw Margaret at once. She was lying on the floor beside the settle, in a defensive half-curl. Her face was buried in her arms and she was sobbing in a soft, weary, settled way, as though she had been doing so for a long time. Her head-dress had been torn off and flung across the room and one of her braids was undone so that red-brown hair spilled across a forearm into the dust of the floor. Her skirt was torn and a flap of it trailed at his feet. Meg, arms folded, was standing grimly in the middle of the room.

'What have you done to her?' said Brownpate to Meg. 'And why?'

'I don't mean to be rude,' said Meg. 'But it's private. Really, Master Brownpate, you shouldn't come bursting into other people's houses like this. You can't . . .'

'Perhaps it's as well I did. Margaret.' He knelt down beside her. 'Margaret? Look at me, love.'

He raised her head and turned her towards him. Her face was unmarked except for dirt and the streaks of tears but when she saw who he was, she jerked away and hid her eyes in her arms once again.

'You see? Even she doesn't want you to see her like this.'

'I can well understand it. Nevertheless, I look on myself as having an interest in Margaret's welfare and I want to know the reason why she *is* like this.'

'I'm sorry to disoblige you, Master Brownpate. But really it would be better if you left. There are times when children need correction and what's happened here is between mother and daughter.'

'I said I was betrothed to Philip!' said Margaret. Her voice was muffled but distinct enough to be understood. Suddenly she sat up. She cried out as she moved, but brought herself to a kneeling position, one arm on the settle. 'And so I am and it can't be changed and I'm sorry to disoblige you too, when you've been so kind as to come and . . . but it's your *fault*! It's because of you! It's . . .'

'Margaret,' said Meg. 'Be careful.'

Margaret looked at her mother and rubbed a dirty arm across her eyes. 'If you do this to me again, I'll throw myself in the river like Wilbertha did, I will! Oh why did you ever come saying you wanted to marry me?' She turned wet, angry eyes on Peter Brownpate. 'I've sworn I'll wait for Philip and I thought oaths were supposed to be sacred. Everyone behaves as though breaking my promise doesn't matter and—'

'You had no business to give that promise and it has no force!' snapped Meg. 'And as for drowning yourself, that'll be the day! I'll believe that when I see it. I know you, my girl, you won't do that, you're not the sort. Well, there it is, Peter Brownpate. I'm sorry she's told you what all this was about because it would have been better if you didn't know. But the fact is that she's still got this silly idea in her head and I'm trying to knock it out of her, since talking's no use. Now if you hadn't come charging in at the door, by tonight—'

'By the end of today, you'd have beaten her repeatedly and so badly that she'd agree to marry the devil himself if only you'd stop? It's as well I did come charging in. A chance word that a neighbour of yours said warned me and just in time, it seems.' He looked from one to the other. 'I'm not going to say I'm not hurt. I must be very objectionable to you, Margaret, if you're willing to put up with this to avoid marrying me . . .'

'It isn't that!' Margaret's voice was distraught. 'But I belong to Philip. I always have, since we were children!'

'All right. I'll try to find comfort in that. Because it wounds me, Margaret, that even Philip who may be anywhere by now and may never come back, still has more hold on your heart than I can manage when I've offered you nothing but love. Your mother is right in this; you had no right to promise yourself without your parents' consent, and your oath need not bind you if you change your mind. But . . .' he swung round on Meg '. . . I won't countenance this. Do you think I want Margaret's consent to our marriage forced out of her in this fashion? On my wedding night, I wish to perform an act of love. I'm not interested in rape and that's what it would be. You may as well leave your daughter alone henceforth, because I'm withdrawing my suit. I doubt that Adam would approve of what's gone on here today. I shan't tell him because I don't want to make trouble, but if I hear of this happening again, I might change my mind. Good day.'

'Now see what you've done!' said Meg furiously to Margaret.

Brownpate was already walking to the door. But as he reached it, he turned. 'Margaret. I still . . . I will never force myself where I'm not wanted but if you ever need help, advice, or protection, I'm still here. That's all.'

'Oh, you stupid, stupid girl!' Meg stormed as Brownpate shut the door behind him. 'How could I ever have had a daughter who was such a blind, obstinate fool! Oh, get up, get up, I shan't touch you again, unless you go blabbing to Adam and if you do I swear by every saint that ever was, that I'll break your neck. Get up, come on!' She caught Margaret's arm and hauled her to her feet. 'You'd better get to bed. We'll tell Adam you're ill. Oh, you *stupid* girl!'

One of the most awful things about that awful day, Margaret thought afterwards, as she lay in her bed, resting on her side and wondering if she would ever again be able to move without pain, was that at that point, just after Brownpate had left, her mother had sat down at the table, put her face in her hands and herself burst into wild and heartbroken crying.

If only, thought Margaret, if only I knew *why* she wants so badly to be rid of me.

It was early June, but dismally wet, with rain slanting out of the wide East Anglian skies and an unfriendly north-east wind behind it, when Philip Siwardson came back to Rushley.

He tramped along on foot, helped by a stave and protected from the elements by a stout hooded mantle. Beneath it was a leather tunic, bought secondhand from a retiring man-at-arms who had worn it under his armour. It kept out the wet very well. Philip hardly noticed the weather even though he was marching head-down into it.

He was on his way back to Margaret and in his pack, carefully rolled up, tied and sealed and wrapped in cloth for protection, was a sheet of vellum on which it was clearly stated that Philip Siwardson had worked for a year and a day as assistant to John Le Toitier, thatcher, of Norwich, and had done so as a free man, for a wage.

Philip could not read or write, but he had attended church in Norwich and paid for the priest to come and take dictation from Le Toitier, who was a little amused by Philip's insistence that he needed the document as a safeguard because he was determined to go back to Rushley, and more amused still by his reason for going back at all. One girl was as good as another to Le Toitier and Norwich was full of them.

But he had been amiable enough over the business. Another of his assistants and the clerk who came with the priest had witnessed the document and Philip knew that it was sound. Sir Gilles could not touch him now. If only, if only, Margaret were still waiting.

If only her mother hadn't bullied her into giving way. On parting, he had said to her, lightly: 'You may have the hardest part.' Afterwards, thinking about it, he had feared that it might be all too true.

If all were well, he'd bring her away at once. Le Toitier had given him a month's leave of absence but the sooner he claimed Margaret and got her out of Rushley, the better. He hoped that his father Siward had got by all right and wouldn't expect Philip either to stay with him or take him to Norwich too because he wasn't going to do either. At a safe distance in Norwich, free of the burden Siward had become, he had found it possible to think of his father with affection but he knew quite well that the affection wouldn't survive for five minutes if Siward tried to fetter him again.

He approached Rushley prudently, at the end of the afternoon when whatever the weather most people, including the lord's men, would be indoors, eating. But he did not feel as nervous as he had expected. His document was valid and, besides, mastering a trade and acquiring his freedom had given him a new self-respect. Although he did not know it, he even walked and held himself differently.

When he came in sight of it, the river was running high, leaden-coloured, pocked with rain and ruffled by the wind. It was hardly a beautiful sight, but it meant that his journey was nearly over. Another ten minutes of steady plodding brought him in sight of the village, and the first dwelling he came to was the crude wattle cottage he had built for his father and shared with him. This was his first objective. Siward might or might not be pleased to see him but Philip had sent him money once or twice, when he heard of someone travelling towards Rushley, and with luck, his father would shelter him. Siward ought to know, too, whether Margaret were still free. He quickened pace.

There was a ragged hole in the roof, the kind of hole which gales made in badly done thatching. Well, he'd had it in mind that he ought to rethatch that roof even if it meant staying in Rushley awhile. He would do it properly this time. Then as he came closer, he saw that the door stood drunkenly ajar, half off its hinges. He broke into a squelching run along the muddy track. The door grated across the earth floor as he shoved it open. He stepped into the one room which was all the dwelling boasted. It was draped with cobwebs in every corner, and on the floor was an old pallet sprouting a revolting growth of toadstools. The fire-pit was empty except for what might have been the remains of very old ash in the depths of it. The storage jars, the few pots and utensils, had all disappeared. In any case a blind man could have told from the smell of damp and corruption that the dwelling had been long disused.

He withdrew slowly, wondering what to do. No one had seen him yet. The village street was deserted, with rain blowing along it. He could go to one of his aunts and ask her to hide him and to give him news.

But he was a free man now. He could prove it. The fact of his freedom rose up in him and rebelled against concealment. He wouldn't skulk in the shadows, finding things out obliquely. He wouldn't steal Margaret away in the night, either. Those were schemes hatched by the villein he no longer was.

No. He'd walk boldly, straight through the village to his uncle Adam's house, bang on the door and ask outright where his father was and if Margaret were still single.

He strode off, rehearsing his questions in his head. Trying not to dread the answers.

The door was opened by Meg, who stared at him as though he had come back from the grave and then, seeing how wet he was, automatically stood back to let him come into the warmth. Her first words, however, addressed to him as he stood steaming by the fire-trench, were not at all warm. '*You*. I never thought to see you again, I must say.' And, her tone made clear, she'd never wanted to, either.

His mantle was heavy with water and dripping on the floor. He took it off and Meg removed it impatiently, hanging it by the door. 'Well, Philip,' she said as she came back, 'I suppose I should offer my husband's returning nephew food and drink. Sit on that settle there and put your pack on the floor. I take it you want to see Adam. You'll have to wait till he comes.'

She moved to the fire-trench and began to stir a cooking pot. Her step was slower than it used to be and the braided hair which showed beneath her coif seemed to have lost all colour. 'Your father is dead,' she said abruptly over her shoulder. 'Did you know?'

'I was about to ask. I saw that our cottage was deserted. What happened?'

'When you were gone,' said Meg, 'there was no one to do his work on the lord's land but him. His neighbours had enough to do already. So they made him get to it. He was very shortwinded, Adam said, but they thought that would pass, once he was in practice again. Only it never did, and last harvest, when they were scything the wheat, he just fell down in the field choking for breath and died. There's stew here and some bread and ale. That do you?'

'Yes, of course. Thank you. I'm sorry about my father.' He found he meant it. He had realised at once that Siward might be dead but hearing confirmation of it hurt. 'I will see the priest about him. I can have a Mass sung for him, perhaps. I sent him some money from Norwich. What happened to it?'

'Adam's got it, put by.' Meg spoke sharply, set her mouth as though she were trying to hold something in check inside it and then said, angrily and unexpectedly: 'It wouldn't have happened if you'd been here!'

'Maybe,' said Philip. 'Maybe not. Who knows?' He didn't want to argue with Meg or, indeed, to discuss Siward with her at all. Siward's death and what it meant to him were his business, not hers. There was no sign of Margaret, he observed, and Meg hadn't mentioned her. 'Where is Margaret?' he asked, baldly.

'Everyone's about, here and there. The boys are in the workshop. They're taking to the pottery work, I'm glad to say. I've good, dutiful sons,' said Meg pointedly and added, before he could speak again: 'We gathered, from the messengers that came bringing money to your father, that you were safe in Norwich. But you've taken a chance, coming back. Sir Gilles was that hot after you. He had the dogs out, once he found you'd gone.'

'I've been working for a Norwich thatcher and he taught me the trade properly. I'll be going back there soon. I'm a freeman now!' He put down his bowl of stew and reached for his pack. He pulled out the precious scroll and undid it. 'Here's the proof, written by a priest to my master's dictation, and signed and witnessed and sealed, all as it ought to be. This says I've worked a year and a day as a freeman for John Le Toitier. And that's why I've come back, Mistress Meg, and I think you know it, don't you? I've come to marry Margaret and take her to Norwich with me. Is she still free to wed? Once again I ask you: where is she?'

'With Adam in the byre,' said Meg shortly. 'We've a cow calving late and giving trouble. No, Philip, she's not wed yet. And you'll forgive me for saying: more's the pity!'

Philip wasn't listening. He had turned his head towards the door. Beyond it, there were voices. Margaret and Adam came in together, laughing, out of breath from running through the rain, shaking it from their cloaks as they entered. Adam's hair was thin on top now and he had the first signs of the joint-evil that afflicted nearly everyone in this part of the world who lived past forty. But just now, exchanging banter in Margaret's company, he did not seem much older than Philip and looked, indeed, very like him.

The sight of them, as always, made Meg's heart twist within her. But neither was attending to her, for they had stopped short just inside the door to gaze in astonishment at the guest.

Then: 'Philip!' Margaret cried, and ran forward and straight into his arms, the two of them coming together as though neither was a complete being while they were apart.

'Well, well!' said Adam, smiling sentimentally.

And Meg, watching, had a distracted and unreasonable feeling that she could with the utmost enjoyment have killed all three of them.

'I can't make sense of you,' complained Adam. They lay close, whispering to each other behind the curtain which separated them from Margaret. 'Time and again you've said you want to see Margaret married, that this house is too crowded. Sometimes I think you dislike your own daughter. But when Philip walks in and offers to take her off your hands and clean out of your sight, and make her a freewoman, too, all you can find to say is that you wished he'd stayed in Norwich and preferably died of the ague there. *Why?*'

'You'll never understand!' muttered Meg angrily.

It was beyond her to explain because she didn't understand it herself. She didn't understand at all how it was that she could hate her daughter and fear her daughter and at the same time love her and want the best for her and want her to stay in the same village where Meg might see her sometimes. Every time she thought of Margaret, all these warring ideas foamed together inside her head as though someone were beating eggs in it.

The one single thing in all the muddle that she did understand, she couldn't mention to Adam.

She knew perfectly well, of course, that when he and Margaret went to the byre to help with a calving or when Margaret went to the workshop when Adam was there to help him prepare clay, there was no harm in it. The only man Margaret ever thought about was Philip, anyhow.

But after Philip went away and Brownpate officially withdrew his suit, Adam had started all this business of giving Margaret a hand with her jobs or asking her to do the same with his to 'cheer her up', as he said, and it had become in Meg's eyes far too much of a habit. Adam had never found out about that savage beating; both Margaret and Brownpate had had the decency to hold their tongues and although half the village must have heard the uproar, no one had mentioned it to him. By ancient, tacit village custom, gossip rarely was repeated to the people it affected most. But he had noticed Margaret's dejection. He had stroked her hair and called her his little girl and after that, this new kind of friendship began.

Meg had watched them, time and again, going out of the door together; had heard them talking of the day's doing together.

Had seen Adam's eyes on Margaret's hair and compared it despairingly with her own. Had looked in her old silver mirror and seen her own worn face. Whitish-green it was, most of the time, and weary, weary.

'If it hadn't been for Philip,' she said now, through her teeth, 'Margaret would have been Mistress Brownpate by now. Yes, I want her married but no, I don't want Philip to marry her. I wish he was dead. Then maybe she'd stop mooning after him. There's other men besides Brownpate and . . .'

'Meg, Meg, this isn't like you. I know you've no high opinion of the boy, but to say you wish he was dead . . .'

'I do wish it!' No one would ever know what it had cost her to sit him on her settle and give him food and make polite – well, fairly polite – conversation to him. She'd given him a bowl of stew and it had been all she could do not to hurl it into that amiable, open countenance of his instead. She had no warring feelings about Philip. She hated him with a fine, unwatered fury.

'I don't want her to go to Norwich,' she said. That was true, anyway. 'God knows what sort of life she'll have there with him. Freeman or no, he's just a thatcher's assistant, from what he says. I want to see her with a man who has a proper home and land and stock, the sort of thing she's used to.'

'I can agree with that,' Adam said thoughtfully. 'The only thing is, she seems to have set her heart on Philip and she's been very resolute . . .'

'Obstinate!'

'Maybe. For myself, I'd be sorry to see her go away to Norwich. I like having her about . . .'

Yes, I know!, Meg thought bitterly.

'. . . but I can respect the way she and the boy have held to one another. I suppose you want me to refuse consent?'

What I wanted you to do, you should have done a year ago. You should have made her marry Brownpate but you wouldn't, would you? 'Yes!'

'I doubt if there would be any point. You saw what happened when they met, didn't you?'

'Yes,' said Meg grimly.

'If I don't consent, well, can't you see what would happen? We can't keep the girl chained up. She and Philip would simply run off together.'

'So you'll consent.'

'I may have no choice. I'm sorry, Meg, if it means so much to you. I'm worried about her future with him too, but . . .'

I must be out of my head, Meg thought, lying in the darkness. I *want* her gone, I *want* Adam to myself. I ought to want her to go away to Norwich. But I don't, it isn't right for her and Philip's not right for her; just a thatcher's assistant; what kind of life will that be? Oh, the stupid, silly girl; if only Adam hadn't been so weak, so fond, last year . . . if only Philip had never existed! The only thing that'll cure this obsession of hers would be if he were dead!

Was Margaret asleep? she wondered. Philip was in the loft, with the boys. She had nearly choked on the words when she asked him to stay, but she could see that Adam would offer if she didn't. Philip and Margaret must be powerfully aware of each other's nearness at this moment.

'Philip's certainly kept his word, you know,' Adam was saying. 'It's barely over the year and a day, and here he is, back, with evidence of his freedom. It's the first week in June and if I remember aright, he went after the third week in May last year. He's got on with things.'

In the darkness, before Meg's wide-open, angry eyes, the light of inspiration dawned.

'I shall remember today as long as I live,' Margaret said as she and Philip, hand in hand, walked along the street towards her home. Yesterday's rain had gone. The wind had swung south and across the broad fields of Rushley and Oxfen its caress now was like a hand gloved in velvet.

'And I hope that that will be a very long time,' Philip said, contentedly. It was a satisfying thing to be a freeman, a satisfying thing to be a prospective bridegroom who has just asked the priest to arrange the ceremony. Above all it was satisfying to be walking along like this with Margaret, openly clasping her hand in his.

'It could be,' said Margaret seriously. 'My grandfather was quite old when he died. He was born before the Conquest, imagine! Adam says that my grandfather told him that he could remember *his* grandfather, and knew he was born before the year one thousand and that that was in the days before King Cnut. I'd never heard of King Cnut but my grandfather told Adam that he was a great Viking king who ruled in England before the Confessor. I've spoken to someone who'd spoken to someone who could remember before the year one thousand. Isn't that amazing?'

'Yes, it is!'

276

But everything, today, was amazing, from the warm brushing of the wind to the surge of their own warm, loving blood; from the gilded light of the afternoon on the pastures to the gold of the ring Philip had brought back from Norwich with him. It had been expensive, but four days hence it was to be Margaret's wedding ring. He had not whisked her instantly to Norwich. He was going to marry her openly, in Rushley, as soon as the wedding feast could be put together. Beside Siward's deserted hovel, on the day of his return, he had realised fully that he was no longer a forelock-pulling villein, and that the old plan of running away with Margaret was neither fitting nor what he wanted. Adam and Meg had given consent and the silver that Philip had sent to Siward would now pay the marriage fine.

The Rushley priest was a solemn man who had reminded them gravely of the seriousness of matrimony, adding that before the ceremony could be held, Philip must present himself and the evidence of his new status before Sir Gilles and have his freedom ratified in the manor court. But Adam said that although Sir Gilles always interpreted the law in the way most favour-able to himself, these days he generally kept the letter of it at least in public. The dour priest was responsible for that. He had taken Sir Gilles to task on occasion and Gilles apparently had a certain respect for the church. Armed with his proof, Philip should have little to fear. He and Margaret were serenely happy today, and as they made their way through the village there were greetings and friendly waves; they were surrounded by well-wishers.

In all probability, the whole village knew where they had been and why. 'There are town criers in Norwich,' Philip said to Margaret, 'and they walk through the streets ringing bells and announcing the news. But I think my aunt Helga is just as good!'

Outside the door of Adam's cottage, they stopped and kissed and they knew that had they not been living under Adam's roof, with no chance of privacy, nothing on earth would have kept them from each other's beds that night.

'It's only a few days,' Philip whispered. 'After we've waited so long, how long is that?'

'A few centuries!' said Margaret, but she was laughing.

She stopped laughing, however, and stepped away from him as her mother came along the street from the opposite end. Meg had given her consent but Margaret thought it was only to please Adam. Inside herself, her mother was still angry. Meg's face now was tight and she was trudging tiredly as though she had walked a long way. She greeted them mildly, however. 'Come inside, then. There'll be a bite to eat as soon as Adam comes in from the workshop. You'll have to get back to the cows tomor-row, Margaret, mind, but I suppose I shouldn't grudge you a day off just this once. It isn't every day a girl's betrothed.'

'Mistress Meg,' Philip said as they went indoors, 'I've been wanting to say, ever since this morning, well – thank you for accepting me. I know I'm not what you hoped for, for Margaret. But believe me, I shall always take care of her and do my best to make her a good husband. I want her to be happy.'

'So do I, Philip. I've never wanted anything else,' Meg said. 'Though you may find that hard to believe. Margaret, fetch out the ale. Now, a bite to eat I said but in fact I reckon we ought to have a little celebration meal. There's a cold chicken that I had on the spit this morning and I've made some honeycakes. Margaret, if you'll put some beans in the pot in a moment and get a spicy sauce ready for them . . .'

At least, thought Adam later as the family gathered round the table to partake of the cold chicken and spicy beans; at least in the end the betrothal had gone forward without fuss. Meg had apparently accepted it, not happily – well, her only daughter was going away and quite likely they wouldn't meet again or hardly ever so one couldn't expect that – but without making any scenes.

He wasn't altogether sure about the rightness of this marriage himself but Margaret was certainly ready to be a wife and she'd earned the right to Philip, through sheer constancy.

He raised his beaker of ale. 'I think it's time we drank the couple's health. I'd like to wish Margaret and Philip every happiness in their married life. Drink up, everyone!' He observed with pleasure that even Meg repeated the toast and drained her beaker. 'And what,' he asked as he set his own empty beaker down, 'will you wear for your wedding, Margaret?'

'I've a length of blue stuff put by that'll—'

The blow on the outer door was no polite neighbourly tap. It was made, surely, with a mailed fist or the hilt of a sword. They stared at each other, Meg stopping in mid-sentence, Adam half-rising.

'Open up!' The voice outside had the harsh, unmistakable accent of a Norman man-at-arms. 'Open up in the name of Sir Gilles of Rushley, your lord!'

Across the table, Philip and Margaret sought each other's hands and held fast. The blow and the shout were repeated. Adam went to the door and unbolted it. He started to ask what the matter was but the three men who strode in glanced at him once and then ignored him. The trio consisted of two men-at-arms and Sir Gilles's bailiff. The latter pointed at Philip. 'That's the man!'

'What?' Philip let go of Margaret's hand and struck out as the men-at-arms closed in on him, but was almost instantly helpless in their experienced grip. 'Let me go! You've no right . . . !'

'No right to seize an absconding villein?' enquired the bailiff.

'He isn't a villein! He's a freeman! He's been in Norwich for a year and a day! Let him be, let him be!' Margaret caught at the wrist of the nearest man-at-arms, trying vainly to break his hold on Philip, and wailed: 'We're betrothed! We're to marry in four days!'

'Ah, well, we'll have to see what Sir Gilles has to say about that,' remarked the bailiff. 'March him along!'

There was a babble of protest from Adam and the boys, but long habit of obedience to and fear of the bailiff and Sir Gilles's men kept them standing immobile. It was Margaret who sprang between the men and the door and stood with her back to it, arms wide. 'You can't take him! *No!*'

'Now come along, there's a good girl . . . no, stop that . . . for God's sake someone get this wildcat off me!' shouted the bailiff as Margaret responded to his attempt to shift her by clawing his face. He jerked her hands away and was savagely kicked. Meg pulled Margaret aside. Philip, now shouting incoherently, his eyes wide with panic, was dragged out of the door. He clutched at the doorpost and looked back at Adam. 'My pack! It's in my pack, the vellum that proves I'm free. I was going to take it up to the hall and present it tomorrow! Find it and bring it, for God's sake!'

'We will, don't worry! Don't be afraid! We'll have you free in a day!' Adam called.

Margaret tried to run after them as they took Philip away but Meg, her fingers biting fiercely into her daughter's arms, held on to her. 'It's no use, girl. It's no use.'

'How did they know he was here, that's what I want to know? We made sure he kept in the village where the lord's men mostly don't come! He said they mustn't see him until he went up there with his document and made it all square. Who'd tell *them?*' Margaret wept.

'Goodness knows,' said Meg, shaking a scandalised head.

'His pack,' said Adam, 'he said he had proof of his freedom in his pack. Where is it?'

'In the loft, by his bed. One of you boys go and get it,' said Meg. 'Hurry!'

She said it too willingly, as though Philip were a truly loved member of her circle. She had said *goodness knows* with too much innocent bewilderment.

A dreadful certainty began to congeal in the pit of Margaret's stomach.

It was a horror but not a surprise to her that when the boys brought Philip's pack and they upended it on the table, the document which she had seen for herself yesterday, lying on this same table when she came in with Adam, was not there.

Adam and her mother said it would be no use and that it might make things worse, going and making trouble with the great people. Margaret, acquiring mature powers of deception on the instant, sighed and agreed and ten minutes later said she would make sure that all was well in the byre; it had been kind of Joan to see to the cows today, but she was sometimes careless. She'd left a broom propped up against the wall in there once and it had fallen down and frightened the cows.

Her brothers, with the best of intentions, nearly frustrated her at this point, by offering to go themselves. 'No. Thank you. But I want . . . I want to be by myself for a bit!' said Margaret violently, and seized her cloak and went. As she left she heard Adam say: 'Let her go, Meg. She wants a good

279

cry, on her own. God knows, I feel the same. That boy's my nephew. But what we can do, except look for that scroll . . .'

Dear Adam. But he wasn't daring enough. She had learned a great deal about courage, over the last year. She set off with a purposeful step in the direction of the byre in case anyone were watching, but as soon as she was out of sight she changed course and made off through the summer dusk, to Oxfen.

She was going, in desperation, to the one person in the whole world who might, just might, have influence with Sir Gilles of Rushley: the woman famed throughout the region for her mercy and goodness, his mother, Lady Cis.

She had never been to Oxfen manor-house before. Oxfen itself she had known all her life but never once had she had occasion to take that right-hand fork which led direct to the house where Lady Cis had lived since her husband's death. It was nearly dark by the time she reached the fork and the slender crescent of a new moon gave no useful light; almost, she missed the way. Nightfall seemed to come down like a shutter as she turned on to the manor-house track. There were faint scuttlings in the grass to either side and a fox loped across the path just ahead of her, the outline of its sharp nose and low-carried brush just visible.

She had hardly ever been out after dark in her life, either. It was a time of fear and mystery when elf and demon might be abroad and ghosts walked. Normally, it would have frightened her. Tonight, she did not care. When she broke into a run it was not from fear of ghosts but with the urgent need to reach Lady Cis quickly, while Lady Cis was still awake.

The palisade gate was shut when she arrived. There was a small postern gate let into it and on this she pounded until she heard a door open somewhere on the other side. The postern opened and a wizened, gnome-like face, weathered to a walnut shade and covered with lines like a pottery glaze which had gone wrong, and lit by a flambeau in its owner's hand, peered out.

'All right, here I am. What's all this about, young woman, at this hour of the night, too?'

'I'm sorry. But please let me in; I've got to see Lady Cicely!' Margaret panted.

The ancient old man's eyebrows rose into his corrugated brow. 'Got to, is it? No question of may I, please? She'll be in her bed by now and not to be disturbed. What's it about and who might you be?'

'I'm Margaret Brittschild from Rushley and it's life and death and it's about . . . it's about Sir Gilles.'

The gnome's swift up-and-down glance said a great deal about Sir Gilles and the kind of young women who might want to complain about him to his mother. Margaret bristled. 'It's nothing like that! I've never met Sir Gilles, so there. But if I don't see Lady Cicely . . . if you won't let me in, I'll sit out here till morning. If you'll let me through and my lady's asleep,

I'll wait in the hall till morning! But see her I must and the soonest minute I can.'

The old man quite obviously didn't want to let her in but he was Lady Cicely's employee and her household knew that she didn't like petitioners to be turned away. Grumblingly, he stepped back and Margaret scrambled through the postern. Inside was a tiny thatched dwelling which was presumably the gatekeeper's lodge where the gnome lived. A track ran across a grassy space towards the manor hall itself and its satellite buildings. It was an old-fashioned place, still much as it was when an Englishman built it before the Conquest. Gleams of light here and there, from windows unshuttered in the warm night, showed that a few people were still awake although, as she watched, two windows darkened.

The gnome put two fingers in his mouth and whistled and a manservant appeared from somewhere. 'She wants to see the lady, so take her up to the hall and get Dame Elinor to take charge of her.'

Dame Elinor, it seemed, was Lady Cicely's senior attendant. She was herself a lady of breeding, tall and dignified, with an eagle beak of a nose. Candelabra in hand, she was still up and doing the rounds of the hall with the steward, extinguishing the flambeaux and examining the banked fire before retiring.

'A wench to see Lady Cicely – *now*?' she said to the manservant who had brought Margaret in. 'My lady is in bed long since.' She used English, though strongly accented. She looked disapprovingly down at Margaret from a superior five inches of height and the candles in her left hand threw a giant aquiline profile on the tapestry wallhanging beside her.

'I said, I would wait in the hall until morning,' said Margaret. 'And see her first thing if I can't see her now. At least I'm here. But, please, I *must* see her, as soon as I can. It's life and death and . . .' prudently, she changed the way she had put it the first time '. . . though I've never met Sir Gilles myself, it's to do with him.'

'I hardly think—' began Dame Elinor in forbidding tones, and then was cut short by a much lighter voice with a crackle in it. This voice too spoke English. 'What is it, Elinor? Who is this?'

'Oh, my lady!' Elinor turned to the woman who had just come in by a side door. 'Oh, you should be asleep by now. Didn't you take your mulled wine?'

'Not yet,' said Lady Cicely, coming forward, followed by a younger woman carrying another candelabra. 'There's a new moon. I always liked seeing the new moon and I was watching it for a while before I drank my posset and went to bed. I saw this young person being brought in. If I heard aright as I opened the door just now, she wants to see me and it concerns my son. I'd better hear what it's all about.'

Margaret, realising in whose presence she now was, had curtsied hastily. 'Well,' said Dame Elinor, clearly not pleased with her, 'you've got your wish. Here's my lady. Tell her all about it, whatever it is.'

Margaret rose from her curtsy to look into the face of the woman she had hoped would be Philip's saviour. And experienced despair.

She had caught occasional glimpses of Lady Cicely and knew that she was not particularly old; in middle life, that was all. But she had never before seen her close to and knew no one in her household. Now she realised that it was true that Lady Cis was only in her mid-forties, but . . .

She was ill. Nothing but mortal illness could create that brittle gauntness, that too-bright colour on a skin almost transparent. She did not look like a match for an arrogant lord in the best of health. She did not look, Margaret thought frantically, like a match for a mouse.

But she was here now, and must try. 'My lady . . .' she began and then, simply because Lady Cis's eyes were so kind, the memory of Philip's hand in hers as they walked home through the June afternoon and the contrast between that perfect happiness and the horror of seeing Philip dragged away, overwhelmed her. She struggled for words and knew that if she tried to speak she would cry. She was determined not to cry. What use would that be? She looked at Lady Cis with dumb desperation. 'My dear child!' said Lady Cis. 'What is it?'

'My dear,' said Lady Cis, 'I will do what I can but I must tell you that I have no power beyond that the love a mother can call from a son and my son is . . . always respectful but he goes his own way.'

She had brought Margaret into her private chamber. The manor-house still had the old English arrangement of separate buildings for use as sleeping-chambers for its owners and their guests. Here there were hangings and settles, a down bed for Lady Cis and truckle beds, also well-furnished, for the ladies who shared her room, and a table on which stood the posset to which Dame Elinor had referred, still untouched.

Lady Cis had sent for plain wine and they had drunk that instead. Margaret, fortified and soothed, had told her tale at last. 'You say,' said Lady Cis, 'that the document that proves your young man's freedom has disappeared?'

'Yes. But I saw it yesterday and so did my stepfather. And my mother.'

'And what do you think has happened to it?'

Margaret turned her head away. 'I don't know. I'm afraid . . .'

'Yes?'

'My mother doesn't like Philip. She doesn't want me to marry him. She's . . . I'm afraid . . . someone must have taken the news up to Sir Gilles at the hall, too.'

'It may not have been your mother,' said Lady Cis gently.

'I can't think who else would have known to take it from his pack, and *wanted* to.'

'Well,' said Lady Cis with a sigh, 'whoever told, and whoever took the scroll, the scroll is gone. A pity. It was of crucial importance. Well, we must do what we can without it. First, we need someone to testify to the date on which Philip left Rushley. From what you say, he came back only just after completing a year and a day in Norwich. Dear me. It would be

282

easier if he had waited longer. I daresay his kinsmen and friends hid his disappearance for a time, too? That's what usually happens. They'll be afraid to admit they lied. Finding willing witnesses may be difficult. But we must start somewhere. Now, are you calmer?'

'Yes,' said Margaret gratefully. The wine was warming and despite her sickly air, Lady Cis seemed to know what to do. It might be all right after all.

'Then I'll tell you what we'll do,' said Lady Cis. 'In the morning I shall send my chaplain to Rushley to speak to your priest, Father Dunstan. He's a stern man, but honest. He may be able to suggest suitable witnesses. Can you suggest any yourself?'

Margaret bit her lip. Even with Lady Cis, she was chary of naming names. She would sooner leave that to Father Dunstan. 'People *did* try to shield him. So they might be scared. But it was kind of them, natural! Oh, why wasn't I brave enough to run away with Philip at the start? Then he would never have had to come back for me. I've put him in such danger!'

'Nonsense.' Lady Cicely's fragile voice rustled like dried leaves but it was still capable of asperity. 'From what you say, he wouldn't have taken you and I'm glad he had so much sense. It was very wrong of him to run away in the first place.'

'He did it for me. I *have* put him in danger.'

'He made his own choice,' said Lady Cis. 'But because I am a tender-hearted woman and I understand what made him so forget his proper duty, I am sorry for you both. As things stand, the law should by this time be on his side, but . . .'

'But *why* was it wrong of him to go?' said Margaret. 'I don't see *why*. Why are people bound to stay in places, bound to serve other people, against their will? He only wanted to call his soul his own.'

'None of us can do that.' Lady Cis's voice faded a little, as though her strength were faltering. 'Our souls belong to God, my dear, and he calls them to him when it pleases him. As for our bodies, they are set where it pleases him to put them. One could say that Philip has defied the will of God in running off to Norwich. But as I said, I am sorry for you both and compassion is accounted a virtue. When one is in my case, one hoards virtue, like gold. Now, let us consider this question of the witnesses. I don't know how much worth they will have, without proof that Philip was working in a town as well. I don't know whether kinsmen would be accept-able, either. But any oathswearers are better than none, especially if Father Dunstan will back them up. I think, too, that you and I had better go straight to Rushley hall in the morning. I will see if I can do anything for your young man before any proceedings begin. They are likely to be held tomorrow,' said Lady Cis. 'My son is in the habit of taking action briskly. Tonight, you shall have a pallet in here. I can promise nothing, but I will do my best. I will also send word to your family to tell them where you are.'

Lying in the darkness later, in this strange room at Oxfen, Margaret, who seemed in the space of a few hours to have travelled from heaven to hell and to have lurched half a dozen times over between wild hope and hopeless despair, lay racked with fear of the morning.

Lady Cis was going to do her best but her strength seemed to come and go like a fitful wind, and there was something very disquieting in her unquestioning acceptance that Gilles, her own son, would be as merciless as he knew how. How many other times had she known him to be merciless, so that she, his mother, did not even waste a few sentences on a token defence of his character?

Margaret lay with her face buried in her arms and wondered where these ideas had come from. They seemed to spring from a layer of knowledge that was far older than she was herself. She shut her eyes tight as if trying to shut them out. She did not want such disquieting wisdom. It was easier to trust, easier to hope, without it.

Chapter Seventeen

In Extremis

'I don't know how to ride,' Margaret said. Before de Mandeville's visitation, Adam had kept a pony for carrying packs and sometimes people, but although they had recovered better from the disaster than some, they had never managed another pony or even a donkey. When he took his pottery-ware to market, Adam hired a pack-animal. Now Margaret stood with Lady Cis in front of the Oxfen manor-house and looked in alarm at the pony which had been saddled for her.

'I can follow you on foot,' Margaret said. 'I can run most of the way.'

'No, we must get there quickly and together,' said Lady Cis firmly. 'There's no time to waste. I've sent my chaplain off to Rushley at a gallop; his old mare won't have moved so fast in years. You can ride with Gervase.' She beckoned to the manservant. 'You're to take Margaret up behind you.'

'Madam,' said Dame Elinor worriedly, 'I'm afraid this will be too much for you. Even though I shall be with you . . .'

'There's a life at stake,' said Lady Cis, 'and mine is forfeit anyway. I can hardly spend what remains more wisely than in defending someone else's. Can I?'

'No,' said Dame Elinor, clearly understanding the precept. Her eagle glance at Margaret, however, was anything but friendly. 'But those who care for you, madam, would like to see you take your ease and save yourself what suffering you can.'

'Or lengthen it,' said Lady Cis. 'Here's Gervase, Margaret. Put your foot on his and take his hand – that's right, up you go.' A horse was brought for Dame Elinor, and a young groom came up with a lightweight bay mare for Lady Cis herself. With his aid, she mounted. He settled her and adjusted the girth with great care. It was clear to Margaret that there was no one in this household who did not love and watch over their mistress.

If only, if only, she could inspire the same emotion in her son.

At Rushley hall, the steward Gerbert met them at the door and said: 'My lady, your son is about to hold a trial. An absconding villein, I believe. The sitting is just beginning but I'm sure it won't take long. If you would care to wait in the solar . . .'

'If the absconding villein is called Philip Siwardson,' said Lady Cis, managing to sound almost sharp, 'I'm here on his behalf. Kindly conduct us all into the hall at once.'

It was going to be formal. In no more than fourteen months, Gilles of Rushley had learned a good deal. When he first inherited, he had dealt with miscreants such as thieves or poachers then and there, because it was easier and extremely satisfying and the fact that it was technically against the law didn't matter. It had been a long time since the law had had any teeth.

But Father Dunstan had had something to say about it, and some remarks about purgatory and hellfire which made even a healthy young man think, and then, sheer chance had opened Gilles's eyes to some new possibilities. When a party of villeins walking home, spades over their shoulders, after a day's work on the demesne farm, came across the scene when Gilles was having a poacher – a man from Oxfen, whom they all knew, who had been caught snaring hares – strung up on the oak tree which marked the demesne boundary, he had observed the impression it made on them.

These things, after all, could be more effective with an audience. Next time, he tried out the system of a formal trial which the villagers could attend, followed by a formal execution, complete with priest, which they were invited to witness too.

It was not only effective; it also appealed to something dramatic in his spirit. It gave him more subtle and varied parts to play than simply that of rough, decisive war-lord.

He could be lord of the manor presiding over his manor court, grave judge evaluating evidence and passing sentence, and superintending executioner, all in the same morning; and while he was at it, he could enhance his dignity by appearing, however mendaciously, to be an upholder of justice.

On one or two occasions he had even allowed a minor offender to be found not guilty, although this didn't happen often. Clemency, Sir Gilles felt, was like strong drink and should be taken in limited quantities.

Philip Siwardson was the first absconding villein he had had to deal with and therefore offered a new variation. Sir Gilles, therefore, proposed to give him the fullest possible treatment. Gilles's household included five hired knights with squires, and a dozen men who did whatever tasks presented themselves about the place but who were equipped as men-at-arms and trained with weapons every day. All but four of these were in the hall, fully armed and standing on either side of Sir Gilles's chair of state on the dais. The clerk, Wilfrid, was seated at a desk to one side, with vellum, pen, ink and sander in front of him, waiting to make notes of the proceedings.

Others of Sir Gilles's employees stood in the body of the hall and there too, in an uneasy group, were a substantial proportion of Rushley's male population. Among them, grouped together, were Adam, Thurgar and Agmund along with Lady Cis's chaplain. Father Dunstan, who was also

Gilles's chaplain was beside him, looking severe, as usual. Lady Cis's entrance caused a stir.

'Mother!' said Sir Gilles, disconcerted. When encountering his mother, he usually knelt and kissed her hand, as a respectful and dutiful son should, but to do anything of the kind now would ruin the authoritative impression he was creating. 'What brings you here?' he said, and remained in his chair.

'I may have something to contribute to this court,' said Lady Cis. 'These ladies and I wish to sit down. On the dais, please.' She took Margaret's arm and led her firmly forward. Dame Elinor followed. Gervase stood aside, but stationed himself close to the dais, and his mistress.

Margaret had understood only a little of this exchange, which was in French. She was intimidated by the atmosphere in the hall, by the mailed figures of Sir Gilles's men and above all by Gilles himself, who was wearing a long, formal, mulberry gown but had a sword across his knees. She wanted to hang back but Lady Cis's thin, hot fingers were insistent. She remembered that if she were frightened, Philip would be even more so. She went forward with a pretence at willingness, looking about her for Philip. He didn't seem to be present.

One of the squires drew a wide bench seat to a position near the front of the dais, to Gilles's left, and here they sat down, Margaret and Dame Elinor one on each side of Lady Cis. Gilles turned to stare at them. Margaret reminded herself that he was an enemy and tried to stare boldly back at him but failed.

'Who is this, Mother?' he inquired.

'A seeker after justice,' said Lady Cis. 'Is this court going to be heard or at least translated into English?'

'It will be held in the dialect which we can all understand. I have concluded that the effect is greater if the audience knows what is happening. Wilfrid's notes will be in Latin, of course. Ah. Here comes the prisoner.'

Two men-at-arms had been fetching him. They thrust him ahead of them through the door. He stopped short, staring round him. His flaxen hair was tangled and there were with bruises and a graze on one jaw. He was filthy, too. He must have lain all night in straw, for bits of it were sticking to him. All trace of his new freeman's dignity had vanished. He was quite obviously terrified. He caught sight of Margaret and gasped.

'Philip, I'm here! Lady Cis has come to—'

'Ssssh!' Lady Cis's hot fingers burned through her sleeve again. 'I'll speak at the right time. Not yet.'

'Bring the prisoner forward!' said Gilles, paying no attention to the women. Philip's escort marched him to the foot of the dais. 'Wilfrid,' said Sir Gilles, 'recite the charge, if you please.'

'The prisoner is Philip Siwardson, villein of Rushley, and the charge is attempted absconding and also an attempt to marry and remove a villein girl from the village without applying for permission or paying the proper fine for such a marriage.'

Margaret made a jerky movement. Lady Cis nudged her reprovingly.

'You,' said Sir Gilles, addressing Philip, 'you are this Philip Siwardson?'

'I'm . . . I'm . . .' he stammered and then, admonished by a prod from one of his escort, got out the words: 'Yes, that's my name. But I'm not a villein!' he added loudly.

'I hope for your sake that you can prove it. Meanwhile . . .'

There was an interruption as the door opened and Meg was pushed unceremoniously into the hall by two more men-at-arms. She was dishevelled and visibly both angry and alarmed. Her eyes darted huntedly from side to side as she was led up the hall. She caught sight of both Adam and Margaret and they appeared to frighten her even more than Sir Gilles did.

'Ah,' said Gilles. 'Meg Potterswife, just at the right moment. Stand there, Meg, look at the prisoner and tell us if you know him.'

'That's Philip Siwardson. But, sir . . .'

'Thank you, Meg. Now please repeat for us all to hear, the testimony you gave me in private yesterday.'

In the crowd, Adam gulped, his face an almost comical mask of disbelief. His eyes met Margaret's. Miserably, in unnecessary corroboration, Margaret nodded.

'But you said I needn't . . . you said no one need know . . .' Meg cried out.

'I've changed my mind. If this trial is to be properly held, then all the relevant testimony must be heard.'

Meg stood trembling, her hands twisting together. If the prisoner, her victim, had been anyone but Philip, Margaret would have run to her to comfort her. As it was, she leaned against Lady Cis and stared down at the floor.

'Well, Meg. Come along, we're waiting. This court has been convened on the strength of your information. I hope you're not going to tell us now that you've wasted our time,' said Sir Gilles.

No, Meg wasn't going to do that. She could recognise the threat in his voice as well as anyone. She raised her head and said: 'All right. That's Philip Siwardson, as I said. And he ran off from Rushley last year, the day before your bailiff's man came looking for him and I know that was the sixth day of June because it was a Friday and on the Sunday in church, Father Dunstan gave out the date like he always does and he said it was June the eighth,' finished Meg, in a gabble.

'It's not true!' Philip turned a blanched face towards her. 'I've got the dates on my vellum. I worked for John Le Toitier from—'

His escort clouted him into silence. 'You'll speak when you're asked, and not before.'

'But . . .'

'Quiet, you!'

'Adam, the vellum!' Philip shouted.

Sir Gilles raised a hand. 'I will hear what the prisoner has to say.'

288

'My lord!' Eagerly and thankfully, Philip burst into speech. 'I worked for Master Le Toitier, thatcher, of Norwich, from the twenty-ninth of May last year to the thirtieth of May this year. That's a year and a day. I've got a scroll, with it all written on and witnessed; Master Le Toitier did that for me . . .'

'I'm glad to hear it. Where is the vellum?'

'Adam!' said Philip urgently, for the second time.

Adam, carefully not looking at his wife, came forward. 'The vellum has disappeared, my lord. But it was real, all right, I saw it myself.'

'Can you read?'

'I . . . no, sir,' said Adam. He looked confused.

'You saw *a* vellum, then. You can't testify as to what was written on it.'

Father Dunstan stepped to the foot of the dais. 'There is something I wish to say, Sir Gilles.'

'Yes, Father Dunstan?'

'Adam Millerson here and two of his kinsmen, his brothers-in-law Thurgar and Agmund, are prepared to testify to the date on which Philip Siwardson first left Rushley.' It was clear that Lady Cis's chaplain had done his work well and persuaded Father Dunstan to do the same. Thurgar and Agmund hesitated momentarily, glancing at each other, but then, to Margaret's mingled pride and alarm, they came to stand beside Adam.

'You are Thurgar and Agmund?' said Sir Gilles. 'Which is which?' He listened, smiling slightly, as they identified themselves. 'And you are prepared,' he said when they had done so, 'to swear that Philip Siwardson left more than a year and a day ago?'

'Yes, sir,' said Adam, speaking for all of them.

'But all three of you,' Sir Gilles pointed out, 'are Siwardson's kinsmen. My bailiff has spoken to me about this. You tried to hide his disappearance. You lied to my bailiff.'

'According to my parishioners,' said Father Dunstan, to Margaret's everlasting gratitude, 'they did not know to begin with that Philip had left Rushley.'

'That's right,' said Adam eagerly. 'We didn't know where he was. He could have had an accident in the marshes, anything. We tried to keep him out of trouble while we looked for him.'

'And that, my son,' said Lady Cis, speaking up unexpectedly, 'is natural and right. I'd have done it in their place and so I hope would you.'

Sir Gilles did not acknowledge her but did not pursue the matter either. 'You say, Adam Millerson, that you and your kinsmen here with you will swear to the date when Philip Siwardson left Rushley?'

'Yes, sir. On the night of the twenty-fourth of May.'

'Are you sure? You keep a calendar, do you?' This produced laughter from Sir Gilles's men.

'Sir, as I said, we were worried about him. His father Siward was alive then and he was worried most of all. We kept count of the days. *I* can

289

remember what date was given out in church the next Sunday, too,' said Adam, glancing grimly towards Meg. 'It was the next day, and Father Dunstan said it was the twenty-fifth of May. So it was more than a year and a day before Philip ever came back, and he came back the day before yesterday, on the third of June.'

Agmund and Thurstan said: 'Yes, that's right,' in duet, and Father Dunstan added: 'To the best of my recollection, Philip was not in church on Sunday the twenty-fifth of May. I can call that to mind because, of course, I learned of his disappearance shortly afterwards and I can remember the sermon I was preparing at the time. I do keep a calendar. I make one, with all the church festivals entered on it and I note the subjects of sermons against the proper dates. I looked this one up.'

'Are you sure that Philip Siwardson was absent on that Sunday?'

As Lady Cis had said, Father Dunstan was honest. He now proved that this could be an exasperating virtue. 'I think he was absent. But I'm not sure I could take an oath on it.'

'Is Hubert the Bailiff here?' said Sir Gilles.

'Yes, sir.' The bailiff came forward.

'Let's hear your testimony, then. Did Philip attend for his usual duties on my land during the week before you found that he had gone? The week *before*. The last week of May.'

'No, sir. He didn't. I had word he was sick, and someone sent a boy of ten along instead,' said the bailiff. 'I told Master Wilfrid to note it, as I always do with absences. It will be in his records.'

Wilfrid, called upon, duly confirmed this.

'You see,' said Sir Gilles pleasantly to Philip, 'you're getting a fair trial. I call honest witnesses.' Something in the way he said it suddenly chilled Margaret. He sounded so extremely pleased with himself. He addressed Meg. 'And what have you to say to that, woman? Where was he in that week before *you* say he left?'

'I don't know, how would I know?' Judging from her expression, Meg would have liked nothing better than to bolt out of the hall. 'Maybe he really was ill. I don't know.'

'But you're sure he disappeared on the fifth of June, not earlier? I do *hope* you're sure,' said Sir Gilles, with the assured smile of a well-off and handsome young man and a voice as silky as the coat of a well-fed tomcat. 'It would be such a pity if you weren't. After all, this court is taking up a lot of time for a great many people.'

'I'm sure, yes, I'm quite sure!' Meg was sweating. 'Of course I'm sure. Only I never thought, you never said, I'd have to stand here in front of the very man himself . . . I'll swear if you like. I'll do anything!'

'She's lying!' shouted Philip. 'It's all lies, because she doesn't want me marrying Margaret . . . !'

'Oh yes,' said Sir Gilles. 'The little matter of taking a villein girl off the estate without paying for her . . .'

Margaret cried out: 'But we were going to see to all that!' and Philip said loudly: 'Yes, that's right!'

Adam broke in. 'I'd have seen to it that permission was asked and the fine paid!'

'I certainly understood from Philip that he meant to see that all was correct before I joined him to Margaret in wedlock,' Father Dunstan interposed.

'The wedding isn't till Monday!' Adam shouted 'How can he be accused of taking Margaret away when she's still here? There she is, not six feet away from you! Meg, Meg, why did you do this?'

'I did what I thought was right!' Meg held up her head but she wouldn't look at him. 'It's a sin for people to run off and desert their proper places. Father Dunstan said so once, in a sermon!' She turned for support to the priest and the villagers. Father Dunstan studied her without speaking and the faces of the villagers were stony. She flinched away. 'I've been dragged here like a prisoner. I've done nothing wrong!'

'Unless,' said Father Dunstan, 'you are now committing perjury, in order to stop a marriage of which you disapprove. It is a sin to leave the place to which God has called one, yes, but the law graciously lays down circumstances in which a man may by honest industry for a year and a day be quit of that sin. I was given to believe that Philip had so absolved himself, and it seems we have witnesses here ready to swear to it. Have I your permission, Sir Gilles, to administer the oath to them?'

'To all the witnesses, both for and against?' enquired Sir Gilles.

'I want to go home,' Meg whimpered.

'My lord,' said Adam, cutting across her. 'I repeat. I and my brothers-in-law here are ready to swear that Philip Siwardson left Rushley between the twenty-fourth and twenty-fifth of May last year. May we do so?'

Sir Gilles sat back. The assured smile was still on his face. He let a silence develop and go on and on. Then he said: 'It does seem as though there is a doubt as to when precisely Philip Siwardson left Rushley last year. But all the witnesses, on either side, appear to be relatives of his with a personal interest in swaying the verdict. In any case, even if there were clear proof that it is more than a year and a day since he went away, that is not enough. All these anxious witnesses merely obscure the real issue. To pass from villeinage to freedom, a man must also prove that he has worked for a year and a day within a walled town. Philip Siwardson claims to have sworn testimony to this from an employer in Norwich but if so, where is it?'

He paused. Margaret sat very still. She dared not look at Philip. Beside her, Lady Cis let out a small, sad sigh.

'There is one more witness to be called, however,' said Sir Gilles smoothly. 'Mother! Since you have taken the trouble to come here today, I take it that you have some interest in this man's fate, and perhaps something to contribute to this enquiry. Would you be kind enough to declare it?'

Lady Cicely took Margaret's hand, pulled her up and led her round to kneel in front of Sir Gilles.

'My dear son, as you must have realised, this young woman is Margaret Brittschild, who is betrothed to Philip Siwardson. She sought my help in obtaining justice for him. She will swear on oath that he has indeed fulfilled the conditions which would make him free. She has sworn to me too – and I believe her – that she has seen the vellum which was his proof, and that it has now disappeared and that she suspects that someone has made away with it. Please, my son, accept the oaths of these honest men of Rushley, and let the said Philip Siwardson go free, with your consent to his marriage with Margaret, if the due forms are observed.'

While Lady Cis was speaking, Margaret raised her eyes to Sir Gilles's face and tried to use them to plead with him. He smiled down at her. 'What a moving appeal,' Gilles said. 'It goes to my heart to refuse the pleas of my own mother and of this charming girl.' A terrible stillness settled on the hall. 'But evidence of the manner in which Philip Siwardson has lived since he left Rushley is essential and seems not to be forthcoming. On its own, the sworn testimony of the witnesses here present are insufficient. Indeed, it would be unacceptable anyway. His kinsmen have already lied for him once, and the woman Meg Potterswife is understandably anxious to protect her daughter from this questionable character. Furthermore, one cannot rely on a peasant understanding the gravity of such a thing as perjury, and I would not imperil their immortal souls by leading them to take what may well be a perjured oath.'

He paused. The silence fell again.

Lady Cis cleared her throat. 'It would be possible, my son, to send to Norwich for the man whom Philip says was his employer.'

'That's right!' Philip cried eagerly. 'John le Toitier! He'd speak for me!'

'I wonder if he is any more real than the vellum which has so strangely vanished?' said Gilles. 'I fear it would be a waste of time to search for him.' Lady Cis made as if to speak again but Gilles raised a denying palm. 'No, Mother. Though it wounds me to do so, I must forbid you to say any more. You have made your appeal. But my judgement is this. There is no acceptable testimony either way but my doubt of this man's guilt is not great enough to outweigh the far greater principle that for a villein to abandon his lord and his land is a crime of the utmost seriousness, endangering the rights and the prosperity of his lord and, thereby, the ability of his lord to discharge his own obligations to those in turn above him. To do that, a lord must have the use of all he owns including his villeins. Let there be no mistake about it. Villeins own nothing but their bellies. Therefore, it is as it says in the Bible, best for the offending limb to be lopped from the body of society, before its contagion can spread to the damage of all. I find Philip Siwardson guilty of absconding from his place as my villein and planning to deprive the estate of a villein woman. Take him out and hang him.'

Into the frozen pause which followed, he added: 'Father Dunstan, do your office and shrive the man first. I would have him go to his death in a state of grace.'

'John Le Toitier's real! He'd testify!' screamed Philip. He tried to break away from the men-at-arms who had seized him. Pandemonium broke out. Meg slumped down, fainting. Margaret shrieked: '*Philip!*' and tried to get to him but ran into Adam, whose arms closed round her. 'Margaret, come away, you can do nothing for him now . . .'

'It's all been just a put-on show! You were going to do this all the time!' Margaret, beside herself, twisted in Adam's grasp and shouted at Sir Gilles. He took no notice. Adam tried to quieten her. 'Margaret, hush. Don't . . .'

'Philip, *Philip* . . . !'

She saw him for the last time as he was hauled towards the door of the hall, his eyes staring with terror and his mouth gibbering. She struggled wildly against Adam, but he would not let her go. Lady Cis was beside them. Her veil was awry, showing her pitted forehead, and she was swaying, supported by a tightmouthed Dame Elinor, but her voice still held authority. 'Get her away from here, quickly. If she doesn't want to go home, take her to Oxfen hall. I'm a little unwell but I'll follow when I'm able. I'll keep her with me there. But take her out of here, Adam Millerson, and make haste!'

No one interfered as Adam half dragged and half carried Margaret from the hall and ran her across the courtyard to the other gate. Once beyond it, he simply kept on going, hurrying her away from Rushley hall as though the nightmare there were a pestilence that she might catch if she lingered, and following the path for Oxfen without hesitation. There was no question of taking Margaret home to the cottage he shared with Meg. He did not know what he was going to do about Meg, what he would say to her when he saw her again, how he would live with her henceforth, how he would explain any of this to their sons. For the moment, he was concentrating on Margaret.

Lady Cis had said: 'Take her to Oxfen,' so he was doing it. They were going through Narrow Wood when Margaret stumbled. He tried to hold her up but she resisted and slid to her knees. 'It's happening now!' she said, and buried her face in her hands.

Adam did not ask her how she knew. Instead, he knelt beside her, took her hand and began to recite the paternoster. Feverishly, Margaret joined in. They did not know and would never know whether their valediction had reached Philip as his fear and agony were reaching Margaret now, or whether they had sent him help in even the least degree but it was all that they could do.

While they knelt in prayer and Philip Siwardson was dying in the courtyard at Rushley hall, June breezes rustled in the trees and birds kept calling, dove and cuckoo and blackbird. They reached the end of the prayer. As they did so, the black horror which had possessed Margaret's mind let her go and she knew that Philip's spirit had let go too and was drifting out of the world.

'It's over now,' she said. 'It's over. Oh, Philip, *Philip* . . . !'

'Hush. Oh, Margaret, I'm sorry, I'm so sorry. I'd make it come right if I could. If I could wave a wand and bring him back to you, I would. Shall we say the prayer again?'

'No. What's the use? Oh, why can't that cuckoo be quiet?' sobbed Margaret.

Gently, Adam drew her to him. His intention was only to comfort, but when his arms were round her and the firm warmth of her was pressed against him, his arms tightened before he could stop them, seeking to press her more securely to him still.

He was a man without a wife now; he might go on living under the same roof with Meg for their sons' sake, but there would be no more to it than that. Sex had been almost non-existent between them now for a long time, but there had been companionship, friendliness. That too was now over.

And as Meg had known all along, desire for Margaret had been present in him, unadmitted but growing, growing, since she was a child. Now, fresh from its long dormancy, it awoke, and it was hot and hungry.

He began to kiss her, exploring the taste of ears, eyes, nose, mouth. He broke away once. 'Margaret, stop me, stop me, push me away, run!'

But Margaret did not want to run. She did not want to be alone. Loneliness, of a most terrible and permanent nature, waited for her outside the circle of Adam's arms and she was not yet able to face it. She clung to Adam as protection, glad of warmth, of intimacy; glad, since real love and real security were lost, to be granted their illusion. What did it matter, anyway? Philip was dead.

She did not try to prevent Adam from loosening her clothing and his, and she held him to her as he nuzzled and caressed and turned his face this way and that against her breasts and her stomach, until at last he entered her, when she welcomed him equally for the closeness and the jab of pain, for nothing should be painless in this time of sorrow.

Adam, not Philip; stepfather instead of bridegroom; love twisted instead of love hallowed; the scent of foliage all round and last year's leaf-mould under her back instead of a priestly blessing and a marriage bed.

The cuckoo, indifferent, went on calling.

'Very well,' said Dame Elinor. 'You may go to Rushley to visit your family. You can have the rest of the day. But take the clean napkins to Lady Cicely before you set off.'

'Thank you,' said Margaret humbly.

She carried the pile of napkins to Lady Cis's bedchamber as requested. Lady Cis, having returned from Philip Siwardson's dreadful trial a month ago, had gone straight to bed. Since then, except for a few occasions when she had asked her attendants to carry her into the hall so that she could sit up for a while in a chair, she had stayed there, refusing to see visitors. She had sent Sir Gilles away when he came to enquire after his mother's health.

But she had been very kind to Margaret, and Margaret, in desperate need of kindness, had taken the utmost care not to offend either Lady Cis or her attendants, whose number she had joined. They had never had a villein girl in their midst before and didn't like her much, and she knew that only Lady Cis's direct command kept them from being openly unpleasant. But she had done whatever menial tasks were thrust at her, and never pushed herself forward and in time she might have made a place for herself among them.

Except that there wasn't going to be any time.

The girl who was reading to Lady Cis did not pause or acknowledge her as she entered with the napkins. Margaret, however, instead of putting them quietly into their chest and going away again, cleared her throat and indicated that she wished to speak to her mistress. Lady Cis made a sign and the reader stopped reluctantly in the middle of a passage from St Augustine.

'Yes, dear?' said Lady Cis.

'Madam, Dame Elinor has kindly given me permission to go to Rushley for the day. I'm anxious to see my family and visit some friends. I came in to tell you, to make sure that it is all right with you and ask if you have any errands there.'

'No, dear. But certainly it is all right with me. I am glad you want to see your family. I think perhaps you should find out what is really happening.' Lady Cis still listened to news from outside when her women brought it to her. She knew that Adam was still living with Meg and apparently treating her considerately, but that hardly anyone else in Rushley would speak to her, while Meg herself was said to be behaving as though she were mad, continually muttering to herself, or crying, or both at once.

'I hope to be back safely before nightfall,' said Margaret.

She hoped that no double meaning was apparent in her voice. Fortunately, Lady Cis did not seem aware of any. 'There'll be a new moon again tonight,' she said. 'If the sky stays clear, I shall ask to be carried where I can see it. You shall see it with me.'

She did not add: It may well be my last. But it was probable. Even in the last few days she had grown thinner and her cough had worsened. She coughed up blood every time, now. Margaret understood all too well the words which had not been said.

She had come to love Lady Cis and she grieved for her, but there was more to it than that. It was because she knew that she would not for much longer have Lady Cis as employer and protector, that she was going to Rushley today.

She set out from Oxfen with resolution, but not with hope. It would be foolish, very childish, to be hopeful. But she must try, she must make this one attempt to provide for the future. Up to now, she had done everything amiss. Peter Brownpate had once praised her for steadfastness, but steadfast was the last thing she had been. She had let Philip down at every turn. If she had been brave enough to insist on running off to Norwich with him, he would not have had to come back to Rushley; if she had fled with him at once when he reappeared, instead of letting him talk about his new dignity as a freeman, he and she would be in Norwich together now. And if she had stayed with him to the last instead of letting Adam take her away, then she would not now be in this disastrous position.

When Lady Cis was gone, Margaret would have nowhere to turn except for one slender possibility. There was, she thought, just one chance for her. She owed it to herself and to the other person for whom she was now responsible, to try.

But she dared not hope, for she was not going to hide behind pretence. If she were given the help she sought, then the giver deserved honesty.

She did not know that this back-to-the-wall integrity which had suddenly risen up in her was part of her inheritance from her forebear Ivon de Clairpont, any more than she had known, in Narrow Wood, that she shared Philip's dying because of the sixth sense inherited, like her fox-coloured hair, from Gunnor. But she obeyed it instinctively.

No lies. No deception. No timidity. One single bid for life and if that failed, she would not see Lady Cis's new moon rise tonight.

She had chosen her day with care, knowing the routine of the person she wished to see. Haymaking and sheep-shearing were over; the weekly schedule would be back to normal. And as she expected, Peter Brownpate was at his workshop, occupied with his carpentry.

He was in fact out in his woodyard, conferring with a customer who wanted a handcart made. His eyes acknowledged her as she came into the yard and she sat down on a pile of planks to wait for his attention.

The customer went away. Brownpate picked up a saw and began methodically to clean it. 'Margaret? You're looking for me?'

'Yes. I need to talk to you. It'd be better if we weren't interrupted.'

Brownpate raised his eyebrows and she thought in panic: I'm making a mess of it already. I sound so downright. 'Please,' she said. 'It's important, or I wouldn't ask.'

'Come into the shop. I'll bolt the door.'

With the workshop door closed, the place was dim even on a bright July day. They sat where they could make the best of the light through the one window. 'I'm glad to see you're all right,' said Brownpate. 'I heard you were with Lady Cicely. That's good, seeing what's happened. I was sorry, Margaret, sorry about your mother and most of all about Philip. I wouldn't wish such a thing on any man. I didn't think he stood much chance, knowing what our delightful Sir Gilles is like. That was why I didn't attend the trial. I didn't want to witness it. Lady Cicely is taking care of you?'

'Yes. But . . .'

'But? You want something of me, Margaret, or you wouldn't be here like this. No need to go all round the bushes about it. What is it?'

'You said once, if I ever needed help, or advice, or protection, you would still be here. You see, I remember what you told me.'

'Yes. I remember too. And now you do need help, or advice, or protection?'

Margaret nodded.

'Well?'

'I can't think how to say it.'

'Try words.'

'It'll sound awful. So bald. So bold.'

Brownpate did not help her any further. He waited, silently.

'Would you still be willing to marry me?' said Margaret at last.

'Ah. I was beginning to think it might be that. But I can only think of one reason why you should ask. You haven't forgotten Philip in a month. You're with child by him, is that it?'

'No,' said Margaret. Her mouth felt stiff, as though it would rather have said yes. To be having Philip's baby would be so much more forgivable and comprehensible, after all.

'No?' Peter Brownpate sounded disbelieving.

'After judgement was passed,' said Margaret, 'Adam took me away. We went through Narrow Wood and we knelt to pray and . . . he was trying to comfort me and somehow it got out of hand . . . I can't explain, I didn't know what I was doing and, well . . .' Her voice became loud. 'It just happened, just the once. We didn't mean it to happen, I never thought . . . I didn't want . . . but anyway, there it is. We did it and now I'm with child by Adam.'

Brownpate stared at her, visibly aghast.

'I can't stay with Lady Cicely,' said Margaret. 'At least, I mean, I expect I could. She's so kind and good; she'd try to help however angry she was with me. But she's ill. I can't trouble her with this and besides . . . she's very ill indeed. She . . . she can't live long. I could only think of you.'

There was a long silence.

'I'm sorry,' said Margaret at last. 'I just hoped . . .'

She stopped, because she had sworn to herself, all the way here, that this outrageous appeal could be made only openly and frankly, that she must not try to coerce him with emotion. But emotion was too near the surface. She shut her mouth on it.

'Was it rape?' Brownpate asked. 'Did Adam force you?'

'No.' She shook her head. 'I let him. He even said to me to stop him, to run away, but I didn't.' How many times, in the past month, had she tried herself to understand how it had come about. 'I wanted someone to hold me. I was glad,' she said. There was another silence.

'I loved you, you know,' said Brownpate at last.

The past tense was answer enough. But she sat there numbly listening to the rest.

'I really did,' he said. 'In a way, I still do, but there are limits. I have my pride. If it had been Philip – that I could respect. But not this. The man is

297

your stepfather. And – dear God – from what you say, this was the very day, the very hour of Philip's death!'

'It was because of that. I can't explain properly. I don't know how to make you understand. It doesn't matter. You're . . . not willing. All right. That's all right. I expected you to say no. I just thought . . .'

'Does Adam know?' Brownpate asked.

'No.'

'I will keep my promise to this extent,' he said. 'I'll offer you advice. You'd better tell him. After all, he's responsible.'

'It's all right. I've decided what to do if you didn't . . . if you said no.' Margaret stood up. Her knees were shaking horribly but she made them take her weight. 'I can't tell Adam. I don't want him to know. He couldn't help me; he's got enough to worry about, with my mother. It's all right. Thank you for listening to me, Peter. Goodbye.'

'Where are you going?' He rose to unbolt the door for her. His voice was a little sharp, as though he were concerned about the answer.

'Home,' said Margaret.

Home, after all, was a word with many meanings. It could mean the house where you grew up, or the house where you were currently living; it could also mean, simply, the place where the person you loved most of all awaited you.

Margaret walked steadily away from Peter Brownpate's workshop and did not look back. She must not hesitate. She must not pause to think. She must shake free of the world which had cast Philip out and was about to leave her destitute, and follow him to wherever he might be now.

Once she had despised Wilbertha for drowning herself but she understood her somewhat better now. She was even grateful to Wilbertha, for showing her the way.

The village was quiet. The men were about their work and the women mostly in their gardens or cottages. She walked past them and set out steadily towards the place where the mill had been, where the leat which had once turned the wheel of Rushley mill, still ran deep and swift.

No looking over her shoulder. No hesitation. There was the water; the solid ground seemed to be flowing back under her feet as she advanced. She must let it flow completely away from her. She had only to go on walking steadily. The day was warm; the shock of the cold water would not be too terrible. In a few moments now, it would be over.

She stepped off the edge of the world into the brown, racing water. And stopped short, suspended in mid-air. Then she realised that at the last minute she had heard feet running behind her and that strong hands had caught her round the ribs. She was being hoisted back to safety with no more than one wet foot.

'What the devil do you think you're doing?' demanded Peter Brownpate furiously, dumping her down on the bank. He stood over her, hands on hips, and glared at her.

'I was drowning myself!' said Margaret.

'I followed you from the workshop,' Peter Brownpate said. 'You said you were going home but you said it in the queerest voice I'd ever heard and how you could go to your proper home, things being as they are, I couldn't see. I felt worried over what you were going to do. Quite rightly, it seems! You stupid little *fool!*'

An answering anger spurted up in Margaret. 'I'd like to know what business it is of yours! You said no, go away. That's all right; I didn't expect you to say yes. It was an terrible thing to ask you but I gambled . . . I took a chance. And you said no and that's fair enough, so would I in your place, but since you've said no, what I do about it ought to be my affair!'

'I don't agree! Just as a matter of interest,' said Brownpate, 'did it never occur to you to take some potion or other and get out of the mess that way?'

'Yes, of course it did. But I don't know what to take or who to ask. There's no wise-woman hereabouts; Father Dunstan won't allow that sort of thing. You know that. I didn't want to ask anyone, anyhow. I don't want anyone to know. I've mucked up everything. I thought: I'll get right out of it and then I'll be with Philip and I'll never be able to muck up anything ever again.'

'What do you mean, mucked up everything?'

'I should have gone with him to Norwich in the first place. Then none of this would have happened.'

'Did he ask you to?'

'No, he wouldn't let me. But I could've got round him if I'd tried. I was scared to go and that's the truth. I'm always scared of the wrong things at the wrong time. Yes, and proud of the wrong things, too! I could still have gone straight back with him, when he came to fetch me, but no, I was that proud of marrying a freeman, I let him talk me into saying yes, let's marry here in Rushley Church where the whole world can see! Oh, it was so wonderful, the thought of being free! As if it ever happens, for the likes of us! So you see I'm not steadfast like you once said; I'm feeble, or I was. I'm putting that behind me now and I'm going to do what I should have done to start with, which is join Philip. And you can't stop me. If you carry me right away from the river now, I'll only come back another time.'

'Stand up,' said Brownpate. 'Come on, up, up! That's it. Now then. Listen to me. You are not going to drown yourself. I will marry you. I'll give this child a name. It'll arrive early, if anyone troubles to calculate,' he added thoughtfully, 'but I expect they'll think what I did, that it's Philip's. Well?'

'I promised myself,' said Margaret, 'that I would not try to force you, that I would ask in plain words and nothing more. No tears and no threats.' She could keep her voice cold but she couldn't keep hope out of her eyes. Nor could she keep her eyes from meeting Brownpate's. His gaze held her fast.

'You aren't forcing me. You walked away without any tears, without any threats. I followed you of my own free will, and rescued you because I chose to. Now I'm choosing to marry you. Only . . .'

'Only?'

'I'll give you the protection of my ring and my roof. Do you also want my bed, Margaret? Will it be a true marriage? It's for you to say.'

If her eyes were saying what their owner's voice would not, the same was true of his. His eyes were hazel, she thought, the same colour as Sir Gilles's, but utterly different in the searching kindness of their expression and as she looked into them, she understood what it was he sought.

'It will be a true marriage. If you will make me a wife, then I'll . . . I'll be a wife.' But he needed something more than that, and she knew what it was and what it would cost. A moment ago, she had thought she was going to Philip. Now, she must turn her back on him for ever. Steadily, she said the words that were required. 'Philip is dead and nothing can bring him back. I'll wrench myself from his memory. I'll learn to love you.'

'I need your love, Margaret. One-sided love would do me harm and . . . mine for you is still alive, you know.'

'I know. I won't fail you.'

'Tell me something. There's something I'd like to know. I know that you and Philip were – friends since you were children. But when he came back from Norwich, and said he was a freeman and would give you freedom too – you said the thought of it was wonderful. Did you mean that?'

'Why do you ask?'

'Because I am a villein and I shall never be anything else and nor will our children, if we have any. I am wondering . . . just for a moment you glimpsed a chance of becoming free. I don't know how much difference it makes in practice. Bond or free, we all still have to earn to eat and most people don't especially want to go off and make fresh starts in strange places. But – will you mind?'

'I shall never be free now, whatever I do, whether I marry you or not. Shall I? So there's no use in minding. Yes, it was wonderful. I meant it; I won't deny that. It was . . . magical. I've been told that my grandfather once threw away the chance of becoming free. I don't think my mother ever forgave him and I can't forgive him, either. He must have been clean crazy. How could he? How could anyone?' For a moment, her jaw muscles clenched in a rage which took Margaret herself by surprise. She remembered Sir Gilles's words: *villeins own only their bellies.*

Then she saw Peter Brownpate watching her face. He hadn't heard those words. Better not repeat them to him. Better not go on about freedom and Philip and Grandfather Ivon who had had strange, odd eyes, one blue and one brown; but had had ideas that were even odder.

'But it's all over now,' she said. 'I shan't think about it again. I'm not that silly. I'll just be glad,' said Margaret, 'to be safe.'

He was wiser than to attempt a passionate embrace just then. They sealed their pact not with a kiss but with a clasp of hands. 'It is still your steadfastness that I admire,' he said.

PART VI

Dangerous Dreams,
AD 1215

No freeman shall be arrested, or imprisoned, or dispossessed, or outlawed, or banished, or in any manner ruined, except by the lawful judgement of his peers or the law of the land.

Magna Carta

Chapter Eighteen

The Irrelevant Charter

It had always been a source of mild amusement to Margaret's family that she not only knew the date of her birth, but set store by it. She never paid much attention to the birthdays of her children (her flaxenhaired eldest daughter, Eve, had gathered as time went on that she had been born a month earlier than her mother always claimed and reckoned that this was why). But she invariably celebrated her own.

This time, however, the pattern had been slightly altered. This time, her family were doing the celebrating. After all, it wasn't every day that a woman reached the age of eighty, least of all with almost all her faculties intact. Margaret could not now walk very well and had a stick to lean on. But her sight and hearing were still good and her mind as sharp as ever.

This was actually to be a double celebration, for if one Margaret had just reached the age of eighty, another one had just been born. Eve had paid her mother the compliment of naming a daughter after her and the daughter in question, had at last – after four sons punctuated by miscarriages and still births – produced a daughter of her own and was carrying on the tradition.

When everyone had finished their work for the day, the whole family would gather under Eve's roof, to honour the birthday and the baptism which had both graced this day.

So, as the morning brightened, Margaret sat at the door of the cottage where it was her choice to live alone, and waited to be fetched to the baptism which the Rushley priest, young Father Thomas, would conduct just before noon. Two of Eve's strapping grandsons would carry her there between them. How many women, Margaret wondered with satisfaction, lived to see their great-grandchildren grow so big?

This, the morning of the thirtieth of June 1215, was peaceful, full of the gentle sounds of breeze and bird; the kind of day to induce nostalgia. In any case, Margaret had noticed of late that in her it needed little inducing. As the time ahead of her lessened, she looked back more and more, and it was an odd thing, but the older she grew, the further back memory seemed able to go.

There had been a time when she never thought of Philip Siwardson at all. At first, she had forbidden herself to remember him. Later, she hadn't wanted to. The love she had set herself grimly to manufacture for Peter Brownpate had in the end come easily, of itself. She didn't know quite when or how, but all of a sudden, there it was. She was Peter Brownpate's wife and she was happy.

She was relieved, too, for Peter's happiness was bound up with hers and he had earned the right to it. Their companionable partnership had endured for more than twenty-six years, as they worked side by side and reared the children, thankful to be living in the steadied world which King Henry FitzEmpress had created when he came to the throne the year that Eve was born. He was known as FitzEmpress to emphasise the fact that he was the son of Empress Matilda and therefore a direct descendant of Henry the First. But he acceded easily anyway, since King Stephen's unpleasant son Eustace, mercifully, had died.

For a long time, Margaret had lived in the present moment and been content with it. And when Peter Brownpate died, at first it was their years together which she remembered.

It was only lately that her mind had shown this curious disposition to go further back in time, back past the weary deaths, apparently from sheer despondency and exhaustion, first of Meg and then of Adam, back past Eve's birth, back past her hurried wedding to Brownpate, back to the scene beside the millrace, and on beyond, with time unreeling swiftly past her mind's eye, to Oxfen and Lady Cis, to Narrow Wood and so, at last, to Philip.

To discover that even now, more than sixty years later, his face was still engraved on her brain.

If they had married, what would their children have been like? Eve, and the family she had had with Brownpate, would never have existed. Hard to imagine that. In particular, she had been proud of her third boy, another Peter. He was gone now, a victim of the marsh fever which had taken his father. But he had been the one who took over his father's carpentry shop and did so well with it. His elder brothers had had little interest in it and Brownpate hadn't forced them.

Adam, pleased that she was marrying Brownpate after all, had given her three cows as her dowry and the elder boys became interested in cattle. They had built up their own herds and could be said to have done well too but she knew Brownpate had been a little disappointed, all the same. The younger Peter had made it up to him.

Perhaps it was fortunate that Brownpate was gone before the younger Peter's son had taken a partner into the workshop and then let the partner buy him out because he, too, was more interested in animals; horses in his case. As a lad he played truant from the carpentry in order to earn a few farthings up at the hall, helping the grooms in the stable.

Though no one, thought Margaret, could say that her horse-loving grandson, who also bore the name of Peter, hadn't been a success in his own right. He was settled now as one of the grooms at Rushley hall and he was so highly valued that although it was rare for a lord to take a villein far from the manor, Peter the Groom regularly went along when Sir Henry set off to attend on his own overlord, Roger Bigod, the present Earl of Norfolk.

He had indeed been gone for most of this month; they had thought they might have to hold the party without him. But Sir Henry had ridden home yesterday and today, when Peter had finished his work at the hall, he would be here.

The only thing really wrong with the third Peter in Margaret's opinion, was that even at the age of twenty-eight, he still seemed to her more a boy than a man, although he was married with a child, and he supported his wife Joanna and his daughter Mary competently. He was not, as a villein, paid for his services when he followed Sir Henry away from Rushley, but he was given gratuities. Sir Henry was a very different man from his father Sir Gilles. He was more like his grandfather, Sir Aubrey. She, Margaret, was the only one left in Rushley who could remember Sir Aubrey.

Her mind was drifting. What had she been thinking about? Oh yes. The children who wouldn't have been born if she had married Philip. She *couldn't* imagine a world without Peter the Groom, without Eve, without . . .

Margaret shook her head impatiently and wished her family would come to fetch her. She no longer wanted to sit here alone with her memories; to remember Philip was painful still and what was the use, anyway? It was all over and done with so long, so very long ago.

The party was being held at Eve's cottage because Eve had done most of the organising. But the dwelling was nowhere near big enough for so many and it was as well that the evening was fine, allowing the gathering to overflow out of doors.

It was a notable assembly, for by this time Margaret's kinsfolk included most of the families in Rushley and a good many in Oxfen, although all were villeins. The freemen, especially the Grosnez clan, still held themselves apart.

There was plenty to eat, since everyone who came had a contribution to make. Ailred the Smith, the father of the newly christened infant Margaret, and his sons, built the outdoor cooking fire, and the child's mother brought a vast chicken pasty. Others arrived with such things as a brace of ducks (plucked and drawn and ready to cook, along with a dozen blue-green ducks' eggs), baskets of bread and honeycakes, and a cauldron of stew.

Those members of the family whose lives revolved round cattle walked in with cheeses and a whole calf ready for the spit. Stephen Carpenter, the friend to whom Peter the Groom had sold his carpentry business, counted as a member of the family since he was actually a distant cousin. He had recently married a girl whose family were the best brewers and the most enterprising winemakers in the village and they arrived pushing a handcart laden with four barrels, containing respectively ale, mead, dandelion wine and elderflower wine.

'You'll have us all reeling,' said Ailred the Smith, with a grin of anticipation.

The Eelfishers were not relatives but they were invited because it was worth it; ask them to any celebration and they could be relied on to turn up not only with fresh eels but with trout and perch as well.

Peter the Groom himself came late and last but happily brandishing a plump hen, already roasted, which he had been given by the cook at the hall, who was allowed to make such gifts at his discretion.

'Well,' Margaret said later, when trestles and benches had been brought from Eve's house or borrowed from neighbours, and she was sitting in the place of honour at the board, 'this is a feast. I can remember times when we had nothing to eat except black bread and thin stew. Times have changed since I was a girl. Not that that's to say they couldn't change back again,' she added. 'Things happen, all in a minute.'

Her family smiled, a little patronisingly. They were fond of her but impatient with her tendency to reminisce about hard times gone by. Margaret was aware of this and eyed them knowingly. Hah! Sir Henry wouldn't last for ever and his heir was an unknown quantity; she wouldn't be surprised if some of her descendants were in for a rude shock one of these days. She refrained from enlarging on this, however. After all, she was a principal guest at this party.

The shadows began to lengthen and the breeze was growing cool but the fire had been built up and they were all warm with food and good drink. One of Eve's grandsons liked music and he had made himself a lute to a new pattern, with a flat back and six strings and a deeper, more vibrant voice than the ordinary lute. He called it a guitar. He sat by the fire with it across his thighs and began to play. Someone joined in with a reed pipe and one of the Eelfishers produced a hand-drum and started tapping out a jigging rhythm. Ailred shouted: 'Let's dance!'

'Just a minute!' Peter the Groom called. 'Let's do it properly, the way they'd do it in a big hall. I've seen how they go on in the great houses now. The guests of honour ought to have thrones!'

Rapidly, benches were pushed back out of the way, and a highbacked settle was turned into a throne by draping it with red cloth and padding it with cushions. Margaret was picked up bodily by Eve's grandsons and set upon it. Their sister Margaret, who after recently giving birth was not yet strong enough to dance, was placed beside her, with the baby on her knee.

'There you are, Grandmother,' Peter the Groom said breezily, smiling at her. In some ways, his open, ingenuous face reminded her more of Philip than of Brownpate who had been his grandparent. Eve, whose father had been Philip's uncle Adam, hardly reminded her of them at all. Only her name, a secret tribute to her parentage, ever kept Margaret in mind of it nowadays. (Philip and Adam had of course been very like each other. Suddenly it occurred to Margaret to wonder if the resemblance between them had had anything to do with her extraordinary surrender in Narrow Wood.)

'Do you know what we're going to do now?' Peter was saying. 'We're going to dance, and as each couple come past your throne, they'll salute you. That's the way they do things in the great houses. I've seen it now.'

Margaret wanted to say: 'What's the good of us pretending to be like them?' but once again quelled this urge in the name of courtesy, and was glad she had done so when as the dancing began, the granddaughter and namesake beside her went all starry-eyed and was holding up her baby's tiny hand to wave at the bows and curtsies and the blown kisses.

And it *was* a pretty idea, Margaret admitted after a while, also raising a hand to wave. It was a beautiful party altogether, and a beautiful evening, with mackerel clouds, tinged now with orange in the west. Likely enough the fun would go on by firelight long after the stars were out.

'This is wonderful!' said her granddaughter suddenly. 'Wave, baby! Look at all the nice people bowing! I wish it'd never end!'

Yes, it was a pity, Margaret thought, listening to the merry music and watching the laughing weatherbeaten faces, the tossing plaits and bright skirts of the young girls, a pity that one couldn't stop time and hold the moment. But the merrymaking, however fair, however prolonged, would relentlessly pass and tomorrow the fire would be a heap of grey ashes and they'd all be one day older and some would be nursing hangovers and this happy, united evening would be sliding back into the realm of memory.

And then, like a breaking cloudburst, the retrospective mood from which, earlier, she had been glad to be rescued, returned overwhelmingly. The music, the laughter, the firelight gathering strength as the dusk descended, spun together and lost their meaning as once more she understood that to bring this evening into being, to bring half at least of those happy faces into being, Philip had had to die choking at the end of a rope and Brownpate's young wife Mary had been slaughtered like a calf.

'Grandmother!' Her granddaughter's voice was alarmed. 'Grandmother dear, what is it? You're crying. Aren't you well? Peter, Peter!' She signalled urgently at Peter the Groom, fetching him and his wife out of the dance. 'Grandmother's upset. I think perhaps she's overtired.'

'I'm not overtired. I'm all right. I was just . . . just overcome for a moment.' Margaret stuck out her chin and wiped her eyes. She couldn't . . . dear God, she mustn't try to! . . . explain this. She mustn't blight the party.

Peter squatted down beside her. 'Have you been thinking of the past, Grandmother?' He did occasionally have this uncanny knack of guessing at people's thoughts and his guesses tended to be at least half-right. 'Thinking of all the people who aren't here? Don't, Grandmother, please. There are times to come as well as times past, you know.'

'I know, but I don't have many still to come,' said Margaret reasonably.

'You may still have some, though, and I hope they'll be good ones. The world's changing, Grandmother, I've seen it for myself on this last journey with Sir Henry.'

Over the food, earlier, people had asked Peter about his latest journey and he'd talked a little, though, being a well-mannered young man who was aware that he was not the guest of honour, he had visibly not talked as much as he wanted to. But they had all gathered that this time he had followed his lord right down to the south of England, to a place near London, and that he had actually seen King John close to. Margaret, to distract him from further enquiries into the workings of her mind, said: 'Tell us.'

'Well, it was all to do with the reason why Sir Henry had to go south with the earl. It was for a special meeting with King John; west of London, it was. It was by the River Thames,' said Peter eagerly. 'I've never seen such a river – so *broad* – and with meadows on either side as wide as wide. We went to a place called Runnymede and it looked as if all the barons in England were there. There were tents pitched all over the place with banners flying, and knights riding about with lances, and . . . when we first got there, I had to hold Sir Henry's horse while people were finding out where we were to go and would you believe it, the king walked past me so close I could have touched him. I could actually have reached out and touched King John himself!'

'The barons don't like him,' remarked Margaret. Except for children, the simple-minded and a few anchorites who had shut their ears to the world, there was hardly a soul in the land who didn't know that.

'No. But he's tried to give justice to poor men,' said Peter.

'Provided they know their place and don't ask for impossible things like their freedom, if they happen to be villeins,' said Margaret cynically. 'I listen to the news, my lad, when the minstrels come round or when our good Father gives out the latest proclamations in church. Never mind me. I'm just a grumbling old woman. Go on. What happened next?'

'What happened next? The king signed a charter! That's why we were there. He and the barons all gathered together for the signing and then heralds rode round the encampment and stationed themselves in various places and read out what the charter said, to everyone who wanted to listen. It must have been read out in Norwich by now and I expect you'll hear about it in church soon.' He looked round and caught the eye of Father Thomas. 'You're sure to get word, any minute. Oh, it was a marvel!'

'Was it, now?' said Margaret. 'And what did it say?'

'Oh, all sorts of things. It was very long. Some of it I couldn't make much sense of. But I remember one special thing it said, and that was the part I thought was a marvel. It said that no freeman shall ever again be arrested or imprisoned or thrown off his land or outlawed or banished except by the judgement of his equals and in accordance with the law of the land. There were cheers when that was read . . .'

'Who from?' said Margaret. She looked with some exasperation at her descendant. 'The freemen who were listening? Well enough for them but what are *you* rejoicing for? None of that applies to you.'

'None of it ever applied to them, either, as far back as any can remember. Sir Henry told us that, on the way home. On the road, evenings, he'd be with the earl's folk, but at midday we just had quick snacks by the roadside and he'd stay with his own and talk to us. The thing, Grandmother, is that it's a first step. The world's going to change. Oh, that's not what Sir Henry said; I've worked it out for myself, but I'm right, I know it! First the freemen: one day, us. One day maybe we'll all be free and there won't be villeins any more at all.'

'Now that,' said Margaret, 'is the most unlikely idea I ever heard. Do you really think that *they* . . .' she did not have to explain who she meant by *they* '. . . would ever let go of us? I know, my boy. I've seen what they're like when their human cattle try to escape. Even Sir Henry won't stand for that and he's better than most. He has runaways brought back and fined. Most lords are harsher and I've seen, close to, what happens then. Some dreams are dangerous, and if I were you, I'd take care to remember that.'

Her granddaughter Margaret, who was not particularly clever, looked puzzled. Her world was bounded by Ailred and the children and the daily routine of home and forge and the animals they kept; this talk of kings and charters and the ways of the lords, confused her.

But Peter the Groom was smiling and now his face seemed less young, less ingenuous than she had ever known it. Looking at him, Margaret saw that the mature man had emerged from the boy at last.

'You believe that, Grandmother? That nothing will ever really change?'

'Things change a little,' Margaret conceded. 'I said earlier, we're all eating well these days but I've seen times when we didn't. And I've seen days when we were attacked by great lords behaving like mad dogs. I've seen houses burning here in this village and bodies lying on the ground with the blood soaking into the earth around them. There's been nothing like that round here for a long time now. So that's different. But the bad times can come back and very likely they will. Changes aren't all good and there's some things don't alter at all, nor ever will, if you ask me.'

'Grandmother,' Peter the Groom said, 'When I was small, you told me stories sometimes. You would bring out a queer old pendant you used to wear round your neck . . .'

'I've still got it,' Margaret fumbled for the cord and drew out the cracked old dagger-hilt. 'You mean this?'

'Yes. You've still got it, after all this time! It belonged to some far-off ancestor, who was a freeman, didn't it?'

'And always wanted his descendants to be free as well. Yes, that's the story that goes with it. And I also told you that we'd have had our freedom, too, if *my* grandfather hadn't been the stupidest man in creation.' Margaret's sudden anger took her by surprise. It was, after all, so very long now since her grandfather Ivon died, since Adam had told her a story about him for the last time. None of it should matter now.

And yet it did matter, and she was full of a useless fury against the blind obstinacy of a man long dead, and the dangerous optimism of the living one now in front of her.

'My grandfather Ivon had the chance of proving his right to freedom, and he threw it away and all our freedoms with it. He said he'd rather stay a villein than admit he was Norman-bred, which he was. Well, chances like that don't come twice, and I've seen where it gets you if you go dreaming that they will. You're a fool if you do, and you'd better believe me, for your own sake.'

To her added fury, her voice sounded petulant even in her own ears. She was old, so old, and the days of her power and her authority were gone. Peter the Groom was looking at her and smiling, as though he thought he knew better than she did. Had she really, a moment ago, imagined he was a mature man? He was just a baby. He didn't know what the world was like.

'I don't know why I've kept this old thing.' She stared at the dagger-hilt with distaste. 'It came down from my father's side of the family. These lines carved here were supposed to be the emblem of our free ancestors. Well, it all used to mean something to me but not anymore. It's all so far back. I just wear it out of habit now. You can bury it with me.'

'Don't talk of that tonight, Grandmother. Grandmother, listen.' Peter put a hand over one of hers. The twilight was all round them and the firelight was glowing on his hair. That fugitive resemblance to Philip was a matter of facial expression, not colouring. Peter's hair was not flaxen but the warm red-brown which hers had been before it became white and so thin that now she took care that her coif should always hide it completely.

From Gunnor had come the fox-coloured hair and from Gunnor the faculty which had permitted or compelled Margaret to share in the moment of Philip's death. And although neither Margaret nor her grandson had ever heard of Gunnor by name and had no idea of her part in their heredity, it was Gunnor's voice which spoke through Peter the Groom now, as he said, with a calm certainty which quietened Margaret's rage and made her, for a moment, almost believe him: 'One day, Grandmother, our descendants will get their freedom again. Believe me. I *know*.'

310